Praise for A FEIGNED MADNESS

"Debut author Mitchell brings the courageous, determined Nellie Bly to vivid life in this fictionalized account
of one of Bly's most daring escapades: her ten days in the
notorious asylum at Blackwell's Island. Mixing known
history with intriguing speculation, Mitchell depicts the
horrific conditions of the asylum, Bly's ambitious rise as a
newspaperwoman, and the magnetic draw of forbidden
love with equal skill."
—*Greer Macallister,*
USA Today *best-selling author of* The Magician's Lie
and The Arctic Fury

"This vivid, enthralling novel of daredevil reporter Nellie
Bly's undercover exposé of the abuses at Blackwell's Island
Asylum for Women took me by the throat and never let
go. Nellie Bly's ambitions, talents, pugnacity, and huge
heart shine throughout. *A Feigned Madness* is a knockout."
—*Kim Taylor Blakemore,*
author of The Companion *and* After Alice Fell

"A page-turning thrill ride through an often overlooked
historical atrocity, *A Feigned Madness* vividly recounts
the horrors of Blackwell's Island and the mistreatment
of its inmates. As a reader, I could really feel Nellie Bly's
tenacious thirst to see them have justice."
—*Nicole Evelina,*
USA Today *best-selling author*

A FEIGNED MADNESS

A
FEIGNED
MADNESS

TONYA MITCHELL

Tonya Mitchell

cennan

Published by Cennan Books, an imprint of Cynren Press
101 Lindenwood Drive, Suite 225
Malvern, PA 19355 USA
http://www.cynren.com/

Printed in the United States of America on acid-free paper
ISBN-13: 978-1-947976-20-7 (pbk)
ISBN-13: 978-1-947976-21-4 (ebk)

Library of Congress Control Number: 2020940207

The extract in chapter 5 is from Nellie Bly, "The Girl
Puzzle," *Pittsburg Dispatch,* January 25, 1885, 11.
The extract in chapter 13, p. 156, is from Bly in the
Pittsburg Dispatch, May 24, 1885, 8. In chapter 13, p. 157,
"A Plucky Woman" is from Bly, *Pittsburg Dispatch,* May
31, 1885, 7. Bessie Bramble's article extracted in chapter
20 is from the *Pittsburg Dispatch,* October 4, 1885, 12.
The extracts in chapter 22 are from Bly, "The Floating
Gardens," *Pittsburg Dispatch,* May 9, 1886, 9. Photograph
of Nellie Bly on p. 372 is copyright H. J. Myers, circa
1890. Image obtained from the U.S. Library of Congress,
https://lccn.loc.gov/2002697740.

Author photograph by Peggy Joseph Photography
Cover design by Tim Barber

For Ron,
who always believed

What a mysterious thing madness is.

NELLIE BLY

Too much sanity may be madness. And maddest of all, to see life as it is and not as it should be.

MIGUEL DE CERVANTES

THE LANGUAGE OF FLOWERS

In Eastern lands they talk in flow'rs
And they tell in a garland their loves and cares;
Each blossom that blooms in their garden bowr's,
On its leaves a mystic language bears.
The rose is a sign of joy and love,
Young blushing love in its earliest dawn,
And the mildness that suits the gentle dove,
From the myrtle's snowy flow'rs is drawn.
Innocence gleams in the lily's bell,
Pure as the heart in its native heaven.
Fame's bright star and glory's swell
By the glossy leaf of the bay are given.
The silent, soft and humble heart,
In the violet's hidden sweetness breathes,
And the tender soul that cannot part,
In a twine of evergreen fondly wreathes.
The cypress that daily shades the grave,
Is sorrow that moans her bitter lot,
And faith that a thousand ills can brave,
Speaks in thy blue leaves "forget-me-not."
Then gather a wreath from the garden bowers,
And tell the wish of thy heart in flowers.

JAMES GATES PERCIVAL. 1872

Prologue

Unwashed bodies, urine, feces—the stench was a blow. I raised my hand to cover my mouth, fearful I might gag. The room was dim, the only light streaming through slats over the sparse windows. As my eyes adjusted, details took shape. The room was large, its floor covered with a thin scattering of hay. The clink of a chain brought my attention to the right. Through the gloom, my gaze met the sight of a woman slumped against a wall. Her hair was loose and hung in knots, her legs bent, her knobby knees exposed. She moaned piteously and reached out a trembling hand. A moan from the other side of the room—another woman. And another. I counted six chained to the walls amid their own filth.

"This is inhumane," I said, my voice slicing the air. "You've got to release these women at—"

The nurse's hands were around my throat in an instant. I tried to gulp air, but her nails bit into my flesh, my fingers digging at hers to no avail.

"I may not be able to lay a hand on you now," she said viciously, "but your time is coming. For now, you can watch. Watch and learn." She spat into my face, a globule landing below my eye.

She pushed, backing me up against a wall. When she released me at last, I gasped for breath, feeling faint. In the next moment, a heavy metal cuff enclosed my wrist, entrapping me with a resounding clang.

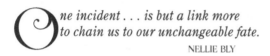

*One incident . . . is but a link more
to chain us to our unchangeable fate.*

NELLIE BLY

NEW YORK CITY, SEPTEMBER 1887

I am not ruined.

I mouthed the words as my cab-for-hire lumbered through Manhattan, dodging pedestrians, wagons, and coaches as it went. The city was already teeming with life in the early-morning hour, each conveyance fighting to get somewhere. *I am not ruined. I shall prevail,* I breathed again. Poverty was not the same as failure, after all. The former did not necessarily produce the latter. Not yet anyway. I still had time—though precious little of it remained—to turn things to my advantage.

Yesterday I'd stepped off the elevated train and walked toward the station exit with the vague notion I'd forgotten something. When I'd looked down at my hands, I'd stopped dead, causing a man walking behind me to stumble into me and angrily veer away, muttering sharp words as he went. *My reticule.* It wasn't dangling from my wrist. In the instant it took me to realize what I'd done, that I had, in fact, left my reticule on the train, everything changed. I'd spun around, only to see the train lurch away in an angry belch of steam, carrying the last few dollars I possessed with it. With the little money that remained in my reticule, I'd known I could get by a bit longer. I would find work. There was still hope. But all bets were off as I'd watched the train lumber away. I was utterly destitute. *Penniless.* The word brought a clenching to my stomach, and for a moment it was all I could do to squeeze my eyes shut to the swarming street before me, blotting out the grim reminder that New York City, with its crush of people, its seething streets, its packed tenements, was not a friendly city in which to go hungry.

In the hours that had followed since, I'd thought of little else. My deficiency was a torment that would not leave me, like a sliver of glass under a fingernail that could not be expelled. I was already two months late on my room and board. I had no money for my notebooks, for postage, a pair of winter boots. Of all the hardships I had suffered, this was the worst. I had only myself to blame.

My funds had been slowly dwindling since I'd arrived in the city four months before, but in the flash it took to step from the train, I'd become as needy as the immigrant poor. For the hundredth time, I cursed my inclination to daydream while riding the train, for it was daydreaming—that most seductive of habits—that had cost me my purse. In all probability, if my scheme did not succeed today, I would lose a great deal more than the last of my pocket change.

I glanced down at the reticule in my lap, which I'd borrowed from Mama this morning. It had seen better days. The green velvet was going bare in spots, and the gold edging had been resewn around the seam. But it was what it held that counted. Inside was a list penned in my own hand, a list like none I had ever put to paper before. It was my future, this slip of paper folded twice over, something that would be or not be, and it was everything. Or nothing.

The odor of horse manure and refuse, borne on a breeze from the river, brought me up sharp. I wrinkled my nose and was pulling a handkerchief from Mama's reticule when my cab-for-hire suddenly lurched to avoid a stopped dray cart. I managed to keep my seat, but the constant starting and stopping of the vehicle, combined with the clamor of hooves and shouts from the newsboys, was giving me a headache.

At Ann Street, the driver turned left onto Park Row. The triangular green spread lush and manicured on the left. Beyond loomed the columned facade of City Hall. On the right, a formidable block of buildings made up what the city called Newspaper Row. The highest and grandest of these—the buildings that housed the *New*

York Times, the *New York Herald,* and the *New York World*—rested at the northernmost end, but it was the *World* that dominated. Rising to fifteen stories, its building was the tallest in the city, the tallest on the planet. The enormous golden globe perched at its top was purported to reflect light forty miles out to sea. How soldier-like they all looked: straight, tall, a row of steadfast unity. But it was all show. They may have been soldiers, but allies they were not. They were bitter enemies, fighting a daily war not with cannons and bullets but with words and opinions.

The cab drew to a stop at the corner and the horse sneezed, sending a cloud of flies into the air. I alighted before the driver could assist me, eager to be rid of them both. I pressed five cents I'd borrowed from my landlady into the man's gritty palm. For a penny, I could have ridden the elevated train, but I couldn't stomach the thought of taking the very form of transportation that had caused my slide into poverty. I prayed the extravagance would, in the end, be worth the expense.

At the entrance to the *World,* I checked my reflection in the glass door. Staring back was a woman in her early twenties in full skirts with a tiny waist. Dark brown, upswept hair peeked from beneath a large hat perched jauntily at an angle. My black kid gloves clutched a reticule that was far too light. I was wearing the best I owned, and though these were not the height of fashion, they gave the impression, I hoped, that I was a woman of the world.

I stepped inside the vast three-story lobby, whose walls were made, I had read, of Corsehill stone imported from Scotland. Four female torchbearers wrought from bronze gazed loftily down upon the building's occupants, representing art, literature, science, and invention. My eyes swept the vaulted ceiling, the intricate ironwork of the staircase. Men stood in clusters, their banter and cigar smoke rising in a thick, heady miasma that filled the echoing chamber. But it was what I couldn't see that held my attention most: the low rumble of the presses beneath the polished marble floor. I could feel the vibration in my chest, a reminder to all who entered that, however elegant the furnishings were above, the belly of the beast was below, hard at work banging out the city's news, broadsheet by broadsheet. The *World* boasted, or so I had read, that six acres of spruce trees were felled a day to feed the press's voracious appetite for paper.

I approached the guard standing behind a desk near the elevator cages. He folded his arms and scowled when he spotted me, preparing for battle.

"Good morning," I said. "I would like to speak with Colonel Cockerill."

The guard didn't smile, nor did he consult the appointment book on his desk. He had endured enough encounters with me to know better. He nodded to a few men walking to the cages, and then his eyes, cool and distant, fell again on me.

"Colonel Cockerill is expecting me," I said. The lie came easily to my lips. Destitution had emboldened me in ways I could scarcely have imagined a day ago. For a woman who prided herself on reporting the truth to thousands of readers in Pittsburgh, I was now counting on deception to worm my way forward in New York. I wondered, in that flash of an instant, if I was going too far. But then there was my lost reticule to consider.

So far in our frequent confrontations, I'd given the guard a winning smile, hoping to melt the glacial expression he wore when confronted with trespassers who desired to get past the cavernous lobby. Today, however, I'd decided to take a different tack. Smiles and an affable nature had opened few doors for me at the *World*. Whoever said you could catch more flies with honey than vinegar was not a woman in the particular straits in which I found myself. I knitted my brows and set my jaw, hoping my stern countenance would convince him that I was no timid female he could send away with a flick of his wrist.

I needn't have bothered.

"There's nothing in the book," the guard began, "about the colonel having a meeting with a *lady* this morning." His eyes raked over me, his inflection clear. Ladies, those perfumed confections of virtue and manners, didn't make appearances at newspaper offices. Certainly not alone, without male chaperones to accompany them.

"I've come to discuss a story I believe he would be interested in publishing." I fished in Mama's reticule and produced my list. "The colonel—"

"What kind of story?"

I narrowed my eyes. My existence in New York City, not to mention whether Mama and I would eat in the near future, depended on this condescending man who knew nothing of column inches and bylines. Who surely did know, and cared the less for it, about the plight of women who, by circumstances rarely of their own choosing, were forced to eke out a living without a man in a man's world. "When I spoke with Colonel Cockerill for my story for the *Pittsburg Dispatch* a few weeks past—you do recall that, don't you? That I had an interview with him?" His only response was to quirk a brow. "Colonel Cockerill told me I should come to him *straightaway* should I uncover anything of interest." I waved the paper. "I gave him my word I would come to him. *First.*"

"That's as may be, but without an appointment . . ." His words trailed off and the guard shrugged, a smile tugging at the corners of his mouth. He was enjoying this.

"Very well." I thrust the paper back into Mama's reticule. I wasn't the least surprised the guard had denied me access; he'd done so more times than I cared to admit. "I was simply doing the colonel a courtesy. I know he would be loath to think I failed to come to him with what should prove to be quite a story for the paper." I arched a brow. "I'm sure another paper will know what to do with it. The *Sun* or the *Morning Journal* perhaps."

When I had played this scene out in my mind earlier, this was the point at which the tide turned. The guard would apologize when I told him I would go somewhere else with my story. Not because he cared a fig about me, but because he'd be terrified of being blamed for letting a potential front-page story slip through his fingers. As I'd imagined it, he would call up to Cockerill's office and alert him of my presence at once. I might as well have spoken in a foreign tongue, however. The guard didn't move. If anything, he looked even more disinterested. Oh, what a fool I was to think those papers—those particular papers—would mean anything to him.

The guard cleared his throat, preparing to evict me from the lobby like so much vermin. But then, just when I thought I had no alternate plan, that I was sunk and would return home to tell Mama the worst, his demeanor changed. He straightened and brought his arms to his sides, his scowl transformed into humble servility.

"Good morning, sir."

I spun, skirts swishing, and there was Colonel Cockerill. I felt a flush of heat rise to my cheeks. I should have been relieved, yet I felt caught out instead, as if I'd just been spotted swiping a bun from a baker's stall.

"What's this about the *Sun* and the *Journal*?" Cockerill asked.

"Good morning, Colonel." I was surprised at how smooth my voice sounded considering my heart was beating like it wanted to break free of my chest. "I was just telling this man I have something I would like to share with you, but he seems to think an appointment is of greater importance than a newsworthy story."

Cockerill's eyes flicked to the guard. "Is that so, McCready?"

McCready turned pink and opened his mouth, but the only thing that came out was an unintelligible sputter. Had I not been in such dire circumstances, I would have laughed out loud.

The managing editor regarded me with narrowed eyes, weighing, I gathered, whether I was worth his time. My schemes to get an audience with Cockerill had always been precarious. If his clenched jaw was any indication, this one would be my last. "Well," he said finally, his lips tight, "far be it from me to get in the way of a newsworthy story." He nodded curtly to McCready, then extended his arm and bid me follow him to the elevators.

Moments later, we filed into a crowded lift. The elevator operator, a man in a black uniform and white gloves who tipped his head deferentially to Cockerill as we entered, closed the gilded cage doors. With a jerk, we were lofted high, a box drawn up by a puppeteer's string. Floor by floor, men in worsted suits and bowlers spilled out as the operator heaved wide the doors. When we arrived at the twelfth floor and the doors slid open to let a gentleman out, I recognized the space at once, not for its vastness—the *World* employed a legion of staff—not for the stale cigar and cigarette smoke that clung to the air, not even for the smell of press paper and ink. It was its busy, hivelike activity. Men scurried about, their shirtsleeves rolled to the elbows, pencils perched behind their ears. Others talked in groups. Despite the early hour, jackets had already been discarded and hung from chair backs. Desks were arranged haphazardly; piles of paper and books covered every surface. As I watched, a balled-up piece of paper sailed across the room, then another, followed by a burst of laughter. If the underground pressroom was the belly of the beast, the newsroom was the heart. I longed, in that instant, to step from the lift and join them, to walk the rows of desks, my hand trailing bookends and inkwells as I called a greeting that was answered by those who knew me as one of them. I wanted my own desk, my notebooks and pens and dictionary and framed photographs arranged just so, waiting for me to sit down and begin the business of writing for the day. Where else but here did I belong?

The operator drew the doors closed with a bang, startling me back to reality. To my consternation, I found that Cockerill had been studying me, his focus shifting back to the doors once the elevator started moving again. If he'd seen the look of longing that must surely have been visible on my face, he showed no sign of it. The car was empty save for the three of us now, and we rode to the top floor without speaking—Cockerill undoubtedly using the silence to rattle my nerves, me to improve my chances of reaching his office before he could change his mind and have me thrown out.

The elevator let out onto a circular room with a dome-shaped ceiling, the golden aerie that sat atop the *World*. With its frescoed ceilings and statues, marble molding and chandelier, it looked more like the entrance to a palace than the top floor of a business office. This was the domain of Joseph Pulitzer, the most esteemed publisher of Newspaper Row, and Cockerill was his right-hand man. I had gotten this far only once before, when I'd interviewed Cockerill for a story for the *Pittsburg Dispatch*. I had no such excuse now, no newspaper backing my presence here in the quest for facts. I had only my resolve to keep myself from plunging further into poverty, which in that moment seemed absurdly paradoxical, surrounded as I was by so much opulence.

I followed Cockerill down a hallway covered in rich carpet. A man sitting at a desk bid him good morning and hopped up to open the door to his office. With a practiced flourish, he flipped on the electric lights, a luxury Pulitzer could well afford.

The managing editor's office was a large, well-appointed room paneled in rich walnut and laid with plush Turkish carpet. A framed masthead of the *World* hung behind his desk. Cockerill's man had stacked the morning editions to one side of his massive desk, fanned out to reveal other mastheads that printed the city's news.

Cockerill removed his coat and hat and hung them on a hall tree near the door. When at last he took a seat, he regarded me with a bold stare. His features were not in themselves intimidating: average height; brown hair parted to one side; a large, well-trimmed mustache; dark, heavy brows. I guessed him to be in his mid-thirties. His eyes, a clear shade of green, bespoke his intelligence. Now they regarded me with mild curiosity and not a small amount of irritation. "Now then," he said, leaning back in his chair. "It's Miss Cochrane, isn't it? You are to be congratulated on your piece for the *Dispatch*. You have a rather uncanny ability to, as they say, stir the pot."

A few weeks earlier, I'd devised a way to gain access to the city's most prominent newspapermen. I'd received a fan letter from a young lady in Pittsburgh who desired to become a journalist and wanted to know if New York City was the best place to start. I couldn't have concocted a better opportunity to approach the newspaper gods of Gotham. I had the young lady's question printed in the *Dispatch*, along with my reply to her that I would endeavor to find out.

I set upon a series of interviews with the city's newsmen. I spoke to Charles Miller of the *Times*, Robert Morris of the *Telegram*, George Hepworth of the *Herald*, Charles Dana of the *Sun*, and Cockerill himself. These respected men of Newspaper Row were all cut from the same cloth. Women, they told me, were not fit for journalism. It was not in our fragile natures, nor in our best interests, to pursue such a profession. I asked questions and took notes with ladylike deference, while inside me, hell's inferno raged. It'd been a miracle I hadn't come across the desks of those pomaded, mustached gentlemen and strangled them all.

My story, a tale of proud men who would never dare hire a woman to do what a man could do better, was printed in the *Dispatch*. It might have ended there, but Joseph Howard, a syndicated columnist who abhorred Pulitzer, used it to his advantage.

"What was it Howard called us men of Newspaper Row?" Cockerill asked, bringing me from my thoughts.

He called you insufferable idiots. "He criticized your lack of . . . vision, Colonel." In fact, Howard had said Cockerill's opinions were rubbish and behind the times. He'd called him and the others out for their stupidity.

"Yes, but what was his phrase?" Cockerill mused. "Lamentable something. I found it quite amusing."

"'Lamentable ignorance.' He condemned the lamentable ignorance of newspaper editors in general."

"Yes, that's it. Our collective, lamentable ignorance." A scowl crossed his features. "It's not every day someone calls me an idiot, Miss Cochrane. And the *Boston Globe* had the audacity to reprint Howard's rant and spin the whole thing up again."

That reprint included a list of women reporters, I among them, whose very success refuted the editors' claims. The *Journalist,* the New York trade magazine, soon spread the story to the journalism community at large.

"I wrote a good story," I said evenly. "It was published around the country."

"One must be careful not to bite the hand that feeds one," Cockerill said. His smile did not reach his eyes. "Don't tell me you've come to get a retraction from me."

"On the contrary. The *World* employs two women reporters, more than any other in the city. I commend you as a matter of fact." There it was again: deception. I did not know who I despised more in that moment, Cockerill or myself.

A man with half his intellect would have been gratified by the praise, but Cockerill wasn't a fool who could be disarmed with a compliment. "What's this then about going to the *Sun* and the *Journal?*"

This was it, then. From here, my circumstances would turn one way or the other. It was too late to turn back. I could not, quite literally, afford to. "Is it correct, Colonel, to say it is in your best interest to make sure the *World* never misses a good story?"

"Of course."

"And unconscionable for you to pass on a story one of the *World*'s rivals would print exclusively?"

A pause. "Go on."

"I understand Charles Dana is an enemy of Mr. Pulitzer."

"Pulitzer has many enemies, Miss Cochrane, including the owner of the *Sun*."

"I also know the *Journal* is published by Pulitzer's younger brother, Albert."

"Your point?"

"Mr. Dana would like nothing better than to trump the *World*. As for Albert, outsmarting the *World* would be quite a victory, would it not? There has been no love lost between the Pulitzer brothers since Mr. Pulitzer purchased the *World* and hired Albert's employees out from under him."

I could see from the set of Cockerill's mouth that his patience was wearing thin. I hadn't told him anything he didn't already know.

"I have come here first, Colonel," I said. "I have no reason to go to the *Sun* or the *Journal*, or any other newspaper for that matter, unless my attempts here do not . . . bear fruit."

"That sounds rather like a threat, Miss Cochrane."

It was exactly what I wanted him to think. I smoothed the top of my skirts. There was a rent in one of my gloves. I hastily moved my hands to my sides to hide it. "I have been in New York since May. I have proved myself quite capable of writing for the *Dispatch* as a correspondent in this city, as well as maintaining a steady following of readers in Pittsburgh."

He was assessing me closely, his curiosity getting the better of his impatience.

I withdrew the paper from Mama's reticule and slid it across the desk. "I've taken the liberty of putting together a list of story ideas I'm willing to undertake, with your permission."

"You hardly need my permission to undertake a story, Miss Cochrane."

"I do if I wish to do so on behalf of the *World*."

Cockerill relaxed into his chair, my veiled threat forgotten. We were on familiar ground again: my ardent plea for employment. "As you know, Miss Cochrane, we do not have a position for another woman reporter on staff. I said as much when we last spoke."

"Forgive me, but I'm hardly proposing to write society news, or report upon the latest fashion in hats."

He lifted his brows. "And so you condemn the work of your fellow sisters in journalism who write of such things?"

I was prepared for this trap, as I'd heard the same from my editor in Pittsburgh two years before, when I'd pleaded with him to give me assignments beyond women's topics. "Certainly not." I smiled. "I'm simply saying I am willing to do more."

"And what of your loyal Pittsburgh readers?" Cockerill ventured with mock horror. "Surely you're not thinking of abandoning them."

Oh, but he was insufferable. It wasn't enough to deny me employment on the basis of my sex; he would ridicule me in the bargain. But I would not let him see my anger. It was what he wanted. An irate, irrational female was far easier to banish from his lair than a clever one who could play his game.

"I would have more readers here, Colonel," I replied, keeping my voice even. I indicated the paper. "See for yourself."

Cockerill picked up the paper at last. He read in silence, his features betraying nothing.

I had tried, in the harrowing hours following my reticule tragedy, to find a story that would pique his interest—something newsworthy, sensational, and sufficiently vulgar, the kind the New York papers hungered for. I had come up empty. Instead, I'd made a list of stories I could investigate on my own—by going undercover. My desperation was so extreme that I would make the news myself. It was the only way to get Cockerill's attention, to prove I had as much mettle as his male reporters, although as far as I knew, none of them had ever proposed the type of bold ideas I was putting before him now. Every idea required some form of deception, some stunt in which I portrayed myself as someone I was not. There was scarcely no identity I was unwilling to assume.

"Well, Miss Cochrane," Cockerill said, his eyes on my list, "you certainly have a flair for the theatrical. A clerk for a fake adoption agency selling black market babies to the highest bidder. A beggar who infiltrates the criminal world of Five Points." He looked up. "Any of these would be difficult, if not impossible, to carry out."

"I am determined to succeed."

We looked at one another for what seemed an age, neither of us willing to be the first to look away. In that instant, I had the impression Cockerill saw me not as a woman but as a reporter.

He reached into his desk drawer and pulled out a slim leather case. "I'm placing in your trust the sum of twenty-five dollars, Miss Cochrane. You are to come back in one week, at which time I will have decided what to do with you."

"You are . . . retaining me?"

"Yes." Cockerill opened the case, counted bills, and extended them toward me.

I leaned forward to accept them, overcome with relief. But when I tried to pull the bills from his grasp, I found he was clutching them tight.

"I cannot promise you anything, Miss Cochrane, but should you take this, it is with the understanding that you will go nowhere else with your list."

"Naturally."

"Most especially the *Sun* or the *Journal*." Cockerill's green eyes bored into mine. I knew then I had been correct in selecting those particular papers. If Pulitzer so much as got a whiff that I'd come here first and been sent away only to knock on the door of his brother's paper or his most formidable rival's, and my story made news—

"I'm waiting, Miss Cochrane."

"Of course, Colonel. You have my word."

Cockerill released his grip, and the bills were in my hand.

The managing editor folded my list and placed it in the breast pocket of his coat. "Now, if you will excuse me, I have a newspaper to run."

A dismissal, but I didn't care. Within a few minutes I was decanted to the lobby, and in another I was again on the street. The first round was over. I hoped it wouldn't be the last. It was not the end, not yet. While I hadn't come away with the assurance of a story, much less employment, I could pay the back rent. Relief washed over me, the tension I hadn't realized I'd been holding in giving way. I was not ruined. Tears swam before my eyes. I placed a hand against the building to steady myself. I could pay back to Mrs. Tuttle the cab fare I'd borrowed. Buy Mama a new dress.

What the next meeting with Cockerill held I didn't know. Either his prejudice would hinder my progress or his desire to sell papers would win out in spite of it. I had so often found that the change-able nature of a woman is but a trifle compared to the mercurial workings of a man's.

But I couldn't think of that now.

A spreading warmth bloomed within me, the first ray of hope since leaving my reticule on the el. The colors seemed to deepen around me. The trees across the street, not yet dressed in the ruddy tones of autumn, shimmered a brighter green. The columns and dome of City Hall blazed a blinding white. And the crowd that flocked the streets—the men, women, and children who scurried along—walked with livelier steps, as if they, too, shared my newfound hope.

The air itself felt electric with all that was to come.

2

*One's imagination is a wonderful
thing when one once gives way to it.*
NELLIE BLY

NEW YORK CITY, SEPTEMBER 1887

Mama put down the black stocking she was mending, a tattered thing that spoke to the hardship into which we had fallen. "Stop worrying, Pinkey. You've given your list to Colonel Cockerill. I'm sure he will respond favorably. Until then, worrying over those clippings will only make you more anxious."

My mother only used my childhood nickname when we were alone. It embarrassed me for many reasons, most especially because it evoked a past altogether different than our life was now. The pink frocks and stockings in which Mary Jane Cochrane had dressed me, her eldest daughter, the great house on Mansion Row with a small staff, the horses and music lessons, were painful memories. It was a time we rarely spoke of now.

From my position on the davenport, I surveyed the newsprint surrounding me. I had been snipping, studying, and organizing stories from the New York papers since my arrival in the spring. I had culled topics from every quarter: politics, business, entertainment, medicine. There was Mayor Hewitt's increasing unpopularity among the immigrant class for his bourgeois nativist views; the impending trial of Jacob Sharp, the infamous horse car magnate who bribed the city's alderman to expand his street transit franchise into lower Manhattan; the fetes of the city's idle elite contrasted with the fourteen-hour workdays of the poor.

"You should tidy those up before Mrs. Tuttle arrives." Mama stabbed the stocking with her needle and glanced up at me, a smile in her deep blue eyes. "She cherishes you my dear, but she does abhor a mess."

I sighed and adjusted my position, avoiding a wayward spring that threatened to escape the old davenport and impale my back. "Oh, Mama. What difference does it make? I shall put them all away when I'm finished." I picked up a clipping. "I cannot help wondering if there is an idea here I've overlooked." The clipping in my hand was about the suffragist movement that had played out over the summer, one of various editorials both condemning and supporting the women's vote. Most of the authors were men with the same view of women in politics as they had of women in journalism. The words still rankled, no matter how many times I read them.

My thoughts were interrupted by a knock. A second later, Mrs. Tuttle entered our sitting room with a tray, closing the door with her formidable posterior, adorned in an equally formidable bustle. "Afternoon, ladies," she said, moving to the table next to the davenport and setting the tray down with a flourish.

"Good afternoon, Mrs. Tuttle," Mama said. "How kind of you to bring something up."

Mama and I held an elevated status in Mrs. Tuttle's Upper West Side boardinghouse for women because she thought me famous. No matter how unsuccessful my attempts to gain employment at the *World,* Mrs. Tuttle refused to believe that the notoriety I'd enjoyed in Pittsburgh wouldn't come in due course in New York. She brought up tea in the afternoons when she had the time, as much because she thought it fitting for "a famous lady what writes for them papers" as because it afforded her time off her feet to discuss the latest news on my employment situation without the other women boarders looking on. In Mama she saw a woman as worthy as the Madonna.

"Ah, I see you're looking over them papers you've cut up again," Mrs. Tuttle said, placing her hands on her hips and casting a critical eye over the piles littering the room. "Anything interesting today?"

I hadn't the heart to tell her I'd stopped buying newspapers two weeks ago. I could no longer afford them. I'd paid our back rent with a portion of Cockerill's retainer and had saved the rest, fearful that if Cockerill sent me away without a story, I'd need the money to get us by until I found a position at another paper. There was also the possibility he'd want his twenty-five dollars back if he sent me packing, a thought that made me shudder every time I thought of it. "No, I'm afraid." I pushed aside some clippings. Mama took a seat beside me on the bumpy davenport. Mrs. Tuttle handed us each a saucer with a biscuit and poured tea.

"Only two cups?" Mama asked. "Won't you be joining us?"

"I'm afraid not, Mrs. Cochrane. I've just learned the widow Johnson is moving out and I've rooms to clean if I'm to show them tomorrow." She handed us our tea in mismatched china cups and tut-tutted. "Not at all like you ladies, our Mrs. Johnson. She's working class she is, but that's no call to up and go without no notice. She don't come from your kind of stock."

Mrs. Tuttle was a champion of good breeding. After Mama told her of our illustrious though short past in Apollo, Pennsylvania, and our subsequent financial difficulties that arose when my father died when I was six years old, the landlady had taken us under her wing. It was not lost on me that we were of a "stock" that had let two months of rent lapse. It didn't seem to matter to dear Mrs. Tuttle, but it bothered me. I didn't want to be in anyone's debt, certainly not one so kind and compassionate as she.

"I can't stand the thought of you ladies pining away," Mrs. Tuttle said, "waiting for word from that man from the paper. One needs nourishment in times of trouble, I always say."

I hid my smile behind my teacup. Mrs. Tuttle found food necessary in all occasions—weddings and christenings, births and deaths, weekdays and the Sabbath, rain or shine. No situation on earth was not made better by stew or cake, depending on the occasion.

"We are hardly pining away," Mama ventured with a smile. "Elizabeth is going for a walk soon, and I've plenty of things to mend to keep me occupied."

"Well then, I'll take my leave and come back for the dishes later," Mrs. Tuttle said. She made to leave, then stopped. "Oh, dear me. I almost forgot. A letter arrived for you this morning, Miss Cochrane." She reached into the voluminous folds of her skirt and withdrew an envelope.

I took it and glanced at the return address. "It's from QO."

Mama looked away, tears of disappointment welling in her eyes. It had been weeks since we'd heard anything from my siblings in Pennsylvania, most especially my younger sister Kate, whose daughter Beatrice, not yet three years of age, was Mama's eldest grandchild. Formerly, nary a week had passed without word from Kate, extolling the feats of little Bea. I could only assume Kate had her hands full with my rambunctious niece. Letters or no, Mama could hardly endure being at such a distance, a distance all the more intolerable when a letter did not arrive from Kate. I wondered, not for the first time, if it had been wise to ask her to accompany me to New York.

When Mrs. Tuttle was gone, I laid my hand on her arm. "Don't worry, Mama. We shall hear something from Kate soon."

"Read your letter, Pinkey," she said, dabbing at her eyes with a handkerchief. "I'm spoiling all your fun."

I tore open the envelope and read aloud:

12 Sept, 1887

My dearest girl,

I hope this letter finds you and your mother happy and well. I received your letter Monday last and was sorry to learn you have not found employment beyond your work for our fair *Dispatch*. Patience is more than a virtue; it is vital when endeavoring to achieve anything of value. New York and its towering monument to journalism, the mighty World, is a worthy pursuit, my dear. Remain steadfast, and all will be well! If not, I shall receive you with open arms and see that Madden does too, if I have anything to say about it. My work here remains much the same, though the atmosphere here is much changed by your absence. The days feel rather dull without your bright face to bring them joy.

Have you had occasion to run into George McCain? I cannot think you will be there much longer without bumping into him on Park Row. He seems most anxious to make your acquaintance once more. I am certain the two of you will work out a sound compromise for your work in that great city you share.

Your loyal friend and Quiet Observer,
QO

"Dear Mr. Wilson," Mama said, after taking a sip of tea. "Such a kind man."

"I shall write to him when I'm back from my walk and tell him of my visit with Colonel Cockerill," I said. "Though I suppose I shouldn't get his hopes up if Cockerill sends me on my way without a story."

"Pinkey," Mama said, "Mr. Wilson makes a good point. It is unlike you to give up, but you must realize, should Colonel Cockerill refuse you, we can always return—"

"I'll not go back to Pittsburgh, Mama." I placed my teacup on the side table with a jarring rattle and stood, my anger rising. "Whether Madden, the devil, welcomes me back or not, I shan't go." I shrugged into my coat hanging on a peg by the door. I refused to meet her eyes.

Mama changed the subject, landing on the one topic I was even more loath to discuss. "How very odd you have seen nothing of Mr. McCain."

As my back was turned, Mama did not see the hot flush that flooded my cheeks. In truth, I had seen him twice near Park Row but had avoided him.

George McCain was the last person on earth to whom I wanted to speak.

⬿

From our furnished rooms on Ninety-Sixth Street, Central Park was a straight walk east a few blocks. I passed boardinghouse after boardinghouse, their thin, bland facades indistinguishable from one another, each its own microcosm of strife. I heard the wail of a baby somewhere in the near distance, the slamming of a door. Someone had upended a trash bin on the sidewalk. I lifted my skirts and moved around the remains of a boiled cabbage and the carcass of a chicken, picked clean. Oyster saloons unfurled disagreeable scents—sawdust, cigars, raw seafood—into the air. I wrinkled my nose and pulled my coat more tightly around me, as if its thin protection could ward off the privation.

The closer I got to Eighth Avenue, the nicer the boarding-houses, the more agreeable the air. When I reached the busy street at last, I crossed, narrowly dodging an omnibus as I ran. I breezed up to the two young women waving to me from the Gate of All Saints.

"Elizabeth," Fannie Merrill said, taking her gloved hands in mine. "We've been dying to hear about your meeting with Cockerill."

"Yes," Viola Roseboro said with a smile, her teeth flashing. "You must tell us everything and leave nothing out."

"Well then," I said, looking from one to the other, "I shall keep you waiting no longer." Arms linked, we strode through the gate into Central Park. The afternoon was crystalline—a day of brilliant sun, cerulean sky, and rustling leaves that signaled the coming bite of autumn. We took the path that headed to the Great Meadow, a breeze rippling our skirts. In fewer than five minutes, I related my morning at the *World* the previous day.

When I finished, Fannie stopped and turned to me. "If Cockerill gave you money to keep silent and wait, it can only mean one thing." My friends exchanged meaningful looks. I waited, hoping they would voice my own suspicion.

"He's going to Pulitzer with your list," Viola said. "He wants to get his approval before he assigns you anything. I'd bet a week's wages on it."

My eyes widened. "Do you really think so?" The thought of the well-known publisher reading my list, actually holding it in his hands, sent a thrill up my spine. I smiled. "I find it comforting Cockerill is under someone's thumb, that his power isn't absolute."

Fannie laughed. How alike we were. Her fiery opinions and belief in equality for women were so much like my own. She'd arrived in New York for the same reason I had: to become a journalist in the greatest city in the United States. She'd joined the ranks of Newspaper Row in the spring. She and Viola were the only two women on the staff of the *World*. I'd met them in the newspaper's lobby during one of my frequent attempts to see Cockerill about a job, and we'd taken to each other immediately. The three of us had met for coffee at the Cosmopolitan Hotel the next day and formed a friendship that had strengthened my resolve to remain in New York.

"Not even the assignment of a *mere woman* to a story is something Cockerill would fail to bring to Pulitzer's attention," Viola said dryly. "He wouldn't dare. No detail is too small, too unimportant, for Pulitzer. Cockerill is powerful enough, but Pulitzer runs a tight ship."

"How intolerable for his employees," I said.

"It drives the men to distraction in the newsroom," Fannie said. "They say he reads every item six times before he allows it to go to print and makes the most miniscule of changes." I pictured the tall, spindly publisher hunched over a fancy desk, reading his newspaper with an enormous magnifying glass. "It galls me that no male reporter with the kind of experience you have would ever need draft such a list to find employment at his paper."

Viola gave my arm a squeeze. "Yes, but let's hope Cockerill sees the risk Elizabeth is willing to take. Risk breeds interest, and interest sells newspapers."

Imbued with a boundless energy, Viola had managed to get hired shortly after Fannie joined the *World*. Like Fannie, she was trapped within the confines of the ladies' pages. Cockerill's insistence that she continue covering what she referred to as petticoat journalism was wearing thin Viola's patience with the colonel.

"Did Cockerill mention any of your ideas in particular?" Viola asked.

"No, other than they would all be impossible to accomplish."

"Humph," Fannie said, cocking a derisive brow.

We walked on, comfortable in the afternoon sun. After a few moments, Fannie stopped again, her deep-set brown eyes searching mine. I could tell by the look on her face she had something to say. She exchanged glances with Viola again, and I had the impression that whatever it was, they had talked of it between themselves. "I just wanted to say—to say—"

"What is it?" I asked, looking from one to the other.

Viola cleared her throat and squeezed my arm again. "It's just that, there are other papers besides the *World,* you know."

I smiled thinly. Was that all? "You sound like Mama. She thinks I should have given up on the *World* months ago." *Especially since I left my reticule on the train two days ago and drained what remained of our finances.* I hadn't breathed a word about my misadventure to Fannie or Viola. I was too afraid they'd pity me and offer me money. I couldn't abide either. "I've decided, if my meeting with Cockerill next week isn't successful, I'll go to the *Sun.*"

Just saying the words made me feel defeated, but the look on my friends' faces was far from pity; they looked relieved. "That a girl," Viola said. "If Pulitzer won't have you, the *Sun* most surely will."

A gust of wind blew across the grass as we began walking again. I'd had my eye on the *New York World* even before I'd left Pittsburgh. The paper was almost mythical in its rise to the top in the four years Pulitzer had owned it. It was the biggest paper in a city of big papers, the one that boasted the largest circulation. It was the *World* that covered the best news, news the city clamored for, news that sent its rivals scurrying for the details of the stories the *World* ran first. I wanted to work there above all else. But what I needed—needed desperately—was a job that would keep me in New York. Even if it meant not working for the *World*.

"Just think of the look on Cockerill's face if your story makes headlines in the *Sun,*" Fannie said with a mischievous grin. "He'll be positively green. And Pulitzer will be apoplectic. He hates Charles Dana with a passion."

"I think you're getting ahead of yourselves," I said soberly.

"I'm not done with the *World* yet. And even if I do land at the *Sun*, it doesn't mean they'll accept any of my outlandish ideas. They'll probably give my list to the men and put me on the women's pages."

"Oh," Fannie said through clenched teeth, her dainty hands balled into fists. "Doesn't that just make you seethe? Imagine, your stories snatched out from under you like that. I think I'd kill any man who had the nerve to steal my ideas and make a sensation of himself doing it."

"You're forgetting one thing," Viola said. "Men are lazy. Why go to so much trouble when the papers pay them well enough and they're working their easy, regular beats? We saw your list, Elizabeth. If Cockerill and Pulitzer don't see your potential, Dana will, and he won't have to raise a finger. You'll be the one in danger. If the story's bad or doesn't come off, he's lost nothing."

They waited, watching me closely. A dog barked in the distance. A couple walking arm in arm sauntered past.

Fannie said delicately, "You could remain a correspondent for the *Dispatch* as you're doing now, you know. There's no harm in that." And then she added, her voice low, "Are you quite certain you're willing to put yourself in jeopardy to get a job here, Elizabeth?"

Madden's assignments had been sporadic since I'd arrived in New York, which meant I often went weeks without recompense. He had no motivation or inclination to give me regular work, for he knew I was only biding my time before I left the *Dispatch* for good to take a position at a New York paper. Fannie's and Viola's incomes were greater, and they didn't have their mothers to support as I did. I cursed myself again for leaving my reticule on the train. How careful I'd been to guard my savings, only to lose what remained in a single train ride.

"I don't see that I have much choice," I said at last.

Viola's features softened. "Your finances. We know it's been a struggle."

You have no idea. "Yes," I said. But it was more than that; I'd never been one to let a wishbone grow where a backbone should be. "I was referring more to my pigheaded desire to be a journalist at any cost." I grinned widely.

Fannie and Viola smiled. Eyes twinkling, Fannie clutched my arm again. "'Pigheaded' is such an ugly word. I prefer 'brave and spirited.'"

We set off again, our mood bolstered. We walked in companionable silence, our arms linked. The working class was still at their labors at this time of day, the rich more partial to the bridle paths and the Mall, so the northern portion of the park was nearly deserted. After a few minutes, we reached the rim of the Meadow and turned left. A soft breeze touched the brims of our hats as a gaggle of geese searched for food among the grasses.

Just through the trees, the waters of the Pool shimmered in the sun. It was one of my favorite spots. Surrounded by foliage, the enclosure surrounding the lake was a private paradise, tranquil and quiet, so different than the fast, bustling streets of the city. We passed some women wheeling prams and took the path that skirted the water. A lone egret poked among the reeds on the opposite bank. Large weeping willows cast their tresses to the water. I recalled a line from Emerson: *I am a willow of the wilderness, loving the wind that bent me.* I was not like the willow. I was an oak, unwilling to bow in the face of adversity. I was stubborn and resilient.

"I will stay in New York," I said quietly. "I shan't give up."

3

There is no greater abnormality than a woman in breeches, unless it is a man in petticoats.

ERASMUS WILSON

PITTSBURGH, PENNSYLVANIA, JANUARY 1885

The newspaper clipping in my reticule had no distinct weight, yet I could feel its presence as tangibly as I would have a stone's. I knew its contents by heart: *If the writer of the communication signed "Lonely Orphan Girl" will send her name and address to this office merely as a guarantee of good faith, she will confer a favor and receive the information she desires.*

One sentence. A handful of words. Yet to me they meant, or could mean, a great deal. In the day that had elapsed since I'd spied them in the letter to the editor section in the *Pittsburg Dispatch,* I'd thought of little else. I'd sent off the requested information straightaway and been rewarded with a note from the managing editor himself.

Despite the butterflies in my stomach that grew stronger as I neared Fifth Avenue, I smiled. I was neither lonely nor an orphan girl, but I couldn't help but feel that my clever pseudonym had played a role in my summons to the paper, even if I didn't yet know what the summons would bring.

A cold westerly wind nipped at my nose as I reached the corner of Wood and Fifth.

Across the street, a few buildings from the corner, the *Dispatch* building rose to a slender four stories, a vertical slice of gray weathered stone. In the chilly morning air, my breath was a ghostly vapor that mingled with coal dust and the faint smell of sulfur, consequences of a city grimy with the manufacture of Mr. Carnegie's steel.

I wanted to tuck my chin inside the collar of my coat, but vanity had won out when I'd left the boardinghouse this morning. My black wool would've proved a better defense against the weather, but my shawl showed off the dress of Persian blue I'd borrowed from Mama to greater effect, and I wanted to look my best.

The street bustled with early-morning commerce. Cabs-for-hire and private carriages rushed past, their drivers hunkered down in the cold. A bank was opening. A grocer was setting out winter vegetables on crates: parsnips, potatoes, turnips. The heady scent of fresh-baked pretzels and roasted chestnuts from a nearby food stall touched my nose, reminding me I hadn't eaten anything for breakfast. My hunger was quickly eclipsed, however, by the shout of a newsboy on the corner across the street.

"Get your *Dispatch* here! Two pennies! The notorious servant girl murderer strikes again! Another girl slaughtered in Texas! Police baffled!"

Another victim bludgeoned with an ax. How ghastly. How many victims did this make? I hadn't yet had the chance to read the day's edition. I realized, given my destination, that this might be a mistake. I stepped from the curb, digging in my reticule for change as I went. Quite unexpectedly, I heard a shout from the left, and then a horse was rearing above me, so close I felt its breath as it whinnied in fear. Suddenly, I was hauled backward. I landed hard in a tangle of petticoats and limbs as I saw the horse's hooves make contact with the street in the spot where I had just been. The driver of the cab raised his fist at me and yelled something foul as he thundered away. For a moment I could only stare after him, though whether I was more aghast at his rudeness or my own stupidity I didn't know. A polite cough drew me to my senses, and I realized, looking down, that there was an arm around my waist.

I turned and saw a man watching me curiously, his legs pinned beneath me. "Are you hurt, miss?" he asked, concern on his face.

"No, I don't think so."

He considered me a moment longer, then, apparently deciding that he believed me, removed his arm from around me.

I scrambled up, color rising to my cheeks. "I'm—" *An idiot.* "Terribly sorry. I—I don't know what came over me."

The stranger pulled himself to his full height. He was well over six feet, slender, and dressed in a well-fitting black coat and matching leather gloves. He bent to pick up his top hat, twirling it once in his hands with such dexterity it seemed a gesture born of long habit. "Sounds to me like a good story came over you." Amusement flickered in his eyes. "Timmy has quite a way with words. I'll have to caution him to be less dramatic when there's a lady approaching traffic."

It took me an instant to realize he was talking about the newsboy. The lad gave a wave across the street, and the man lifted his chin in response. With a quick gesture, the stranger returned the hat to his head, raking a lock of dark hair from his forehead before he did so. "You're certain you aren't hurt? I can hail a cab if you'd prefer not to walk."

"No, no," I said. "I'm only going—" I looked fleetingly across the street at the *Dispatch* building. "A short distance." I couldn't tell him the full truth, that my destination was the very place whose headline had so distracted me that I'd nearly been trampled to death. I suspected he'd only been teasing about the newsboy's role, but his joke was closer to the truth than I wanted to admit.

"Very well then," he said with a smile. "Would you permit me to escort you across the street so that you may arrive to wherever it is you're going in one piece?" He quirked a brow and said with mock solemnity, "I would consider it a huge insult to my pride should anything ill befall you. Not when I could have prevented it." There it was again, that amusement in his eyes. He offered his arm.

I saw no reason to decline him. He had, after all, saved my life. I slipped my arm through his, and after waiting for a break in traffic, we strode together across the street. The rush of heat to my skin where his arm touched mine was due purely to his proximity, yet I felt myself blush again. What was the matter with me? He was a complete stranger. In another minute I would never see him again.

"So sorry, miss," the newsboy said as soon as we'd reached him. "I thought you was a goner for a minute there."

"What's this?" the stranger said, tousling the boy's mop of ginger curls. "You sound as if you had no faith in me at all."

"Oh no, sir," Timmy replied. "I knew you'd save her once I seen you. You was quick. She never seen you coming, nor the horse neither." He turned to me, coloring slightly. "Begging your pardon, miss. I don't mean to sound fresh, just telling it like I seen it."

"That's quite all right," I said. "Timmy, isn't it?"

"That's right."

"Well, Timmy, you have quite a talent. I should like to read more about the ghastly Texas murders. May I have a paper?"

The boy obliged, and I tucked it under my arm, handing over two pennies. "And now I really must be going." I turned to the tall stranger. "Thank you for appearing when you did, sir. I shouldn't like to think about what might've happened if you hadn't." I swallowed, a shiver navigating my spine. The shock of it still hadn't left me.

The stranger tipped his hat. "You're most welcome. Do be careful on Fifth Avenue, mind. It's full of newsboys, though none as talented as Timmy here."

The boy beamed, and the stranger tousled his hair again. I turned to go, but not before I saw the man drop coins into the boy's palm. "Now tell me," I heard him say as I walked away, "what does the *Dispatch* have to say today?"

Timmy laughed as though the man had made a jest, but his reply was swallowed up by the chugging of vehicles and clopping of horse hooves as I made my way to the newspaper office's entrance a few doors down. Bold yellow letters painted on the glass informed me that the paper was the largest in the city, boasting a circulation of more than thirty-five thousand. Butterflies stirred in my stomach again. Would the managing editor of such a colossus waste his time asking me here if his intentions were not earnest? And just what *were* his intentions?

I was surprised to find the lobby deserted. A reception desk welcomed visitors just past the entrance, with a row of chairs off to the side. However, there was no receptionist at the desk to assist me, nor a directory indicating what floor I wanted. I took a seat and withdrew the paper from beneath my arm. The headline about the grisly murder glared at me in thick angry letters, but my head shot up almost immediately when two men entered from the street and headed for the stairwell, talking in low tones as they climbed. I returned my attention to the story but realized, as sensational as it was, that I was too distracted to read. What was I to do if the receptionist didn't appear? Did I dare seek out the editor on my own? I was biting my lip in frustration when the door from the street opened once more.

"So my eyes weren't playing tricks on me after all," my knight errant said with a grin. "I thought I saw you walk in here." He removed his hat and glanced at the reception desk. "Ah, no Gregson I see."

I rose to my feet. "Gregson?"

"Receptionist." He mimed drinking and frowned. "Probably

still in his cups from last night. Poor fellow. Not all that depend-
able, I'm afraid."

My heart sank. *Please let the reason I'm here be unrelated.* I did
not want to be a receptionist. I would be horrible at it.

"Have you come to place an advertisement, madam? They can
assist you on the second floor if that's the case."

"No, I'm here to see Mr. Madden."

His eyebrows rose a fraction. "I see." He looked down at the hat
in his hands and said carefully, "Madden doesn't generally speak
to walk-ins. I can give him a message if you like. Or you could
send him a note yourself, by post. He doesn't always have time
to respond to public inquiries, of course, but he reads everything
that comes across his desk."

He was making every effort to be polite, but I knew when I was
being dismissed. I lifted my chin. "I'm not here to make a 'public
inquiry,' as you put it. I happen to have an appointment with him."

The stranger's eyes widened, and then something like relief
came over him. "Forgive me. We have a great many people come
in. Most of them simply want to run an advertisement. Those are
handled easily enough. But there are those who oftentimes wish
to express their difference of opinion, quite heatedly I might add,
concerning some piece the paper has run."

He'd described the situation that had brought me here so
closely, I felt my hackles rise. "I see," I said flatly. "How very
unpleasant. Readers who disagree."

He caught the change in my tone, and his expression sobered.
"It isn't the difference of opinion he takes issue with."

"Oh, then what is it? The fact that he must converse with the
public at all?"

The ire that had led to the letter I'd written Madden came
flooding back. Those insufferable articles about a woman's place in
the home by the equally insufferable columnist Erasmus Wilson. It
had taken all my control not to tear each one to bits after I'd read it.

"It's not that," he said. "If Madden were to meet with everyone
who wished to give him a piece of his—or her—mind, he'd get
very little done. He simply doesn't have the time."

"Well then, I shall endeavor not to waste it," I shot back. "Please
kindly direct me to where I can find him. With his time as precious
as it is, I imagine he frowns upon visitors who are late."

There was a beat of silence between us. A floorboard creaked.
A horse whinnied outside as it clopped by. The stranger did not
stir. He was fixing me with the most penetrating gaze, trying, it
seemed, to plumb the very depths of me. After another moment,

he said, low, "You must forgive me again. I believe I've insulted you. That was certainly not my intention." He extended his hand. "Please allow me to introduce myself properly. George McCain, city editor for the *Dispatch*."

I took his hand. "Elizabeth Cochrane." His eyes were a deep gray, the color of the sea below churning clouds. It was his continued assessment of me, however, that unsettled me most. I withdrew my hand and looked away, my anger giving way to sudden awkwardness.

"Madden's office is on the top floor, Miss Cochrane. Please follow me."

We climbed four flights to the top. By the time we reached the final step, I was out of breath. While the lower floors had opened up into wide rooms full of people at desks, this floor revealed only a narrow hallway flanked by doors, most of them closed.

McCain led me to an office at the end of the hallway. The door was open, but no one was seated at the desk. He indicated a chair outside the door. "If you'll have a seat just there, I'll see where Madden's gone off to." He disappeared down the hallway.

From what I could see, Madden's office was exceedingly tidy. Save for the few cigar butts in the ashtray on his desk, it was devoid of any personal effects that might have given hint to the kind of man he was. As the managing editor for the city's largest newspaper, there was surprisingly little paper. Just two neat piles of correspondence graced his desk. Beside these, pencils lay in neat, vertical rows. I wondered if dust was allowed to settle here and, if it did, who removed it—a cleaning service, or Madden, with his meticulous orderliness?

Down the hall, McCain was knocking softly at a door. He pulled it open and ducked his head inside. I couldn't hear the conversation but guessed he'd found Madden, because in the next instant, McCain was waving for me to join him. As I reached his side, he pressed his lips together in a smile. He gestured toward the open door, gave me a conspiratorial wink, and strode away.

"So this is the Lonely Orphan Girl, is it?" a man with a handlebar mustache said, his lips clenched around a cigar. He was seated across a desk from another gentleman, this one seemingly older, though with the heavy smoke that hung about the room, it was difficult to tell for sure.

I didn't know if the question was directed at me, but I lifted my chin and nodded nevertheless.

"Come in, come in." The older man behind the desk beckoned me. "George, move down a seat and let the poor girl get off her feet." He turned to me, the blue eyes behind his spectacles bright and twinkling. "The first time anyone climbs those steps, they're ready to collapse. Lucky for me I'm a robust old man, or I'd have expired long ago."

"Gad, but she's young." I swung my gaze to the man with the cigar and found him eyeing me warily through the haze. "May I ask how old you are?"

I straightened my spine. "Twenty, sir. I'll be twenty-one come May."

He sat blinking at me for a moment, then rose with a grunt, extending a fleshy hand. "George Madden," he said around his cigar. "I'd thank you for coming, but I expect Erasmus already has a pretty speech prepared to that effect."

I took his hand. The editor's face was pale and flaccid beneath his bowler hat, his potbelly straining against the buttons of his suit—all things that hinted at an older man. But he didn't look a day over thirty or thirty-five. I suspected the running of a newspaper had taken a toll on him. He didn't appear to be a man who had the leisure to spend time out of doors. Judging by the rather shoddy condition of his jacket, he didn't look like a man who would have a spotless office either.

"Elizabeth Cochrane. Thank you for inviting me here." *I think.*

Madden grunted again and said rather cryptically, "Whether an arrangement can be made that is fortuitous for us both remains to be seen, Miss Cochrane." Without taking his eyes from mine, he continued, "Erasmus, I leave her to you. You're much better at this sort of thing than I am. Now, if you'll both excuse me, I've got copy to approve before the sun sets on this day."

He left the room, closing the door behind him.

In the uncomfortable silence that followed, I realized two things. First, the office was the opposite of Madden's: papers, magazines, and newsprint littered every surface with no apparent order; bits of paper, receipts, and photographs were tacked to every perpendicular surface within an arm's reach of the desk; cubbyholes on the credenza behind the desk were crammed to bursting with paper, pens, and what looked to be the remains of a sandwich. Second, Madden had called him Erasmus. This, then, this gentleman peering at me from over the top of his glasses, was Erasmus Wilson—the man who had caused so much bitterness to spew from my pen.

"You may close your mouth, Miss Cochrane, and take a seat." The kind look on his face belied the sternness of his words.

There was nothing to do but oblige, and so I did, arranging my skirts around me.

"Madden has a rather direct manner about him. It's jarring at times, but he means well." Wilson chuckled and then waved a hand in the air, as if noticing for the first time how thick the smoke was in the room. He spun in his chair and opened a window behind him a crack, letting in a thin stream of bracing January air. "There, that's better." He leaned back in his chair and steepled his fingers, the tips of which were smudged black with ink. "You have obviously gathered that I am Erasmus Wilson, author of the *Quiet Observations* column that so, er, moved you to write us."

"I have," I said.

"And yet you are puzzled, I think."

"I was under the impression I would be speaking with Mr. Madden. Forgive me, but he's the one who requested I write the paper and supply my name and address so that an appointment could be arranged."

A small smile crept onto Wilson's face. He turned to the credenza behind him, lifted two piles of paper, and placed them on the desk between us. "Do you know what these are, Miss Cochrane?"

"Correspondence of some sort."

"Exactly so." He thumbed one of the stacks. "Most correspondence comes addressed to the editor, some of it positive, some of it not. Such is the way of the newspaper business. We can't make everyone happy. Madden is dutiful in reading all of it. A good managing editor needs to stay current with his readership." Wilson sighed and removed his glasses, rubbing both eyes with a thumb and forefinger. "However, correspondence over the last week has more than tripled, most of it to do with my reply to a reader who signed himself—"

"Anxious Father," I finished. A man with five unmarried daughters. *I am at a loss how to get them off, or what use to make of them,* he had written. Wilson's written response was deplorable. He blamed parents for failing to rear children for the roles they were intended for, namely, daughters who could cook and clean house to perfection. Any woman who desired anything else was venturing outside the only sphere to which she belonged: home.

"Ah, I see the very name still hits a nerve."

"I don't believe women are out of their minds for desiring to be more than someone's humble daughter or wife, Mr. Wilson."

"And yet, civilization has been forged by women who stayed at home and made their world a little paradise, Miss Cochrane."

I had a sudden image of Mama at our kitchen table, exhausted from her workday, cutting a sweet bun into five equal portions because it was all she could afford to buy her children for dinner. "Not all women have the luxury of staying home, and many who do don't wish to be there." My anger was a black hole inside me. Why had I even come? Did he or Madden think to change my mind? Wilson was nodding solemnly. "The women of this city—mothers, unmarried women, widows, young girls like yourself—have been writing in and telling us so, although none with quite the—" his eyes searched the ceiling, looking for the right word, "*vigor* you did."

"Give them time, Mr. Wilson," I said with a tight smile. "Although, now that I think of it, they're probably too busy working to pay their rent and feed their children."

Wilson studied his hands, looking a bit sheepish. "I am an old-fashioned man, Miss Cochrane."

Old-fashioned indeed. One of Wilson's lines to Anxious Father, in commenting how ghastly it was for women to seek roles intended for men, had been *There is no greater abnormality than a woman in breeches, unless it is a man in petticoats.* How my sister Kate had laughed when I, seated at the kitchen table of our boardinghouse, had read that aloud. I had not found it at all funny.

"I write my column from the perspective of a country gentleman waxing nostalgic about times gone by," Wilson was saying, "but we are in a new age, are we not?" He slapped his knee with a flourish. "Why, just yesterday I read in our very paper that the Boggs & Buhls Department Store installed its first telephone. And if Thomas Edison has anything to say about it, the gaslights that illuminate our streets will be powered by electricity soon."

And yet you would keep women in apron strings. I leaned forward. "Is it so hard to imagine women in different roles? Even Ms. Bramble called you out on your reply to Anxious Father." Bessie Bramble was the sole woman on the *Dispatch* staff, a seasoned journalist I greatly admired who'd used her column to respond to his nonsense.

Wilson searched his desk and retrieved a newspaper from a pile, searching with his finger for the entry he was looking for. He then read aloud, "'Cooking and housework are drudgery so why should women do that unless they are compelled to, any more than the brethren should all go out and hew logs?'" He chuckled. "Oh yes, Bessie had a few words to say about it."

"I must say I agree with her."

"Well then," Wilson said, "you should know that it's because of Ms. Bramble, in part, that you've been summoned here. Madden plucked your reply from the pile overtaking his desk and tossed it to me. He was struck by your earnestness, if not by your—" he coughed delicately into his hand, "penmanship. I agreed, on both counts. When I showed your reply to Bessie, she suggested Madden bring you in at once."

I let out a long breath I didn't know I'd been holding. Bessie Bramble had read my letter. She'd thought it good enough to ask me here.

"Miss Cochrane, have you any idea how many papers serve this city?"

"Four?"

"Seven. For a city of sixty thousand people, that's five too many. The competition is fierce." He gestured once more to the stack of letters on his desk. "More than one of these stated, in no uncertain terms, that my outdated notions were responsible for them taking their business elsewhere. Most of them, naturally, were women."

I didn't blame them, but I remained quiet. I sensed something good was coming and didn't want to press my luck.

Wilson leaned forward and peered at me over the top of his glasses. "Have you any journalism training?"

"No."

"Schooling?"

"I attended normal school some years ago." Attended, yes. Graduated, no. But I wasn't about to offer this up.

"Are you employed?"

"Horrific as it must seem to you, Mr. Wilson, I tried my hand at nanny work and housekeeping and found myself unsuited to both." There was no reason to beat about the bush, and anyway, he knew my stance on women in tiresome roles. "I haven't yet found anything amenable to my skills."

"And so how is it you are getting by, if I may be so bold?"

"I live with my mother. She runs a boardinghouse in Allegheny City. My siblings and I help out as best we can."

"Orphan girl indeed," he said, his blue eyes dancing. "And your father?"

"Deceased."

Wilson nodded, rubbing his chin absently as he tried to fit the pieces of me together. After a moment, he said, "Very well. What I ask of you is this: I'd like you to pen a reply to Anxious Father's latest letter." He rummaged on his desk again and held up a folded piece of paper. "Your answer will serve as a sort of test. We will pay you for it, but I cannot promise you we'll print it. Along with your penmanship, your grammar leaves something to be desired, and in any case, Madden makes the final decisions. I can, however, promise you that I will take you under my wing and teach you what I can about being a writer—a *possible* writer—for the *Dispatch*."

"And if my opinions do not agree with yours?"

He chuckled. "My dear girl, that is precisely what we want you for."

I blinked, quite unable to believe what he had just said.

"In return, Miss Cochrane, you must teach me the mind of the modern woman."

Energy rightly applied and directed will accomplish anything.

NEW YORK CITY, SEPTEMBER 1887

The leaden sky was filled with the promise of rain as I waited at the Ninety-Third Street station. Never once had I ridden a train in New York that was not a congested human pen within, and this damp, gray afternoon was no exception. When the train arrived, huffing and hissing as it slid to a halt, I managed to squeeze into a seat while others less fortunate were made to stand shoulder to shoulder while the train bounced, swung, and bumped from one station to the next. A penny fare hardly warranted lavish surroundings, but I would have liked to experience a journey just once that did not assault my nose and eye in equal measure. The malodorous vapors issuing from Washington Market combined with the grit and grime belched from the foundries of the Lower West Side invaded the senses of even the most robust New Yorkers. These were no less repugnant than the stench within of unwashed bodies and the sight of poorly shod children holding fast to their mothers' hands, faces black with soot from their fourteen-hour workday in the factories.

A young girl of no more than eight or nine stood next to my seat, our faces level. Her cheeks were covered in grime, her hair a riot of tangles, but it was her eyes that caught my attention. Round, brown, frozen. We stared unblinking at one another. It did not appear an adult was with her, no parent or guardian. Where was she headed? Where did she belong? I bit my lip. I no longer carried all the money I owned in my—Mama's—reticule. Fate had taught me a lesson, but I no longer trusted myself to leave the train with my purse in tow either. I had wrapped its strings twice around my wrist for good measure, but I unwound them now, reached inside, and withdrew a nickel. I didn't yet know what my meeting with Cockerill would yield, but even my situation was not as dire as I imagined the young girl's to be. She wasn't even wearing a coat. I hoped the coin would relieve—at least for a little while—the detachment I found in the depths of those chocolate brown eyes. The girl snatched it quickly from my open palm, as if I might change my mind and think better of it. I was rewarded with a small smile, and then she turned from me, but not before I saw the shame in her face.

I alighted at Barclay Street and walked four blocks, dead-ending into the stretch of granite that was the post office, an eyesore of monstrous proportions. Situated on a triangular plot of land across from City Hall Park, its corner towers and center dome reminded me of a squat, turbaned old man. I turned left and approached the park. A day without sun and warmth had kept crowds from the green, and I was able to cross without circumnavigating around pedestrians, groups of children playing, and street vendors selling hot buns to hungry parkgoers.

Across the street, the *World* building loomed like a stone beast. On such a dreary day as this, the golden dome would reflect no light out to sea, but as it was higher than Lady Liberty's torch, I imagined it would be the first of the city that immigrants approaching from the harbor would glimpse.

Inside the lobby, the bulbous-nosed guard acknowledged, with an almost imperceptible nod of his head, that I was permitted to advance to the elevators. I foolishly expected Cockerill to be present at our agreed upon time. He was not.

As a child, I had never been patient. I awaited the birth of my youngest brother Harry with anger, not comprehending why Mama could not bring him forth sooner. At five, I learned to saddle my pony myself, unwilling to wait for our gardener, a slow-moving old man who had worked for my father for years, to do it. After Papa died, my impatience manifested in other ways. Though I had always enjoyed books, I found it hard to sit still in school and was often disciplined for being too active, too precocious, in my nature.

By the time I had reached fifteen years of age, I had accepted my inability to remain still, preferring exercise and lively conversation over endless hours bent over books.

At twenty-three, none of my restlessness had tempered in the slightest.

When Cockerill did appear three-quarters of an hour later, it was with the speed of a man who would just as soon run me over in his carriage as pull to a stop.

"Miss Cochrane," he said, breezing into his office. He stood over his desk, thumbed through some small memorandums, and, without looking up, said, "As it turns out, there is a matter we would like you to investigate. A matter similar in scope to one of your suggestions, with a slight twist."

I waited, wondering if his "we" meant he had consulted Joseph Pulitzer in the matter of my employment.

Cockerill seated himself and looked at me at last. "One of your ideas involved an investigation into the goings-on inside a mental institution."

"Yes, I came up with the idea because of the two guards who were indicted for manslaughter when they killed a lunatic." That trial had led the *World* to run two editorials calling for an overhaul of the institution because it was overcrowded and mismanaged.

"That's correct," Cockerill said, nodding. "That was the facility on Ward's Island that houses the men. We are interested in what you can learn of the other institution, the one for women on Blackwell's Island. Do you recall the story the *Times* ran about a month after the Ward's Island incident?"

"Something about nurses who pressed charges against two physicians."

"Yes, they were all eventually suspended, but the fact is, Miss Cochrane, we have been, thus far, unable to investigate the atrocities—alleged atrocities—being committed in these institutions. As a body of the press, we have not been allowed on the islands. We would like you to lift the curtain of secrecy."

"And the twist?"

"We would like you to gain admittance into the Blackwell's Island insane asylum not as a nurse, as you proposed, but as an inmate."

A shiver ran down my spine. The silence that enveloped Cockerill's office seemed to thicken, as if the contents of the room were poised for my reaction. *An inmate.* "But how will I get in?"

"I'll leave that to you, Miss Cochrane."

"I shall have to feign insanity."

"Naturally," he replied. "Your job is to observe, nothing more, but leave no stone unturned. Find out what you can and write up things as you find them."

"And how am I to get out?"

"Leave that to us," Cockerill replied offhandedly, as if I had just asked him how to hail a cab or some other trivial matter. "In ten days' time, which we feel is a sufficient duration to gather what information you can, we will get you out, even if we have to reveal who you really are and for what purpose you feigned insanity." Cockerill laced his fingers together and leveled his gaze at me. "Your task, for now, is to get in."

There was no mistaking the authority in the statement. I could take it or leave it, and because I could not afford to leave it, I nodded my agreement. How simple the motion, that little bob of my head, that sealed my contract to become, for ten days, a lunatic.

Some moments later, I rode the elevator to the lobby, my mind racing, my impatience gone. I had at last succeeded in getting an assignment from the *World*. It was not employment, but it was a chance. I would not likely get another.

Upon reaching the street, I found to my relief that the sun was peeking through dispersing clouds. The sidewalk was beginning to dry. I decided to take a circuitous walk around the city, my mind more focused on the story Cockerill had given me than on the path in front of me. Doctors, nurses, a remote facility, lunatics. They would all be thrust upon me—or I upon them more like—in a matter of days. Presently, I found myself face-to-face with the Halls of Justice. It was a rather majestic-sounding name for a bleak granite building referred to as the Tombs. I walked warily past, thinking of the prisoners inside. It was widely known as a dark, unsanitary place filled with criminals who had committed any number of crimes—theft, burglary, or worse. I shivered, goose-flesh creeping along my skin, and then chided myself for my own foolishness. Would the insane asylum on Blackwell's Island be any more comforting than the Tombs? Were not the insane at Blackwell's prisoners too, closeted away, kept from society, without freedom of movement, without free will? If the facade of the city prison unnerved me, how on earth was I to endure the interior of an asylum, as a lunatic?

I headed west toward Broadway. I had thought that getting an assignment from Cockerill would bring relief, even joy. Instead, my anxiety had intensified to something akin to dread. My task would not be easy—all of the ideas on my list were challenging ones, fraught with any number of difficulties, most especially assuming the guise of someone I was not. But a *lunatic*. Did I have the means to pull it off? At a crowded intersection, I climbed steep steps leading to the station platform, lost in my roiling thoughts. My legs felt leaden. At the landing, I worked my way forward, elbow to elbow with passengers awaiting the next train. A question presented itself, as stark as it was unbidden: was I afraid that I'd never manage to get on the island, or was I afraid that I would?

A few minutes later, the train lumbered in, belching steam from its fuming underbelly as it slowed to a halt. I pushed my way through the crowd, determined to be among the first to board. I didn't revel in the thought of standing for the six-mile journey uptown. After dropping a penny into an attendant's palm, I climbed aboard and pushed my way to a seat at a window.

The train jerked, then slipped away from the platform. I settled back, determined to take in my surroundings to shut out the possibility that I had just made a horrible mistake. A hodgepodge of tenements, boardinghouses, and shops stood huddled against each other on either side of the track, immovable watchers of the constant, never-ceasing flow of people who were the lifeblood of New York.

There is no better place to observe the complexity of life in New York than upon an elevated train. There one could view the most squalid lodgings of the poor and the vast homes of the rich in the time it took to sneeze. Misery amid plenty. Cheap wages against old money. Immigrants and Knickerbockers. Laborers who worked fourteen-hour days while the Astors and Vanderbilts held their soirees and balls farther uptown. The working class, who couldn't afford to live far from where they labored, lived among the vapors of gasworks, slaughterhouses, and rail yards in the lower reaches of Manhattan. As one moved north, the air was fresher, the buildings newer, the houses grander. Still, it often surprised me that the haves and have-nots could live so close together, leading such disparate lives.

Amid the two extremes, the middle class of New York seemed almost invisible, yet this was the class to which I belonged—those who must work, if not in the factories, foundries, and wharves, then in the shops, offices, or a skilled trade. *Work*. I was back to my conundrum.

I sighed in frustration as the train came to a stop. Straight ahead was the lush foliage of Central Park. I frowned. The line dead-ended here. In my befuddled state, I'd taken the Sixth Street Line instead of the Ninth, which ran all the way up to Ninety-Sixth Street toward home.

I cursed under my breath, shuffled out of my seat, and stepped off the train. Looking heavenward, I saw clouds to the west, but the sun was bright and the temperature perfect for a walk. In the next moment, I was dashing across Fifty-Ninth into the park.

The breeze moved over the surface of the Pond, a dogleg-shaped body of water that held court on the southeast corner of the park. I was content basking in the warmth of the autumn afternoon, far from the crush of the city. Few pedestrians were about. Perhaps the threat of rain earlier had kept them away. It was just as well. I needed time to think. Had I made a gaffe in accepting Cockerill's assignment? Had he been merely testing me to see if I'd still accept when he'd insisted I impersonate a lunatic instead of a nurse? The more my mind worried over it, the more I realized that it was immaterial whether I'd walked into a trap. I had accepted the assignment. There was nothing for it now other than to go through with my ruse.

My first meeting at the *Dispatch,* when QO had given me my first chance to write for the paper, seemed like child's play now. If I wanted to work in New York as a reporter, I needed to prove myself. No one needed to know how terrified I was, for I was terrified.

I was just returning to the path that encircled the Pond when I heard someone call.

"Miss Cochrane?"

I froze. Nothing but trees ahead and the path that wended through them. There was no one, and yet, I knew that voice. I knew it as well as my own.

"Miss Cochrane? Can it really be you?"

I spun. I had played out so many scenarios over how George McCain and I would finally meet in New York that I thought him an apparition. Something conjured from the fanciful realm of my imagination. I'd pictured meeting him on the el, at the library, in City Hall Park, each time bringing into sharp focus my initial surprise and, later, the residual pain such imaginings left behind. But he did not disappear this time when I blinked, vanquished like so many other fleeting imaginings. He stood not twenty paces away. Not a figment, but very, very real.

He was even more handsome than my daydreams had evoked.

He stood, lean and lithe, in a dark overcoat, a rakish lock of dark hair falling forward onto his brow as he doffed his top hat. I broke the rigid posture in which I had been holding myself and offered him my hand as he approached. "Why, Mr. McCain. Is that you? What a pleasant surprise."

McCain bowed over my hand, his stormy gray eyes never leaving my face. "It seems I always happen upon you in a profusion of nature."

A flash of McCain fingering daffodils on a table quoting Wordsworth. *And then my heart with pleasure fills, and dances with the Daffodils.* Standing before me in a white summer suit and boater, his carriage waiting behind him, the sweet smell of clover around us.

Already my body was betraying me. My heart was beating an unsteady staccato, and a flush was creeping up my cheeks.

"Erasmus tells me you've been here since the spring," he said, straightening and removing his hat. "I've had not a word from you."

"I fail to see a reason why you would expect one."

His eyes searched mine. I could see that my words had wounded him. "You might have asked for my address and written me."

"For what purpose? To tell you Madden has given me permission to write about puffed sleeves and skirt lengths? Such work hardly treads upon your turf."

His eyebrows rose a fraction. "We are fellow correspondents for the same paper, Miss Cochrane. That doesn't make us enemies. In any case, I know you are only temporarily with the *Dispatch*. You made it clear in your note to Erasmus you were headed here to work for a New York paper."

My heart sank. If McCain knew about my proud, cursory note—*Dear QO, I am off for New York. Look out for me*—he knew I'd left without Madden's approval to correspond on behalf of the *Dispatch*. I was doing so now only because QO had persuaded Madden to keep me on until I found a position. It was a wound to my self-respect that he knew, but I would not let him see it. I lifted my chin. "I say again, Mr. McCain: I shall not tread on your turf. That was never my design."

A softness came into his eyes. "Must we pretend this discussion is about 'treading on my turf,' as you put it?"

I looked away.

"You are angry with me for leaving Pittsburgh."

"Nonsense. You had an opportunity and took it." I fingered a leaf from a rhododendron bush and felt heat rise to my cheeks again.

Something in my face must have changed, because he took

a step closer. "I've wanted to ask Erasmus a dozen times where to find you here, but I couldn't bring myself to do it. It was too dangerous, not to mention self-indulgent."

He was devilishly handsome. Oh, how I wanted to sink into him and feel his arms wrap around me.

A flock of geese flew over, their honks reverberating around us. I began walking along the path again, back in the direction I'd come. McCain kept his strides even with mine.

"It was good of Erasmus to negotiate a truce of sorts with Madden," he said, switching to a lighter subject. "I know the work you're doing here for the *Dispatch* isn't what you want, but something will break."

"Perhaps it already has." The words were out before I could stop them.

"Oh?"

I kept walking, mentally berating myself for saying too much.

McCain stopped me. "Are congratulations in order? Heavens, why didn't you say so before? This is excellent news."

He looked so happy for me that I wanted to weep. "It's not—not a sure thing. Not yet anyway."

His brows came together in confusion. "What do you mean?"

"I must—" I looked away and back again. "The *World*—it's complicated and unfortunately, I'm not at liberty to say."

A knowing look crossed his features, and he swore softly under his breath, closing his eyes for a brief instant. When he opened them again, he said, "I don't blame you for seeking employment at the *World*. It's the best of the best. But you must be careful."

"Really, Mr. McCain," I said, making my voice light. I began to walk once more. He had guessed more than I wished him to know. "I don't see—"

He came to stand in front of me so that I was forced to stop and look at him. A bird called in the distance, and the wind stirred the lock of hair on his forehead. "I told you once that I would not interfere in your life. But I am bound by our . . . friendship, and by my honor, to warn you."

"Warn me?" I looked up at him, aghast. Of all the things I thought he might say, that he could say, it was not this.

"I hold Cockerill and Pulitzer in the highest esteem as newspapermen, but they're men who firmly believe in the doctrine of 'the end is worth the means.'"

I was taken aback. "You know Cockerill?"

"Everyone on Newspaper Row knows Cockerill." He looked like he wanted to say something else but thought better of it, twirling the hat in his hands instead. Then he stopped, looked at me, and said, "Like you, they'll do anything to get a story. Unlike you, they won't put themselves at personal risk. Do you understand what I'm saying?" He ran a hand through his hair, looking more exasperated than I'd ever seen him. "Cockerill isn't to be trusted. Pulitzer is no better. Do not put yourself at risk for the *World*. It's too dangerous." He couldn't possibly know about the list I'd given Cockerill, or learned of my assignment. I'd only just accepted it myself. I took a deep breath and said with more courage than I felt, "You take me for a fool, Mr. McCain, if you think I'll do anything I shall regret."

There was a beat of silence. McCain's eyes never left mine, and when he spoke next, it seemed he was choosing his words carefully. "I know the kind of stories you wish to pursue, and I know how badly you want to work for a New York paper. You are a champion of equal rights, the downtrodden—the very same whom Pulitzer attempts to win over with his paper." He looked away, his face reddening in anger. Then he turned to me again. "Do you not find it odd he condemns the wealthy of New York to gain the support of the immigrants who buy his paper, yet keeps company with the same elite?"

"I—I fail to see the importance—"

"I fear you'll take on something big at the expense of your own safety, Miss Cochrane. Cockerill's hatched some horrific scheme you've agreed to, hasn't he?" McCain stepped closer and grasped my arm. He was so close that his breath stirred the hair at my temple. "Tell me. Tell me I'm wrong."

I could only gaze back at him, unable to utter a word, for if I did, I would tell him everything. But I couldn't take the risk. If I let the cat out of the bag and he went to Cockerill, I would never write for the *World*. Ever.

"Do not allow them to take advantage of you in your desperation, Elizabeth. I beg you."

His voice was low and husky, and for a moment, neither of us moved. I was aware of the dark lashes that framed his eyes and the heat of his body, the tantalizing pull of his mouth. I forced myself to lower my gaze. I didn't know what excited me more—the feel of his hand on my arm or that he had used my given name.

"Forgive me," McCain said. But he didn't release me.

"I—"

"Please, allow me to finish," he said softly, his eyes moving over my face, my hair. "I said more than I should have that day at Schenley, but I wouldn't take the words back even if I could." He raised his hand and brought it to rest against my cheek. "You know, you are the most intelligent, most independent woman I know, and yet you bring out the most protective instincts in me."

I didn't know how many minutes passed before I pulled away. Too many, and not enough. I gathered my skirts and stepped around him. "I must be getting home. It's growing late and Mama will be worried." I walked a few paces away, then turned. "And I don't need your protection. I'm quite capable of taking care of myself."

He stood looking after me, his hat in his hands, his expression somber. "I know." A whisper. For a second, he looked aged, as if the utterance of the words had cost him his youth. We could only stare at one another, each lost in memories, and then I turned again and walked away, this time not looking back.

⁂

"Oh, Pinkey." Mama slumped back against the davenport and gazed at me as if I had lobsters crawling from my ears. "Please tell me you're pulling my leg."

It had all come out in a rush: the meeting with Cockerill, taking the wrong train, the walk in Central Park, the dash to the station so I could take the Ninth Avenue line home. I had only left out running into George McCain. Mama had listened patiently, even with some excitement, but had turned ashen when she learned of my ten-day assignment.

"What did you think, Mama?" I said, my voice rising. "You saw my list. None of my ideas were going to be easy."

"What did I think?" Mama sat up straight. "I thought a man with Colonel Cockerill's clout would choose a story that wouldn't so endanger my daughter." I had no reply to that. Mama rose and walked to the end of the davenport and back, her hand on her forehead, eyes downcast, one end of her shawl dragging along the floor. "Blackwell's Island. I can't think of a more despicable place. You know what's there besides the asylum, don't you? A prison, almshouses, a hospital for the chronically ill." She sat down again. In the late afternoon sun slanting through the window, she looked older. I wondered, not for the first time, if bringing her to New York had been a good idea. She was away from the rest of her children and her beloved grandchildren. Our precarious financial situation and, now, my risky assignment were more than she had bargained for.

"Blackwell's Island is not a place people return from, Pinkey," Mama breathed. I sat down beside her. She reached out and squeezed my knee. "You must be careful. This is all very dangerous, especially for a woman."

"I will come back, Mama," I said. "Cockerill promised. Ten days isn't that long."

Mama walked to the window. "Why couldn't he accept your original idea? Impersonating a nurse would have given you some level of authority, of respect. An inmate, on the other hand . . ." She let her words trail off, unwilling, it seemed, to breathe life into her fear.

I was having the same reservations, but I wasn't about to say so. I was determined to see this through. "I would've had to supply references and proof of training I'm sure, none of which would guarantee my employment." In truth, I suspected it was the drama of the tale told from a lunatic's perspective that Cockerill wanted to exploit. It was what would sell the most newspapers. "I hardly need these things if I'm to assume the role of a madwoman."

Mama closed her eyes. "I cannot pretend I like this, Pinkey." When she opened them again, I saw a spark of anger. "It pains me to see you take on such a dangerous thing, for a newspaper that may well decide, when all is said and done, not to employ you."

My eyes widened. "You don't think I'll do a good enough job for Cockerill to offer me a position?"

"That's not what I meant. I have all the confidence in the world in you, but I don't have the same confidence that Cockerill will reward you in kind."

She had voiced my own concern. I didn't know whether to put my faith in Cockerill, whether I could trust him. But there was something else too. "Must you make me say it, Mama?"

She stormed back to the davenport, pointing a finger at me. "Don't you dare tell me you must take this risk for us to stay here. You'll find something. We won't starve. There are other papers and there are certainly other stories. And for heaven's sake, if all else fails, there are other professions."

"Not for me."

Mama sighed and covered her eyes with her hand, massaging her temples. "I suppose you wouldn't entertain the idea of writing QO and asking for his advice?"

"There's no time for that, Mama. I'm to start right away." I was certain QO would advise me against stepping foot on Blackwell's Island.

Mama sat down and pulled her shawl around her, biting her lip in concentration, then brightened. "I have an idea. Why not ask Mr. McCain? Didn't QO mention in his last letter that he's here too, corresponding for the *Dispatch*? I'm sure he—"

"*No.*" The word came out more forcefully than I had intended. I recovered quickly. "I don't know where to reach him." This much was true. "Besides, Cockerill insisted on absolute secrecy." Also true. While I wasn't about to tell her about my complicated history with George McCain, at least I hadn't lied to her.

"Well, then, there's nothing I can do to change your mind, is there?"

"Not a thing."

⁂

The more I tried to free my mind of George McCain, the more images came forth. McCain bowing over my hand. *I always seem to come upon you in a profusion of nature.* The impassioned look in his eyes at his warning: *Cockerill isn't to be trusted.* From the beginning of our acquaintance two years before, it seemed the very essence of him had been burned into my conscious, like an afterimage of the sun behind closed eyes. Would I ever truly be rid of him?

Mama's mention of him had further unhinged me. She knew nothing, of course, of what had happened between us. She couldn't have known that bringing him up would arouse such anguish. As I studied my reflection in the lavatory mirror, I could see in the pallor of my face and the slight tremble of my hands that running into him had truly shaken me. Even now, the recollection of his utterance of my given name, the feel of his hand on my arm in Central Park, sent a jolt through me.

Enough. I closed my eyes, willing myself into the present.

When I opened my eyes once more, I saw a look of firm resolve in my features. I moved my head this way and that in the mirror, forcing myself to concentrate on the matter at hand. My assignment, my opportunity, my future. I stared at my face as if it were a stranger's, but found only the things I had seen all my life: the hazel eyes so like Papa's, the narrow nose that was the twin of Mama's, the scar on my cheek from falling from a tree when I was five. I had to erase, I had to un-become. I had to remove the complexities that made me myself, so that I could embrace becoming someone else, someone new. But how to transform myself? How to alter my appearance so that all vestiges of my self disappeared, replaced with a look that conveyed a different person entirely? I practiced various leers in the mirror: first squinting, then opening my eyes wide. Squinting made me look too hard and calculating; wide eyes gave the appearance of one frightened, and though that effect wasn't bad, I decided that a lazy, distant gaze conveyed the look that was most convincing—that of a woman who had lost her mind. I smiled and frowned, grimaced and laughed. A frown looked a good deal more serious, but a forced grin, when paired with the faraway look, really did make me appear quite crazed. I removed my remaining hairpins. My tresses tumbled past my shoulders. For years, I had battled keeping my thick, unruly locks in order. Now the stubborn tendency of my hair to do what it liked was a benefit beyond measure.

Mama had laid out my things beside the sink. I took the comb and began teasing, producing a thick, brown nest. I then drew up the hair framing my face and replaced the pins, a difficult task now that my hair had been given free rein. I pulled some stray locks free so they hung limp at my temples. By the time I was finished, I looked appropriately disheveled, as if I hadn't combed my hair in ages.

Good.

I emerged into the hallway from the common bath we shared with the other boarders, guided by the glow of my candle. I padded down the hallway and found the lamp turned low in our little sitting room when I entered. There was no light beneath our bedroom door—Mama had retired for the evening. I turned up the lamp. Wrapping a shawl around my shoulders and taking a seat at my desk, I opened the drawer with a key I kept in my skirt pocket. Inside was a neat stack of stationery, a pen, two pencils, a writing notebook, and a Bible.

I penned two short letters. The first was to Fannie, telling her I'd received an assignment from Cockerill at last, but that it was veiled in secrecy. I explained I'd be gone ten days and to look in on Mama when she could. The second letter was to QO. I told him I was about to embark on a story for the *World,* that he would be proud of the lengths I was going to be employed by the greatest paper in the country. I said nothing more. He, and everyone else, would find out in due time where I was going, if I was successful. *And if I came back.*

I replaced my pen and stationery and picked up my Bible. It was old, the cover a faded brown leather. Not for the first time, I wondered what Mama would think if she knew what I kept hidden inside it.

I opened it to reveal a pile of small cards, each bearing a colored illustration of a flower with its name printed in bold beneath. I had placed them in sequence, in the order I'd received them. On the reverse side, all bore a date that had been written in by hand, and nothing else, save one. They had no message. The meaning was in the flowers themselves. A secret language known to lovers. I picked up the last one in the stack, the last sent. A yellow, trumpet-shaped flower—Carolina jasmine. *Separation.* Scrawled on the back were two words: "New York."

I swallowed and felt my throat constrict, the sting of tears. I closed the Bible, careful that the cards remained tucked inside. The insertion of the key, a quick twist of my wrist, and the drawer was locked once more. It was a ritual. Even so, I was never without guilt when I did it. Mama thought it was my writing, my journalism work, I locked away. In truth, it was the work of another I wished to conceal.

5

*eigh! Nelly, Ho! Nelly, listen love, to me.
I'll sing for you, play for you, a dulcet
melody.*

STEPHEN FOSTER, "NELLY BLY"

PITTSBURGH, JANUARY 1885

Less than two weeks after my first meeting at the *Dispatch,* I sat at our boardinghouse kitchen table reading. The weather had turned. The snow had snuck in overnight like a thief: silent, quick, and furtive. I'd awoken to a glittering mantle of white—a white so bright it stunned the eyes. But I knew it wouldn't last. My first winter in Pittsburgh four years before, a cold one when Mama, my four siblings, and I had arrived freezing and hungry, had taught me as much. Soon the snow would mix with coal dust and the burning crude from the refineries, churn with the mud and grit of the streets, and turn the city a filthy gray. But for now, it was still brilliant and pristine.

Out the window, Mama was striking the rug with the carpet beater, sending up a cloud of dust with every blow. Her breath misted the air with each whack, and her skirts billowed each time she drew her arm back to swing. Partially concealed beneath the hood of her cloak, she might have been a young girl and not a middle-aged woman fate had, twice, dealt a terrible blow.

I wrapped my shawl more snuggly around me and returned my attention to the table where Werner's *Practical English Grammar* regarded me, its cloth cover a cheery spot of red in the watery sunlight coming through the window. Madden had rejected my first two replies to Anxious Father out of hand, citing my grammar as too poor to wade through (though he had, in fact, waded through both my submissions, making angry, red-pencil corrections, which he'd then thrust back at me with a scowl). My third submission had paid off, due in part to my perusal of Werner. Next to the book, yesterday's edition of the *Dispatch* lay open. Printed across two columns was the third piece I'd written. Madden had apparently felt it good enough to grace the pages of his paper. He'd headlined it "Girl Puzzle" and placed it on page eleven along with my pseudonym. He'd dropped the "Lonely"; I was now simply "Orphan Girl."

In my piece, I'd asked readers to consider Anxious Father's complaints. I'd asked them to ponder young women and the limits society placed upon them through the eyes of the female working class—the ones who made up much of the city's labor force and, through no fault of their own, had little or no training, talent, or money.

> The schools are overrun with teachers, the stores with clerks, the factories with employees. In fact, all places that are filled by women are overrun, and still there are idle girls, some that have aged parents depending on them. We cannot let them starve. Can they that have full and plenty of this world's goods realize what it is to be a poor working woman, abiding in one or two bare rooms, without fire enough to keep them warm, while her threadbare clothes refuse to protect her from the wind and cold, and denying herself necessary food that her little ones may not go hungry—

The sound of the kitchen door opening brought my attention from the paper. A gust of cold air preceded Mama as she swept in, dropping the rug onto the floor and heaving a sigh. "Goodness, it's cold out."

"Perhaps you should have waited until later," I said. "It'll be warmer in an hour or two."

Mama removed her cloak and hung it on a hook near the door. Her hair, which she'd swept up in a bun, fell in wisps around her face. "In an hour or two I'll be blacking the stove and sweeping the foyer, Pinkey." I shot her a reproachful look. "Oh, it's just a pet name. Don't make a face," Mama said, putting the kettle on the hob. "It'll give you wrinkles when you're my age, and you shall regret it." She turned from the stove and reached for the tin of tea on a nearby shelf. "Would you like a cup, or are you too busy with your writing this morning?"

It was the time of day I liked best. Our boarders had already been served breakfast and left the house for work. We would not see them again until dinnertime, and while Mama would be busy with the various duties required to run the house, she always made time for a cup of tea late mornings.

"I have never refused a cup of tea in my life, Mama."

"And yet, since your victory with Mr. Madden and his *Dispatch,* you've been preoccupied. Twice you've failed to come down to supper."

I had ensconced myself in our shared bedroom, leaving the boarders' meal preparation to Mama and my sister. Kate, two and a half years my junior, had been none too pleased. Her six-month-old daughter Beatrice had wailed for her attention and she'd had none to give, thanks to two fewer hands to peel, chop, and set the table. Mama had been more understanding. She'd seemed delighted with my good fortune. But then Madden had paid me for everything I'd submitted thus far, even though only "Girl Puzzle" had appeared in print. I'd turned over my earnings to Mama each time, which she had put to good use running the boardinghouse.

"I'll try to be better about helping, Mama," I said.

The kettle whistled, and Mama removed it from the burner. When she had poured two cups and brought them to the table, she sat down. "You will do no such thing, not if it gets in the way of your writing."

I smiled. "Kate would disagree if she were here."

Mama returned my smile. "Kate is not your mother." She spooned sugar into her tea, stirred, and brought the cup to her lips. After taking a sip, she said, "I know it bothers you, me calling you Pinkey." I added sugar into my own cup. The coal in the stove shifted. Outside a chunk of snow fell from the eaves. When I made no reply, she continued. "It's true we shall never have that life again, but must I forgo your pet name? It's one of the few things I—we— didn't lose." Her voice broke, and she drew a handkerchief from the folds of her skirts to dab at her eyes. When she had composed herself, she placed her hand on mine. "Elizabeth."

I looked up. Her eyes were a deep blue, her bone structure delicate and balanced. Her hair, a medium brunette I had inherited, was only slightly graying. And yet, the long hours required to run the boardinghouse—the endless cooking, scrubbing, cleaning, polishing, laundering—had played a role in the lines at the corners of her eyes and her blistered, work-roughened hands. And she was thin. Too thin.

"Your father was a wonderful man," she said ruminatively, looking down at her teacup. "The fact that he left us so soon was a misfortune for all of us, but you mustn't shut out—"

"We have been over this before, Mama," I snapped. I pushed my tea away and loosened my shawl, the kitchen suddenly warm despite the winter chill outside. "He abandoned us."

My mother frowned. "He did not abandon us. He *died*. It is hardly the same thing."

"Without a will, Mama. He died without a will. It amounts to the same thing."

"And so you continue to think him despicable because he did not have the foresight to know when he would die." She raised the cup to her lips to drink but decided against it, setting the cup down with a *plink*. "A man who, just days before his death, was in perfect, robust health."

It was true. There had been no hint of his impending demise. My father, the esteemed Judge Michael Cochran, had been stricken with a sudden, mysterious paralysis that confined him to bed. He died within a matter of days. But he'd been twenty-seven years my mother's senior. Mama had been his second wife. His first marriage produced ten children. After his first wife had died, he'd married Mama, and when he, in turn, gave up the ghost, the children from his first marriage demanded an equal share of his estate when he passed. Mama, my siblings, and I were left with little to live on once his assets had been sold to offset his debts and his first family had been awarded their portion by the court. I'd never believed his eldest children deserved an equal share. At the time of his death, most were married and had families of their own. Three of my mother's stepchildren were older than she. My father had left us, his young second family, with no provisions for our security. He had owned a good deal of real estate; founded a large mill in a town, Cochrans Mills, that took his name; and served as an associate justice for the township. Why had he worked so hard accumulating wealth only to be foolish by not making certain that the wealth would remain with his beloved young wife and her children? I could not forgive him for it. At times I hated him.

"Robust health or not, he was nearly sixty, Mama," I said.

My mother waved her hand dismissively and stood, bringing her cup to the sink. "I don't know why I'm discussing this with you. You were just a tiny thing when he passed. Your father would be rolling over in his grave if he knew you thought of him as some sort of . . . of villain."

"I do not think him a villain, Mama," I said. *It's Albert who's the villain.*

It was as if the thought of my brother had conjured Mama's own. Leaving off the conversation, she switched topics, saying, "Albert is coming to supper. Please tell me you'll be at the table."

A flare in my chest. I wrestled it down, determined to reply with composure. I did not particularly enjoy my eldest brother's company. "What brings him here?"

"Why, he wishes to see us, of course. It's been weeks since he visited."

It was no use. My anger could not be caged. "The only time Albert comes around is when he wants something, Mama. That, or something's happened he wishes to boast about."

"Oh, Elizabeth." Mama threw up her hands in exasperation. "He's your brother, for heaven's sake! He's making his way on his own, as we all are. Why must you fault him so?"

Because he's selfish. Because he left us to fend for ourselves as soon as he was old enough. Albert, with my other elder brother Charles following soon after, had headed to Pittsburgh for work and left Mama, Kate, little Harry, and me to survive on our own in Apollo after Papa's death, sending money back only sporadically, and only—as I came of age and realized Mama wouldn't do it—at my insistence. Those had been tumultuous times, when Mama—lost, gullible, and seeking a partner in little Apollo—had made an awful mistake: she'd married a man who was as different from Papa as night was from day. Oh, how I'd hated him. The day of her divorce from Jack Ford, after six and a half long years, had been one of the happiest of our lives.

"I wish you and Albert would make your peace," Mama was saying. "He's getting married soon. Surely—"

"Don't you wonder why he's never brought Jane here? I'll tell you what I think. Because he doesn't want Jane to see the boarding-house. It embarrasses him. I'll bet he's told her how well off we were in our Apollo days and she knows nothing of the time after Papa died." I had no such proof, only a niggling feeling, but it was just like Albert to do such a thing.

My mother sighed and smoothed her skirts, doing her best, it seemed, to quell her own temper. "You judge him too harshly, Pinkey, just as you do your father."

Because they let me down when I needed them, when we all needed them.

"I don't want to quarrel, Pin—Elizabeth," Mama said. She walked to the table and sat down again, her eye falling on the paper in front of me. With great forbearance, she changed the subject again. "Tell me, what has Mr. Madden asked you to write next?"

I shrugged. "He hasn't given me a topic. Mr. Wilson said I'm to choose my next theme myself. Something I'm passionate about. Something I could weigh in on that would interest other female readers like me."

Despite the hurt and anger she still must have been feeling regarding my comments about Papa and Albert, Mama smiled. "How lovely." She placed her hand on my shoulder. "Whatever our differences have been this morning, I want you to know how proud I am of you. Your papa would be pleased. You will make something of yourself one day, you know."

I didn't know if I believed her. There were too many times life had seemed to be going in the right direction when fate had suddenly intervened and pulled the rug out from under me. Papa's sudden death and Jack Ford coming into our lives were proof of that.

"So," Mama said, "you must've given some thought to what you'd like to write about. What's it to be?" She cocked a brow, a smile playing about her lips.

She was truly happy for me, which made my next comment all the more difficult. I bit my lip. "I fear you won't like it, Mama."

Her eyebrows rose in surprise. "Oh? I very much doubt there is anything you could write I wouldn't like."

"Very well." I squared my shoulders. *So be it.* "I should like to write about divorce."

The color drained from Mama's face, and a hand flew to her breast. "Elizabeth, you wouldn't."

"There will be nothing personal in it, Mama. I promise. Nothing of . . . the family. People here need never know. It's just that—" I choose my words carefully. "I have ideas about marriage laws and divorce. I'd like to voice them. I think, if Mr. Madden and Mr. Wilson will listen, they'll like what I have to say."

"I see." The smile was gone. With a sigh, she rose and walked from the room, saying as she went, "I shall leave you to it."

"I'll make no bones about it, Miss Cochrane," Erasmus Wilson said from across his desk. "I thought a topic so contentious as divorce would be a mistake for you, especially so soon after you started here." He twisted in his chair and reached for a pile of papers behind him. He placed the stack on the desk between us, then used his forefinger to push his glasses up on the bridge of his nose. "Forgive me, but I've read a good many of these, though they're addressed to you. Madden asked me to so that we might get the gist of what readers thought of your 'Mad Marriages' piece." He smiled. "You do have a way, I think, of getting just to the point that so many," he gestured to the correspondence, "find refreshing. I commend you."

My divorce piece had run three days ago. I'd had no idea, up until that moment, what readers had made of it. I felt the wind suddenly depart my sails as a kind of euphoria came over me. I'd come prepared to defend my views, thinking perhaps readers hadn't agreed and the mail would say so.

It looked like thirty letters, perhaps more, lying on his desk. "Thank you," I said rather clumsily.

Wilson riffled through some newsprint on his desk, fishing out the edition open to my story. "I thought it quite innovative, your idea to prevent criminals and drunkards from marrying, although it would be difficult to enforce naturally."

I thought of all the years in Apollo Mama had wasted after Papa's death, married to Jack. "New marriage laws would have to be adopted," I said, my mouth suddenly dry. "If it became illegal for someone to lie about his history—if he were a drunkard, or dishonest, or an abusive sort of person—things would change. A man would be less prone to hide his unsavory past."

My voice was trembling. I didn't dare say more. A slow anger was building inside me. It had been six years since I'd climbed the witness stand, testifying before the Armstrong County Court of Common Pleas. *Mother was afraid of Jack Ford, sir. I have heard him scold Mama often and use profane language toward her and call her names. Whore and bitch and—*

"Miss Cochrane?" I blinked, coming to myself. Wilson was staring at me, his blue eyes wide behind his glasses. "Your face is mottled. Are you unwell?"

"I'm fine. Just a bit warm, that's all."

Wilson looked sympathetic and turned to crack open the window behind him. A brisk wisp of air blew itself across the desk, caressing my cheek. I pretended to be relieved, and when he was certain I was feeling better, he snatched up the paper once more. "A young man drawing a comfortable income," he read, "has a widowed mother, who has doubtless worked hard to give him a start in life, and helpless sisters. He lets his aged mother work, and allows his sisters to support themselves where and how they will, never has five cents or a kind word to give at home, dresses in the height of fashion, has every enjoyment, gives his lady friends costly presents, takes them to places of amusement, tries to keep it a secret that his mother and sisters work. If the fact becomes known, he will assert positively that it is against his most urgent desire. Will he make a good husband, think you?" He laid down the paper. "That bit got the attention of a good many mamas and daughters."

It was a thinly veiled jab at Albert, one Mama had seen through instantly. It had taken much cajoling to convince her no one would be the wiser. No one knew Orphan Girl's true identity, and it wasn't like I'd called Albert by name for the cad he was.

"By Jove, what a nerve you hit," Wilson said, his mouth down-turned in a grimace. "If the postal responses are any indication, there seem to be a good many sons out there who have shirked their responsibilities to their families. It is a wonder to me, Miss Cochrane, how you can speak so intelligently of a subject so foreign to you."

If Wilson was fishing, I couldn't see it. His expression was too genuine, too open and guileless, for me to think his intentions were other than earnest. The columnist had been nothing but kind and supportive since I'd stepped across the threshold of the *Dispatch* building, wanting only to teach me what he could of writing for the paper. Perhaps Mama was right; I was being too harsh. I couldn't forgive Papa or Albert or the despicable Jack Ford, but I would not judge Wilson without cause.

My ease must have shown on my face, for he replied, "There now, you look better." He scooped up the letters on his desk. "Where's your bag? You'll want to take these home and read them. It's one of the perks of being a journalist, reading one's mail. I doubt, from those I read, you'll find a complaint among them."

I dropped the letters into my shoulder bag and then looked expectantly at him. "What's to be my next assignment? Has Mr. Madden said?"

"He hasn't breathed a word to me," Wilson replied, then winked. "There's only one way to find out." He rose from his chair. "Let's go find him."

Madden's office was empty, so I followed Wilson down the steps to the third floor, where, just beyond the landing, the room opened up into a large area crammed with desks. Half of them were occupied with men, their shoulders hunched over their work as they wrote in notebooks, paged through books, and thumbed through newspapers. Others stood about in groups chatting. Nearly all were in shirtsleeves. Sheets of newsprint littered the floor here and there. Someone had opened a window to allow fresh air into the room.

"Dunlap," Wilson called to a man sitting at the desk nearest us, "where's Madden?" The man pointed across the room. Sure enough, there was the managing editor, surrounded by a small group of reporters, the thick miasma of cigar smoke wafting above them. "I might've known," Wilson said with a chuckle. "If in doubt, follow the smoke."

As we made our way across the floor, I felt the room grow still. Conversation ceased; heads swiveled as we passed. Madden broke off from his discussion and widened his eyes as we approached. "Ah, Erasmus," he said. He inclined his head to me. "Miss Cochrane."

The room was now completely silent. The men in Madden's circle were looking at me. I felt my face grow warm as I nodded to each man in turn. The last of them, the tallest, was George McCain, my rescuer from certain death just a few weeks before. He, too, had discarded his jacket and was in shirtsleeves, which he had rolled to his elbows, revealing lean, muscled forearms.

Madden made introductions, none of which I heard. I was aware only of McCain, though I was trying my best to be unaware of him. I would not look in his direction. Something about being in his presence unsettled me.

"You read the 'Mad Marriages' piece?" Madden was asking, between taking great puffs from his cigar. "We got a healthy dose of feedback from that one. This, gentlemen, is Orphan Girl herself." I stood, dumb as a clam, looking at the floor. I wanted nothing more than to be counted among them, to fit in. Why, then, was I tongue-tied?

"Miss Cochrane," a voice said at my ear, "it is a pleasure to make your acquaintance again."

I raised my gaze and looked into McCain's eyes. Was I mistaken, or did a flicker of compassion flash in them before they turned serious once more?

"What a wonderful grasp of Governor Pattison's recent proposal for divorce reform you have," McCain said, more loudly. "Your research is impeccable."

"Thank you." I prayed he would not ask me what sources I had used. The truth of it was I'd merely searched my memory. I'd followed marriage and divorce reform discussions in the newspapers as a matter of course as soon as I'd been old enough, given my wretched familial circumstances that had necessitated it.

Wilson turned to Madden. "When you have a minute, we'd like to have a word with you."

"Oh?" Madden said. He puffed a smoke ring into the air and rocked back on his heels. The button holding his jacket closed looked poised to spring.

No one stirred. I did not care to discuss what Madden wished me to work on next in the presence of these men. Perhaps McCain felt my unease, for he said, turning to the editor, "Have you given any thought to a suitable pseudonym for Miss Cochrane?"

Madden frowned, an irritable expression coming over his features. "She has a pseudonym, McCain. It's 'Orphan Girl.' That's suitable enough."

"Come now," Wilson entreated, "'Bessie Bramble' is a fine pseudonym. We can certainly do better for this young lady."

"Bessie Bramble already had that pseudonym when I hired her," Madden said.

"Just so," Wilson went on, "but I agree with McCain. 'Orphan Girl' is a mere description, a rather unfitting one at that."

Madden grunted and turned to the short, rotund man next to him. "What do you say, Sutton?"

"It is rather a sad little moniker," Sutton replied. He smiled impishly at me and winked. "You aren't by any chance a real orphan, are you?"

"No, sir, I am not."

The men broke into laughter, and I felt a spark of anger rise in my chest. Imagine a group of women standing about, deciding what false name to give a man, a man who was not allowed to use his real name in print. It was ridiculous.

"Perhaps we should ask the lady herself what she prefers." This from the ginger-haired man standing next to the man called Sutton.

"I think the answer to that is obvious," I shot back. "I should like to be called by my real name."

Perhaps their laughter might have been more welcome this time instead of the sudden hush that ensued. Was it possible the room had gone even more still? Madden was regarding me closely, his eyes narrowed to slits as smoke swirled around him. "I think," he said slowly, "that would be a most unsound idea." He broke his stare and called out into the room, "What say boys, eh? What shall we call this young lady?"

"Betsy! Betsy Ross," someone called. "There's a real American girl."

"Nah," another answered, "'Betsy' is too close to 'Bessie.'"

"I've always been partial to 'Willomena Henrietta,' my mother's name," another said. "God rest her soul."

"Typesetter's nightmare, Fisk," was the reply. More laughter. "She needs a real Pittsburgh name, something that calls to mind the city."

"Well, we can't very well call her 'Coal Dust,' can we?"

"How about 'Black Fanny'!" Hoots of laughter.

I stole a look at McCain. He was looking out at the newsroom like he wanted to strike someone.

"I'd like to know what this city's known for, if it ain't soot and coal," a voice said from the far side of the room.

There were general murmurs of assent, after which the room fell silent once more, each man working over what name I might be called or what quip he could offer that would elicit further amusement. Madden was taking it all in, puffing all the while on his cigar.

It was Wilson who broke the silence. "Stephen Foster."

The room exploded, one man shouting above the din, "That's no name for a lady, Erasmus."

The columnist raised his palms and pumped the air, quieting the room. "Now, now. I meant the noted songwriter. Our city is proud of him. It's been thirty years or more now, but he wrote many songs here."

"'Swanee River'?" someone shouted.

"That's the one," Wilson replied.

"How about 'Jeanie with the Light Brown Hair'?"

"Typesetter's nightmare, Fisk."

More guffaws.

"Didn't Foster write 'Oh! Susanna'?" someone volunteered.

Madden pulled his cigar from his mouth. "'Susanna' isn't bad. 'Susanna' what?"

There was no immediate response. Then someone called, "What about 'Nellie Bly'? That's a swell song, if I ever heard one."

Madden ruminated, rocking back on his heels as he gazed at the ceiling. Then he shoved his cigar back into his mouth, chomping down on it. "Nellie Bly. I like it. Miss Cochrane, you now have a new pseudonym. You're to use it henceforth." He nodded to the men around him and strode away.

※

Bessie Bramble regarded me over the rim of her teacup, a bone china more delicate than any I had ever seen. Everything about the room was delicate: the lace doilies on the side tables, the flounced curtains, the floral pattern of the Aubusson rug. There was no sturdy, utilitarian furniture like that in our boardinghouse, no worn floorboards that creaked from the habitual tread of lodgers. This was a woman's room, done up in blush pinks and creams, framed by armchairs and a sofa too small and feminine for a man's taste. Here was a room that suggested long, leisurely hours spent reclining with books. I had never seen the like, could not comprehend that any room in a home could be reserved strictly for the use of the fairer sex. Knickknacks littered every surface: porcelain birds, vases, photographs. A white piano in the corner of the room faced the garden, a large fishbowl atop it within which swam a goldfish.

"What do you think of the nom de plume they've given you, Elizabeth?" By her 'they've,' I assumed Ms. Bramble had heard the story of how I'd come by it.

"I think it fine enough as names go," I replied. I then added, because I felt Ms. Bramble a kindred spirit, "But I think it disgraceful I must use one at all."

Ms. Bramble lowered her teacup to her lap. She was a short, bespectacled woman with a full figure who looked to be in her mid-forties. Though she sat perfectly still, one ankle crossed over the other, teacup in hand and head slightly tilted, her eyes continually moved over me, assessing. There was not much, I realized, that Bessie Bramble missed. "Maddening as it is, it will protect you, my dear."

I considered this, not sure whether I understood. "You mean a false name will protect my reputation, lest anyone find out who I really am and, and . . ." I trailed off, not sure what would happen if anyone outside my family learned I was writing for the *Dispatch*. Would they really care? And if they did, what of it? I was no blueblood with a family name to uphold, no debutante looking to make a spectacular match in the marriage market.

"How much did Erasmus tell you about me?" Ms. Bramble asked.

"He told me you had endeavors other than journalism and that you might tell me about them, but that he was not at liberty to disclose them himself."

"Good man," she said, nodding. "Erasmus knows my real name, as does George Madden of course, but they are among only a few. A very few." She placed her teacup on the side table beside her chair and poured it full again. She dropped in a sugar cube and stirred the contents ruminatively, as if considering how much to say. When she looked up again, her expression was serious. "May I count you among my confidants, Elizabeth?"

"Of course."

"Of course," she repeated with a chuckle. "I wonder if you know what that means. You live with your mother and siblings, is that right?"

Wilson must have told her as much. "Yes."

"Well, if I tell you who I am, it means you may not return home and, in turn, tell them. You must keep everything I tell you to yourself."

"I understand."

"Well, then, my real name is Elizabeth too. Elizabeth Wilkinson Wade. My husband is a banker, which is how we are able to afford this home."

I'd assumed the fine furnishings were the result of Ms. Bramble's—Ms. Wade's—reporting career. She was as well known in the city as she was respected and championed all manner of things, principally political, social, and cultural issues—or, to put it more aptly, their reform. "Oh," I said rather inanely. I was beginning to feel uncomfortable under Ms. Bramble's scrutiny; it was a blustery winter day outside the window, yet the room felt suddenly warm.

"I say these things because you will earn a meager wage as a writer for the papers, certainly less than your male counterparts." She took a sip of her tea. "If you have come to the *Dispatch* to make a fortune, you are better off finding something else."

"I didn't come to the *Dispatch*," I said. "Madden found me."

"Oh, yes, I've heard the story. I was the one who urged Madden to bring you in." She leaned back in her chair, tilting her head. "What I am saying is, you must expect to work hard and be paid little. Oh, I know. Your wage now is likely more than what you've ever made before, am I right? But you must realize you'll be working doubly hard to stay on staff while your fellow reporters will be making more and doing decidedly less."

I hadn't considered this, although given all I knew—the disinclination of editors to hire women, their insistence on using a pen name, the way many viewed women journalists as social pariahs—it hardly surprised me. "It isn't fair."

"Life rarely is."

A branch scratched against the windowpane. It was enough to break Ms. Bramble's rumination. She rose and approached the window, where the goldfish swirled in its circular world. She produced a small tin from a nearby drawer, opened it, and dropped bits into the bowl. The fish rose to the surface and began to nibble.

"Education is of great interest to me," she said presently. "I

feel it vital for all children, regardless of gender or class, and I
have written—heatedly at times—about the importance of better
schools, and better curriculums. I have criticized most of the
school administrators in this city and been very outspoken about
their mismanagement. I see you are nodding your head. You are
aware of this, then?" She paused, taking me in.

"Oh, yes," I said. "I read everything you've written." I'd meant
it earnestly, but blurting it out as I had felt like the worst sort of
pandering. "That is, I mean—"

"Then it may surprise you to know that I currently hold the
position of principal of the Ralston School for boys. Prior to that,
I was assistant principal at the Pike Street School, another boys'
school for a good many years. This is where the importance of
keeping one's pen name a secret is crucial. You see," she rubbed
her hands together and replaced the tin in the drawer, "such cutting
remarks would have been impossible under my real name." She
paused, waiting for her words to sink in.

"You mean the schools would have . . . fired you?"

"I have gone on record—as Bessie Bramble, mind—saying that
school officials will hire a man so green the cows would eat him,
give him the highest position at a school, and then wonder why his
results are a failure, time and time again. What man wants to hear
this from a woman, even if she is an administrator at a well-known
school?" Ms. Bramble returned to her chair, regarding me with
an intensity that was now familiar. "A moment ago, you could
not imagine what might happen to you should someone discover
you write for a newspaper. In my case, should my name and my
newspaper persona be linked, I would lose my academic position,
something I have worked many years to achieve. There might even
be repercussions for my husband and children."

My eye fell on the cluster of photographs on a nearby table.
For the first time, I saw Ms. Bramble as more than a formidable
journalist who spoke her mind and stirred others to action. I saw
her as a wife and mother. A woman with fears and joys, triumphs
and failures, of her own.

"Do not think for a moment, Elizabeth, that it doesn't anger
me, this business of pen names. But if men with small minds insist
upon it, then let us use it to our advantage! Men would have us
use false name to preserve our reputations; I say we use them to
state our minds in a way that gives us a freedom our real names
never could—as a catalyst for change."

"That is what I wish to do," I said breathlessly. She had
summarized it so succinctly. All this time, what had begun in me as

a dislike for housework, for nannying, for doing what I ought rather than what I wanted, was really something bigger, much bigger. "Yes, I see it in you. You have a strong will and a sound mind, if your divorce piece is any indication. I have long advocated for change in that quarter. Divorce has touched you deeply somehow, I think." She narrowed her eyes, but just when I thought she would inquire further, a small gold clock on the mantle chimed the hour. "Goodness, it grows late. My husband will be home soon, and we've plans this evening for dinner."

She rose. We exited the room and made our way to the foyer, where she handed me my coat at the door.

I extended my hand. "Thank you, Ms. Bram—Wade," I said.

"Oh, no," she said, with emphasis. She did not take my hand. "I am Ms. Bramble to you. I cannot risk you calling me anything else should you see me at the *Dispatch*."

"You have my word on it," I said.

"Good. Then I've a bit more advice before we say our good-byes. You are very young. I should have liked to have had such guidance when I was starting out." She watched me shrug into my coat and then, when she knew she had my full attention, she continued. "State your mind directly and succinctly. Do not pander to your audience; they will know it instantly and loathe you for it. Never, ever apologize for your opinions in print. You must always appear the authority."

She drew open the door. We were greeted by a gust of bitter wind. Snow covered the hedges, the grass, the limbs of trees reaching their barren branches to the sky. A lone crow flew overhead, and I had a sudden, unaccountable sense of foreboding.

Ms. Bramble placed a hand on my arm, drawing my attention back to her. She was a good three inches shorter than I. Her eyes behind her spectacles were gray and intelligent. "Most of all, trust no one."

I drew in my breath. Somehow, this was the last thing I'd expected her to say. "Not even Madden?" She nodded. "Why?"

"Because he is a man tasked with selling newspapers. Should you become inconvenient to him, he will let you go in an instant."

"And Mr. Wilson?"

"Erasmus is a kind soul, but he is under Madden's power, which means he'll be of little use to you when you need him."

I nodded and turned away, stricken. I was halfway down the path when she called my name. I turned. Ms. Bramble was standing in the same spot, one hand against the doorframe. "Remember what I said. Trust no one."

6

It is only after one is in trouble that one realizes how little sympathy and kindness there are in the world.

NELLIE BLY

NEW YORK CITY, SEPTEMBER 1887

The Temporary Home for Females at 84 Second Avenue was located on the Lower East Side of the city, along a block of sagging row houses clustered together like sordid thieves. I'd found it in the city directory, and it seemed as good a place to start as any. I approached the three-story brick ediface clad in the oldest, most out-of-fashion items I owned: a plain gray flannel dress, brown gloves, a black straw hat with a veil, and a dark blue coat. I pressed the bell. A young, fair-haired girl answered.

"Is the matron in?"

"She's busy," the girl pronounced with a bold stare. And then, eying the battered valise I carried, she said, "Go to the back parlor."

I did as I was told, walking through the entryway into a small, dim room. A wardrobe stood against the wall, a small table to the left, a few ratty chairs. The organ looked as if it hadn't been used in years.

I sat for a good while in the shuttered room, long enough to wonder, yet again, if the path I'd chosen to get on the island was the right one. As I figured it, there were two ways I could be committed to Blackwell's Asylum. One was to feign insanity at the house of friends and get myself committed on the decision of two doctors. This course required friends I didn't have (ones who didn't work for the *World* and would thus cast suspicion). Additionally, these friends would have to do some acting themselves; they'd need to feign poverty for me to be sent to the public institution that was Blackwell's. Too many things could go wrong, and it would take too much time to execute in the bargain. I didn't have time. Cockerill wouldn't wait forever, and every day wasted was a day the memory of our arrangement would grow dimmer and dimmer in his mind. I couldn't take that chance. The other was to go through the police courts. My stomach clenched just thinking of the next twenty-four hours, but before I could think any more of what awaited me, an older woman strode into the room.

"Oh," I said, my eyes wide. "Are you the matron?" I had not lifted my veil. It was what a normal person would have done coming into a home, and most certainly into a dark room. But I was no longer a normal person.

"No, the matron is ill. I'm her assistant." The room was too dark to get a good look at her. I had only the impression of a thin woman with hair pulled back into a bun. "What is it you want?"

"I'd like to stay here a few days, if you can accommodate me."

"We are very crowded at present." A pause. I sensed that she was taking me in, tattered clothes and all, though in the darkened room I wondered just how much she could see. "You will have to share a room with someone else. We have no single rooms left."

"How much do you charge?"

"Thirty cents a night."

I'd only brought seventy cents. The less I had, the sooner I could be put out. I paid her for one night's lodging, counting out the coins in the low light.

"And what is your name, miss?"

"Nellie Brown." Cockerill had instructed me to use this name, as the initials agreed with the pen name I'd been using since my days at the *Dispatch*.

"Well, then, I'm Mrs. Stanard."

I would have liked to see her features better, to inspect the room more closely, but I resisted asking her to open the shutters. It was something a sane person would request.

Mrs. Stanard left on the pretext of being needed elsewhere. I hastily recorded her name in the little notebook inside my reticule.

Fifteen minutes later, a bell clanged. Through the doorway I saw women making their way to the back of the house, feet

tramping on floorboards. I caught the scent of food cooking somewhere. Bread? Meat? Was I entitled to a meal, having paid for one
night's lodging? Would someone think to summon me from the
back parlor?

I was relieved when Mrs. Stanard reappeared and led me down
a back stair to the basement. There, a few women sat around tables.
The fair-haired girl who'd answered the bell was playing the role of
waitress. I sat down at an empty table. She approached me, crossing her arms. "Boiled mutton, boiled beef, potatoes, coffee or tea."

I blinked, thinking for a moment I was expected to choose
just one of these. "Beef and potatoes, please. And coffee, with
some bread."

"Bread comes with," she replied with the same unnerving stare
and then stomped off to the kitchen.

Wall-mounted gas lamps threw wan light onto a floor that was
bare of rugs. The furniture wanted polishing; no linen was on the
tables nor pictures on the walls. The tiny, street-level windows were
grimy with dirt and grease. It appeared there was no heat, either.

Whatever profit the matron earned from housing women in
her home, it was not used to improve the surroundings.

As for the diners, there were six, plus a few children. Despite
my dislike for the place so far, I was glad Mrs. Stanard and her
superior did not reject mothers with little mouths to feed.

The fair-haired girl returned and banged a tray down in front
of me. The meat had a grayish cast, and the potato, cooked in its
skin, was so shriveled it looked like a giant raisin. I went through
the show of eating while I studied my companions from beneath my
veil. I had seated myself near two older women who were tucking
into their meal as if it were their last. They were dressed in clothes
similar to my own—old, somewhat soiled clothes past their glory.
Two women closer to my age sat at another table, two children
beside them: a young girl in braids of perhaps five, and a boy of no
more than eight. The third table was occupied by two others who'd
looked up when I entered and then resumed eating. No one spoke.

This was a perfect time to begin my ruse, to convince these
women of my insanity. Yet in the silence, with only the clink of
utensils against plates, I didn't know where to begin.

As the women finished, they went to a desk in the corner, where
Mrs. Stanard collected money. In the better light, I could see that
the assistant matron was approaching middle age and that her
coal-black hair was drawn back into a tight bun. While she didn't
look unkind, an air of severity was discernible in the harsh lines
around her mouth and the plain gray dress she wore.

"That will be another thirty cents, for your lunch and dinner both," she said at my approach.

I dropped the coins into her palm. Already my funds were perilously low. I hadn't enough money to spend even one more night.

I ventured upstairs, fetched my valise where I'd left it in the back parlor, and sought out the front parlor, which had better light and less of a disused air. One of the young women from the basement was reading a tattered copy of *Godey's Lady's Book* while ostensibly watching the children I'd seen in the basement. Her daughter turned the pages of a picture book, while her son performed a litany of unmannerly amusements: pulling at his sister's braids, throwing books on the floor, licking the front window, speaking in a loud voice to no one in particular. After each, his mother looked up and muttered "Georgie," which served little purpose. Georgie paid her no mind.

An older woman I'd not seen before was seated on the sofa in shabby dark maroon taffeta. She was trying her best to doze but having a hard time of it. No sooner did her chin meet her chest than she was startled awake by the mother's "Georgie." I watched this scenario play out again and again, wondering who would be the first to give up: the oblivious mother, the disobedient son, or the drowsy woman.

Two others who looked very much like sisters were seated together on a settee in kerchiefs, knitting needles clacking together like chattering teeth. The bell began to ring almost continually, the fair-haired girl directing women to the back parlor like cattle or lost sheep. How many other women would join us when the workday came to a close?

I was itching to write the details in my little notebook inside my reticule but dared not. But perhaps there was a way I could use it to my benefit. I pulled out the notebook. On the same page I'd written the assistant matron's name, I began to draw. I sketched a leafless tree and drew the faces of the women seated in the room. Young Georgie was the knot of the tree in the center, one hand jutting out from the bark toward his sister in the tree, pulling at her braid. I drew his mother above too, her mouth open, screaming "Georgie!" The prim ladies in kerchiefs had knitting needles for mouths. It was ghastly, this picture, and yet it was, I thought, exactly the sort of thing one might expect to find in the notebook of a lunatic.

I was writing the address below the tree when Mrs. Stanard appeared beside me. I pretended not to notice so she could get a long look at what I was doing.

After a small silence, she cleared her throat. "What's wrong with you? Have you some sorrow or trouble?"

I pretended to be startled. "Yes, everything is so . . . sad."

"You mustn't worry," Mrs. Stanard replied, with more cheer than she'd shown since I'd arrived. "We all have our troubles, but we get over them in time. Are you looking for work?"

"I don't know," I said, trying to look confused, as if I couldn't recall why I was there. "It is all so very distressing."

"Perhaps you could be a nurse and wear a nice cap and apron," the assistant matron ventured, as if a change of clothes might improve my outlook on life.

"I don't know. I have never worked." Better for Mrs. Stanard to think I had no plans for employment—that sooner or later, my funds would run out.

"But you must work," Mrs. Stanard said with alarm. "Everyone here does."

"Do they?" I looked around with wide eyes. "They look frightening to me. They look like . . . like crazy women."

The knitters stilled their needles.

"There are good, honest workingwomen here," Mrs. Stanard pronounced, her voice now stern and low, the kind of tone a mother uses with a child who might embarrass her in public.

"There are so many crazy people about," I insisted, loudly. "They frighten me so. One can never tell what they will do. Look at all the murders committed and the police never catch the perpetrators." I finished this last with a sob.

Mrs. Stanard gave a convulsive start. "We do not keep crazy people here."

By morning, if all went as planned, I hoped Mrs. Stanard would not be able to state this with conviction.

※※※

When the supper bell rang, we trooped down to the basement again. We were a larger group now, the dining room crowded with at least six more women. The buzz of conversation filled the room as the children from the parlor ran between the tables while their mother chatted with a woman seated next to her. The knitting sisters sat at their own table, content, it seemed, to keep to themselves. The woman in the maroon taffeta appeared revitalized; she talked animatedly with three others at her table. All the while, the fair-haired girl busied herself between bringing food and stomping back to the kitchen. This time, there was no menu from which to choose; the meal consisted of a thin soup, a roll, and a cup of tea. When the server approached, she set my tray down with a bang. I jumped, emitting a small cry. The chatter ebbed as the women swung their attention to me. Even Georgie and his sister halted in their play, their eyes large as they took in the strange woman with the dark veil seated alone.

Now was the time to begin my show of madness in earnest. I picked up my tea, raised it in salute, brought it to my lips, and drank it through my veil, spilling a good amount as I did so. Georgie broke out in a guffaw, which his mother silenced by demanding that he and his sister sit down. Mrs. Stanard, seated at the desk in the corner, narrowed her eyes and took my measure.

"What's she doing, Mama?" Georgie's sister asked loudly.

"Never mind," her mother hissed. "You mustn't stare."

"Not in her right mind, that one," a young red-haired woman at the table nearest me muttered.

Seated next to her was a plump, middle-aged woman with large brown eyes. "Poor dear," she said.

My soup smelled no more appetizing than it looked, and after lifting a spoonful to my lips, I grimaced and pushed it away.

By now, most of the others had resumed their chatter and were eating. "You should eat up, dear," the middle-aged woman said, leaning toward me. "There's nothing else until breakfast."

I brought a hand to my breast. "You mean I can't have anything brought to my room?"

My neighbors exchanged glances. "If you haven't noticed," the redhead said, "this isn't the Waldorf Astoria."

Her companion tried the soup. "I believe it's lentil," she volunteered. She turned to me. "Taste it. You don't want to grow hungry before morning."

I responded by turning to the wall, lifting my veil a little, draining my teacup, and replacing the veil—as if loath for anyone to see my face. When I turned back around, I found Mrs. Stanard at my table.

"Is there something I can assist with?" She looked, with her eyebrows knitted and her mouth in a firm line, quite irritated. She eyed the spilled tea on the table in front of me.

"Is it true I can't have a tray brought up if I get hungry?" I asked. "I don't particularly like supper. It's rather . . . dull."

The assistant matron let out a sigh, her shoulders slouching in exasperation. "This is the last meal of the day. If—" she glanced around the room and then said, lower, "if you don't like what has been served to you, you'll have to make do until morning. This is not a hotel."

I crossed my arms. "Well, I never."

"And as you've paid for your supper already, I'll not give you a refund."

By now, most of the women were pushing back their chairs. Mrs. Stanard returned to her desk, casting one last look my way before taking her seat.

I followed the women up the stairs. I decided, after coming into the front parlor, to continue my conversation with the redhead and the plump woman, who were seated on a small sofa engrossed in conversation. Judging by the way they looked at me as I approached, I guessed they had probably been talking about me. I took the empty chair next to them. "May I join you?"

The redhead looked none too pleased, but the older woman nodded. There was a small pause. By the way she looked pensive and bit her lower lip, I reckoned she was casting about for a topic that did not involve my strange behavior. "We were forty in the omnibus this evening," she said finally. "Goodness, it was packed. Do you think a gentleman offered me his seat?"

The other woman shook her head in dismay. "I don't know what this world is coming to."

I saw my opening. "The world is indeed a crazy place." I stared at them with wide eyes. "It is all quite frightening."

"I could not agree more," the redhead said despite herself. "I don't like the city much, with all its filth and people about. Wretched place." Her older companion patted her hand, but the redhead was focused on me. "Why is it you're wearing a veil? Shouldn't you remove that?"

I decided to lift it from my face, all the better for them to see my expression. I fixed them with a faraway look, the one I'd practiced in the mirror at home. There was an uncomfortable silence, and then the middle-aged woman cleared her throat. "What is your name, my dear?"

"Nellie Brown."

"Well, Nellie, do you happen to know about the Boston boats? I should like to know when the ferry departs."

I blurted out the answer before I knew what I was doing, horrified I'd forgotten my role. I was so occupied in mentally chastising myself that I didn't realize she was speaking to me again.

"Your job, my dear. What is it you do?"

"Oh, I don't work. I think it's quite tragic there are so many women working in the world. I daresay I don't think I would like it."

The ladies exchanged glances.

"Well, none of us *like* it," the redhead said tartly. "But we've got no choice about it, do we?"

The knitters on the settee had stopped again and were looking on.

"I had no choice but to find work," her companion said with more kindness. "I lost my husband years ago, and I came here and found work as a proofreader. For a medical dictionary of all things." The redhead nodded; this information was not new. "Bah, the things I can tell you of illness."

"I shall miss you, Mrs. Caine," the redhead sniffed. "I don't know what I shall do without you."

The older woman, Mrs. Caine, turned to explain. "My health hasn't been good of late. I must return to Boston, where I have a sister who has agreed to take me in. I'm lucky, I know, to have family who can care for me. So many others have no one."

Just then, the fair-haired girl stomped into the parlor and announced it was time for bed. I busied myself with picking up my valise so that she and I were the last to leave the room. As we approached the stairs, I said, my voice trembling, "I'm frightened."

She turned sharply. "What?"

I placed a hand at my breast and said nonsensically, "I'd like to stay on the stairs if I could. It's safer there." The last of the ladies were going up, the pinched-faced redhead bringing up the rear. She was looking down from the landing, listening to our conversation.

"No one sleeps on the stairs here," the girl barked, eyeing me with suspicion. "Everyone will think you're crazy."

"But I'm frightened!"

"Don't be an idiot. Now come along."

To my disappointment, most of the women had left the landing. With so few to witness any trouble I could stir up, I allowed the girl to lead me.

"You're to room with Miss King," she said as I followed her up the stairs. "We don't tolerate late hours here, so get to bed and extinguish your lamp."

We passed bedrooms that opened off the hallway on both sides. I glimpsed sparse furnishings within—iron bed frames, chipped washstands—before doors were shut tight. She stopped at the last room and ushered me in. Standing in the middle of the room gaping at me in horror was the redhead. At the sight of me her eyes widened, and without so much as a word, she rushed past us out of the room.

The chamber was as tiny and sparse as the others: there was a double bed against the wall and a small table with a mirror, chair, and wash basin opposite. I sat down on the bed with my valise, deliberately leaving my notebook open beside it. My reflection in the mirror revealed a young girl with ratty hair streaming from beneath a battered hat. I was taking off my coat when Miss King and Mrs. Caine entered the room. Miss King was avoiding my gaze while her companion searched for something to fill the awkward silence. The fair-haired girl had already disappeared back down the hallway

"Would you like me to remove your hat?" Mrs. Caine inquired, all kindness.

I nodded and took a seat before the mirror while Miss King, whom I could see in the reflection, sat down on the bed looking daggers at me. Mrs. Caine removed my hat and began pulling hairpins. My hair, which I'd further teased when I'd awoken this morning, issued forth in a matted pile. I pulled a comb from my reticule, and Mrs. Caine began her deliberations, gently working the comb through the tangles.

"Now, then, that's better, isn't it?" Mrs. Caine soothed, smoothing my hair.

Miss King twitched on the bed. "Why is it you're so frightened?"

"I don't know," I replied, looking down at my hands and sniffing. "I'm so confused sometimes. I . . . don't always remember things. And the women here . . ." I looked up and stared at Miss King through the mirror, whispering, "I think they're all crazy." I began to sob in earnest.

"Poor dear," Mrs. Caine said. "Isn't there someone to look after you? Where do you come from?"

"I don't know." I withdrew a handkerchief from my reticule and pressed it to my eyes. "I can't remember. I don't want to work and I've lost my trunks I think."

My sobs brought some of the women to the doorway. I pretended not to see them. "It's unsafe here. There are too many murders in this city, which means there are too many *murderers.*" I hissed the last word and then looked around and jumped, as if startled by the onlookers. "Oh! It's them! The crazy women. Have they come to get us?"

"Poor loon," one of them clucked.

"She's a loon all right," said Miss King. There was a fierce burn in her eyes, and she looked as if she might spit on me.

"She's a crazy one, she is." It was the woman in the maroon taffeta from the parlor, now wide awake. She looked like a plump exotic bird in her faded yellow dressing gown with an equally faded night cap. "She's like to murder *us* before morning."

I was shocked. Could it really be this simple to convince them I was mad?

Mrs. Caine, who was working my hair into a fat braid, was not swayed. "She'll be fine by morning, I'm sure. She's just a bit melancholy, that's all." She cast a stern look at the hovering women, a look that sent a message: they must all return to their beds and mind their own business. I was disappointed when they obliged.

"Melancholy, is it?" Miss King asked. She'd found my notebook and was staring at the ghastly illustration I'd sketched earlier. "She's crazy, and I'll not stay with her for all the money of the Vanderbilts. Come, Mrs. Caine, have a look."

Mrs. Caine crossed to the bed. The two exchanged a conversation in low tones as they peered at my notebook. I pretended to preen in the mirror.

It was soon apparent that Miss King would take Mrs. Caine's room and the latter would stay with me. When Miss King finally left, the older woman closed the door and turned down the lamp.

"You must undress now, my dear. It's growing late."

"I won't. It isn't safe."

After several more attempts, Mrs. Caine gave up and allowed me to sit on the side of the bed and stare in bewilderment at the door, as if I expected visitors to come in and cut us to bits at any moment. Mrs. Caine removed her garments and at last lay down, pleading with me once more to relax and let sleep come. "All will be better in the morning, dear. You'll feel better if you lie down and rest."

I did lie down but refused to close my eyes in case I fell asleep and ended everything I'd started. I focused my eyes on the ceiling. Mrs. Caine extinguished the lamp. Every few moments, she sat up and stared down at me, looking to see if my eyes were closed. Realizing at last that I wasn't going to sleep, she began asking questions. Where was I from? How long had I lived in New York? Where was my family? How had I come here?

To these questions, I had but one response: I didn't know because I couldn't remember.

When at last Mrs. Caine fell asleep, I listened to the settling of the house. Someone down the hall had a persistent cough. A dog barked in the distance. Mrs. Caine's snore sounded like a high police whistle.

No more than an hour later, I was startled by a cry from the hallway.

Mrs. Caine woke with a start and sat up. "What is it?"

"Someone screamed!" I clutched Mrs. Caine. "You see? It's not safe here."

It took all my control to remain in bed. Getting up and seeing what had happened was something Elizabeth Cochrane would have done. Nellie Brown would not have moved. Nellie Brown was led by an irrational fear, a fear that kept her rooted to the spot.

Mrs. Caine opened the door and went out into the hallway. Voices down the hall, murmurs, an agitated voice that rose above the others and gradually abated. In another moment, Mrs. Caine was back.

"What is it?" I said. "Has someone been murdered?"

"Goodness me, no," she replied. "Miss King had a nightmare."

"A nightmare?"

The older woman paused, as if considering whether to answer. "She says she dreamed of you."

"Me? Whatever for?"

"You were crazed and coming after her with a knife, bent on killing her." Mrs. Caine sighed. "Can you imagine? A sweet thing like yourself?" She patted my arm. "Now lie back down, dear. There's nothing to be frightened about."

Mrs. Caine was asleep almost immediately. In the darkness, I wondered again if it could really be this easy to fool them. Even so, I had to be careful. I was certain the police would not be so easily duped.

❧

Morning arrived, a gray glow in the window that spilled dull light into the room and woke Mrs. Caine from her whistling slumber. She was surprised to find me still clothed, staring up at the ceiling.

"Would you like to go home today, Nellie?"

"Where is home?"

Mrs. Caine's face fell. She had truly believed my memory would be intact come morning. She dressed in the chilly room and told me to stay put, she would just pop down and speak to Mrs. Stanard. Despite her reassurances, I could see she was agitated. My lack of memory upset her.

She wasn't gone ten minutes. She spent the next hour helping me with my hair and fetching water for the wash basin, as if she were in no hurry for breakfast or to take the ferry to Boston. All the while, doors opened and closed down the hallway. The others were preparing for the day. I soon realized it was Mrs. Caine's ploy to prevent me from mixing with the others. She patted and consoled me, telling me all would be well amid my tears and declarations of amnesia.

After I was dressed and had gathered my things, we went down two flights to the basement. I was certain Mrs. Caine had prearranged this with Mrs. Stanard. The breakfast hour was past, but a cup of coffee and a muffin lay on a table occupied by Mrs. Stanard.

The assistant matron wasted no time. "Where are your friends? Is there no one who can take you in?" She pushed the muffin toward me and indicated the coffee. Gone was yesterday's consideration. Mrs. Stanard was now preoccupied with how to be rid of me.

"I don't know what we can do," Mrs. Caine said. She brushed a stray lock of hair from my face, a gesture so like Mama's it made my heart ache.

"I want my trunks. Where are they? Do you know? Will the crazy women be back?"

"You came with no trunks, Nellie," Mrs. Stanard said, her lips tight. "Nothing but your reticule and a small valise."

"That isn't true!" I pushed back my chair. "I brought my things with me and I won't leave without them! Did the others take them? The crazy women? It was them, wasn't it? They've stolen my things and they'll come back for me!"

The women exchanged glances. Mrs. Stanard nodded ever so slightly, rose, gathered her skirts, and walked up the stairs.

"Poor child," Mrs. Caine murmured. "Poor, dear, sweet child."

*I looked around at the strange crowd
about me, composed of poorly dressed
men and women with stories printed on
their faces of hard lives, abuse and poverty.*

NELLIE BLY

NEW YORK CITY, SEPTEMBER 1887

Thirty minutes later, Mrs. Caine led me upstairs to the dark, vacant back parlor. "Just rest here, dear."

"Are you going to look for my trunks?"

"Mrs. Stanard is seeing to it, I'm sure." Mrs. Caine moved to the front parlor. From my seated position, I could see Miss King on the settee, throwing unpleasant looks my way. Her night terror had been replaced by indignation. I wondered if the events last night had kept her from going to work. Mrs. Caine looked simply anxious, which only fueled the curiosity of the few women who still remained, who were craning their necks to get a look at the mad girl sitting in the dark.

"I'll be glad to get rid of the likes of her," Miss King hissed.

Mrs. Caine, who was peering out the front window looking up and down the street, did not reply.

The woman in the maroon taffeta agreed. "She'll get what's coming to her, where she's going. Mrs. Stanard is seeing to that."

I took this to mean the assistant matron had left the house to see to the matter of what could be done with me. So far, so good. Mrs. Caine began to pace between parlors, asking me questions each time she entered the room. "Are you sure you don't know anyone who can help you?"

"I don't know."

"And you have no family, no one at all?"

"I may, but I don't remember."

"You cannot recall where you live?"

"No." Though I hated to see the stricken look on her face, I couldn't resist adding, "Do you think my trunks have been stolen? Shall we search the others' rooms?"

A few minutes later, the front door opened. Mrs. Stanard had returned. She breezed into the back room followed by two men in police uniforms. "This is the girl I told you about," she said, walking to the window and opening the shutters. Somber light revealed that the assistant matron was out of breath from her excursion, her slicked-back hair escaping its prison and giving her a disheveled air. "This is Nellie Brown."

The officers were a study in opposites: one was tall and slender, the other short and rotund. The tall one said, "Will she go quietly?" as if I were deaf.

"Of course she will," Mrs. Caine said, taking a seat beside me and wrapping an arm around my shoulders.

"She will or she'll be dragged through the streets," the short officer said, eyeing me.

"There is no call to be unkind," Mrs. Caine snapped. "Nellie will go quietly."

I rose. "Where am I going?"

"These kind men are going to help you find your trunks," Mrs. Stanard said. She helped me on with my coat and handed my hat to me. "Wouldn't you like to go with them to find them?"

"Oh, yes," I cried, "but I don't want to go alone!"

A titter of laughter from the front parlor. Mrs. Stanard threw a murderous look through the door, but she volunteered to accompany me, saying to the officers, "You're to follow us at a respectable distance, mind, until we're clear of this street. This is a reputable house, and I'll not have the neighbors saying otherwise."

It was apparent Mrs. Stanard, in her haste to arrive with the officers, had forgotten that they had entered through the front door.

I picked up my reticule and valise, and in another minute, Mrs. Stanard and I were emerging from the house into the dull gray of the street. I pulled my coat around me, and we set off at a brisk pace. There was no one about but a stray tabby that sat watching us from a fence post, tail flicking. The officers met up with us at the next block, and within ten minutes, we'd arrived at the station house.

Inside, the officer at the desk spoke in low tones with Mrs. Stanard while I looked around. The room was full: men, women, and children sat, leaned against walls, or milled about. The air was full of the odor of unwashed bodies, the hum of conversation like the buzzing of a thousand bees. Written on their faces were the hard lines of misery, of strife, that came from lives spent in fierce, continuous work above which no amount of labor would raise them.

When I saw a broad-shouldered man with piercing dark eyes speaking with a few officers not five feet away, my heart leapt. It was Captain McCullough, whom I had met and interviewed at Cooper Union a month past for a story for the *Dispatch*. Surely he would recognize me! I lowered my head and used my veil to full effect, hoping to remain another faceless unfortunate in the crowd.

The officer speaking with Mrs. Stanard called to me. "You are Miss Nellie Brown?"

"Yes," I replied quietly, hoping I wouldn't attract Captain McCullough's attention.

"And is it true what this lady says? You've lost your memory?"

"I came for my trunks, Officer," I told him. "Is this where you keep them?"

"I told you, she doesn't remember anything," Mrs. Stanard said. "She doesn't know where her family is, how she got to the Temporary Home, not a thing." Then, more hushed: "We cannot have her back there. She upsets the others."

After another low discussion, they agreed that Mrs. Stanard and the taller of the two officers, a man named Tom Bockert, would take me to the Essex Market Police Station in a horse car.

We emerged onto the street once more, and I breathed a sigh of relief that I had escaped being recognized. We walked to the corner, the air brisk with a cold, light wind. Pedestrians trudged by, headed to their destinations with their heads bent low, oblivious to the deceit I had begun. Officer Bockert attempted to hail a cab-for-hire while I kept up my charade with Mrs. Stanard.

"I do not like the people on the streets here," I said. I looked around in wide-eyed fear at the people walking by. "Who are they, where are they going?"

Mrs. Stanard searched for a cab without meeting my eyes. "They are going to work, Nellie."

"I think there are too many people in the world for the amount of work to be done."

This nonsensical remark brought Officer Bockert's attention to me. He gave me a look of pity and was about to reply when his focus was directed behind me. I turned. A small band of children dressed in attire a good deal shabbier than my own were looking me up and down.

"What's she in for, eh?" a scrawny, soot-faced boy without a coat asked.

A second boy, sporting a black eye and hair that looked like he had cut it himself, added, "Where'd you get her?"

"She gonna hang for her business?" the first boy asked. He sneered at me, as if my fate were his affair, this boy of no more than eleven years.

The other children chimed in, jeering, shouting, sticking out their tongues. One of them threw an apple core and hit me in the arm. I covered my head and cowered, as if the noise was too much for my delicate ears.

"Run along," Officer Bockert told them, making a shooing motion with his hands. "Off with you now." When they didn't move, he dug in his pocket, pulled out some coins, and flung them in the air a short distance away. The urchins ran to collect them and were gone.

At last he secured a horse car, and we hopped in and turned south on the Bowery Road. It was noon; the streets were moving masses of people, wagons, carriages, and horses. By the time we'd reached Delancey, I knew we were near our destination. I pretended otherwise. "We have gone an awfully long way. Are we going to find my trunks?"

"Yes," Officer Bockert assured me, with a look at Mrs. Stanard. "We're on the way to the express office now."

We turned onto Essex a moment later and stopped in front of a brick building. Men and women stood outside despite the chill, as if this were a soup kitchen that fed the hungry and not a police station.

"There are a lot of people here," I said.

"People just like you," answered Officer Bockert, as if he were speaking to a child. He jumped out with my valise, paid the driver, and assisted us down. "They've all lost their baggage. This is where everyone goes who loses his things."

Inside was the same as the prior station: bodies stood, leaned, or sat, waiting for their turn to be heard for some offense or crime. All wore expressions of want, of despair. Well-groomed officers regarded me with bland faces; they had seen this before. What was one more unfortunate?

Officer Bockert told us to wait where we were and disappeared into the crowd.

At the far end of the room behind a waist-high wooden partition loomed a large, elevated desk. Behind sat a rather beefy man with muttonchops and half-moon spectacles, dressed in a robe. My heart began to race. Would I be able to trick the judge, as I had the women at the Temporary Home? Reporters hung out at such places looking for stories to pursue. What if the few I had met recognized me? What if George McCain himself strode through the door? I swallowed, trying to tamp down on my fears and get ahold of myself, just as an officer seated at a desk motioned for me to approach.

"State your name, please," he said without looking up.

"My name is Nellie Brown they tell me," I said in a thick Spanish accent. I don't quite know why I did it. To get his attention perhaps, or throw off any reporters should they think I looked familiar. Well, it was too late now. Mrs. Stanard was staring at me in confusion. "I've lost my trunks and need to find them."

"When did you come to New York?" The officer's pen was poised over his notebook.

"I didn't come to New York."

That made him look up. "But you're here now."

"I never left."

"But you're from somewhere with that accent."

"She's obviously from the West," an officer looking on offered.

"No," said another. "That's an eastern accent if I've ever heard one."

The two argued as if they were experts in diction. We left them to it when the desk officer handed us his notes and told us to wait in line for the judge.

"Judge, here is a woman who cannot remember who she is or where she comes from." The officer in charge had a booming voice that cut through the din like a blade. Silence. All eyes turned in our direction. Mrs. Stanard, Officer Bockert, and I approached the bench.

The judge was a man in his middle years. The eyes looking over his spectacles narrowed as he gazed down at me. "Lift your veil so I can see your face."

"Who are you?" I demanded in my Spanish accent.

"I am Judge Duffy. This is my court, and if the Queen of England were here, she would have to lift her veil if I said so."

I did not move.

"Come now," the judge said. "Do as I ask so that I might see your face."

I obliged him this time.

The judge looked me over, studying my face, my attire, my reticule, and the valise I clutched. "Now, what's all this about?"

"This man," I motioned to Officer Bockert, "promised to help me find my trunks and brought me here."

The judge turned to Mrs. Stanard, who stood pale, looking up at him as if she might faint. As a reporter, a police station and its inner workings were not unknown to me, but Mrs. Stanard was as yet uninitiated. I had a vision of the assistant matron returning home and downing a shot of brandy to calm herself, splayed out on a sofa. "What can you tell me of this girl?"

"She came yesterday to the home where I work and spent the night. I know nothing else about her."

"What kind of home?"

"The Temporary Home for Females." Mrs. Stanard gave him the address, told him her position there, and gave him a brief summary of my stay, ending with my sleepless night and inability to remember whence I'd come.

The judge nodded. "Did she pay you?"

"Yes, I did," I piped up, hoping to call attention back to myself. "I paid for the room and the meals, which I can tell you, sir, was some of the worst fare I have ever had."

A ripple of laughter swept through the court. Judge Duffy banged his gavel. "Enough." When his courtroom had settled once more, he turned his attention back to me. "You are from Cuba?"

"Yes." I smiled broadly. "How did you know?"

"A guess. What part of Cuba?"

"On the *hacienda*."

"Ah, a farm. Do you know Havana?"

"*Sí,* it is near home."

"I see." A benevolent smile. "Now, be good and tell me where that is."

"I can't." I clutched my head. "My head aches so; I can't remember. I forget things. Everyone is asking me questions and making it worse."

The judge did not reply for some moments. Then, to no one in particular, he said, "She seems well dressed enough and a lady.

Her English is perfect, and I'd stake everything on her being a good girl. She must be someone's darling."

Another burst of laughter. I willed myself not to smile. Mrs. Stanard looked outraged. Such levity would never get me off her hands.

"That's enough." He banged his gavel again. "I meant someone —her mother, her sister perhaps—must be looking for her." More quietly, to me he said, "I shall be good to you, my dear. You remind me of my sister, who is dead. Now sit down and rest for a bit."

Mrs. Stanard and I had just taken our seats when an officer approached me. "Forgive me, miss, but a reporter just came in. Perhaps if you speak with him, he can have your likeness drawn for the papers—"

My heart leapt again. "Oh no," I cried. "I don't want to see any reporters." I lowered my veil and placed my palms at my temples. "My head aches and I shall scream if a reporter comes near me, I swear. The judge said I was not to be troubled."

The officer winced and moved away, but I wasn't sure he wouldn't be back with the reporter. I needed to act fast. I stood and began to pace the courtroom as Mrs. Stanard clung to my arm and begged me to sit and be calm.

"I won't stay here! I want my trunks. Oh, why won't they give me my trunks!"

This outlandish behavior provoked a shout from the back of the room. "Send her to the island!"

"Oh, don't!" Mrs. Stanard cried, wringing her hands. "She's a proper lady! That's no place for her."

"There's been some foul work at play," Judge Duffy said from his bench. "Perhaps she was drugged and brought to the city." He sighed. "Very well." He glanced at a court clerk sitting to the side. "Perhaps by the time the drugs wear off, she'll remember who she is and put all this behind her. Make out the papers, and I'll have her sent to Bellevue for examination."

It was, of course, the very thing I wanted.

8

With all my bravery I felt a chill at the prospect of being shut up with a fellow-creature who was really insane.

NELLIE BLY

NEW YORK CITY, SEPTEMBER 1887

"Put out your tongue," the court surgeon said.

After my spectacle before the bench, Judge Duffy had motioned Mrs. Stanard and I into a small, closet-like room off the courtroom. In the dusty little space, the judge loomed large. He towered over the surgeon, Mrs. Stanard, and me, telling the former that I was to be handled with kid gloves, repeating again that I favored his deceased sister and deserved the doctor's utmost attention. The surgeon had listened with courtesy, but as soon as Duffy left in a swirl of robes, his civility evaporated, replaced by a brusqueness that spoke to his desire to be rid of me as soon as possible.

"I said, put out your tongue," the court surgeon repeated. He was a compact little man with protruding front teeth, a quivering nose, and twitchy movements—a mouse in a three-piece suit.

I clamped my mouth shut and crossed my arms.

"For the last time, put out your tongue when I tell you."

"I'll do no such thing." I persisted with my accent.

"You will. You're sick, and I'm a doctor."

"I won't. I'm not sick and never was. I only want my trunks."

In the end, my curiosity won over. I wanted to see what his examination—the examination of one believed to be a lunatic—consisted of. He inspected my face and hands and took my pulse. Next, he withdrew an instrument from his bag with two prongs, one for each of his ears, then placed the small metal piece connected by a tube at the other end to my chest. How did the heart of an insane person beat? Did it beat differently? Was there some telltale abnormality that I lacked that would call me out as a pretender? I held my breath while he listened until, by the time he was done, I was gasping for air. He didn't seem to notice, or perhaps he didn't care. Finally, he examined my eyes. He held a small light half an inch from my pupils and instructed me to look at it. I did, unblinkingly, and though I wished to look away, I did not. The surgeon then jerked the light source away and studied the effect. Finally, he pulled back and pocketed the instrument while spots swam before my eyes.

"What drugs have you been taking?" he asked.

"I don't take drugs."

Mrs. Stanard, who had stood speechless during this exercise, spoke up. "I daresay her pupils have been enlarged since she came to the Temporary Home, now that I think of it. They haven't changed since."

"She appears to be under the influence of belladonna," the surgeon said importantly, jotting down information in a notebook. When he was finished, he snapped it closed and said to me, "I shall be taking you home now."

Home. A strange euphemism for Bellevue Hospital, for this was almost certainly what he meant. It was the last link in the chain that led to the land of the damned. I was getting closer.

The court surgeon took my arm and guided me down a hallway toward a side door that led outside. Just before I stepped through, I looked back. Mrs. Stanard, her hair still in disarray, smiled tremulously from the other end of the hall and gave a tiny wave. I wondered if she felt guilty now for summoning the police. She couldn't know that I had orchestrated it all, that she and Mrs. Caine had fallen perfectly into my plan. A part of me hated the subterfuge, but the other part of me, the part that needed desperately for this plot to work, was relieved. If I could fool the doctors at Bellevue, which, I reckoned, wasn't going to be easy, I'd be on my way across the river soon.

The court surgeon marched me down steps to where a small crowd waited around an ambulance wagon. There must have been thirty people, perhaps more—men, women, and children with both curiosity and unkindness on their faces. The sort, based on their ruddy complexions, the drab, unkempt look to them, who'd experienced misery aplenty and wanted to take a gander at another in similar straits. They parted like the Red Sea as we neared them. No one uttered a word. The only sound was the scrape of boots as they drew back. Then, by some unspoken command, someone barked, "Lock 'er up and throw away the key!"

The crowd erupted. The floodgates had opened.

"She's a goner now!"

"No rest for the wicked!"

"Put her with the rest of the crazies!"

I responded by putting my hands over my ears and cowering while a policeman behind us blew a whistle and advanced into the throng. "Break it up now," he said, making a shooing motion with his hands. "That's enough of the likes of you. You've taken your fill, now go."

The onlookers began to disperse, and we made our way to the rear of the wagon. No sooner had we climbed in and started off, however, than another clamor arose. I looked out the side window. It was the pitter-patter of little feet. Children were chasing after us, their faces bobbing beside us as they ran. They beat on the side of the wagon and threw stones. "A ne'er do well!" a young girl cried, her face smudged with grime. "Another ne'er do well for Blackwell's!"

They continued to rap on the glass and fling rocks until the horse pulling the wagon gained enough speed to leave them behind. For all they knew, I was going away to be locked up forever, yet they cared not a whit. I swallowed, my mouth suddenly dry. I was a spectacle, another soul on the way to condemnation.

The court surgeon refused to meet my gaze as we jostled along, only stealing glances when I was looking out the window. I wondered what he thought he could discern in me when I wasn't looking, what circumstances had led him to become a doctor of the courts when he seemed to care so little for those he studied, if my examination was any indication. I soon forgot him and concentrated instead on the world outside the window. We were traveling north up Second Avenue, the sky low, gray, and layered with ominously dark clouds. When we passed Stuyvesant Square, I knew we were not far away.

At last the horse slowed its gait as we turned east onto Twenty-Seventh, and there, one block dead ahead, was Bellevue. The towering brick structure rose as if to touch the leaden sky. It was like a fortress. Bellevue was widely known for housing a separate insane pavilion within its grounds, but it had grown overcrowded the last several years, and so the city's insane were, pending a positive examination, sent across the East River—the men to Ward's Island, the women to Blackwell's. The insane ward was the last resort for the city's unwanted, a place no sane person would ever conspire to go. I shivered and then chuckled at the irony of it. On the seat opposite, the court surgeon stiffened and moved farther away from me.

The old iron gates opened at our approach. "How many have you?" a gruff voice called when the wagon had pulled to a stop.

"One," I heard the driver say, "for the pavilion."

The door swung open, and a rough-looking man peered inside. With the doctor's nod, he seized my arm and attempted to haul me out. I threw a venomous look at the surgeon.

"Leave her," he said. "She will come quietly."

I alighted from the wagon with my valise, smoothed my skirts, and squared my shoulders. After climbing shallow steps to the doors, we entered a vast lobby and soon came upon an office where a man at a desk nearest the door began at once to ask questions, the same questions I'd been asked all morning at the police stations. I refused to reply, and the surgeon informed the man that it was of no consequence; he had all the information needed for my admittance. He handed over the paperwork. The desk clerk glanced at it and, seeing that all was in order, nodded to another large brute waiting behind us.

"How dare you touch me!" I said as soon as his meaty hands made contact with my arm. "I will go with no one but this man." I indicated the surgeon. "Judge Duffy said he was to look after me, and I'll not go with anyone else!"

The surgeon nodded and the brute released me. He picked up my valise. We followed him through a series of hallways and doors, lobbies and sitting rooms, passing nurses in starched aprons, doctors in white coats, custodians with brushes and mops. Corridors seemed to stretch into oblivion. It was a city, this place of death and misery, a city of shining floors and windows and echoing corridors. I longed to pull out my notebook and put details to paper.

Soon we were outside again in the chill September air. We passed manicured grounds with stately trees and curving sidewalks and entered another, smaller building. A nurse seated at a desk lifted her head when we entered.

"This girl is to wait here for the boat," the surgeon said. He turned to leave.

"You mustn't go," I pleaded, more for the nurse than the surgeon. I grasped his arm. "I'm frightened and I have yet to see my trunks!" "I am just going to take my dinner now," he said, his little eyes landing everywhere but on me as he lied. "I shall come for you after." I didn't need him anymore—I was at Bellevue—but there was something so odious about him that I didn't want to let him off so easily. "Then I'll accompany you," I said. "I'm hungry myself." "I'm afraid I have appointments back at court," the surgeon said, disengaging my hand from his elbow. His lips curled in disgust.

Just then, a horrible, anguished cry rose from within the building, and it was no act that I shivered as gooseflesh crept along my skin.

The surgeon noticed my response and said meaningfully to the nurse, "What a racket the carpenters are making, don't you think?" He turned to me, his mouse's nose aquiver. "They are doing some construction in the yard. It's the men about their work, that is all." He patted my arm, the gesture at odds with the coldness in his eyes. "I shall return as soon as I am finished." He stepped briskly away before I could detain him further.

There is a peculiar aspect of hospitals, of whitewashed walls and sturdy benches, well-scrubbed floors and basins. They are sanitary and useful, as they are meant to be, but lack the warmth, the spirit, of things cherished. This utilitarian atmosphere was clearly evident at the Bellevue Asylum. It exuded cleanliness and order, but there was something else beneath the surface. I couldn't shake the feeling that, beyond the sitting rooms and closed doors, things were not what they seemed.

Before me stretched a long hallway, its wooden planking scrubbed raw. At the end were large iron doors fastened with padlocks. Wicker chairs were arranged at intervals, and two women, seated separately, sat disconsolately upon these. Immediately to the right was a small sitting room with a sign marked NURSES, to the left a room designated DINING. It was cold, terribly cold. The windows that flanked the hall were open.

A middle-aged woman who introduced herself as Nurse Ball instructed me to take a seat and left. I walked down the hall, my boots echoing against the sparse white walls. I approached a young woman who looked similar to my age and sat down beside her. She did not look up. She was dressed in a coat a good deal more careworn than my own. On a chair beside her was a bundle of clothing secured with a belt.

"Good afternoon," I said. "My name is Nellie Brown. I've just arrived."

The girl met my eyes, a dullness in their depths that brought pity to my heart. Her hair was a deep auburn, her face covered in freckles that stood out against her pallid skin. She was not unhandsome, but her hair needed washing, and there was a hollowness to her cheeks, a whiteness to her lips, that spoke of recent illness.

"Anne Neville." It was a small voice, little more than a croak, and seemed to take all her energy to utter it.

"How it is that you are here, Anne Neville?"

Tears welled in her eyes, and she looked down at her hands. They were calloused and raw, the nails short. "I was employed as a maid and took to fever. When I did not recover as quickly as the family wanted, they sent me away to a sister's home."

"With nuns, you mean?"

"Yes." She wiped tears away with the heel of her hand. "But I had to leave after a few weeks. They couldn't keep me."

I was taken aback. "I have never heard of a nun's home turning out the ill."

"They didn't have a choice. There were many sick there. Too many. It was horribly overcrowded." She shivered. "I don't think many there will see the light of day again. In truth, I think the nuns felt better about sending me here because I was young and not as sick as some of the others. They thought I had a chance of recovering."

"And are you recovering? You have no fever now?"

"I'm better, yes." Her eyes fell. "I fear I have lost my place permanently though. I don't think I can return to the family I was working for. They must have replaced me by now. It's been nearly three weeks since I fell ill."

"Have you no family?"

"Only a cousin in the city. He is—was—a waiter, but he's out of work and cannot afford to keep me." A sob escaped her. "I-I've tried to tell the doctors here that I only need rest, but they won't listen."

"There must be some mix-up. Shouldn't you be in the main building for the ill?"

Anne withdrew a handkerchief from her coat pocket and wiped her nose. "I-I have been unable to convince the doctors that I'm well of mind. They ask me dozens of questions and I respond just as any sane person would, but they don't listen. It's the same with the nurses. They think I'm mad."

I didn't know what to say or how to console her. Here was a young woman who wanted only freedom, while I'd schemed to lose mine. I looked at the other woman seated a distance down. She looked somewhere between fifty and sixty years of age, dark complected and dressed in a thin black coat. She was staring into space, oblivious to everything around her.

"That's Mrs. Fox," Anne whispered. "She hasn't spoken since she arrived."

Before I could reply, the sharp report of footsteps announced someone's approach. A nurse in a dark dress with a white apron and starched cap was coming toward us.

She stopped in front of me and snatched my reticule from the chair beside me. "Take off your hat."

I bristled. "Who are you?"

"Nurse Scott, head nurse," she intoned with severity. "Now remove your hat *at once.*"

"I have come to take the boat," I answered back, "and I will not remove my hat."

The nurse quirked a brow, her mouth set in a firm line. "You will not be taking any boat. You might as well know that now. You are in a hospital for the insane and you'll do as you're told."

My heart skipped a beat. Would I be staying here instead of Blackwell's Island? That wouldn't do. Cockerill would be none too pleased. I cleared my throat and said with more authority than I felt, "I didn't want to come here and I don't want to stay. I won't remove my hat."

Nurse Scott narrowed her eyes. "It will be a long time before you get out with that attitude. I'll use force if I must." She leaned down to me. "It won't go well for you if you resist."

I lifted my chin. "If you take off my hat, I'll remove yours."

At that moment the nurse was called back to the front of the hall, and, with a scathing look at me that signaled the matter wasn't over, she retreated. I decided to remove my hat and gloves; I'd made the impression I'd wanted to make. By the time Nurse Scott returned a few minutes later and ordered the three of us to follow her to the dining room, she looked pleased to see I'd followed her order. But when she snatched up my hat, gloves, and valise, I began my argument once more.

"Why must you remove my things?"

"You're not to have them."

"Why?"

"Rules."

"And the windows? Is it also a rule that these stay open? It's as cold as a tomb in here."

"The chill keeps the air fresh."

"From what?"

"The stench of patients. And you'll not mention shutting the windows again or you'll regret it."

I glanced at my companions. They were looking on with so little interest, I wondered if they'd had the same discussion to no avail or if it was their mental state that kept them silent. "Then surely, if you take my hat and gloves, you can give me something to keep from freezing."

Nurse Scott bristled. "You've a coat, haven't you?"

"Yes, for outdoors. With the windows open and nothing to do but sit, a coat won't suffice. Have you no blankets for us?"

"No," Nurse Scott said. She shut and locked the door behind us as we entered the dining room, which consisted of one long table and a stove at the far end. A plump woman who introduced herself as Mary busied herself with preparing our meal. We seated ourselves at the table, and before long, Mary brought a small piece of meat and a boiled potato on tin plates. They could not have been colder if they'd been prepared the week before. Bread followed, hard as stone. Across the table, Anne Neville and Mrs. Fox stared down at their plates with no intention of eating.

"Do ye have any pennies, dearie?" I jumped. Mary had appeared beside me. Her breath smelled of garlic, and she was missing a tooth.

"Pardon?"

"Would ye have any pennies to give me?" she repeated in a thick Irish lilt. "They'll only take 'em from ye, ye might as well give 'em to me."

I told her I hadn't any money. It was true enough; my purse had only a few precious coins left. In any case, Nurse Scott had taken my reticule.

The meal didn't last long. None of us had more than a bite or two. Up close, I saw that Mrs. Fox was not as old as I'd thought. Though she was pale and looked drained, her hair had not a bit of gray in it. I wondered what had brought her to Bellevue and was about to enquire when the door was unlocked and Nurse Scott stormed in. In her arms was a pile of clothing, which she dropped onto the table.

"Shawls. Three of them. They're all we've got, so don't go asking for anything else."

As we were each grabbing a shawl, there was a sudden pounding outside the room. It sounded as if a great many fists were beating on the exterior door. Nurse Scott spun and exited the room, locking the door behind her.

"What is it?" we heard Nurse Scott say on the other side of the door.

"We've come to see the girl." A muffled male voice.

"What girl?"

"The one from the station." Another male voice.

My heart flip-flopped in my chest. *No.*

"I've no idea who you're talking about," Nurse Scott said, "and if I did, there are no visitors allowed here."

"We're here by order of Judge Duffy," a voice persisted. "He said he wanted a proper write-up to see that the girl with amnesia is recognized by her family and gets home."

Reporters, ever persistent for the truth, would bend words when it suited them. I didn't know if the judge had ordered any such thing, but even if he had, he had no legal power to issue such orders here. Still, I was frantic; I might be recognized by any one of them.

"This is no place for social calls," Nurse Scott was saying. "Now be gone with you or I'll call the guards."

Anne Neville, eyes as big as saucers, looked frightened out of her wits.

"There's something in it for you," a voice on the other side of the door said, "if you'll let us have a few minutes with her. Her name's Nellie."

Another beat of silence. I imagined the mention of money turning Nurse Scott's sour expression to joy. In my mind's eye, she would arrive home and count out her take with greedy satisfaction, all for merely letting some visitors question an inmate for a few minutes. But then, I couldn't think the doctors would allow visitors in, certainly not reporters. And Nurse Scott seemed all about abiding by the rules.

"Wait here," I heard her say.

A second later, the key turned in the dining room door. Nurse Scott bustled in, eyes glinting. "You're dismissed," she said with a flick of her wrist. She narrowed her eyes at me. "Except for you, Nellie."

I felt an awful dread in the pit of my stomach as Anne and Mrs. Fox left the room. I had not anticipated reporters. After I'd missed them at the Essex Market Police Station, I'd put them from my mind. What a fool I'd been. I was trapped, and now there was no time to prepare. Nurse Scott was already unlocking the outer door. There was no time to organize my thoughts, no time to consider what I should or shouldn't say. At the last moment, I threw the shawl over my head so that only my face was visible. It was a feeble barrier, but it was all I had.

The reporters filed in one by one. Six. All men, naturally. I didn't recognize any of them.

When the last entered, Nurse Scott closed the door and leaned back against it. So she would be witness to my interrogation. Perhaps she thought there would be more money in it for her if she stayed. Another few minutes allowed with the patient, another few coins to line her pockets.

The two youngest reporters, barely older than myself, took a seat across from me. The others remained standing, forming a semicircle around me. Six pairs of eyes took in the bareness of the table, the lack of linen, the stale bread on the counter, the untidiness of Mary, who was seeing to the dishes at the sink. They looked at me with what I recognized as a reporter's discerning eye. Already, without me answering a single question, they were working out how they would describe me. A young lady wrapped in a shawl with a kind, clean face or a poor, retched thing sitting alone with wide, wild eyes? It all depended on how they would play it. What would sell the most papers? The poor girl with no memory or the horrid waif who'd lost her mind?

They were dressed in black suits and overcoats, the wools and cottons of the middle class—not grand, but not down-at-heel like the attire I'd donned for my charade. They had notebooks, the small, standard-issue kind all reporters on Newspaper Row carried. I was suddenly glad Nurse Scott had taken my reticule. I didn't want them finding my own notebook inside like the ones they were carrying, or parsing out clues I might've left within its pages. One of them took out a pencil and began to sketch me, the sound of the lead scraping against the paper loud in the room. I would have known them anywhere. With the exception of my gender and garments, I was one of them.

No, I am not one of them. I am a madwoman in a hard, uncertain world with neither memory nor money.

The tallest, a slender, bearded man with red hair, said, "We're here, miss, to ask you some questions, to see what we can learn of you."

Ordinarily, I would have been flattered to have the attention of a roomful of men. When I wasn't fighting to defend my right to be one of their rank, I preferred their company to that of most women; I found men far more direct and comprehensible than members of my own sex. But nothing about this occasion was ordinary. I'd lied my way here, and these men might well find me out. I couldn't let that happen. I had a sudden vision of Cockerill at his desk, telling me I'd failed: *I'm sorry, Miss Cochrane. Your fellow*

reporters sniffed you out. Thank you for your efforts, but you see, this business of reporting really is far better suited to men.
I took a deep breath and regarded them with wide, guileless eyes. This was a game, and I could play it better than them. "Why would you wish to learn something of me?"
"We're reporters, miss," a portly man with a shock of gray hair and a matching beard said. "If we write you up in the papers, perhaps someone will come forward to claim you."
I wanted to know what papers they represented, but this seemed an unlikely question from a woman who couldn't remember her past. "Do I need claiming?"
A few of the men blushed. The red-haired man said, "Is it true you don't remember who you are?"
"My name is Nellie Moreno."
Glances at each other. Furious writing in notebooks. Nurse Scott, arms akimbo at the door, frowned. The gray-haired reporter said, "The judge told us you were Nellie Brown."
"I'm not Nellie Brown. I'm Nellie Moreno, from Cuba."
"But you don't recall how you came here, from Cuba?"
"I remember Mrs. Stanard's Temporary Home. I spent the night and had two meals, but I don't remember anything before that, except..." I let my voice trail off and my gaze go vacant, as if I were lost in my own crazed thoughts. They leaned closer. I could feel their apprehension. "I lost my trunks. They were stolen. An officer was kind enough to take me to the police station to look for them, but he never did find them. Such a great many people there, looking for trunks. A pity."
"What was in those trunks, Miss Moreno?"
"Why, I have no idea."
A pause.
"Miss Moreno," a man of middle height with blond hair said, "the court surgeon at the police station thought you might be under the influence of drugs."
"That scrappy mouse of a man? I don't take drugs."
"Might someone have given you some?"
"I don't know. I have headaches, you see, and I can't remember."
"Are you employed, Miss Moreno?"
"Employed? Why should I be?"
"Well, if you aren't married or living at home, you must be working. That, or you are very rich."
"Oh no, I don't work. I'm not trained for anything, and besides," I leaned forward and lowered my voice, "there are too many crazy people about. Look at all the murders that go unsolved, and all

the awful people in the world who never get caught. Dangerous people, everywhere. I couldn't work with such people."

The artist was making quite a sketch. He had portrayed me sitting at the table, a thin girl covered in a shawl with enormous eyes and a petulant mouth. My first venture into the New York papers would be in the role, not of a reporter, but of a lunatic.

The red-haired man spoke again. "And how are they treating you here?"

"Well enough," I said. A disdainful sniff. "The food is awful, and they keep the windows open on a day as cold as this. It's rather ridiculous to sit about in a coat indoors with a shawl over one's head, don't you think?"

There was a murmur of agreement. Nurse Scott saw the way the interview was going and decided to end it. "That will be all. You must leave at once."

The nurse escorted them out, and I was once again locked in the dining room. I'd answered their questions. I'd confirmed what they already knew. Was there enough for a story? Would Cockerill be disappointed or pleased to see something printed about my escapade in the competitive papers? I was still thinking when Nurse Scott told me to join Anne Neville and Mrs. Fox in the hall.

9

I began to have a smaller regard for the ability of doctors. . . . I felt sure now that no doctor could tell whether people were insane or not, so long as the case was not violent.

NELLIE BLY

NEW YORK CITY, SEPTEMBER 1887

When Nurse Scott led me from the dining room, I saw that my companions had returned to their chairs and were huddled into their shawls dozing. My own shawl was moth eaten and stank of mildew. I sat down next to Anne. I draped the black, misshapen thing around me but found I couldn't endure the stench, so I flung it aside. I would just have to bear the cold.

"What, you don't like it now?" Nurse Scott scoffed. She stepped closer, so close I could smell her faint scent of talcum. "People on charity should be happy to get what they get." She turned and left, saying over her shoulder, "Those too uppity for their own good will come down soon enough."

With nothing else to occupy me, I decided to slip beneath the shawl after all and close my eyes. I hadn't slept more than an hour or two at the Temporary Home. My mind had been too full of worry about how far my ruse would get me. I needed rest.

I was in a state of semisleep when the shawl was yanked

from my head. Nurse Scott glared imperiously down at me. An elderly man in a white coat stood beside her, blinking behind thick spectacles that made his eyes look enormous. He held a stack of paperwork.

"I am Dr. Field. State your name for me, please."

"Nellie Brown." I was using the Spanish accent, wondering what he and the nurse would make of it.

"And how are you feeling, Nellie?" the doctor asked.

"Fine."

"Ah, but you are sick, you know. Where do you come from?"

"Home."

"And where is home?"

"Cuba."

"When did you leave Cuba?"

"You know my home?"

"Very well," he said with another owlish blink. "I remember you, don't you remember me?"

I knew for a fact I'd never seen him before. "Yes, yes, I do remember you, though I've forgotten your name."

Dr. Field made notes, felt my pulse, listened to my heart, and inspected my tongue while Nurse Scott looked on suspiciously. It was the examination of the court surgeon all over again. Was the pronouncement of my insanity really nothing more than checking my pulse and studying the interior of my mouth? I couldn't think so.

When he had completed his exam, he said, "What do you do in New York, Miss Moreno?"

I'd just told him my last name was Brown. This meant Nurse Scott had informed him of the reporters' visit. Was it his intention to use the name I'd given the reporters? Was he trying to trip me up? "I don't do anything."

"You don't work?"

"No, señor."

"She didn't have that accent earlier and that's two names now," Nurse Scott interjected, looking from me to the doctor. "She's making it up, I tell you."

Dr. Field ignored her. "Tell me, Miss Brown, are you a woman of the streets?"

I noticed Mrs. Fox and Anne looking on, and I felt my face grow hot. "I don't know what you mean."

"Do you allow men to provide for you and keep you?"

"I don't know what you're talking about. I've always lived at home."

"Are you in the habit of taking drugs?"

"Certainly not."

"Has anyone given you drugs?"

"Why should they?"

"Indeed. Now tell me, do you ever see things, Miss Moreno, things that aren't there?"

"Why, everything I see is there."

Dr. Field scowled. He was growing impatient. "I mean things that people *tell you* really aren't there."

"Like what, ghosts and such?"

"Yes."

I crossed my arms and said haughtily, as if insulted by the question, "What do you take me for, a demented idiot?" I hoped that by professing my sanity, Dr. Field would be more likely to believe the opposite was true.

"Your paperwork says you believed murderers might come after you and the other women at the Temporary Home."

"Well, of course. People are murdered in their beds every day. It only stands to reason sooner or later one might come after me. Or you, for that matter." I leaned forward in my chair and said softly, "You never know where they might lurk." I looked up and down the hallway, as if expecting a man with an ax to appear at any moment.

After a few more questions, the answers to which offered him nothing of value, the doctor and nurse left me. As they moved back down the hall, I heard Dr. Field say, "Positively demented. A hopeless case."

Another female patient arrived in the evening. She came in accompanied by a boy about sixteen years of age. Judging by his accent, I concluded they were German. The boy, most likely her son, was doing all the talking with Nurse Scott. I gathered his mother spoke little English. Her son turned to her before he left and embraced her, at which the poor woman broke down crying. She made to cling to the boy, but Nurse Scott intervened, instructing Nurse Ball to take the poor thing down the hallway while the boy exited the building.

As she neared our seating area, I could see that she was frightened. What had happened to make this skittish woman look like she was going to bolt at the slightest sound? That the woman had led a difficult life was apparent in the deep lines of her forehead, her work-ravaged hands, and her clothes, which, though clean, were shabby.

"This is Mrs. Shanz," Nurse Ball said. She indicated for the older woman to sit. "Don't think she knows a word of English. Lord, but we get all kinds." She gave us all a sharp look. "You're to make her feel welcome, hear? The doctors don't like when the likes of you bawl and make a fuss." She turned to Mrs. Shanz. "Do you sew? We've got some mending to keep you busy." The older woman only stared back at her. Nurse Ball mimed a needle going into fabric, and Mrs. Shanz responded by vigorously nodding her head. The nurse darted away and came back with some mending, which Mrs. Shanz took up immediately.

When the supper hour arrived, the four of us assembled in the dining room while Mary set down a piece of bread and cup of tea at each place. When she saw that I was having none of it, she brought me a soda cracker and a cup of milk. I was starving; I hadn't eaten in more than a day, but I could only think of Mrs. Shanz, who was taking in her food as if she hadn't seen such fare in years. Without a word, I slid my plate and milk over and gave her an encouraging smile. Mrs. Shanz nodded, and soon the food was gone.

⁓⁓⁓

"Have you fallen recently, Nellie?" Dr. O'Rourke said.

I stared at him, my eyes wide with what I hoped was a look of vacuous innocence. I had been escorted by one of the nurses after dinner to a small examination room within the main building. There Dr. O'Rourke had taken my pulse, listened to my heart, and checked my reflexes. These he had performed perfunctorily, as if he knew he would find nothing to indicate my condition. I considered his question. Should I pretend I had fallen? Would this explain my memory loss? If I owned to it, he might assume my condition was temporary and had nothing to do with insanity. "No, Doctor."

"Very well then." He placed his hands at my temples. "Tell me if anything hurts." He felt around my skull with his fingers, working from my forehead to the back of my head, all the while watching me for any sign of discomfort. At last, he dropped his hands and frowned. "Have you felt any dizziness of late?"

"None at all."

"Well," he said, stepping back, "you seem the picture of health to me. Your heart rate is normal, and your reflexes are fine. I can find no bump or bruise of any kind to indicate you've taken a spill. Sometimes such an event might bring on loss of memory." He frowned. "Of course, just because I can't see evidence of one doesn't mean you don't have a mild concussion."

I did not want him to believe I had a concussion, or any other condition from which I might recover. I needed to be sent up the river to Blackwell's Island. I bit my lip. *Think.*

"Nellie?"

I started. Dr. O'Rourke was looking at me with interest. There was a beat of silence, then he pointed to a sign on the far wall with rows of random letters on it, each row getting gradually smaller the farther down they went. "Please read to me the smallest line you can see."

I read him the lowest line on the chart. There was no use in pretending my eyesight was poor. Surely lunatics had good vision.

"Hmm." He sat back on the edge of his desk and crossed his arms, staring at me curiously with dark, narrowed eyes. So far, Dr. O'Rourke was the only doctor among those who had studied me who had gone beyond a cursory exam. I suspected he was no fool.

"Tell me, Nellie, do you see visions, hallucinations, that sort of thing? Things that might appear and disappear?"

I had already told Dr. Field I did not. Contradicting myself now might be too much. I very much felt that if Dr. O'Rourke could trip me up, he would. "No."

He picked up a file behind him and flipped through the pages, then tossed it on the desk with a sigh. "Dr. Field seems to think you are quite out of your head. What do you say to that?"

It was the first such question I'd been asked. For a moment my mind raced, trying to think of something that would instantly brand me a lunatic.

"I'll tell you what I think," Dr. O'Rourke said. "I think you've thought about every question I've put before you."

"Well, naturally, I—"

He lifted a hand, stilling my words. "Let me finish. As I was saying, you've put some thought into each of your responses. The mentally ill don't typically think like that. Instead, your behavior is more like one who *wants* to be believed she is, shall we say, of unsound mind. Furthermore, there is nothing that indicates to me that you are in any way unwell."

My heart skipped a beat. I wanted to tell him he was wrong, but no lunatic would try to convince a doctor of her own insanity. On the other hand, if I agreed with him, I might be just convincing enough to be charged a normal person, not a madwoman at all.

"I generally don't work with the mentally ill patients," Dr. O'Rourke went on. "It isn't my field of study. It's up to the doctors in the pavilion to qualify your case. But Dr. Field asked me to have a look at you to see if there were any physical reasons that might explain your behavior over the past few days."

I bristled. "I don't know what 'behavior' you mean, Dr. O'Rourke. I've answered everyone's questions honestly. I just want to put this behind me and find the trunks that were stolen from me at the Temporary Home. Does the report say anything about that? And as far as my memory—" I managed to tear up a little and went on. "I can't tell you what I don't know."

Another beat of silence. I could not look at him. I feared he would be able to see right through me, though I expected he had already.

"I find it most interesting you claim to know only your name yet you've supplied us with two of them. Brown and Moreno. Which is it, Nellie?"

"Brown. I am Nellie Brown."

"From Cuba?"

I stiffened and tried to look affronted. "No, New York."

He stared at me for a long moment. "Well, Nellie Brown from New York, I will give my report to Dr. Field. The nurse is waiting for you outside. You may go."

I came to my feet, but before I could quit the room, he said, "I have the distinct impression you're deceiving us all, but I'll be damned if I know why you're doing it."

I refused to look at him and kept going, for surely the look of fear my face would tell him he was right.

༄༅

An hour later, just as the nurses were lighting the lamps, another woman arrived. She was young, younger than Anne Neville and me. Once she had taken a seat in a wicker chair near us, I wasted no time.

"I'm Nellie Brown," I said kindly. "I have only just arrived today."

The palest of blue eyes set into a small, heart-shaped face stared back at me. "I'm Tillie. Tillie Maynard." Like Anne, signs of illness marred her otherwise striking features: her skin was pale and damp from fever, the area beneath her eyes hollow and tinged a grayish blue. Her head was wrapped in a white-and-red-striped kerchief. "I'm suffering from a nervous debility."

It sounded more like a proclamation than a confidence. I had the impression Tillie Maynard was repeating what she'd been told. "I'm sorry to hear it," I said.

"My friends have sent me here to be treated for it, you see," Tillie continued. She looked at me as a child might look to her mother for approbation.

"I hope you feel better soon." What sort of friends would send a young girl here? I had the sudden impression that Tillie, so young and in her fevered state, had no idea she was in an insane ward. Unfortunately, however, my fact gathering was cut short when Nurse Ball arrived and announced it was time for bed.

We stood and waited for her to unlock the iron doors at the opposite end of the hall. When they opened, her lamp revealed another long hallway with doors on either side. As Nurse Ball unlocked each room, the lamp throwing shadows against walls and giving an eerie cast to our surroundings, she pointed to who was to occupy it, telling us to get undressed, change into a gown, and get into bed. "No dawdling. It's to bed for the lot of you."

My room was only a bit larger than the bed, with no furniture or wall decorations, a chamber pot in the corner, and a window with iron bars—details I saw in a flash before Nurse Ball and her light were gone and my door was shut and locked. How was it possible that it was even colder in this room? I undressed quickly, my skin rippled with gooseflesh, and felt for the short, thin gown I'd seen lying on the bed. It was over my head in an instant, its weight wholly unsuitable for the cold. My coat and shawl were welcome layers. Through the thin walls next door, Nurse Ball was explaining to Mrs. Shanz in slow, careful English what she was to do.

The sole blanket was too small to accommodate me or the bed, but it was welcome nevertheless. I used it to cover my legs and stockinged feet. When all was quiet and I was at last settled, I heard voices from the entry hall, the echoes of speech carrying into the dormitory, as Nurse Ball had left the padlocked doors open.

"It's late," I heard Nurse Scott say harshly. "They've gone to bed."

"I've just come from the police court and learned of her," a male voice replied, "or I would have come sooner."

I sat up in the darkness.

"Well, you're a bit late now, aren't you? The others came hours ago."

"I shall only take a moment. I just have a few questions to ask her."

"As I said, they're all in bed, and we don't allow visitors. You'll have to get the news from your friends or read it in the papers yourself."

"I wonder if . . . I wonder if I might inspect her clothes and see what I can determine from them."

"Certainly not!" Nurse Scott's indignation reverberated all the way down the hall.

It couldn't be.

"Can you describe her then, this Nellie?" the man said anxiously.

But it was.

"Early twenties. Thin with long brown hair. Now that's all."

There was a sound of hushed giggling from outside my door. If there was a reply, I didn't hear it. My door opened, and two young nurses burst in with a lamp.

"Are you Nellie Brown?" a girl with a large bosom and a nest of black curls inquired.

"I am."

"There was a reporter just here for you." The girls looked at each other and giggled again, as shadows danced around the room. "He was a right looker, weren't he?" the black-haired girl said.

"What's he come here to find out anyway?" the other inquired when she had sobered. She was a head taller than her friend and appeared just as daft. "We don't get reporters here for the likes of you."

"I don't know what you mean." My heart was beating fiercely.

"She means for you *crazies,*" the black-haired nurse said, crossing her eyes and attempting a look I could only assume was meant to mimic a lunatic. "The reporters ain't interested in you."

"I heard you don't know who you are or where you come from," said the tall one. She eyed the other nurse meaningfully and said to me, "I'll bet he's really your beau and you've—"

"Whatever is going on here?"

The three of us started. Nurse Ball stood in the doorway.

"We was just collecting Miss Brown's things," said the dark-haired girl.

"Then be quick about it." She clapped her hands and advanced into the room.

The taller girl turned to me and said, "I'll just put your initials on these, Miss Brown, so we don't mix them up." She picked up my clothes, nodded to Nurse Ball, and left with her friend in tow.

For a moment, Nurse Ball lingered at the door, staring at me as though I were a puzzle she couldn't decipher. Had she overheard what I had? Was she suspicious reporters and now another late visitor were taking an interest in who I was, who I might be? In the next instant, she was gone, and I was alone in the cold dark once more. But sleep would not come.

I was certain the reporter looking for me a moment ago was George McCain.

10

*ove and marriage form the basis of
every plot.*

NELLIE BLY

PITTSBURGH, APRIL 1885

I stood across from the entrance of the exhibition hall watching the crowd. The grand circular foyer was jammed. Fair weather had brought out the masses, and they were eager to shed their winter disposition and venture, once more, beyond the stuffy confines of their parlors. Colorful floral arrangements sat on tables and pedestals, above which hung a crystal chandelier the size of a cabriolet. Off the foyer, corridors of rich red carpet led into grand salons. The scent of flowers hung in the air, an intoxicating bouquet of roses, hyacinths, forsythia, gardenia, and jasmine.

I spotted McCain at the entrance almost immediately. It wasn't difficult; he stood a head taller than most men. I watched him move through the throng, his head down as he shouldered through the crowd, stopping to let ladies with formidable bustles pass and to nod greetings to the gentlemen he knew who crossed his path. When his head came up and he met my gaze, I was startled. He'd caught me staring. Flustered, I looked down at my notebook and pretended to write. When I looked up again, it was into his eyes. He was so close I could reach out and touch his coat.

"Oh," I said stupidly, "you startled me."

He smiled, flashing a row of even white teeth. "Please forgive me, Miss Cochrane." He withdrew his top hat, twirling it once in a gloved hand. A lock of dark hair fell forward onto his brow. I was transported, for a brief instant, to that chilly January morning when he had saved me from certain death on Fifth Avenue, when I'd seen him twirl his hat for the first time after we'd disentangled ourselves from each other. To my consternation, I blushed to the roots of my hair. If he took notice, he was too polite to remark on it. "In truth, I thought I might find you here. I overheard Madden saying something about your coverage of the show." He turned and watched the people. "A good turnout, I think."

A bark of laughter sounded at the door. A group of gentlemen had just entered, each with a pastel-clad lady on his arm.

"What brings you to the flower show, Mr. McCain? Are you a botanist?"

"Not in the slightest." He dropped his smile and looked suddenly sheepish. "Would it surprise you to learn I happen to be a haphazard gardener? It's a fine spring Saturday afternoon, and I thought a visit might give me some ideas for my fledgling garden at home."

He was serious, perhaps even a little embarrassed by the admission. I liked him the better for it. "If that's the case, Mr. McCain, you've come to the right place."

An uncomfortable pause. I'd given him the liberty to excuse himself and peruse the halls, but he didn't move. He indicated the notebook in my hands. "Do I impede your fact gathering, Miss Cochrane?"

"There aren't many facts to gather, I'm afraid. In any case, I've taken my notes."

"Then may I have the honor of walking the floor with you? I shall try my best to amuse you with the thimbleful of knowledge I possess on floriculture." It was a simple request, and yet I could not help but sense something indefinable and delicious between us. Was I imagining it, building castles in the air where there were none? He was a fellow journalist, a coworker who'd come to enjoy the flower show and nothing more. There was also the fact that I'd been insufferably bored since I'd arrived, mentally berating Madden for assigning me such a dull story.

I took the arm he proffered and stepped into the crowd, aware that my heart was beating rapidly. He led us out of the foyer, which had become overcrowded and warm. Or was it I who was warm, with my hand clutching his sleeve, my skirts brushing against him? I forced myself to concentrate on my surroundings. I was being silly. Around us strolled women in new dresses and hats, men in coats and top hats, children in short breeches and dresses. It was a pleasant scene—I would relay it to the letter for readers—and yet, it all seemed so insubstantial.

"Your brow is furrowed, Miss Cochrane. Is it my professed ignorance of flowers that distresses you, or my rakish means of keeping you from your story?"

"Fact gathering, you said." I didn't want to sound critical, but frustration had burned within me all morning. "I only wish there was something of import here to report, Mr. McCain. Something of substance. More than, say, a few paragraphs on the beauty of tea roses and how their colors bear a striking resemblance to the shades of the ladies' gowns this season."

"You dislike Madden assigning you ladies' topics."

"I find them tedious."

We had entered one of the grand salons. Each bloom—and there were thousands—seemed to compete for attention. Around us were rows upon rows of flowers blooming in pots, arranged in bouquets, hanging from garlands from the ceiling. Across the room, a harpist played before a bank of windows. Sunlight slanted into the room, washing the harp a glittering gold. The musician's fingers were bright spots moving over the strings.

He stopped and turned to me, his expression thoughtful. "Your series on the plight of the city's poor factory girls was very good, very good indeed."

An eight-part serial that had run for two months. I was enormously proud of it. As city editor, McCain was responsible for the city's hard news. As my stories tended to be features, they didn't fall under his jurisdiction. I was thrilled to know he read them nevertheless.

McCain smiled. "I wager the topic was your idea."

"Yes, I thought women forced to earn a living in such a way because they had no other alternative might be of interest to readers."

"And you were right. Erasmus told me himself how pleased he was with it. And again, I thoroughly enjoyed your divorce piece. I rather agree with you on allowing one to file for divorce if a spouse is convicted of a crime."

I raised a brow. "Even if the husband is the one convicted?"

"Of course. And it's quite genius, your suggestion to disallow a couple to marry if they're both in great debt. Your ideas may be unconventional, but they are brilliant, Miss Cochrane."

I felt heat rise to my cheeks. "Yes, so brilliant that, after receiving mail from readers applauding my themes, Madden assigned me a story on trees." I couldn't keep the derision from my tone.

"Your story last week on Arbor Day."

I nodded. "Followed by this." I indicated the room. "It's beautiful here, I don't deny it, and as a means for raising funds for the city's library association, admirable, but—"

"But you would rather be investigating the city workers who find themselves in poverty? Or perhaps interviewing young women on their own who must rely on themselves to earn a living?"

I felt strangely exposed and understood at the same time. "Madden will be content with a few paragraphs describing who among the upper class attended today, nothing more."

McCain didn't reply. He seemed to be struggling for words. Or perhaps he was growing uncomfortable for bringing up a topic that had so obviously provoked me and he wanted now to abandon the conversation. "And now you are silent, Mr. McCain."

"I'm endeavoring to find a gentlemanly way to say Madden is an ass."

I blinked at him for a moment, then smiled. McCain broke into a grin too, and then we were both laughing.

Presently I sobered. Madden had become insufferable. He ignored the letters coming in from women who admired my stories and continued to assign me topics—fashion, theater, town gossip—he thought women should be reading instead.

"I think we are of one mind on many things, Miss Cochrane," McCain said, and then he looked away, as if his words bore an intimacy he hadn't intended. His eye fell on a table nearby covered with yellow flowers. "Ah, the genus *Narcissus*. A flower of meadows and woods. The native flower of Wales, if I'm not mistaken."

"They look like common daffodils to me," I replied. According to the placards on the table, there were six varieties, ranging from deep gold to white.

"And you find them common?"

"Well, they're certainly not ugly," I said, "but they're plain, are they not? Hardly exotic, like so many of the species here."

"The narcissus—or the daffodil or jonquil as they are better known—is quite extraordinary," McCain said, fingering a petal. "They were cultivated in ancient times for medicinal purposes." He touched another bloom and then looked up at me, a spark of mirth in his eyes. "Narcissus even makes an appearance in Greek and Roman mythology."

"The story of Narcissus the hunter, you mean."

"The very one."

"Who fell in love with his own reflection and drowned."

"I ask you, Miss Cochrane, how common is that?"

There was something playful in his expression. I sensed that beneath the facade was a man of great intellect who used humor both to charm strangers and to guard his innermost thoughts. I wondered which it was in this case.

"Do you know," McCain said, indicating a white variety marked *Narcissus papyraceus,* "that daffodils that grow near water are said to be Narcissus looking at his reflection?"

"Is this a mythology lesson, Mr. McCain?"

"No, I'm on to poetry now. Wordsworth must have had the *Narcissus poeticus* in mind when he penned, 'And then my heart with pleasure fills, and dances with the Daffodils.'"

"Your scope of subjects dazzles me."

"I'm boring you."

"On the contrary, I find this discussion immensely more satisfying than looking for who among the elite is here, or comparing flowers to ladies' fashions."

"Nonsense," McCain said. He looked about the room, then indicated a tall, slender woman in a frothy peach gown. "See that woman in the plumed hat? See how her hat mimics the daffodil's high center crown? And those outrageous plumes, of which there are six, look somewhat like the six petals of the daffodil. Even her neck resembles the flower tube from which springs the lively bloom. It's easy once you know what to look for."

I suppressed a giggle. "I can hardly put that in my article."

"Ah, you laugh. I'm not boring you now, Miss Cochrane. Let us find another." McCain searched the room again, his height an advantage in the game. "Ah, see there? The woman in the hat with green leaves? Give me your impression. What you do think of her?"

"I think she is the picture of fashion in pale green silk."

"Hmm . . . I do hope the yellow berries on her bonnet are not real or, in any case, that she doesn't get hungry."

"Because?"

"Because those small orbs on her hat look like bittersweet berries, which are poisonous," McCain said. "After paying top dollar for that hat and hoping everyone will admire it, imagine her embarrassment should she discover she is showcasing a most deadly agent."

I laughed. "Such amusing stories, Mr. McCain. A pity I can't use them."

"Consider them a way, perhaps, to give Madden a reason to take you off the flower show."

"I wouldn't dare."

We spent another hour admiring the blooms, listening to the

harpist, walking the corridors. Time passed quickly in his company, so quickly I was disappointed when he glanced at his watch fob and declared, "Alas, the hour grows late, Miss Cochrane. I must be going, I'm afraid."

He bowed over my hand and begged his apologies. I watched him retreat into the crowd until I couldn't see him any longer.

I didn't know yet that I was tethered to him. It had begun the day he'd saved me on Fifth Avenue, but it would strengthen over the talk of flowers. A language, a clandestine link, we would master over time.

"The white roses are simply splendid," Jane said, "but the lilies! I have never seen the like."

"The lilies are indeed lovely," Mama said.

It was the second day of my coverage of the show. Mama, I, and my eldest brother's fiancée, Jane, were seated at a small table in the café off one of the salons. It was overcrowded, the air near stifling. I watched my brother Albert make his way to the refreshment line while Jane prattled on.

"I cannot decide. If I go with a conventional flower for the wedding, I feel as if no one will notice. If I choose a flower more daring, what if I choose wrongly? What do you think, Elizabeth?" Jane's blue eyes implored me.

I thought she should stop prevaricating and decide, else I would bat her over the head. "Whatever you wish, Jane."

"But I must decide, and soon," Jane replied. She thrust out her lower lip in a pretty pout, one Albert likely found charming but rose my hackles. In her pink dress and matching hat, she was the picture of demure beauty. Beneath was a woman who would never be independent, would always need those around her to make decisions for her. To Albert, Jane was the perfect picture of a wife: obliging, sweet, and, most importantly, obedient. Jane would never defy him, and to Albert, with his pompous, self-assured air, obeisance was a must. I wondered if Jane had considered what marriage to Albert would be like beyond their wedding day.

"Perhaps I should go back and have a look at the crocuses, Elizabeth," Jane said. "What do you think?" She fluttered her fan, the tendrils of her hair dancing around her face.

"Crocuses?" Albert said, setting down a tray of iced beverages and taking a seat.

"Jane is seeking your sister's advice on flowers for the wedding," Mama said.

"Heavens, Jane," Albert replied, shooting a glance at me. "Elizabeth is the last person you should ask about such things. She has no desire ever to be a bride, isn't that right, Sister?"

I quirked a brow at him and turned to Jane. "I know very little about flowers, as it happens. You'd best seek someone else's advice on the subject."

"Well, since you're reporting on the flower show, I thought you might have gleaned *something*," Jane said with a sniff. She set her eyes on the glass Albert had placed before her. "Oh, lovely! Whatever is this, Albert?"

"The latest thing, they tell me," Albert said. "Grapefruit juice."

"Oh, I've never tried it," Jane cried, putting her gloved hands together. "How lovely."

I sighed and looked around. We were surrounded by clusters of people talking, sipping, trying to stay cool in the close air. A few men had unbuttoned their jackets or abandoned them altogether. Ladies were wilting in their dresses. When a group of women talking near the counter moved away, a tall gentleman in a fawn suit came into view. My breath caught. George McCain was coming from the refreshment line. For reasons I didn't care to think about, I felt myself blush.

"I've never heard of grapefruit," Jane was saying, raising her glass and peering into it. "I wonder where it comes from."

I forced my attention on the table lest McCain catch me gaping again. "South, I suppose," I said distractedly, "unless they're imported."

The four of us took a unified sip, our faces transforming into grimaces as the taste hit our respective tongues.

"Goodness," Mama said. Her lips puckered. "That is the most bitter thing I believe I have ever tasted."

"It's not at all what I expected," Jane said.

"Ghastly." Albert pushed his glass away. "I cannot imagine it will last long here once the masses have tried it."

I busied myself with my drink, hoping McCain wouldn't overhear our inane conversation. I had just taken another horrid mouthful when I heard, "Is that you, Miss Cochrane?"

My eyes flew up, and I choked down a swallow. There he stood—tall, somehow graceful in the heat, holding a glass of lemonade—while Mama beat my back and murmured, "Goodness, Elizabeth. You mustn't gulp."

"Mr. McCain, how nice to see you." I inclined my head and set down my glass. There was a beat of uncomfortable silence. "Um, this is my mother, Mary Jane, my brother Albert, and his fiancée, Miss Jane Hartley."

McCain smiled at Mama. "I see now where Miss Cochrane gets her fine features."

Albert's eyebrows rose. He looked with interest at McCain. "Have we met, sir?"

"No, we have not." McCain offered a hand as Albert came to his feet. "George McCain, city editor for the *Dispatch*. I had the good fortune of coming upon Miss Cochrane here the other day."

"Good God, they have more than one reporter covering flowers?" Albert blurted.

"Don't be silly, Albert," I said. "Mr. McCain is here for enjoyment only."

Albert grunted and said low, "I should think a day of it would have been sufficient."

Had I been able, I would have kicked him under the table. McCain pretended not to have heard.

"Miss Hartley, a pleasure to meet you. May I congratulate the two of you on your impending nuptials?"

"Have a seat, Mr. McCain," Mama said, gesturing to the empty chair beside her. "We have plenty of room."

"I don't want to interrupt."

"Not at all," Jane said. "We were just discussing this." She raised her glass. "Albert was kind enough to get all of us grapefruit juice to try, but it's very bitter."

"I'm afraid I missed out and opted for plain lemonade," McCain said as he and Albert took their seats.

"Not all things that are common are plain," I said.

"Not unlike the daffodil." McCain raised his glass and took a drink, eying me over the rim.

I looked away and saw Albert scrutinizing him, as if McCain had uttered something in a foreign tongue.

"The juice doesn't taste at all like a grape," Jane said, frowning into her glass. "I wonder why it's called 'grapefruit.'"

"Probably because it looks like a grape," Albert said, a sudden authority.

"Actually, grapefruit grow in bunches, like grapes," McCain said, turning to Jane. "Though, yes, the juice is entirely different, isn't it?"

"There, you see?" Albert said crossly. "They look like grapes, Jane, and thus *grapefruit*."

"Actually," McCain said, "the fruit resembles the orange,

though it's bigger in size. I happen to have met a grower some months ago on the train. A man from Texas who'd come from New York City and was on his way home. He was quite happy to have arranged a shipment there for the grocers to try. Seems they're now making their rounds here, though I myself agree with Miss Hartley. It's quite bitter."

Albert, who abhorred being bested by anyone even in the most inconsequential of matters, sighed deeply and pushed back from the table. "Well, I'm refreshed enough. Would you like to take another turn, Jane?"

It was unaccountably rude of him. McCain had barely touched his drink.

"You go on, the two of you," Mama said, making a shooing motion. "Elizabeth and I will wait for Mr. McCain to finish his lemonade."

"I would be honored," McCain said, after taking another sip, "to accompany you and your daughter on your rounds, if I may. I've only just arrived and haven't had the opportunity to walk the floor."

Why was he attending a second time? He knew more about flowers than he'd let on; I couldn't think another visit was worth his time. Perhaps he was on business from the paper or hoping to see members of the mayor's office. Did I dare think he'd asked Madden if I would be here again?

Mama was watching McCain, darting surreptitious glances between the two of us. I knew what she was thinking, and I was relieved when the three of us strolled, some minutes later, into one of the salons.

"You must be quite a flower enthusiast to come again today, Mr. McCain," Mama said with a coy smile.

"I thought my last visit so engrossing, I decided to come again today."

"Did you see Elizabeth's write-up in the Sunday edition?"

I winced. *Oh, Mama.*

"I did," he replied. "Another engaging piece."

In truth, I'd written a short article that was dull as dishwater. I'd been unable to bring myself to mention more than a single line on daffodils. Any more and it would have felt as if I were impeding on a personal conversation we had shared.

McCain turned. "And what will you report today, Miss Cochrane?"

We had arrived at a room off the main salon where a heavy throng walked among the tables. "I'm not certain," I said. "There isn't much new to report, I'm afraid."

"Perhaps I can offer some assistance?" He was all politeness, yet a playful smile twitched at his lips.

I wanted nothing more than to walk with this man I barely knew. His intelligence and wit appealed to me. If only we were alone. If only Mama had gone with Albert and Jane.

He was waiting. Again, I felt something divine, something unspoken between us. Mama cleared her throat and very slightly pressed her forearm against mine, willing me to respond.

"Of course," I said at last.

The room was another bower, alive with color and laden with the heady scent of blooms in pots and artistic bouquets wrapped in garlands strung around pillars.

McCain stopped at a table full of white, pink, and red blooms. "Do you know the carnation, ladies?"

"I am familiar, yes," Mama said. "It's one of my favorites."

"It was also one of my mother's favorites," McCain said. "She grew them for years. I remember vases of them all over the house in my youth."

"How lovely," Mama said. "I have always wanted a green thumb, but alas, I'm not gifted in that regard."

"They are not difficult to cultivate," he replied. "You can grow them from cuttings at the stem here." He fingered a pink variety. "It's easy enough to make a cutting from the suckers that form around the base, or even here on the shoots of the flowering stem."

"Mr. McCain will tell you he knows little of flowers," I teased, "but in reality, he knows a great deal."

"Only what a weekend gardener learns from his labors," McCain said. He turned to Mama. "The carnation is called the 'Flower of God.' Do you know why?"

I wasn't the only one so easily charmed. Mama was captivated. "Tell me."

"The species name is *Dianthus*: *Dios* from the Greek name for God, and *anthos* for 'flower.' It's said, according to legend, that carnations first appeared on earth as Jesus carried the cross. They sprang up where the Virgin Mary's tears fell as she cried over her son's plight."

"I've never heard that before, Mr. McCain," Mama breathed, "and I consider myself a Christian woman."

"It's only a legend, Mama," I said. "There are probably others."

"I wouldn't be surprised," McCain said, his eyes twinkling. "Flowers have a long history associated with them. Their own language. I have always found their history quite fascinating. As fascinating as people, as a matter of fact."

We turned at the sound of a woman laughing. A couple, arm in arm, was coming toward us. The way in which the woman carried herself, a sort of proud saunter and leering eye, gave the impression that she was not a moral woman. The effect was deepened by her dress—it was far too low cut for daytime.

"Oh, I think flowers are a good deal more pleasing to look at than most people," Mama whispered. She stared after them.

"Some," McCain said. He briefly glanced at me and then away. "But not all."

McCain and I took air at a large open window that looked down onto the exhibition grounds. Men, women, and children strolled about on the lawn or sat on benches beneath the trees. Mama had left us, ostensibly to find Albert and Jane.

"I had an ulterior motive for coming here today, Miss Cochrane."

I felt his gaze on me but didn't turn from the window. I couldn't be sure of my face.

"As you know, I have been following your stories for the *Dispatch*. I've had more than one chat with Erasmus Wilson."

"Oh?" I felt suddenly overheated, as if a hot desert breeze had blown through the window.

"He's quite taken you under his wing."

I'd come to adore the columnist. He'd been immensely helpful in honing my writing skills. In turn, I'd helped him understand the mind of the modern woman, as he'd put it. "I call him 'QO' now," I said.

"QO . . . oh, I see. For 'Quiet Observer,' his column."

I nodded. "'Mr. Wilson' has always seemed too formal. He's . . . the father I never had."

"I'm sorry," McCain said. "I didn't realize you'd lost your father."

"Yes, when I was a child." The words tumbled out before I had time to consider them. It was unlike me to share such things with someone I barely knew, and yet with McCain, I felt sometimes that I had always known him. I told him of Papa's first marriage, his passel of children by his first wife, his subsequent remarriage to Mama when his first wife passed. How my parents and siblings had lived happily in a nice home until Papa died suddenly and fate intervened. "Our life was never quite the same after his passing."

"I'm sorry to hear it."

Out on the lawn, two chubby boys chased one another laughing, while their mother looked on. "It's . . . dreadful to lose someone you depend upon so soon. I was angry for a long time. Angry at my father, angry at my half brothers and sisters for demanding their portion of Papa's estate. We had to move, you see."

"It must have been difficult."

I turned from the window to find him studying me. "For my mother the most, I think. To see our circumstances so reduced in so little time. She remarried a few years later. He was a man wholly unsuitable in every way. Our lives were in turmoil for many years, until they divorced." Why was I telling him this? What purpose did it serve that he knew?

"And so you decided to become a journalist? To earn your living by the pen, so to speak?"

"In truth, I think journalism found me. Or, I should say, Madden did." I sighed. "I wonder how long he will keep me on ladies' topics."

Outside the window, the boys were attempting to climb a tree, while their mother spoke to another woman.

"I don't think Madden quite knows what to make of you," McCain said.

I sighed once more. "He's not the only one."

"I know," he said. "I'm well aware of the current views of women in journalism. Working in any profession, for that matter, other than teaching or nursing. I also know that if it wasn't for Erasmus and Bessie Bramble, Madden wouldn't have taken you on."

The words were true but stung nevertheless. Would it never end, this constant struggle to prove myself?

A muscle in McCain's jaw worked. "Miss Cochrane, what I am about to say is the reason I came to see you today. Do I have your discretion?"

I felt as though the air had been sucked out of me. "Yes."

"I know that at least one advertiser has put pressure on Madden to let you go."

I felt the color drain from my face. "What?"

"There may be others. Erasmus carries a lot of weight at the paper. He'd fight on your behalf vehemently, and there is, of course, Bessie Bramble. Madden would be a fool to upset them by firing you outright, but he's resourceful. It's why, I think, he's assigning you ladies' topics. He knows how much you hate them."

I looked away. "And so I'm a problem that must be eliminated."

"If by 'problem,' you mean you're a woman with a great deal of intelligence and mettle, then yes. He's been comfortable enough having you on staff, but advertisers who pay the bills who are threatening to pull their advertisements . . ." He trailed off, his meaning clear.

He would know these things, of course, in his capacity as city editor. All the *Dispatch* editors likely knew. I was silent for some moments, trying my best to quell my anger. "I don't see why my work can't simply speak for itself."

"I've told you, Miss Cochrane," McCain said, his tone gentle. "Madden can't see past your gender."

"You mean he won't."

"Please don't give up," McCain said. His eyes moved over me, flitting to my hair, my face. He took a step toward me and leaned in, his voice soft, barely above a whisper. "Not even when Madden gives you work that's trifling."

The sun shining through the window tinted his hair a burnished golden brown. I was struck again by how handsome he was. A lock of hair had fallen against his brow. I wanted to smooth it back with my fingers. Instead, I looked away and swallowed, forcing myself to speak coherently. "I aspire to do so much more."

"And you will. I'm sure of it." He paused. When he spoke again, his voice was different, less soft, more strained. "I beg you, please don't do anything you shall regret. God knows, I have . . . settled. Done things that were expected of me to please others, rather than what I wanted, things that cannot be undone. I don't want you to fall into that trap."

I searched his face, waiting for him to say more. What things had he done that he couldn't undo? "You have more faith in me than most," I said finally.

"Then trust me when I say you must weather the storm." His gray eyes bored into mine. "I believe that anyone with talent and the will to work hard can succeed—*should* succeed—regardless of gender. It's as simple as that."

"Your views are quite progressive, Mr. McCain."

"I think you exceed me in that vein, Miss Cochrane."

We were standing close, so close I could see the shadow of his lashes against his cheek. We were, I knew, sharing an intimacy greater than the words we had exchanged. And then, quite suddenly, the air shifted. The bubble burst. He was backing away, excusing himself, saying he needed to get back to the *Dispatch*. A few seconds later, he was gone.

The final day of the flower show dawned with an angry black sky. Where sunlight had streamed through windows of the exhibition hall for six straight days, now only somber half-light lingered, like a cautious gray ghost.

For the third time, I wondered what I would write about. I'd written my second installation, discussing no more than the sizable crowds that had attended mid-week. I'd hoped Madden would be satisfied at last and allow me to cover a story of my own choosing.

He'd assigned me the last day of the flower show instead.

Today, it looked as though I'd be discussing nothing more titillating than the foul weather and empty salons. But by some stroke of luck, the rain didn't come. By midafternoon, the clouds began to disperse. With their exit came attendees only too happy the weather had turned. Once again, the aisles grew crowded, voices bounced off the high ceilings, the café bustled. It was in this state of happy commotion that fate turned: a brisk spring wind arrived, thunder cracked, lightning flashed. The salons darkened, and exhibition workers scurried to close windows before the sky opened.

A large crowd was still on its way to the exhibition hall when it did; fifteen or so minutes after the rain began, a sea of citizens poured forth into the entrance exclaiming, wailing, dripping in dismay. Ladies' skirts were sodden, gentlemen's trousers soaked, children's curls limp with moisture.

I was positioned, as had become my habit, against the wall at the far end of the foyer so that I was out of the crowd's way and had a view of the entrance. A mixture of both surprise and joy filled me when I saw George McCain enter. I looked down at my new dress. It was a soft olive green, a shade Mama said matched my eyes. I'd taken more time with my hair. Hastily, I pinched my cheeks to bring color to them.

I was certain he'd seen me straight away and intended to come to me directly, but he was waylaid by a gentleman who recognized him, and the two were now in rapt conversation. I was so intent on looking his way every few minutes that I didn't notice the child beside me at first. She was speaking, but I paid no attention. I kept getting glimpses of McCain talking with his companion, only to have my view blocked as people milled around. I had the impression McCain was trying to get away; more than once, he'd smiled at me, but he couldn't seem to extricate himself.

A cough issued from the child at my elbow, but it was the hand on my arm that finally cast my attention downward. It was not a child but a small woman who stood beside me. She was dressed in a pale blue coat, her matching hat misted with rain.

She extended a dainty hand. "Miss Cochrane, a pleasure to meet you." A voice as high-pitched and childlike as the woman herself, yet she must have been thirty or so, maybe older.

I grasped her hand rather dumbly. "Do I know you, Miss—?"

"You may call me Mary. I feel as if I know you, after all."

I craned my neck. I didn't see McCain.

"This dreadful umbrella," the woman said. A matching umbrella trimmed in pink dripped from one hand. She was attempting to fold it into a collapsed position when she was suddenly racked with coughing. She dropped the umbrella and fumbled for a handkerchief to cover her mouth. I stooped, picked up the umbrella, and worked to close it while the poor woman hacked.

After her fit subsided, Mary said, "Such dreadful weather for a flower show. But I couldn't stay away, not when it was the last day."

One of the spokes of the umbrella wasn't bending. I held the handle with one hand and attempted to bend the spoke at the top with the other.

"I wanted so to come," Mary continued. "I couldn't stay home, you see, not when the sun was shining. How cruel the rain should come now."

The spoke bent at last, and I handed the umbrella back. The tiny woman smiled. Hers was the fragile beauty of a flower. A small, pretty rosebud. The fragility that gave it its delicate beauty was the same fragility that made it vulnerable to the slightest wind. I saw it now, details coalescing: her pale complexion, the crescents of gray beneath her eyes, the lack of vigor to her frame. She was not well. As if in answer, Mary coughed again. The spasm overcame her. I waited for the episode to subside. I felt sorry for her, yet I was vexed. McCain had disappeared.

"Do forgive me. The rain has addled my thoughts. I didn't properly introduce myself. I am Mary McCain."

"Oh," I said, "I didn't realize—"

"He speaks of you with such enthusiasm, you know, such pride for what you're doing at the paper." Mary searched the crowd. A feeble exercise—she must have been a good half foot shorter than I. "Where did he go? He can't go anywhere without seeing someone he knows. Always chatting, always so amiable, George."

This tiny thing was his sister. How interesting. How unlike they were. Mary was a pale beauty with golden hair and light blue eyes—the antithesis of McCain, with his towering, dark good looks. "Do you live in Pittsburgh, Miss McCain, or are you visiting?"

Mary blinked. "Oh, dear me. I've confused you. I'm so sorry. I am George's wife."

The edges of the room receded. Colors blurred. I had the sense that something out of grasp had vanished, never to be attained. There was only this woman, this strange woman and I standing alone. That and the word *wife* floating between us, a gossamer streamer snaking itself around us, around me. I couldn't breathe.

"It's such a thrill to have a young woman like yourself at the *Dispatch*. I can't tell you how delighted I was to learn they'd hired you. Such courage you have, Miss Cochrane. That's what I admire the most. Your courage."

I couldn't feel my hands. I couldn't move. My feet seemed a long way down, as if I'd climbed a tree and left them far below.

Mary said, "George writes of politics mostly, which is all well and good for the men, you know. But the stories you write, those for us women, those are what get my attention. Leave the men their boring topics." A light laugh, like ringing bells. "Give me a good story on, well, your Arbor Day piece was very good, and I did enjoy—"

I watched Mary McCain's mouth move, but I could no longer hear the words. How had I missed this? That McCain was—

"May I call you Elizabeth? Miss Cochrane? Are you all right? You look pale."

That McCain was—

"There you are, George," Mary said, turning. "I have just introduced myself to your Nellie, though I think she might be ill."

Your Nellie. I swallowed and straightened myself, smoothing my olive green dress that matched my eyes. "Not at all, Mrs. McCain. I'm quite well."

McCain was studying me. He looked, as always, slender and handsome and graceful.

I lifted the corners of my mouth. "How delightful to meet your wife."

"Please call me Mary."

"I'm glad the two of you made it when you did," I said. It took great effort to sound normal, to sound sincere. "You might have been swept away by the wind and rain otherwise." Oh, how I wished they had.

"I would not have missed today," McCain said, low. There was no trace of playfulness, of mirth in his eyes now. Instead, he was serious, his mouth drawn, his eyes almost haunted. Why was he looking at me? Why didn't he speak to his wife?

"Nor I," Mary declared. "George has been talking incessantly of the flowers, and we have both been following your coverage."

I couldn't look at him. "Have you? You must look around, Mrs. McCain. There is much to see."

"You will accompany us, of course?" Mary asked.

"I was just going, I'm afraid."

"So soon? But we've just arrived." Mary's dismay quickly turned to eagerness. She put a hand on McCain's sleeve. "Oh, there is Delores Vandergriff. I must go speak to her. Will you excuse me?"

I nodded and watched her go, unwilling, still, to look at McCain.

McCain cleared his throat. "I meant to introduce the two of you. As it happened, I—"

"We made our own introductions." I smiled. "A lovely woman."

"She couldn't wait to meet you," McCain said. I had never seen him so grave, not even when he'd spoken to me of Madden days ago. "She shouldn't be here. She's unwell. The damp isn't good for her."

I made no response. He was a man concerned for the well-being of his wife, an admirable thing. I hated him.

"I must be going," I said. "Do give my regards to your—" My voice broke, and I cleared my throat. "Your wife." I made to get past him.

"Miss Cochrane, I—"

I didn't stop. I didn't turn. I grabbed my wrap from the coatroom and launched myself into the cold, driving rain.

11

*P*oor women . . . they were being driven
to a prison, through no fault of their
own, in all probability for life.

NELLIE BLY

BLACKWELL'S ISLAND, SEPTEMBER 1887

After lunch the following day, I was seated in the corridor with the women I'd met the previous day. Sleep the night before had eluded me. Thoughts of my examination by Dr. O'Rourke had left me tossing and turning most of the night. I had overheard Dr. Field say to Nurse Scott after my examination that I was "positively insane," but after my discussion with Dr. O'Rourke, I was no longer sure my declaration of insanity was secure. His report would indicate I was physically sound, but would he go as far as to voice his concern that I was a pretender? How much sway would his opinion have, if mental instability wasn't his field of expertise? The nurses had made no indication how long any of us would stay at Bellevue nor if, indeed, we were bound for Blackwell's Island at all. How long were the female patients kept here before they were pronounced insane and ferried north of the river? If I failed the test for one so affected, what would become of me? Would they simply put me out? I dared not ask such questions, for I was fearful too much poking might arouse even more suspicion.

Equally disturbing was George McCain's unexpected visit. It

was apparent he had learned from the reporters who had visited yesterday about a woman at Bellevue with no memory. This, combined with the sketch, might well have solidified his hunch that I might be that woman. After all, my ridiculous slip-up in Central Park had all but informed him that something was afoot between the *World* and me. But was he visiting merely to confirm his suspicions, or had he come to talk me out of my ruse? Would he have betrayed me to the staff if I'd refused to abandon Cockerill's assignment? I would not countenance his intrusion. He had no right to impress upon me his own opinions. He had promised me once he would never interfere. Now, with my prospects at the *World* a real possibility, I would never forgive him if he made a mess of things, even if he did so out of concern for me.

The sound of footsteps coming down the hall tore me from my thoughts. Nurse Scott stopped in front of our group of bedraggled women. She eyed the five of us in turn, her expression stern. "We've gathered your things by the door. Pick them up there and follow me. The ferry is here for Blackwell's Island."

Oh, what glorious relief! I was to be shipped off to Blackwell's after all. But my joy quickly evaporated when I saw my companions' faces. How miserable they looked. What was good news to me must have felt like a pronouncement of death to them. For a moment, I felt guilty for contriving to be where they were now being forced to go.

No, they are not my concern. I have a job to do, and I shall do it.

Even so, I expected some show of emotion at Nurse Scott's proclamation, some plea for mercy perhaps, but Mrs. Fox remained as mute and aloof as the day previous, Mrs. Shanz likely hadn't understood, and as for Anne and Tillie, they seemed too weak and dispirited to argue.

At the outer door, I put on my coat, hat, and gloves and picked up my shawl and valise. My companions did the same. Nurse Scott threw open the outer door. Three burly male attendants and an ambulance wagon awaited us on the other side. A cluster of what looked like medical students—young men in white coats with fresh faces—stood in the yard and looked on with curiosity as the brutes seized us by the arms, one of us in each hand, and hauled us toward the wagon. The force was unnecessary; none of us protested. Perhaps the attendants were merely trying to impress the students. That, or women bound for Blackwell's were often hysterical to the point that strong men were required to subdue them.

The day was gray and raw. It had rained overnight. Wet leaves littered the flagstones, the smell of damp earth sharp in the air. How was it the weather had been so glorious just days ago, when I'd walked with Fannie and Viola in Central Park? How the space of a few days had changed things. I was no longer an independent woman working as a newspaper correspondent but a madwoman bound for an asylum.

I was first into the wagon, the attendant pushing me through the door with a mighty shove. I landed in a tangle of skirts on the bench opposite with my valise in my lap. I moved down to allow the others room. Once my companions were all inside, I assumed we would set off and at least have the privacy of a short drive to collect our thoughts. Instead, one of the men climbed in after, clutching a folder. How I would have liked to have a look at the paperwork tucked inside, but I was thwarted from thinking on it further when the door was slammed shut from the outside. The sound of the bolt sliding home was a loud, metallic bang that seemed to go off in my head. With a whistle from the driver, the horses lurched forward. The sickeningly sweet smell of whiskey quickly permeated the air in the wagon. Apparently, the job of a Bellevue attendant did not require sobriety. Nor did it require cleanliness; the beast was in bad need of a bath and a shave. His beige overcoat was stained with dirt that no amount of laundering would ever banish. I tucked my nose into the collar of my coat and sank deeper into the corner.

Through the windows on either side, I could see that we were moving in a wide arc around the grounds, slipping in ruts the rain had pounded to mud. We passed the main compound, and then, quite suddenly, the main gate loomed large. Two men stood on either side, and as soon as we passed through, I heard the great iron doors groan closed. The wharf was a short distance away, on the other side of the broad avenue that fronted the river. After a few turns, we came to an abrupt halt near the water.

The bolt was thrown back and the wagon door swung open, admitting the foul odor of filthy seawater and decaying fish. A policeman glanced inside and gave the attendant a curt nod. I wrapped my shawl around my head, fearful even now that I might be recognized. I waited for the other women to get out. When at last my turn came, I stuck my head out of the wagon and felt the attendant's firm grip on my arm. I threw him a look of loathing and shook him off. Though it was not easy to disengage myself from the wagon with my skirts, I preferred it to his brutal manhandling. My boots sank into mud as soon as they touched down. Light rain and a brisk wind bit at my face as I turned to the water, a churning blue-black mass that stretched for less than a mile to Queens. To the left, somewhere upriver, lay Blackwell's.

A cluster of people stood near the shoreline—more curious onlookers, hungry for a glimpse of ill-fated creatures worse off than themselves. When it was clear that no other inmates were withdrawing from the wagon, the crowd began to press closer, and the uniformed officer moved to block their way.

"Ah, come on, let us have a proper look!" someone shouted.

"There'll be none o' that now," the policemen shot back in a thick Irish accent. "Ye make trouble, and ye'll be going up the river too."

"There's no harm in looking," another called.

"Long as that's all ye do," the policeman replied.

My companions and I walked single file down the bank and onto the dock. At the end, a shabby-looking ferry bobbed in the water, connected to the dock by a weathered plank. One by one, my companions disappeared into the interior. I took one fleeting look behind me and saw the pale faces of the men, women, and children who had come to witness our departure, a motley group dressed poorly, wearing the hard expressions of those who had not lived easy lives. Like the crowd at the police court, not one face held a shred of sympathy.

I was not prepared for the darkness or the stench that awaited me when I entered the cabin. As my eyes grew accustomed to the gloom, I discerned two women on either side of the entrance clad in nurses' caps. My four companions had taken a seat on a low bench. There was no other place to sit. In the wan light coming through the windows, I made out a makeshift bed in the corner. An old woman with wild gray hair and what looked to be a basket filled with bread and scraps of meat stood next to it, staring into space. I stepped farther inside and heard a moan. There, under the filthy blankets of the bed, lay a young girl. She moved her head from side to side and moaned again, and the motion brought the scent of musty linen, body odor, and urine to my nose. I forced my eyes shut to subdue the bile rising in my throat and stepped away.

Just then, the brawny attendant entered the cabin and thrust the folder at one of the nurses.

"They give you any trouble?" the shorter of the two asked.

"Nah, but that 'un there," he pointed at me, "she's got some spirit. Keep an eye, mind." He turned his fearsome gaze on me, his beady eyes full of malice. "You'll get your come-down soon enough where you're going. In the meantime, they ain't above throwing you in the drink to dampen your temper."

The low rumble in his throat must have been laughter, for the nurses joined him.

"Remember that scrawny git bound for the workhouse?" the short nurse said. "All high and mighty, mouthing off about there bein' no way she was goner abide in a place like that?" She slapped her hip in glee. "We threw her in and let her flail, and by the time we fished 'er out, she was 'bout as lively as a dead cat."

Their laughter continued until there was a shout from the captain and the engine sputtered to life. With a nod and one last glower at me, the attendant darted out the door.

I heard the plank come up and shortly thereafter felt the boat sway as we moved off from shore. Mrs. Shanz started to stand to look out a window but froze when one of the nurses, the tallest of the two, pointed a finger at her and said sharply, "You can sit yourself down now, missy. There ain't no standing unless there's no seat for you to sit."

Mrs. Shanz looked at Mrs. Fox, a question in her eyes. Mrs. Fox tugged on her sleeve and patted the bench. Mrs. Shanz sat once again and lowered her gaze.

If not for the caps they wore, I would have mistaken our chaperones for convicts or lunatics themselves. Both were cut from the same mold: coarse looking, sharp featured, and unkempt. They were bundled in shabby coats, below which peeked sodden skirts that wanted mending. Suddenly, the tallest of the two made a low sound in her throat and expectorated tobacco juice. I had never seen the like. The brown glob landed in the middle of the cabin floor among what could only be its cohorts.

Through the window on the far side of the cabin, the East River churned under an angry sky. Across the water, the low buildings and docks of Hunters Point slid into view. When we had advanced another mile or so, a jut of land appeared. A self-contained island all its own. Blackwell's. On its southernmost tip rose a grand-looking multistoried building with a mansard roof. The ferry approached a dock a minute later, and the shorter nurse scurried out to lower the plank. The other hauled the wild-haired woman with the basket from the cabin.

When the first nurse returned, she bent over the girl on the bed. "Get up! Get up now, ye lazy cur." She slapped the girl twice. There was no response. It took all my resolve to remain silent and not reprimand the nurse for behaving so cruelly to a poor, sick girl. Anne and I exchanged glances. I saw in her eyes the same question I had: was this treatment what awaited us at the asylum?

Just then, the other nurse returned, and together, both women pulled the girl from the bed. Her feet were bare and black on the bottom, and she wore only a thin, ragged dress. Oh, the stench that arose when the girl stirred. I covered my nose with my hand and watched the nurses wrap each of the girl's thin, wasted arms around their necks and drag her from the cabin.

I approached a window, using my glove to rub a clear spot in the glass. We were docked on the southwest side of the island. The two women who had left us must be headed for the charity hospital, the mansard-roofed structure that sat resolutely in the rain. In the near distance, I saw the nurses carrying the girl up a walk toward the building. Perhaps she would get the care she needed there. Or was I being a fool? Blackwell's Island wasn't known as a place of rest and healing, of sanctuary and hope. It was where the sick, poor, mad, and criminal were sent, many for the rest of their lives, and I had contrived to come here. I swallowed, my mouth suddenly dry. *Do not put yourself at risk for the* World, *Elizabeth. I beg you.* I shook my head, trying to banish the words, the image of McCain's hand on my arm.

Ten days. A little more than a week. I could do it. I had to.

A few minutes later, the nurses returned, and soon we were moving again, the ferry lurching and bringing forth more fetid odors from the sea. Just beyond the charity hospital, a long brick structure came into view. This castle-like beast, with its crenellations and towers, was the penitentiary. So vast were its wings that it seemed an age before it disappeared from view. For the next several minutes, there was only wild brush and trees with brief glimpses of lower buildings beyond: the men's and women's almshouses, most likely, where the disabled or those otherwise unable to work were housed. Then, suddenly, another large building loomed, longer even than the penitentiary: the workhouse, a place where, it was said, thousands of men were incarcerated for petty crimes, living out shorter sentences than those housed within the penitentiary.

With each new sighting, my dread grew, dread that manifested as an ever-tightening knot in my stomach. My companions exchanged wary glances, and then they, all of them, looked at me. What did they expect me to do? Give them an encouraging smile? I, the woman who had lied her way to Blackwell's? I had not come to make friends. Their situations were no concern of mine. I had come to observe, to fool everyone for the sake of a job. It was as simple as that.

My last glimpse out the window before we docked was of a distant circular tower partially obscured by trees. As we neared the shore, however, it was eclipsed by other trees and scrub along the beach. I felt the ferry slow. We had reached our destination. An open wagon awaited us on the shore, the driver and horse staring disconsolately in our direction. I was the last to step from the ferry. As I did, a cold mist greeted me. I followed the others down the weather-beaten dock, my valise bumping against my leg as I stepped foot onto the muddy beach. One by one, we were handed in by the driver, a man with sharp features and a beak of a nose. Soon enough, we were on a thin, unpaved track surrounded by brush. The rain hadn't ceased and clung to our coats like a cold outer skin. The woolen shawl Nurse Scott had given me was already heavy with water and giving off vapors like a decomposing animal. I cast it off. It landed on the floor of the wagon in a sodden heap.

Mrs. Shanz and Mrs. Fox sat huddled together on one side of the wagon, their heads bent against the rain. Tillie and Anne occupied the bench opposite. The unceasing drizzle was doing nothing for their health. Tillie in particular looked more fragile than she had the day before. The red-and-white kerchief clinging to her skull looked like a bandage from an accident from which she would never recover.

"Now don't you get any plans to up and run on us, else you'll be thrown in the Retreat, and that ain't a place nobody wants to go."

The tobacco chewer. I had the misfortune of sitting between her and the other nurse in the back of the wagon. I couldn't think, even if one of us managed to flee, how we would escape from an island in the middle of the East River. The other institutions would hardly take in runaways, and even if they did, they would scarcely be any more hospitable.

The brush around us began to thin, and I glimpsed a low stone building. With its weeds and sagging roof, I assumed it was abandoned, until the smell of rotting food within touched my nose. Surely this was not where the asylum stored food? I could only imagine how awful the stench would be on a hot summer's day.

The horse took a sudden turn right and began to trot. An enormous edifice came into view. An octagonal stone tower, several stories high and majestic in girth, stood in a clearing in the near distance. It was topped with a dome-shaped mansard roof with dormer windows framed by intricate stone treatments. Two long, three-story wings stretched from the tower to the south and west. These, too, were made of stone, each having at its midway point a set of wide entrance steps leading to an enclosure with columns.

As the wagon neared the steps to the western wing, I glanced up. There, in the windows of the second story, faces peered down at us—faces so ravaged they looked almost skeletal. A few of them had shaved heads. A shiver navigated my spine. How long had they been here? Were these what the faces of the insane looked like?

The wagon pulled to a stop. When we had all alighted, the tobacco-chewing nurse ordered us to climb the steps. They were high and steep, as if designed for legs twice the length of a man's. We struggled to climb in our heavy wet coats, especially Tillie. I grasped her arm and helped her up, fearful the poor thing would lose her footing or, worse, tumble backward. We were inside a sort of side porch, and though it was dank, I was relieved to be out of the rain.

A nurse dressed in a brown-and-white-striped uniform, a white apron, and a cap was waiting at the top of the steps. A ring of keys dangled from her belt by a green cord. It appeared not all of the nurses at Blackwell's dressed as poorly as the nurses on the ferry. She held out her hand to the short nurse, who handed over the folder, now limp from the rain.

"I am Nurse Grupe," she said. "Follow me."

Our party exchanged glances. No one moved. It seemed I was not the only one reluctant to cross the threshold into a madhouse.

"Get on with it," the tobacco chewer snapped.

We entered a vestibule and waited while the door was locked behind us. Then we followed Nurse Grupe down a vast, uncarpeted hallway lacking any sort of ornamentation, nothing but a row of large barred windows along the right-hand wall that looked out onto the grounds. Presently, the hallway led out into a cavernous, multistory chamber with a magnificent circular stair. High above, a domed ceiling with diminutive windows let in what little light there was to be had on such a gray, miserable day. This must be the octagonal tower I'd seen on our approach, the area that connected the two wings. A small sitting space with couches and a few chairs held the only furniture. We continued on through, traversing another long corridor. Up ahead, a nurse approached, followed by another line of women dressed in shapeless beige uniforms. Inmates. As we passed, I noticed with horror that they looked like the women I'd spied at the windows: gaunt, pale, some hairless. All had their hands clasped in front of them, their heads bowed. But as we passed, their eyes flicked up to take our measure.

"Remove your outer garments and put dem here," Nurse Grupe said as we entered a small sitting room filled with women on benches. She indicated a round table. "Reticules too. Jewelry, your bags. You've no use for dem here." A German accent. Well, she would be of help to Mrs. Shanz.

"What about our extra things?" Anne asked. She still clutched her clothing roll, all she had in the world it seemed. "Will you keep them safe?"

"Safe from vat?" Nurse Grupe barked. "You dink dis is some sort of hotel? You dink dese ladies," she indicated the seated women looking on, "will take your dings? You dink dey are dieves?" Anne did not reply. Her hands were shaking. She looked so cold. Around the room, the women sat immobile. They might have been carved from stone.

"Speak up!" Nurse Grupe commanded. Silence. Anne's body began to tremble. When it became clear she wasn't going to answer, the nurse said, "Dat's right, you vill do as you are told. No questions. Now, put everyding on da table like I said. Quickly now."

We obliged, peeling off our coats and hats, giving up our gloves and bags. I set my valise on the table. My notebook tucked inside my reticule would have to go; there was no getting around it. I didn't dare speak out, for I knew the nurse would only make an example of me as she had Anne, and I didn't want to attract any more attention to myself than necessary.

When we were finished, we were instructed to take seats on the benches with the others and await further orders. In the meantime, Nurse Grupe and another nurse scooped up our belongings and carried them from the room. I wondered if we would ever see them again.

I inspected the room, committing it to memory so that I could describe it in detail later. The walls were bare, except for three lithographs: one of the popular actor Fritz Emmet, the other two of dancing Negro minstrels. Odd themes for an institution like this one, I thought. There were no chairs or davenports, and the benches, made to accommodate four, were crowded with six women or more. An old black piano was tucked into a corner. The room's best attributes were large windows that looked out onto the lawn, but as these were covered with the ubiquitous iron bars, they were more a reminder of our confinement than a pleasing feature.

Two nurses sat at the center table talking in low tones. It seemed the staff, if not kind, were fastidious about cleanliness; though the room was bare, it was spotless. The table was covered in clean white linen, and the floor had been recently scrubbed. And yet, there was a listless air of bodies too long idle. Some women sat bored; others stared off as if their minds were occupied elsewhere. All were dressed in the same uniform: a lightweight dress of off-white or beige calico, many of which bore stains. An old

woman with snowy white hair hanging loose hummed to herself
and swayed on her bench like a child.

"*Pssst.*" A young woman sitting on a bench across from me
smiled. "Who sent you here?" she whispered.

Her head was shaved. She, too, looked like she had been
recently ill. But then, most of the women in the room looked wan,
with dark circles under their eyes and haggard expressions on
their faces.

"Doctors," I said.

"What for?"

"They think I'm insane."

She snickered. "They think that about all of us. What's the
real reason?"

"I can't remember anything but my name."

She turned in the direction of the nurses and, after confirming
they weren't watching, leaned over and extended her hand. "Molly."

She was young, eighteen or nineteen perhaps, with a determined zeal in her eyes. Molly inspected me, her eyes roving over
my face, my hair, my hands. It was as if she were searching for
the finest grain of sand. "Well, if you're a lunatic, I can't see it.
What's your name?"

"Nellie."

"Well, Nellie, we can talk as long as the nurses don't hear."

Just then, the snowy-haired woman cackled and muttered, "I
told him not to, but he plucked it right out of the tree!"

"That's enough from you!" a portly nurse shouted from the table.

"That's Mrs. O'Keefe," Molly whispered. "She's as daft as they
come, but you'll get used to her."

There were no books or magazines, no newspapers or playing
cards, nothing to pass the time, except for the piano. "What do
you do here with nothing to occupy you?" I asked.

Nurse Grupe had returned and was motioning for Anne to
follow her. Anne complied, looking as though she was being sent
to her doom.

"Nothing," Molly said, lifting a thin shoulder in a shrug. "Unless
they give us a chore, we aren't allowed to do a thing."

When Anne returned a quarter of an hour later, her eyes were red
rimmed. I motioned for her to take a seat next to me. I wanted to
know how her examination had gone; I needed to learn what mine
might consist of. I didn't need another experience like the one I'd

had with Dr. O'Rourke. As it turned out, there was no time to ask Anne anything.

"Nellie Brown," Nurse Grupe intoned, "you come vid me."

Some moments later, I found myself in a small waiting room down another hallway. Nurse Grupe peeked her head into an office and said, "Nellie Brown for you, Doctor."

There was an inaudible response from within. When the nurse turned back to wave me in, her cheeks were flushed, and she was smiling. I studied her with renewed interest. Something in the pointiness of her chin and the thinness of her lips hinted at a harshness of character that set off warning bells. Her brown hair was drawn back severely from her face, which only added to my impression that she was a woman who lacked compassion.

When she saw me considering her, the smile vanished. "Go," she said, pushing me in. "Dr. Kinier doesn't like to be kept vaiting."

Physically, Dr. Kinier was unremarkable: neither fair nor dark, fat nor thin, handsome nor homely. He was the sort of man who would go unnoticed in a crowd, at a restaurant, at the theater. He did not look up when I entered. He indicated the chair across from his desk with a wave of his hand, and I took a seat.

"State your name, please."

"Nellie Brown."

"And your address?"

"I don't know."

"Surely you know where you live." He looked up. "You are a vagrant then?"

"I don't know."

"What did you say your name was?" He glanced down at his desk. "Nellie Brown." He frowned. "Where have I . . . yes, there was some business in the papers about you this morning." He fumbled through some correspondence on his desk and withdrew a stack of newspapers from the pile. An edition of the *Sun* lay on top.

The headline above the fold was large, the letters thick and sprawling across multiple columns. I read it upside down easily: WHO IS THIS INSANE GIRL?

My heart constricted. One of the reporters had wasted no time in writing up his interview with me. I'd imagined my story buried within the respective papers—if they'd chosen to carry it at all. A curious little anecdote taking up no more than a few column inches. Easily missed. But my story was front-page news in the *Sun*.

My God. What if the other papers . . . A wave of nausea rose in my stomach, and I wondered if I was going to be sick.

Dr. Kinier didn't notice. "Well, Nellie," he said, looking down at the paper with a sigh, "it appears your case has attracted the attention of a good many people. Judge Patrick Duffy of the Essex Market police courtroom, the doctors at Bellevue, and a good many reporters who visited you there. Are you aware of this?"

"I remember speaking with them, if that's what you mean."

"And have you experienced any memory lapses since you woke up at—" he found the line in the paper with his finger, "the Temporary Home for Females on Second Avenue?"

"I don't think so."

"And before the Temporary Home, what do you recall?"

"Nothing. Only my name."

"She is a modest, comely girl," Dr. Kinier read, peering down at the newsprint before him, "with a low, mild voice and cultivated manner—"

Nurse Grupe snorted behind me.

The doctor looked up and smiled. "You've seen this, Mary?"

"I have. It says dat da varden at Bellevue dought she vas nothing more dan a clever little humbug."

O'Rourke.

"Hmm . . . that may be, but one of the other papers said something about—" Dr. Kinier set the *Sun* aside. "Where is it . . ." He unfolded the *Herald* and began turning pages. I felt my muscles relax, if but a little. Perhaps only the *Sun* had featured the story prominently. "Ah, here it is. According to a Dr. Braisted, head of the insane pavilion at Bellevue, 'her delusions, her dull apathetic condition, the muscular twitching of her hands and arms and her loss of memory, all indicate hysteria.'"

I had never spoken to a Dr. Braisted; I was certain of it. He must've spoken with Dr. Field and used that information for his statement to the reporters. In the scheme of things, however, he'd played right into my hands.

"Well," Dr. Kinier looked at Nurse Grupe, "I can't see any reason to do a full examination. What with all the hullaballoo at Bellevue, the doctors were thorough enough. Let's get her weighed and measured."

Nurse Grupe beckoned me to an apparatus in the corner and lowered a bar onto my head to read my height. "I can't see it, Doctor," she said.

Dr. Kinier came from behind the desk and grasped Nurse Grupe's fingers on the measure.

"There, you see," he said softly. "Five feet five inches." He returned to his desk.

With a motion from the nurse, I stepped on the scale. Grupe continued her flirtation. "You shall have to come here and read it for me."

He obliged, and they peered down at the scale together, one on either side of me. "When do you get your next pass, Mary?" the doctor inquired.

"Next Saturday."

"One hundred twelve pounds," he pronounced. They straightened. A smile tugged at his lips. "Are you planning to go into town?"

"Perhaps."

He returned to his desk, recorded my weight, and then glanced again at Nurse Grupe. "What time are you going to supper?"

"I don't know, Doctor," I said. "What time do you recommend?"

The smile slid from the doctor's face, and he reddened. "That will be enough from you." He threw down his pen. "Remove her at once."

Nurse Grupe hauled me from the room by my upper arm and dragged me back down the corridor, hissing profanities into my ear I barely heard.

My mind was spinning. Dr. Kinier's exam had been a farce. I should have felt relieved. Instead, a cold fear was wrapping itself around my chest. My stunt was making headlines. What would Cockerill make of it? Would he see the attention as an advantage, one in which the *World* could swoop in and best them all with the shocking truth, or had the competition stolen the *World*'s story out from under them before I had a chance to reveal it? If so, the story was dead.

There was a third possibility. The *Sun* and the others would keep digging and expose me for the pretender I was. If that came to pass, I was finished. I'd never work in New York again.

12

I was left to begin my career as Nellie Brown, the insane girl.

NELLIE BLY

BLACKWELL'S ASYLUM, SEPTEMBER 1887

When we entered the sitting room, Nurse Grupe thrust me down onto one of the benches. I landed on one of the women, made my apologies, and tried to calm myself. Had I really thought it was going to be this easy, that once I'd arrived at Blackwell's, my worst fears would be over? How stupid I was. Now I had to worry not only about what might happen here but also about what was going on at Newspaper Row. Never would I have imagined that my story would make headlines before I left the island, and by competitive papers besides.

For the next hour, Mrs. Shanz, Tillie, and Mrs. Fox were all called back to be examined by Dr. Kinier. None of them looked optimistic when they returned. I doubted their discussion with the doctor had gone any better than my own. It seemed that having come from Bellevue had condemned me in and of itself, had perhaps condemned us all. I needed to speak with them to see how their time with the doctor had gone. The more I could find out, the better.

I heaved a sigh and looked around the room. I didn't know exactly what I'd expected to find at Blackwell's Asylum, but I was certain it hadn't included sitting idle on crowded benches with women for long spaces of time. Some of the women occupied themselves by whispering with their neighbors, but most said nothing at all. How could they bear the monotony?

I turned to my neighbor, the one on whom I had sat. "Hello," I said, offering my hand. "I'm Nellie."

She took my hand. I expected her to introduce herself, but she did not. Instead, she looked at me uncomprehendingly. She then looked down at my hand, dropped it, and resumed her stare out the windows.

A nurse came into the sitting room and pronounced loudly, "Line up for supper."

I followed the women out to a landing where, to my amazement, we were made to form a line in front of open windows. The day had not improved; clouds the color of steel wool churned in the distance. The cold air blew through the windows, turning my skin to ice.

"How unnecessary to keep us standing in the freezing cold," Tillie said. Her kerchief was still sodden.

"We shall catch our deaths," Anne said, hugging herself.

The women in line seemed accustomed to the windows being open and didn't complain, though they were as affected by the cold as we were; they rubbed their arms and stamped their feet. Some were talking more animatedly now, while others were silent. All the while, nurses walked back and forth barking commands: "Form a line, two by two!" "Keep your hands to yourself. No pushing!"

I was watching an old woman with milky eyes use the wall to feel her way along the hallway when I heard a loud voice say, "How many times must I tell you to keep in line?"

All noise, all movement, stopped.

A tall, raven-haired nurse was staring imperiously down at a young inmate in front of us. The girl murmured something I didn't catch. Without warning, the nurse slapped her across the face. The girl staggered backward and fell into Molly's arms.

"Cross me again and I'll take you to the Retreat," the nurse said. She disappeared down the hallway, the ring of her keys fading as she went.

"Who was that?" Tillie whispered.

"Grady, the head nurse," Molly said. "The devil's handmaiden." She turned to the girl. "Are you all right, Louise?"

The waif nodded and shrank away from us. *The Retreat.* I'd heard it mentioned twice now. Was this why Louise was frightened, or was she frightened of Nurse Grady herself? Whatever its source, the other women shared her fear, for no one spoke. At last, a set of double doors was unlocked, and we entered the dining hall, a whitewashed room of rectangular tables and more benches. Women scurried for a seat. I joined Tillie, Anne, and Mrs. Shanz at a table on the far side of the room.

Each place was set with a small crust of bread, a bowl of gray slop, and a cup of what I presumed was tea.

"*Mein Gott,*" Mrs. Shanz murmured, looking down at her plate. A sudden noise brought my attention to a large woman dumping bowls of the gray substance into her own bowl. She drained a cup of tea and was snatching up another when two nurses ran over. One shoved her onto a bench and removed the things in front of her. The other slapped her hard across the face. I was so transfixed that I didn't notice my bread was missing until it was too late.

"You may have mine if you want," a middle-aged woman sitting catty-corner from me offered. Her brown hair, which was piled on top of her head into a loose bun, was shot with gray.

"That's very kind of you, but you can keep it." Hungry as I was, I had lost my appetite upon looking at the food. The bread didn't look fresh, and whatever substance was in the bowl didn't look good either.

The woman smiled. "Where are my manners? I'm Eugenia Cotter."

"I'm Nellie, and these are my friends Anne, Tillie, and Mrs. Shanz. I don't believe Mrs. Shanz understands much English, I'm afraid. She is German."

"Oh dear," Mrs. Cotter exclaimed. "I shall have to introduce her to Mrs. Roiger. She speaks German."

"Thank you. I'm sure she would like that very much."

"Well, I must tell you if it isn't clear by now," Mrs. Cotter said. "If you don't act fast here, you'll surely starve."

"The bread," Tillie said, her blue eyes enormous. "I've never seen the like."

It was slathered with an odd brown substance. "It's mostly lard, but they call it butter," Mrs. Cotter explained. "Most can't abide it, but sometimes if you ask for bread without it, you can get it." She turned. "Nurse McCarten, may Nellie and Tillie have another piece of bread? Without butter, if you please?"

It was the stout nurse from the sitting room, an unattractive woman with a red, doughy face the color of sausage meat. She lumbered to the table and sneered at me, ignoring Tillie altogether. "Ah, if it ain't the girl from the papers. You may have lost your memory, but you ain't lost your appetite, have you?" She stormed away, with no intention of granting Mrs. Cotter's wish.

I considered the contents of my bowl. Some sort of gruel perhaps. I was about to push it away when I noticed Mrs. Shanz imploring me with her eyes. I slid my bowl to her. "Take it." My tea was the last thing remaining. I took a sip. It was weak and had a coppery tang.

I was regretting the absence of linen to wipe my mouth when I realized how silent the room had become. I followed everyone's attention to the next table, where I saw Louise, the young girl who'd enraged Nurse Grady, looking down at her plate. Her nemesis stood behind her, her hands behind her back, one black eyebrow arched in scorn. Slowly, Louise picked up her spoon, dipped it into the gruel, and brought it to her lips. Nurse Grady leaned down and whispered into the girl's ear. Louise's spoon began to tremble. With great deliberation, she opened her mouth and spooned the gruel into her mouth, closing her eyes and swallowing it down. Every woman in the room seemed to be holding her breath. Nurse Grady straightened and moved off, her beady black eyes sweeping over the tables with a satisfied smirk.

"What did Nurse McCarten mean about the papers?" Mrs. Cotter asked.

I considered how much to tell her. I didn't want to bring attention to myself. "Some reporters came to Bellevue. They found it interesting that I couldn't remember who I was."

"Oh, my dear, I'm so sorry," the older woman replied. "I didn't realize . . . well, you never know what the women here are in for. We've all had our trials. I do hope your memory returns." She chewed on her bread, ruminating. "I don't recall reporters around when I was at Bellevue. How fortunate they were there and saw you."

"I wondered about that too," Tillie piped up. "How did you manage that, Nellie?"

I pushed my tea away. "When I was at the police station—"

"The police station!" Mrs. Cotter dropped her bread. "Good heavens, child. You were arrested?"

"No, I was brought there by the assistant matron of a women's home where I'd spent the night." I briefly explained how I'd awakened the next morning without a clue how I'd gotten there and that the assistant matron had escorted me to the station.

"Ah," Mrs. Cotter said, "and reporters saw you there, I suppose."

"Not exactly. They . . . went to Bellevue on the judge's request to interview me. He asked that they bring someone to draw my likeness for the papers." *And they did more than that. I am front-page news in one of them.*

"Luck seems to follow you." Mrs. Cotter raised her cup in salute
and took a sip. "Someone will surely come forward for you now."

I felt another stab of guilt. These women would, in all probability, stay for years, perhaps their lifetimes. I couldn't think about that
now. In ten days' time, I would be released. Until then, I would play
my part. I was just another unfortunate with an uncertain future.

❧

Nurse Grupe cleared her throat, a challenge in her eyes as they
locked with mine. "I said *naked*."

Never in my life had I been naked in front of strangers; it was
unthinkable I was expected to be now. Forty inmates looked down
at the floor, too frightened to meet the nurse's eyes. All but me
were stripped bare. We stood in four rows of ten before a small tub,
motionless, dispirited, and so chilled to the bone it might have been
deep winter and not September. Crouched on a low stool beside the
tub was an old, shriveled crone with a rag in her hands, a dingy towel
slung on a chair next to her. Low evening light, filtering through the
barred windows, threw diagonal slats across tile that had once been
white but was now gray and bore the scars of perpetual use. Yet in
that miserable gray-white room where there were only the singular
tub, the rows of sinks and toilets, and the ubiquitous tile, I thought
those marks signaled something else. If one were to move one's
fingers across those nicks and cracks and fissures like braille, they
would tell the story of women who had borne witness to more than
just bathing; they'd endured the crushing weight of hopelessness.

A muscle twitched in Nurse Grupe's jaw; her pointy chin
jutted in contempt. "For da last time, remove your clothes, else I
vill strip you myself."

Slowly, and shivering as I did so, I slipped out of my chemise
and stockings and let them fall to the floor. I had already unbound
my hair and so it covered my breasts, but that didn't stop
Grupe. Her eyes traveled down my body and back up again, her
self-satisfied smile an indication of all that was Blackwell's. Fewer
than twenty-four hours inside the asylum, and I'd already learned
an important rule: suffering was something to be brought forth and
stoked continually, fed with the fire of a hundred insults, fueled
with a thousand opportunities to humiliate.

"New arrivals go first," Grupe said, "and as you're a stubborn
little bitch, you're first among dem."

I stepped to the tub. The old crone's lips parted in glee, revealing a row of rotten, tobacco-stained teeth. The two other nurses were poised at the ready on either side of the tub.

"Well, ain't ye a prize piece for one o' the doctors," the crone cackled. Her smile slid from her face, and she jerked her head toward the tub. "Well, in wit ye. We ain't got all day."

The tub was as pitted and gray as the tile. Inside, along the bottom, a sinewy rust stain led to the drain, its hole plugged with the sawed-off end of a broomstick. *It's only a bath.* I stepped into shin-high water so icy it took my breath away.

I brought my arms up to my abdomen in a futile attempt to keep warm, but the nurses were having none of it. They forced my arms to my sides and pressed me into a seated position. Icy water bit at my buttocks, thighs, and shins, my skin already turning pink. Behind me, the old nurse smacked the filthy rag against my back. The smell of the soap—a mixture of lye, ash, and animal fat—was far worse. I resisted the urge to gag as the two other nurses dropped wooden buckets in, filled them, and lifted them over me.

Freezing water rained down my head and face, shocking me into convulsive tremors the nurses rewarded with snickers. Bucket after bucket was upended over me, the water filling my mouth and eyes until there was only the blur of uniforms and the frenzied sloshing of the nurses' efforts. My limbs throbbed. The cold was thickening my blood to sludge.

Suddenly, the dousing stopped. My head was yanked back as the crone began to soap my hair.

"Must you p-pull so?" I said, trying to keep my teeth from chattering. "It won't be any cl-cleaner for it." Already the surface of the water was coated with a thin layer of grease.

Nurse Grupe leaned down to me, a glint in her eyes as she watched me shiver. "Dose who complain have der heads shaved. Vould you like dat?"

"No."

Nurse Grupe straightened, stepped back, and nodded to the crone.

She pulled me backward by my hair and pushed me down into the water so quickly that I barely knew what had happened. I flailed, legs kicking, fingers clawing at the sudden hands at my neck, my lungs burning as I lay submerged. My hair writhed around me like dark seaweed. Muffled laughter as precious air escaped my nose and mouth. Blurry faces white and rippling as they held me down.

They were going to drown me.

And no one would save me. No one.

I thought of all the things I had come to learn and would not. The story of my death would hit the papers and readers would get it wrong, all wrong. Had it come to this? A dingy lavatory among shivering, naked women, just hours after I'd set foot on the island? I had a sudden image of Mama at home in our rented rooms fretting at the window, another of Cockerill sitting at his desk several stories above the city, grimacing as he read the account of my demise in every major newspaper in Manhattan, except for the one for which he worked. In my mind's eye, he shook his head back and forth at what became of upstart women when they attempted to enter a man's vocation, a vocation no woman could perform half as well as a man.

And then, just when I thought I was finished, I was tugged from the water by the roots of my hair. I was half lifted, half dragged from the tub—water streaming, feet sliding—as I flailed for purchase on the tile. A kick sent me sailing across the room. I landed on my stomach, my chin hitting the tile with a resounding crack.

"Dat is vat you get for not obeying orders!" Nurse Grupe roared.

I lifted my head and turned. Hands on hips, she was pacing in front of the women. The keys dangling from her belt rang with every step. Did Dr. Kinier, a man for whom she apparently felt some affection, know of her cruelty?

One of the nurses threw the towel and a thin calico gown in my direction, while the other scooped up my discarded chemise and stockings and threw them in a pile by the door. I rose to my feet. My limbs protested, and my chin was dripping blood, but I dried myself quickly. I was pulling the gown over my head when Grupe came to a halt in front of her next victim.

She cocked a brow and folded her arms, narrowing her eyes as she looked the petite woman up and down. "Isolde Shanz, yes?"

The German woman was looking at Grupe instead of the floor like the others, hoping to catch a word she might recognize.

"Vat are you staring at?" Grupe barked.

Mrs. Shanz replied in German, and Grupe stepped back in exaggerated surprise. "Vat's dis? You speak your gibberish here? To me? Here vee speak *English*. Try again."

There was a stretch of silence. Out of the corner of my eye, I saw Anne and Tillie exchange glances. Mrs. Shanz answered once more in German.

Grupe moved off, walking among us with her hands clasped behind her back, keys ringing. "I am growing tired of you all today. You know vat happens when I get tired, hmm? I get bored. Ven I am bored, I look for vays to amuse myself. Bad dings." She turned and strode to Mrs. Shanz again, tilting her head as she looked down at her prey. And then, once more, she leaned in close. "When I am bored, I do vat I did to your friend Nellie; I tell da nurses to dunk you. But sometimes, because I am so bored, I forget to tell dem to bring you back up."

Molly looked up, a flash of anger in her eyes, but hers was the only reaction in the room.

Grupe must have known then, if she didn't already, that Mrs. Shanz hadn't understood a word. The older woman only looked confused. Her eyes searched Grupe's, and then she looked to all of us, searching for some crumb of meaning, anything to tell her what she had missed.

Your job is to observe, nothing more, Cockerill had said. *Leave no stone unturned. Find out what you can and write up things as you find them.*

I would not intervene. It was what a sane person would do, and I was not sane. I was a lost girl with no memory.

"But . . ."

The word sliced the air like a knife. It was Tillie. Her body was so emaciated, I could see her ribs. It was hard to believe she'd only just arrived today; she looked as withered as the rest of the women.

Grupe walked to her, a smile playing about her thin lips. "You have someding to say, Tillie?"

"I-I don't understand." Tillie blinked. "We met Mrs. Shanz—Isolde—yesterday at Bellevue. That is, Nellie, Anne, and I. Mrs. Shanz can't speak English. She doesn't understand."

"Oh?" Grupe asked sweetly, as if she were learning this for the first time.

"That's right," Tillie replied. "And so . . . and so, it's only fitting . . ."

You fool, I wanted to shout. *Can't you see what she's doing?* Instead, I lowered my head and stared at the floor.

"Only fitting?" Grupe prompted.

"That you help her."

"And vhy should I help her?"

"Why, because you're German, aren't you?"

My eyes flicked up. The smile slid from Grupe's face, and her eyes darkened. She snatched Tillie's arm and hauled her to the tub. Tillie cried out as she struggled. "Please, I was only trying to help! If you were to speak to her in German—"

"Shut up, you filthy bitch!" Grupe bellowed, smacking Tillie across the face.

Tillie staggered back against the tub. As her palm flew to her cheek, Grupe whisked the kerchief from her head. Tillie shrieked and brought her hands to her hair, but the nurses forced them down. Blonde hair stuck out in short, jagged tufts. It looked as if a child had taken scissors to it. Parts of her scalp were visible. Grupe's throaty rasp of a laugh was soon joined by the other nurses', but it was the crone's we heard above all, high-pitched and maniacal.

"You are very cruel!" Tillie exclaimed, her shame turning to indignation. "You should be ashamed of yourselves!"

She was still perched precariously on the lip of the tub. It took only a jab of Grupe's finger for Tillie to fall over the side. She landed with a splash.

"P-please, I've b-been ill," Tillie cried, righting herself in the water as the nurses doused her. "It's t-too cold."

"Is it?" Grupe said. "Perhaps vun of da doctors can varm it for you."

Laughter.

Tillie began to shake. She gasped each time a bucket was dumped over her. Finally, after her body had been scrubbed raw, Grupe said, "Dat will do. You can come out now."

"Thank you, N-nurse," Tillie stammered.

Grupe leaned down and offered her hand, but just as Tillie was taking it, Grupe's hand slammed against Tillie's throat. She was thrust backward into the water just as I had been. The nurses moved quickly, bending to hold her under.

There was a garbled wail below the water. Grupe stepped back. Water was cascading over the sides of the tub and sloshing onto her uniform and boots. "*Scheisse.* Bring her up."

Tillie was hauled out, her body racked with coughs. She, too, was sent flying across the floor. No one stirred. It was clear Grupe expected no one to come to the poor girl's aid, for the nurse looked around the room, challenging anyone to move.

One by one, the others were bathed and pulled from the water. Many of the inmates had violent skin eruptions and open sores. The nurses paid no attention. The fatty soap turned the water to a thick, gray slurry. It was never changed. By the time the last inmate had been bathed, dusk had fallen.

We exited the lavatory single file. Nurse Grupe led the way with a lantern that threw eerie shadows against bare walls, broken only by banks of large, barred windows. The two stout nurses, holding their own lanterns aloft, brought up the rear, barking at us to keep pace and remain quiet. All the while, a slight breeze blew through the passageways that crept over my skin and set my teeth on edge.

We appeared at a set of doors bolted tight, huddled into ourselves and shivering, and waited while Grupe fumbled in the shadows with her key ring. Then, like ghosts crossing the threshold into a different world, we passed through, and the doors were locked once more. The whole of the asylum seemed shuttered, though the hour wasn't late. Perhaps it was a matter of saving the fuel that would've been required to light the rooms come nightfall.

After what seemed an interminable number of doors and turns, we arrived at a door at the end of a wing. After we had passed through, Grupe unlocked another door to the left. Raising her lantern, she said, "First twenty of you here. No running. No pushing." She counted off the women as they crossed the threshold. Mrs. Shanz and Tillie filed in. Nurse Grupe vanished with them after the last of the others had gone through.

That left the remaining half of us for the room on the other side of the corridor. Inside, the lantern illuminated multiple cots and a chamber pot in a corner. The draft coming from the barred windows was perceptible as soon as I walked partway into the room. The inmates scrambled for the cots farthest from these and quickly climbed into bed, throwing the thin blanket atop each over themselves. Anne and I approached the only two remaining beds—those directly under the windows.

"Do you think Tillie and Mrs. Shanz will be okay?" Anne whispered. Her amber eyes were wide with fear. In the shadows, her thin face looked even more pinched. While Anne's bath hadn't been as violent as Tillie's and mine, the nurses had wasted no time humiliating her by calling attention to her skin and bones.

"I don't know," I said irritably. She wanted reassurance, but who was I to give it? What did I know of this place and what horrors awaited us?

"I'm sorry," Anne replied, chastened. "It's just . . . I'm so frightened."

"Worrying won't solve anything," I said firmly.

Anne dropped her eyes. She looked ready to cry, which only made me angrier. She was not my problem. Cockerill had made it clear what my job was, and it didn't include consoling anyone. Anne was rubbing her upper arms to keep warm.

"Is there no heat?" she breathed softly.

"If you want to know, ask a nurse," I spat.

"Heat is turned on in October," a nurse, overhearing us, called from the door, "and I'll remind you that this is a place of charity. You're lucky you've got a roof over your head. Now get in bed." With that, the door slammed shut and was locked. For a moment, Anne and I stood there in the darkness, but there was nothing for it. We padded our way to our cots and busied ourselves with bedding down for the night.

My mattress and pillow were hard and smelled of mildew. The blanket was worse: it was thin and far too small to cover my body without either my shoulders or my legs being exposed. My hair was still wet, and with the air coming freely from the windows, I found it impossible to lie still without shivering. I was still trying to find a comfortable position when the door was unlocked again.

"Nellie Brown?" A nurse cast the lantern high, long shadows moving across the floor as she swung it left and right, revealing the wide-eyed faces of our bedfellows.

"Here."

"Get up. You're to follow me."

My stomach tightened. Anne sat up in bed, but I didn't look at her. I didn't want to see the alarm on her face I knew must be visible on my own. Barefoot and shivering, I followed the nurse to a room next door. After unlocking it, she stepped aside for me to enter. The space was tiny, made for no more than one occupant. A bed, one small, high window, no chamber pot.

"Go on then," the nurse prodded.

I stepped across the threshold. I had been singled out. Why? Was I being punished for refusing to remove my clothes? Had the story in the *Sun* sent off alarm bells?

Suddenly, a boot slammed against my backside. I stumbled forward and landed hard against the bed. With a loud bang, the door shut and the bolt slid home. Darkness once more.

My chin throbbed; it was bleeding again. Patting around, I found a single wool blanket. Like the other, it was too small to cover me and stunk. I climbed in, pulled my knees up to my chest, and lay still.

At first, I heard nothing but the mournful sound of wind in the passageway. As it turned out, however, my first night at Blackwell's was not to be a quiet one. All night long, the nurses haunted the halls with heavy footsteps and clanging keys. Doors banged and locks turned at regular intervals. Three times a nurse unlocked my door, shone a light inside, and locked the door again. It was the same next door and across the hall. What could they be looking for in the dead of night? What did they expect to find except cold, defenseless, frightened women?

Ten days. I could last that long. I would collect details like a magpie gathered shiny things. My notebook was lost to me, but I'd keep notes in my head. I'd remember everything, every unsavory detail. They were the stepping-stones to my future. My magpie's hoard.

I may have made a pact with the devil, but I'd get out. In ten days, Cockerill would see to my release. Then I would leave this godforsaken place without a backward glance. All I had to do was keep pretending I had no memory and observe.

13

*he silent man is always credited
with knowing a great deal more
than the man does who talks.*

NELLIE BLY

PITTSBURGH, MAY TO JULY 1885

"I can't write about fashion anymore, QO," I said. "If I don't find it interesting, why should my readers?"

"You'd be surprised how many women care of nothing but fashion."

QO removed his spectacles and rubbed his eyes. On his desk lay massive piles of papers, notebooks, newspapers, and books. In the five months we'd been working together, his untidiness hadn't lessened in the slightest. It was a habit at odds with his thinking, which was structured and precise. Both were things I'd come to adore about him.

I flopped indecorously into a chair across from his desk. "I'm bored."

Following the flower show, QO had convinced Madden to allow me to continue my series about the young girls who worked in Pittsburgh's factories. I'd set to work and interviewed dozens, most of whom had no other option to earn a living. They were either on their own without a husband or father to support them, or, despite a male head of household, they needed to work to make ends meet. Some already had children. Few had any opportunity for a better job given their lack of education. The unwed had no prospects for a higher station unless they happened to meet a future husband who would rescue them from near-poverty. What chance did a young woman have to meet such a man when she toiled in a factory all day?

Mail had arrived from my readers. *Keep writing. We love your work. How well you understand the plight of us women.* These I placed on Madden's desk. He ignored them. Then, three weeks into my series, he inexplicably pulled the plug and put me on women's fashion: hosiery, lace, jewelry, wraps, collars, kerchiefs. The trappings of a woman's wardrobe many women in Pittsburgh couldn't afford. Madden placed my stories next to recipes, notices for upcoming bazaars, and advertisements for ladies' parasols. Meanwhile, mail continued to come in. But they weren't about my articles on fashion; the letters praised my stories about the poor, the downtrodden, the misfortunate. When would I be writing more? they wanted to know. What would I investigate next? I left these on Madden's desk too. They made no difference. For most of May, I'd been stuck within the ladies' pages. It wasn't that I abhorred the themes entirely; I liked a new dress or pair of slippers as much as any woman. I simply felt my work should be focused elsewhere, where my readers seemed more interested.

"My dear girl, have you proposed something else to Madden?"

"What do you think?"

He chuckled and then fogged his glasses, rubbing the lenses on his trousers. "Of course you have. Tell me."

"I want to write about the Economites." QO replaced his spectacles, blinked, and rolled up a wayward shirtsleeve. I'd never seen him in a jacket. His fingers were perpetually smudged with ink. "The people of Economy, Pennsylvania, QO. The sect who live simply, among themselves."

"I'm familiar, Nellie." He was given to calling me by my pen name now in the vein of protecting my identity at the paper.

"There's something about them I think readers would find interesting. They have almost no contact with the outside world, you know."

"Then how can you be sure they'll talk to you?"

"I've already written one of them, a relative of the founder. She agreed to speak to me."

A smile played on QO's lips. "You've been very tolerant." He folded his arms and leaned back, his chair squeaking in protest. He'd been meaning to oil it for months but had never gotten around to it. "A few months ago, I didn't think you'd have the patience to keep accepting Madden's assignments so quietly. You're growing up."

I'd accepted Madden's assignments because I knew now, thanks to George McCain, that the managing editor was trying to get me to quit. I wasn't going to make it that easy. Just let him try. I could be stubborn when I wanted to be. If Madden wanted to fire me, he'd have to do it outright. As for McCain, I'd been avoiding him since seeing him the last day of the flower show. I came into the office later in the day now, when I knew we'd be less likely to run into each other on the stairs. I didn't linger at the *Dispatch* office any longer than necessary, for fear he might seek me out. But then, why would he? My stories didn't fall under his editorial jurisdiction. Our paths need not cross. But just because I was evading him didn't mean I was going to disregard his warning. I needed to be careful if I wanted to remain at the *Dispatch*—which was why it was more prudent to have QO speak to Madden on my behalf than for me to speak to him personally. I couldn't be sure my anger over the lighter themes he assigned me wouldn't show on my face and eventually come out my mouth.

"Me, grow up?" I said. "Never."

QO smiled. "Very well then. I'll speak to Madden."

I left QO's office and walked down the flight of stairs to the mail slots. From my cubby, I retrieved several letters postmarked locally to "Miss Nellie Bly." One envelope stood out from the rest: it bore no stamp or return address, only "NB." I tore it open. It was a small card depicting a color illustration of a scarlet flower. The caption below it, printed in neat black type, identified it as the red poppy. Handwritten on the back was a date: May 3. How odd. From a reader most likely, but why no explanation? Why flowers?

I had only one connection with such, but I dared not think why George McCain would send it.

A few days later, I returned home to Mama's boardinghouse and was making for the stairs when someone called from the parlor. A young man rose from a chair by the window as I stepped into the room.

"Mr. Gillespie."

"I didn't mean to startle you."

"You didn't startle me at all."

"Your mother told me you were out doing a story. Economy," she said."

"You know Economy?" I asked.

My sister Kate had informed me, after Frederick Gillespie's rather open interest in me, that we were the same age, yet I was always struck by how very young he appeared. His blond hair was parted straight down the middle and slicked down, and this, combined with his eternally pink ears, gave him the impression that he'd just emerged from a bath after a prodigious scrubbing. He was handsome enough, but in a rugged, farm boy–like way, and it was from a farm he'd come. He'd told me once he was the son of a corn farmer, and indeed, Mr. Gillespie looked as if he would be more at home in overalls than in the suits he wore.

"Not at all. I was hoping, Miss Cochrane, that you could sit with me for a bit and tell me more about it." He gestured to the chair next to him with a brawny arm.

If I liked Frederick Gillespie, if I were the least interested in him, I would've been flattered. Now, as he looked at me in earnest, all I could think about was how different he was from George McCain. How wanting. Oh, I had planned on erasing McCain from my memory since learning he was married, planned to pretend he didn't exist, but I'd failed miserably. Especially when I'd received another flower card in my cubby at the *Dispatch* a few days ago. The ox eye daisy. Written on the back was another date: May 16.

"Miss Cochrane?" Gillespie's arm was still extended.

I had a sudden, horrifying thought. What if Gillespie was the sender and not McCain at all? Gillespie had been, in his awkward way, courting me—or trying to—for weeks.

"Miss Cochrane?"

I stared, afraid to mouth the words, and even more afraid of his response. Carefully, I managed to say, "Mr. Gillespie, did you know Economy is known for its wonderful flower gardens?"

"Flower gardens?" His eyebrows drew together in confusion. "No, I didn't know."

"Do you . . . have an affinity for flowers?"

"Pardon?"

I was so overcome with relief that I wanted to collapse to the floor and weep. The cards had to be from McCain. There was no other explanation.

A floorboard creaked at the top of the stairs. At this hour, the boarders hadn't yet returned from their jobs. It could only be Kate, the little minx, or Mama, snooping from above. I wanted to strangle them both.

"How odd to find you here at this hour," I said, in an attempt to buy time. I smoothed my skirts and looked feebly around the room. I didn't care for a tête-à-tête with Frederick Gillespie. I didn't want to lead him on. Besides, I was itching to write up my story on Economy.

"As it happens, I have good news about that," Mr. Gillespie offered, all smiles. "I've been promoted to junior bookkeeper by Mr. Langley. He gave me a raise today, and told me to leave early and celebrate. I could think of no better person to celebrate with than you, Miss Cochrane."

Such words from McCain would've made me blush. From Gillespie, I felt only irritation, both at him and at myself. In my effort to bide time to refuse him, I had only made things worse.

"What excellent news, Mr. Gillespie," I said, "but I'm afraid I can't. My story's due to my editor first thing tomorrow." A white lie that would do no harm. "I must write it up at once. It was kind of you to think of me though." I started to leave the room, then turned. "I'll see that Mama does a special dessert for dinner to celebrate your good news." I left him, hoping he would get the message and realize I wasn't interested, that I would never be interested.

Halfway up the stairs, I heard a giggle.

"Kate?" I hissed when I reached the landing. A door clicked closed down the hall, and I strode down to push it open. There, sitting on her bed, were Kate and little Beatrice.

"Hello, Sister," Kate said, all innocence. "Oh dear, I do believe your auntie is cross," she cooed to her daughter, who was dressed in a concoction of white lace. "Economy must not have been as interesting as Auntie Elizabeth thought."

Fool girl. I could scarcely believe my childish kid sister was married with a baby. Were her husband around more and not always away working for that infernal train car company, they would have a proper home and Kate something to occupy her time besides meddling in my affairs.

"I don't appreciate you eavesdropping," I snapped, pulling the door closed and crossing my arms. "And don't you dare look like that, as if you don't know what I mean."

"Mama says he would make a good husband," Kate said, without looking away from Beatrice. She was holding her at arm's length, watching her little legs kick in the air.

"Tell me you haven't been encouraging Mr. Gillespie," I said. "I've half a mind to tell your husband what you've been up to next time he's here. I hardly think he'd find it as amusing as you do."

"On the contrary, he thinks it's time you married." Kate pulled Beatrice to her. Two pairs of identical blue eyes looked up at me. Only little Beatrice's were void of judgment. "You needn't be so cross. He's a nice young man."

"You sound like Mama."

"And what if I do? You're not getting any younger, you know. There's nothing wrong with a man like Mr. Gillespie. He's only trying to make something of himself, like you." Beatrice began to whimper, her lips downturned into a frown. "There, look at what you've done to poor Bea."

I left the room. In my own bedroom, the one I shared with Mama, I paced the floor. Kate didn't understand. Mr. Gillespie wasn't at all like me. He wasn't the type of man who interested me. He wasn't—I froze and shut my eyes, balling up my fists. Without meaning to, I'd conjured the essence of George McCain again—his dancing gray eyes, his playful turns of phrase. With great effort, I took a seat at my desk, pulled open the drawer, and withdrew my writing paper and pencil. I needed to start my story on the Economites. I must, I would, shut out all thoughts of childish Kate, of Frederick Gillespie with his boyish awkwardness. Of George McCain and his mysterious cards.

I'd traveled eighteen miles to interview Miss Rapp, the last surviving daughter of the founder of a dying society. She'd told me of Economy's heyday, when silk manufacture, cotton production, and wine making were in full swing, when members numbered in the hundreds and the church brimmed to the rafters. Now the factories stood empty, and the streets were almost deserted. The members, upon taking an oath in 1825, had pledged celibacy. They were, quite literally, dying out. There was a story there, one I wanted to tell before their candle went out.

An hour later, I was nearly finished. I ended my story:

> Thus they live day by day, peacefully, quietly, religiously, preparing themselves to meet the God they believe in. They do not flaunt their great wealth in the faces of the deserving and struggling poor; neither do they count their gold like misers. What will become of it all when the last survivor passes away no one outside of a small circle knows.

After my Economy piece was printed in the *Dispatch,* Madden allowed me, for a time, to take on more of my own stories. Whether it was because more readers responded with kind notes saying how much they enjoyed the story or because he was distracted elsewhere, I couldn't say. It hardly mattered. I didn't care why Madden had given me the liberty, only that he'd granted it.

I interviewed Miss Effie Ober, a woman with the unprecedented role of owning and managing an opera company, a woman as independent and noncompliant to social standards as I was—or at least as much as I was able to be. Madden placed my write-up on page seven under the headline I had styled myself:

A PLUCKY WOMAN

It is shameful to state, though the fact remains, that in this enlightened age there are many who think that all labor, except housework, belittles a woman and look with holy horror on one who has courage enough to leave the regular routine laid down for the fairer sex and enter the manlier domain. Plenty of women will eke out a miserable existence at some so-called "light work," while the world is full of good, comfortable places that require only energy and pluck to assume. Some few women can be named who have bravely struck out according to their own pleasure, and have succeeded.

I arranged the cards on my counterpane from left to right, in the order I'd received them. Red poppy, ox eye, flax, cape jasmine. Four so far. All colored, printed illustrations of flowers, none I would have been able to identify (except the ox eye daisy) were it not for the name printed below. They had all been placed in my mail slot at the *Dispatch,* each arriving a different day, though with no regularity. Unlike my reader mail, which was stamped, they had arrived in plain envelopes with only "NB" and the date scrawled in an eloquent hand on the reverse.

No postmark. No return address. Hand delivered.

They could be from no one else but George McCain, but why? What did they mean? I hadn't seen him since the last day of the flower show, that horrid day of rain and realization. I was still spending as little time as possible at the office, doing all my writing at home, never loitering at the office for fear of bumping into him.

Red poppy. Ox eye. Flax. Cape jasmine.

None of the varieties we'd spoken of at the show. None that held any significance to me. Perhaps McCain was simply reminding me of our time together there, or he was merely trying to school me on flowers.

Or perhaps he was playing a game, the rules of which only he knew.

⁂

"I want you to write something about florists," Madden said.

We were seated in his office. I had recently finished a story on the life of a chorus girl, an exposé in which I dispelled the notion of women in that profession as loud, indecently dressed, and low bred. My female readers had responded with enthusiasm. For the past three days, there hadn't been enough space in my mail slot to hold all their letters. The mail clerk had started putting them in bags and leaving them in Madden's office, which, according to QO, had sent him into blasphemous fits. When Madden had ordered the clerk to leave them in QO's office, the clerk had replied, "There ain't a place in there to put 'em, sir." The result was more cursing, which had brought chuckles from the newsroom, the men having heard Madden's outburst one flight down.

"I was under the impression I could continue reporting on meaningful themes," I said as delicately as I could.

Madden looked up from the copy he was editing, his pen poised in the air. A smoking cigar sat waiting for him in an ashtray on his desk. It was beginning to make my nose tickle. It would never occur to him to crack a window for me.

"It's summer, Miss Cochrane. Ladies like a good story on flowers, and florists it's going to be."

I thought of the flower cards at home in my desk tucked inside my Bible. Flowers. Always flowers. Must I never be rid of them? Of him?

The following day, I arrived at a flower shop on Water Street. I waited for two customers to take their leave and then approached a salt-and-pepper-whiskered man in a green apron.

"I'd like to speak to the owner," I said.

"You're looking at him." The man offered his hand. "Will Brady at your service."

"Well, Mr. Brady—"

"Will, call me Will," he said, his crow's feet deepening as he smiled. "Mr. Brady was my father, and he's been dead and gone seven years, God rest him." He pointed to a grainy photograph on the wall behind him of himself and a stooped older man standing outside the flower shop.

"I'm sorry to hear that," I said. "I've lost my father too."

This seemed to endear me to the shop owner, and so after telling him my name, I explained I was a reporter with the *Dispatch* and that I'd come to find out how his business was doing and what, if anything, he could tell me that would interest readers this season.

Mr. Brady snorted. "Well now, I'll tell you a thing or two." He ran his hand down his face. His apron was damp, and a leaf was clinging to his whiskers. He looked tired. Flower clippings littered the counter behind him. I had the sense he hadn't had the time to sit down all day and would enjoy a talk. "It's a sight to see when people come in here to buy flowers. We've got all kinds." He shook his head from side to side.

"Customers or flowers?"

"Both. Let me give you a pointer." Mr. Brady took a seat on a stool behind the counter. "When you come in, all you have to do is tell me what occasion you're buying flowers for and what price you want to pay. You get the most for your money that way and save me time in the bargain."

"That sounds perfectly logical to me."

"There's nothing logical about it, not the way my customers do it. Half the time they make me guess. Do you know why?"

"Because they don't know what they want?"

"Oh-ho! How wrong you are. It's all this hushed-up, private nonsense. They know perfectly well what they're after, but they just don't want to tell *me*." He grimaced and shook his head. "Can you imagine? Do I look like a mind reader to you, Miss Bly? Do I look like an idiot? If they're too embarrassed to tell me what sort of arrangement they want, maybe they shouldn't be shopping for their beau in the first place."

The bell over the door jangled, and a woman came in. While Mr. Brady helped her decide between the asters or the day lilies, my mind raced. *Hushed-up, private nonsense.* I pictured Madden at his desk waiting for my story. He was expecting a write-up on the latest in summer bouquets or perhaps what brides were ordering this season. I smiled. I was beginning to like this story.

When the woman left, Mr. Brady settled himself on his stool once more. "Where was I?"

"You were speaking of customers and their inclination to . . . beat about the bush?"

"That's right. Here's an example. A young man comes in asking for a flower. Just the one. 'A button-hole for yourself?' I inquire. Being answered in the affirmative, I pick a single rose, maybe a white, or a pink. Then we're done, right? I can help the next customer in line. Nope. He suggests I add another and another, and so on, until I have a *bouquet de corsage* of maybe fifteen or twenty roses. Imagine that in a button-hole!"

"He didn't want a button-hole at all."

"Of course not. He just wants to make me think so. Like I won't realize he's built a whole arrangement for his girl he wants to impress. He's too bashful, the dolt, to tell me that outright. Do you have any idea how long it takes to put together that many flowers when each one has to be individually considered? All very well for him, mind you, but I don't have all day. And the customers waiting on the poor sop to figure out what message he wants to convey—you know, whether he's just plain besotted or completely over the moon, for instance—I can tell you, they're not happy."

I had been getting this all down in my notebook, but at hearing this last, I looked up at him.

"The thing is," Brady continued, "a rose just isn't a rose anymore. In comes spring, and this language of flowers nonsense has everyone all strung up and crazy."

The language of flowers.

Brady looked askance. "What, you don't bother with it? Well, you've never been very much in love, have you? The other day a girl comes in with one of those little books the druggists give away. She studies it for three-quarters of an hour, and then I spend two hours getting an assortment for her, and it only cost twenty cents."

The language of flowers.

"The girl sighs, bats her eyes, and asks for catchfly. I walk to the back of the store, get down our *Sentiments of Flowers,* and read the meaning: 'I'm a willing prisoner.' I come back and tell her I'm sorry, I can't accommodate her. Next is Virginia creeper, which means 'I cling to you.' I hunted them all out. Red tulip: 'declaration of love.' I told her I was sorry, they were out of season."

The flower cards. Of course.

"Sunflower: 'adoration,'" the florist continued. "Chickweed: 'let us meet again.' Spindle tree: 'your image is engraved on my heart.'" Will Brady was just getting started. A list of flowers and their meanings spilled forth, like buds bursting into bloom.

⚶⚶⚶⚶

I stared at the cards on my bed. Madden had printed my florist story in its entirety. My write-up, "Thorns Among the Roses," was little more than a dialog between Brady and me. In it I'd deliberately included his "Do you know the language of flowers? What, you don't bother with it?" A test.

This morning, I'd pulled a small package out of my mail slot at the *Dispatch*. It sat upon my lap now, wrapped in plain brown paper. No initials this time. No date.

I opened it. It was a small book. *The Language of Flowers.* There was no inscription on the title page, nothing to indicate the identity of its sender.

The flower entries were listed in alphabetical order. I found each definition easily:

Red poppy	*Consolation*
Ox eye	*Patience*
Flax	*Domestic industry*
Cape jasmine	*I am too happy*

Now that the flowers' meanings were disclosed, I expected some message to reveal itself. I was disappointed. Were they disparate thoughts? Advice? The last seemed the strangest: *I am only too happy.* Why? I stared at the cards, each flower as different as the next. Something tugged at my mind when I checked the entry again for flax. *Domestic industry.* What was it? McCain and I had never spoken of such a thing. It reminded me . . . it reminded me of the story on the Economites. Hadn't I said something to that effect in my piece? I checked the date on the envelope for flax: May 24, the day the Economites story ran. I checked the dates for red poppy and ox eye: May 3 and May 16. May 3 was the first story after my flower show series, when Madden had insisted I cover fashion for several succeeding weeks. *Consolation.* May 16: another banal story on . . . what was it? Ladies' collars. *Patience.*

Cape jasmine was dated May 31, the date of my exposé on Miss

Ober, the bold opera company owner with whom I felt a certain kinship. What was it I'd written? *Some few women can be named who have bravely struck out according to their own pleasure, and have succeeded.* Cape jasmine: *I am only too happy.*

George McCain was commenting on my work, my stories. He was communicating with me in a way I now understood.

Dare I think these missives were an indication that McCain had felt something too in our private discussions? That I hadn't imagined a connection between us? And that the cards, beautiful and anonymous, relayed his thoughts in a way he could never, should never, reveal in a handwritten note?

I gathered up the cards and clutched the stack to my breast until evening shadows slipped into the room.

14

Should the building burn, the jailers or nurses would never think of releasing their crazy patients. In case of fire, not a dozen women would escape.

NELLIE BLY

BLACKWELL'S ASYLUM, SEPTEMBER 1887

I woke to the sound of a key turning. A figure entered the room with a lantern and stepped to the bed. It was a woman: tall, gaunt, and unsmiling. In the flickering shadows, she looked like an apparition from the underworld, a black witch with a sharp jaw, jutting cheekbones, and jet-black eyes.

"Nellie Brown?"

I sat up and pushed the hair from my face. It was still damp.

Nurse Grady brought the lantern nearer and studied me like a vulture assessing carrion. "Just as I supposed. You are not as pretty as the papers are saying." She dropped a pile of clothing on the bed and moved to the door. "Get dressed and go out into the hall."

"Where—"

"Do as I say."

"But it's night. Surely—"

My words died away as she stepped briskly to the bed. "It is six in the morning. If you are not dressed and out in the hall in two minutes' time, you will spend the day without *any* clothes. And I do not mean here, in this room. I mean you will sit with the others, take your meals, and speak with a doctor without a stitch of clothing on you." She quirked a brow and waited. In the passageway outside, a door banged open. A nurse barked an order. Bedsprings creaked. The machine that was the asylum was starting up, the cogs that were the inmates lurching into motion. "And now you have one and a half minutes."

I cast the blanket off and prepared to leave the bed, but the witch snatched my chin in her hand and tilted my face to hers. "One more thing. When I give an order, you are to obey without question. Is that clear?"

Anger, evil, venom, triumph. They were all there in those black eyes, hard as stones. *Ten days. No, nine.* I had endured the night.

"I did not hear your response, Nellie Brown."

"Yes, Nurse Grady."

The door slammed closed. I stepped from the bed onto icy floorboards, thankful the pale glimmer of dawn was now just visible through the window. Using the weak light, I pulled on an underskirt of coarse beige cotton, followed by a stained calico dress that bore an ugly stamp across the bodice: LUNATIC ASYLUM. B. Is. Hall 6. Finally, I pulled on the shoes and stockings with which I'd arrived the day before and opened the door.

The other inmates were emerging from the dormitories, each dressed in the same drab, ill-fitting dress, each hunched into herself to fend off the cold. Their hair, too, was still wet from last night's dousing. I noticed Tillie, her cornflower blue eyes enormous, taking it all in. When a nurse's sharp tone punctured the air, she nearly jumped out of her skin.

"Stand with your back to the wall in a line," the nurse intoned. "No slouching, no touching, no talking."

As we left the dormitory, the sun was just breaking the horizon, slanting light through the now-familiar barred windows. Back through the long corridors we traversed. In the lavatory, we were instructed to form lines to have our hair dressed. When it was my turn to sit, a nurse attacked my head with a fine-toothed comb. My hair was thick and knotted, but there was no show of mercy. When at last she had worked it into a thick plait, she ordered me to a sink to wash. As there were only two towels for drying, I used the hem of my dress to dry my face. The memory of the women's sores and eruptions the previous night, the astonishing lack of hygiene, made me shudder. I wondered how quickly infection would spread in such close quarters with no clean linen.

Next to me, Anne was bent over the sink splashing water on

her face. When her head came up, she too used her hem to dry off. When her eyes met mine, recognition flickered, but she looked quickly away. Perhaps my biting tone the night previous had sent a message that I did not want a friend. I would have to be more civil if I wanted to learn more about the unfortunates of Blackwell's. I resolved to find an opportunity to speak to her.

When the last of the women had finished washing, we were led to the sitting room.

Mrs. Shanz settled on a bench with a woman who must have understood German, for the two were already locked in whispered conversation. This must be the German-speaking woman Mrs. Cotter had mentioned yesterday.

I took a seat next to Anne, throwing her a small smile. Across from us, Tillie was trying to smooth her hair into place, looking very much like she wished to have her kerchief back. Though her hair had dried, it was too short to lie down. As thin and wasted as she was, she looked like a street urchin.

Beside her, Molly looked on and whispered, "It'll grow back. You'll see." She swept a hand over her own scalp. "And you're not the only one without hair. You've got lots of company."

Just then, a nurse entered and pointed to a stout woman by the door. "You there, you'll work in the laundry today." The woman rose and, with bowed head, approached the nurse, who pointed to another woman, this one older and thin as a reed. "Mary, you'll scrub the hall floor." The nurse clapped her hands. "Come on then, let's be quick about it, else I'll give you more to do than that." They left. What a fool I was, thinking it was the nurses who kept things tidy.

I turned to Anne. "I don't think I was very civil to you last night. Please forgive me."

Anne seemed to relax a little, happy, perhaps, to have a friend. "It's nothing. No one is herself here, I think." She looked around the room, her amber eyes taking in the other women. So many of them looked despondent, as if happiness and hope had left them long ago. Anne turned to me again. "You must have been scared out of your wits last night when the nurse came to fetch you. Where did she take you?"

"Just next door. To a . . ." I was going to say private room, but it sounded too exclusive for what it was. "To a small room. There was only one bed."

"Why?" Anne's brow furrowed. "Do you think it has something to do with the reporters?"

"I don't know." I changed the subject, uneasy with questions that focused on me. "Were you able to get any sleep?"

"No. The nurses came and went all night. I don't understand. What do they expect us to be doing other than sleeping?"

A rational question, but rational questions weren't the sort of thing lunatics asked. What was it about Anne Neville that had convinced the doctors at Bellevue she was mad?

"Do you think we'll ever get out of here, Nellie?" Anne asked. "I've spoken to a few of the others and they've been here such a long time."

"I don't know, Anne." How easily I lied. I *did* know I would get out. Yet, I couldn't think others would be so lucky. "Anne, you said that when you spoke to the doctors at Bellevue, you couldn't convince them you were sane."

"No." She was looking down at her work-roughened hands. "The more I told them I was just unwell, the more they insisted I was crazy."

"They must have asked you all the silly questions they asked me," I said, hoping she would divulge more of her time with the doctors. Maybe the doctors at Bellevue had found something that made them believe Anne belonged here. "They wanted to know if I was taking drugs, if I saw hallucinations—"

"It was the very same with me," Anne cut in. "I told them no, of course. They took my pulse and weighed me, but there wasn't much more to the assessments than that. The examination with Dr. Kinier yesterday was even less thorough than the ones at Bellevue."

I considered Anne. She looked no better. She was still pale, with dark circles under her eyes. Her freckles stood out in sharp contrast to her pallid skin. Her damp hair only intensified the effect. It was a wonder, with Anne's illness so apparent, that the doctors at Bellevue hadn't transferred her to the main building and kept her there until she fully recovered. But then, Anne was without family and position. I bit my lip. She wouldn't have been able to pay for her care. Clearly her employers had never had any intention of footing the bill for her recovery. A public asylum, on the other hand, took in the poor and homeless. Was this why Anne and the others, including me, were now at Blackwell's? The realization hit me hard. It was easier to send us over the river than to bear the cost of getting us on our feet again. If that was the case, a pronouncement of insanity at Bellevue was the sentence that would remove us from an already overcrowded hospital and doom us to an existence here—at least for the foreseeable future. Even if we weren't insane. As for Dr. Kinier, he likely didn't feel the need to determine if his most recent arrivals were insane; he already had the assertion from Bellevue. And even if he felt otherwise, his counterparts at Bellevue would hardly like to be challenged in the matter.

It seemed that our circumstances, not a diagnosis of madness, were what had brought Anne and me here. I thought about what I knew about my companions. Mrs. Shanz was unable to communicate her troubles, whatever they might be. It was the same for Mrs. Fox. Anne and Tillie were recovering from illnesses that had necessitated bed rest to such a degree that they had lost their positions. Unless their circumstances were considered a form of madness—and I doubted it—they had all been sent to Blackwell's for the wrong reasons. Which meant others had been too.

"What is it, Nellie?" Anne was looking at me, curiosity in her eyes. "What are you thinking?"

I took her hand. "I was thinking you don't belong here." I was glad to be honest with her. My mission required subterfuge, but I didn't relish lying to a young woman I was beginning to like very much.

Just then, a cry split the air. Mrs. O'Keefe was pulling her feet up onto her bench and peering at the floor. "Do you see them? They're crawling everywhere! Hundreds of them. Oh, I cannot look. Someone help me!"

"There ain't nothing there, you cow," Nurse McCarten said from the nurses' table. "Settle yourself or I'll do it for you."

A stricken look came over Mrs. O'Keefe's face, and she bit her lip, but when she saw that Nurse McCarten was glowering at her, she lowered her feet.

Proof that not all of the women in the sitting room were sane. I wondered, taking in the ones sitting nearest me, how many were not and how I would know if not for an example like Mrs. O'Keefe's?

My gaze fell on Tillie. She was still trying to subdue her hair. "Molly is right," I told her. "You mustn't fret. It will grow back."

"I should never have cut it myself." She dissolved into sobs. From the corner of my eye, I saw Nurse McCarten turn in our direction.

"Hush," I whispered, "and stop pulling at your hair." *It makes you look half-crazed.*

My stomach was growling by the time we were told to proceed to the dining room for breakfast. I had barely touched food since the few bites I'd had at the Temporary Home three days before. After we waited a long time in the hall in front of the open windows, we passed into the dining room. I crawled over a bench and sat down to a meal of five prunes, bread, and cold tea. The bread was the only thing I could stomach. This time it had no butter, and I was able to get most of it down, though it was tasteless and stale.

As weak as I felt from hunger, Tillie looked worse. I met Mrs. Cotter's eyes, and together we watched the young girl pick at her plate without eating a single morsel. I wondered how much longer she could go without proper food. The bones of her arms were thin as sticks.

"I have a good many friends who are worried for me," Tillie said, lifting her chin. She straightened her posture as if aware of our perusal. "I shall get well soon though, I know it. And when I am, they will come for me, and I will leave this abominable place."

"You must eat something then," Mrs. Cotter said with a smile. "It isn't the best fare, but you need it. We all need it."

Tillie looked down at her plate and grimaced.

"Tillie," I began delicately, "do your friends know you're here on the island, at Blackwell's?"

"No."

"Then how will they know to come for you here?" Molly asked. "It's like being cut off from the world, Blackwell's. Once you're here, you're forgotten."

"I shan't be," Tillie responded. "It won't happen to me."

I tried again. "Do you have any family, Tillie?"

"No." She sniffed and averted her face. "You are asking a lot of questions, Nellie Brown, and I won't answer them anymore."

"You don't have to tell me anything you don't want to," I replied. "I was only asking to be polite." Not entirely true.

"I'll tell you why I'm here," Molly answered. "I'm not shy."

I pushed my plate away. I was intrigued to hear her story. Perhaps Molly, too, had been sent here for reasons other than insanity.

"I come from a big family. The youngest of eight. We didn't have much in the way of things. Both my ma and pa drank. They relied on us kids to do all the chores. The washing, the cooking, the cleaning. It wasn't right. Pa would come home drunk and angry, and if things weren't like he wanted them—and they were never like he wanted them—he took to beating us. One by one, my older brothers and sisters left as soon as they was old enough, until it was only me and my folks. Pa stopped working after that. He couldn't hold down a job, and Ma was no better. They expected me to look after them and make a living too."

"How did you do it?" Anne asked.

"I didn't. Decided there was no reason for me to work to buy their liquor, only for them to drink and beat me. I started yelling back. My pa decided that any time I gave him lip, he'd lock me away in the cellar."

"The cellar?" Tillie breathed.

Molly nodded. "It was his way of making me do his bidding. I hated him for it. Ma too. The first time, he wouldn't let me out until I stopped yelling back. Then after that, I got smart. He'd lock me down there in the cellar and I wouldn't say a word, and when he and Ma wanted something to eat, they'd let me out. Soon after, I left too. Pa thought I'd stay. He thought I'd stay because I was the only one left and I was bound by blood—he said that, 'bound by blood'—to look after them because there wasn't anyone else. But I didn't. I ran away. Was all I could do." For a moment, I saw a flash of pain in Molly's eyes, and then the fierce determination returned. "I begged on the streets, maybe a year or so. I had friends too, people like me who really cared and showed me where I could find food, what places would offer handouts and the like."

"It must've been very hard," Mrs. Cotter murmured.

"It was," Molly said, nodding. "It was cold and dirty and there were days I didn't know where my next meal was coming from, but I'll tell you true, it wasn't near as hard as living with my ma and pa."

"And so what happened," I asked. "How did you get here?"

Molly breathed a long sigh. "If you can't find work in a city like this and you're hungry with no place to sleep, sooner or later you start stealing. I stole an apple from a grocer and a copper saw me. Next thing I knew, I was getting sent to Bellevue."

"How old were you?" I asked.

"Sixteen. I've been here three years."

Three years.

"None of the doctors thought I was right in the head for running away from my parents, even when I told them what it was like, what they did and the beatings and all. But I'll tell you, running away was the best thing I ever did, even if I did land in this awful place." She raised her chin and stared at us defiantly, as if willing us to contradict her.

There seemed to be nothing to say after such a story, and so I decided to change the subject. I was about to urge Tillie to take a bite of bread when I noticed Louise, who was seated a ways down our table, staring down at her food. There was a sheen to her cheeks, and her hair was damp and clung to her forehead.

"Heavens," Mrs. Cotter said, following my gaze. She leaned forward and called, "Louise, are you all right? You look feverish."

"I'm . . . not well. My stomach—"

"Are you refusing to eat again, Louise?" a voice said behind us. Nurse Grady.

Mrs. Cotter started to reply, but a warning glance from Molly silenced her. Why was Nurse Grady singling out Louise? Would she notice that Tillie, too, was only picking at her food?

Nurse Grady came around the other side of the table and placed her hands on Louise's shoulders. "I asked you a question, Louise." The girl continued to stare at her plate.

Nurse Grady's hands gripped Louise's shoulders and gave them a firm squeeze. I felt my breath catch. Talk had ceased in the dining hall. My God. We were all frightened of Nurse Grady, and she reveled in it.

"Well?" Grady persisted.

Louise opened her mouth, but not a word came out.

It's not your fault. Tell her you're ill, I thought frantically. I opened my mouth to speak, my heart pounding in anger. How could Grady be so cruel? Then I heard Cockerill's voice, clear as day: *Your task is to observe, nothing more.*

Grady's patience had run its course. She nodded to Nurse Grupe, who flew to her side. The two of them wrenched Louise from the table and dragged her from the room. The last we heard of the frightened girl were her sobs echoing down the hallway.

Discussion resumed again, though more quietly.

"What will become of her?" Tillie asked, eyes wide.

"Most likely the Retreat," Mrs. Cotter said. "Poor thing, to be shut away from everyone." She put her hand over Tillie's and then looked around at all of us. "We must all eat. We must keep up our strength as best we can. We mustn't give the nurses a reason to punish us."

I was just about to ask what the Retreat was when a ripple of whispers ran through the dining hall. I turned in the direction of the entrance. A tall, balding man was saying good day to some of the women and inquiring about their health.

"The head doctor, Superintendent Dent," Molly whispered.

"Why don't they tell him what just happened with Louise?" I asked. I hadn't seen any of the nurses inquiring after the health of the inmates.

"Do you think it would do any good?" Molly whispered. "The nurses don't like us to complain to the doctors, least of all Grady. They threaten to beat us if we do."

I was shocked. But was this really so unbelievable based on what I'd seen—the way we'd been nearly drowned in the bath for sport, the cruel slap Louise had received from Nurse Grady for failing to stand in line for the dining hall? As the superintendent moved about the room inquiring after the women, I noticed not a one of them spoke more than a desultory greeting to him before dropping her eyes.

The superintendent was now speaking to Nurse McCarten on the far side of the room. Suddenly, he looked my way when she pointed in the direction of our table. My heart skipped a beat. I dropped my eyes.

He knows. I have been found out.

I waited for a summons, to be yanked from my chair. A yell. Something. To my surprise, nothing happened. When I looked in the superintendent's direction again, he was gone.

⚘

Dr. Ingram had a head of dark brown hair, a small mustache, and a neatly trimmed beard. I was surprised by how young he was. He couldn't have been more than thirty. The sign outside his door proclaimed he was assistant superintendent of Blackwell's. He wrapped his spectacles around his ears and consulted paperwork. "It says here you are from Cuba, is that correct?"

"Yes." I decided to forgo the Spanish accent for now.

"And you cannot remember how you got here?"

"I got here by way of Bellevue Hospital."

Dr. Ingram looked up and smiled, the first I'd seen from a member of the staff since my arrival. He looked genuinely amused, as if I'd told a joke. "Yes, that's right. I meant that you don't recall anything before that, such as how you came to New York."

"I remember nothing before the Temporary Home, I'm afraid."

He glanced again at his paperwork. "You had some trunks there I understand. You were quite agitated after realizing you'd lost your things."

"I didn't lose them. They were taken from me by those awful women at the Temporary Home." I decided to bring up something new. I had grown weary of the trunk story and felt the doctors would soon tire of it also. Something had been bothering me and, if I worded my questions correctly, might convince the doctor my mind was still disturbed while providing me valuable information. "Dr. Ingram, how many women are at this asylum?"

"Somewhere in the vicinity of sixteen hundred or thereabouts."

"Are you aware that the dormitory doors are locked each night?"

"Of course."

"I cannot help wondering, with the windows barred, what would happen in the case of fire."

Dr. Ingram removed his spectacles. "You are concerned with fire?"

"It terrifies me, Doctor. I-I have always harbored a great fear of fire. How horrible it would be to burn to death, don't you think?" I sniffed and made to look as if I might break into tears.

"You're here to get well, Nellie," Dr. Ingram replied, not unkindly. "You shouldn't worry your mind over such things."

"But I do. If a fire broke out, the nurses would act for their own safety, would they not? Even if they managed to unlock the doors for a few of us, the rest of us would be left to roast alive! Do you not see the danger?" My voice had risen to the point of hysteria. In truth, I really was alarmed at what would happen in an emergency, when quick evacuation was needed.

Dr. Ingram replaced his spectacles and scribbled on the paper before him, no doubt a note on my irrational horror of being burned alive. "Rest assured, the nurses have been instructed to open the doors in the case of fire. You needn't worry."

"But you know positively well they couldn't open them all." I broke down, saying between sobs, "We'd all die a horrible death. The nurses would make it out, but we patients would all be left to burn!" I collapsed into more sobs and pretended to wipe away tears with the hem of my dress.

Dr. Ingram heaved a sigh, removed his spectacles once more, and looked out the window. The grass was a startling emerald green in the autumn sun. Trees waved their russet and yellow leaves in the breeze coming off the East River. "What can I do?" He said it so softly that I almost missed it. "I offer suggestion after suggestion, but it does no good." He seemed to be speaking more to himself than to me. Then, as if remembering himself, he swung his attention back to his desk and replaced his spectacles. "Anyway, you mustn't worry." He scratched again on the paper, adding a final flourish as if to dismiss the conversation.

I sniffed and cleared my throat. "I know what I would do."

Dr. Ingram looked up. "Oh?"

"I would insist on having locks put in as I have seen in some places. By turning a crank at the end of the hall, one can lock or unlock every door. There would be some chance for escape with such a mechanism, you see. As it is now, with every door locked separately, there is none."

Dr. Ingram did not immediately reply. Outside, a bird fluttered past the window, its shadow a fleeting dark shape across the desk. Somewhere down the hallway, a nurse barked an order. "At what institution have you been a patient before coming here, Nellie?" "None." I then added hastily, "That is, that I can recall." "Then I wonder where it was you have seen such locks."

I'd seen them at the Western Penitentiary in Pittsburgh for a story I'd done for the *Dispatch,* but I could hardly tell him so. I continued to dab at my eyes while Dr. Ingram, for his part, stared at me unblinkingly for an interminably long time. Dr. O'Rourke had stared at me in much the same way. Presently, he scratched more notes, then said, putting down his pen at last, "Well, that's that. They'll be no more talk of fire. As I said, you needn't worry. You must relax. You cannot be restored to health by worrying over such things, do you hear?" He gave me a sincere smile and then called for the nurse.

I wanted to press my hysteria case further, but the nurse, sensing my hesitation, grabbed my arm and hauled me up from my chair. As we were leaving, I heard Dr. Ingram mutter, "Interesting." I turned at the door. "There is only one place I know where such locks you describe exist and that is Sing Sing."

He waited for me to reply, and as I could not form a response that would explain how I came to know about such mechanisms without betraying myself, he waved me away. "You may go."

I exited his office, wondering if I'd overplayed my hand. I'd wanted him to believe I was hysterical, but he'd focused more on the logic of my argument. I needed to be more careful.

As I was deposited back into the sitting room, Nurse McCarten was ordering the women out into the hall for coats. My mood brightened; it hadn't occurred to me that we would be allowed outdoors. I followed the others down the hall, past the central tower with the great spiral staircase, and down another hall where row after row of lightweight coats and straw hats hung from pegs. They were all identical and made by the same unimaginative tailor who had crafted the asylum uniforms, which was to say, they were shapeless, bore stains, and looked decades old. Nevertheless, they were better than nothing for fending off the chill.

The nurses instructed us to form a line, and the doors were flung wide. The air, the smell of grass, the sight of blue sky, filled me immediately. Was it only yesterday that the Bellevue ferry had carried me to Blackwell's Island? I felt as if I'd been inside the asylum for ages.

We walked in pairs along a path that led to a spacious graveled area. Groups of women walked in formation, marching the perimeter of the yard. Nurses walked alongside, barking orders, shouting insults, blowing whistles. It was critical, it seemed, that each inmate keep up, stay in line, keep moving. This was the first glimpse I'd had of the other women of the asylum, and they all looked identical. Gradually, however, I began to notice subtle differences beneath the straw hats. Some women wore vacant faces, as if their souls had departed and only their bodies remained to march in time. Others babbled or mumbled, chanted or shouted, cried or laughed.

An old, battered-looking woman with matted hair caught me watching her and leered. Her face was riddled with sores, her mouth devoid of teeth. I looked away. Seeing this, she cackled, a sound that rooted itself in my stomach, which lurched with uneasiness. Another woman stooped to pick up a bit of something in her path. A leaf? A twig? She was not permitted to keep it. A nurse snatched it from her hands and flung it away. What harm was there, I wondered, in cherishing this small comfort?

I took in the green surrounding us. I'd assumed when I'd first seen it yesterday that it was for the pleasure of the women here, but I realized, with a sinking heart, that it was only for viewing. We were forbidden to walk on it, forbidden to enjoy this bit of nature that was a welcome contrast to the foulness within.

A loud ruckus drew my attention to another group approaching the yard. Another line of women was coming toward us, stirring up a great clamor of shouting, screaming, and cursing.

"Who are they?" I whispered to Anne, who walked beside me.

"The women of the Lodge, kept in the building past the south wing," Molly muttered behind us. "The most violent here."

Another group was behind them, louder still. Each was tethered to a rope fastened to her by way of a wide leather belt at her waist. There must have been fifty women shackled this way, interconnected to each other by rope in this bizarre fashion. Like cattle, or oxen. Beasts. The tethered women were pulling a heavy cart carrying two inmates, one with a bandaged head, the other screaming at a nurse who walked beside it.

"You beat me!" the woman cried. "I shan't forget! I know you want to kill me!"

"The women on the rope," Molly said. "The maddest of all."

The tethered women passed. They were filthy, their clothes shabbier than any I had yet seen. The stench of body odor, urine, and feces rose in the air.

The horror, the shock, of what I had witnessed in the space

of minutes, left me speechless. What lives had these poor souls led before they came to Blackwell's Island? What horrors went on inside the Lodge?

"God help them," Anne said, low. "I can't look."

We were nearing the south wing now, and I stopped, stricken.

"What is it?" Anne asked.

A woman behind stumbled into me.

"Keep moving, ye bitch!" cried a nurse, suddenly at my side. I resumed my pace, but Anne had seen it too. It was a sign nailed to the building:

WHILE I LIVE I HOPE

"I suppose it's meant for encouragement," Anne said, after the nurse had moved ahead to shout at someone else.

I didn't think so. It seemed to me a cruel joke. Or perhaps it was an admonition to endure before all was lost.

On our return back to the wing, I glanced up at a second-story window and saw a pale, bald man looking down on the yard. I was overcome with a sudden, fleeting shiver. His arms were crossed, his face impassive. He was only gazing down at the activity below, and yet I felt as if Superintendent Dent was looking directly at me.

As we were being herded out of the dining hall after dinner, Nurse McCarten grabbed my arm. "Not so fast. The superintendent wants you in his office."

While the other women filed past, my mind raced with possibilities. Had she pointed me out to Dent at breakfast like I'd assumed? McCarten's face bore no hint as to what Dent's summons might mean. She wore her customary coarse expression.

She led me past the west wing entrance to the rotunda beneath the central tower, the intersection that connected the western and southern wings. My eyes swept the stunning circular stair that led up to the top floors of the asylum. To God knew what. The stair and the fine furniture were so different from the rest of the asylum that it was hard to believe this was Blackwell's.

Nurse McCarten stopped at a door just off the rotunda and knocked. The door opened, and Superintendent Dent ushered me into his office. To my surprise, I found there were two other occupants in the room. A middle-aged couple was seated across from his desk—not inmates, for they were dressed in the street clothes of the middle class. The woman was crying quietly into a handkerchief, her face downturned and partially obscured by a large crimson hat. The man beside her looked up when I entered, hope lighting his features, and then his face crumpled. It was as if the air had gone out of him. He groaned ever so slightly, and the woman looked up and turned in my direction. It was the same all over again: the searching hope, the immediate pain.

"I'm very sorry, Mr. and Mrs. Newland," Superintendent Dent said.

The woman collapsed into sobs, her shoulders shaking as she buried her face once more in her handkerchief.

Her husband put his arm around her. "Now, now, Millicent," he said softly. "We knew it was a gamble."

"But the drawing in the *Sun*," Mrs. Newland sniffed, dabbing at her eyes. "She looked so much like our Constance, didn't she, Harlan?" She looked at me again, as if to make sure her eyes hadn't deceived her. They were red-rimmed and raw, the deep crimson of her hat intensifying the effect. Without turning from me, she said, "Didn't we think so, Harlan? You said so yourself. 'That could be our Constance,' you said. 'That's the spitting image of our Constance.' But now I see . . . I see . . . she's not Constance at all."

"Your daughter may well turn up," Dent said as Mrs. Newland's sobs subsided. "You must stay positive and see what the police can learn."

The Newlands rose slowly, Mrs. Newland leaning on her husband for support as they took a step toward the door.

"I'm very sorry," I blurted.

No one had expected me to speak. The Newlands looked taken aback. Dent's mouth set in a firm line, the skin white around his lips as he studied me. Apparently, it was not my place to comment. He followed the Newlands out of his office and said curtly, turning back to me, "Wait here."

A few moments later, he returned, closing the door to his office. Taking a seat at his desk, he clasped his fingers together and regarded me closely, his eyes raking over me in an altogether different way than the Newlands'.

"In future when you are brought here in the hope to be recognized, you will refrain from speaking unless prompted. This was only the first family. I presume they will not be the last, Miss . . . Brown, isn't it?" His eyes were of the lightest blue, so translucent they were almost colorless.

"Yes. Nellie Brown."

"Our Cuban visitor."

"Yes, I believe so."

"How's that?"

"Well," my mind raced furiously, "I remember a *hacienda* where I used to live—at least, I think so."

"And yet, you have no accent. Tell me, were you Miss Moreno then, living on the *hacienda*?"

"Pardon?"

"The papers say you've given your name as Brown and Moreno."

"Oh, did I? That's silly. How could one have two names?" I gave him a wide-eyed stare.

His eyes narrowed. "It strikes me, perhaps, that you are married. It would explain two names."

"Oh, I don't think so."

His eyebrows rose. "You sound so sure."

"Well, I suppose I shouldn't be, sure, I mean." Here was someone, I realized, who would not be easily fooled.

The superintendent leaned back in his chair and, with his elbows on the armrests, laced his long fingers together. "Something intrigues me, Miss Brown. I've been wondering why the reporters took such an interest in you. You aren't the first woman to come here with a faulty memory."

"That was Judge Duffy's doing. He sent the reporters to Bellevue to question me and have my likeness drawn up."

"And you told them what exactly, the reporters?"

This was beginning to feel like an inquisition. Dent knew what the papers had printed because he'd admitted to reading them. I leaned forward and said conspiratorially, "I told the reporters those women at the Temporary Home were crazy in the head. Coming and going at all hours, staring at me like *I* was the crazy one. They were like to murder me in my bed, Doctor. I slept not a wink that night, and when I got up the next morning, my trunks were gone. Thieves and murderers all."

"Thieves and murderers," he repeated. "I wonder what a young woman from Cuba would know of such things."

A pause. I had the impression the superintendent didn't believe a word I'd told him.

I decided to change tactics. "Do you think the papers will help me, Superintendent? Do you think someone will come for me, that I shall be rescued?"

"Rescued? What an interesting choice of words." His eyes narrowed once more, the unnatural blue of his irises blazing through the slits. "Do you feel you are in some sort of danger, Miss Brown?"

He was staring at me as if I were a lock he would like to pick. The danger, of course, was that I would be discovered for the pretender I was. At that moment, that discovery felt perilously close. Like Dr. O'Rourke, Superintendent Dent was no fool.

He lifted a corner of his mouth in an attempt to smile, but his eyes were cold steel. "I can assure you this is a very safe place indeed."

And now he was lying. There wasn't an ounce of him that made me feel I was in safe hands. I'd seen enough of Blackwell's Asylum to know nothing could be further from the truth. As Nurse McCarten led me back to Hall Six, the receiving hall for newcomers, I realized the inmates were frightened of more than the nurses. They were frightened of Dent himself.

Hours later, I lay in darkness. I was nearly asleep when I heard it: a woman's tormented scream. And then another. "Please help me, God! I'd rather die than be here!" The sound of running feet. Nurses in pursuit. It was some time before I fell asleep.

15

People in the world can never imagine
the length of days to those in asylums.
They seemed never ending.

NELLIE BLY

BLACKWELL'S ASYLUM, SEPTEMBER 1887

Hunger was a beast I could not satisfy, a great yawning cavern in my stomach that never abated. I woke to it in the mornings, endured it at breakfast when I tried to choke down food that was wholly unappetizing. I felt it in the sitting room, dreaming of the dishes at Mrs. Tuttle's boardinghouse, ordinary fare that now seemed abundant and exotic. By dinnertime, I was light-headed and felt as if I might faint. It was no wonder we were given so little activity; we were not given enough sustenance to endure more. I ate what I could, but it was never enough. Each morning, I tied my underskirt around my shrinking waist and tightened it again throughout the day. I was disintegrating. Melting away. Bedtime was the worst; hunger didn't sleep. It groaned inside me, fueled by my stillness and anxiety, never content.

"You best keep scrubbing."

I started. Next to me, Katie dipped her brush into a pail. When she brought it out again and smacked it on the floor, water splattered our faces. I had seen not a hint of madness in her, only a strong Irish temper for the life fate had dealt her. On our knees in the hall, brushes swishing and heads bent, we could whisper without the nurses interfering. I enjoyed Katie's company and her Irish lilt. It was a way of passing time, and it was better than the benches.

"I've never seen anyone scrub a floor as hard as you," I said.

"I put me anger into it," Katie replied. "The floor don't hold a grudge and smart back like the nurses."

"Why are you here?" I asked, retrieving my own brush from the pail. "You seem a hard worker and are healthy enough."

"Ye mean I ain't mad," Katie said, sitting back on her haunches. She wiped a strand of red hair from her face with the back of her hand. "What's it to ye?"

"I want to know why everyone is here," I told her. "Everyone has a story."

"Well, mine ain't no different from the rest." She started scrubbing again. "My ma and da and sisters died from the influenza, and I went into service. I was a maid for a fine family, the best family I ever knew. The husband, he was a legal man, worked high up in the courts, he did. The missus was a saint or near, ran the house with kindness. Then her daughter, her little Nancy, who was only seven, took ill. The family was in turmoil, and there were doctors in and out." Katie stopped and wiped a tear from her face. "Just a few weeks later, little Nancy gave up the ghost, she did. The missus was fit to be tied. I washed and scrubbed just like I always done, but the missus, she went a bit off. Didn't want the house clean anymore, didn't care about the grates being cleaned or the table laid for supper, nothin'. It was like she died with her bairn."

"She let you go?"

"It wasn't her fault. She didn't know what she was about. Little Nancy's death, bless her, put her in a twist."

"Couldn't you find work somewhere else?"

Katie looked at me askance. "Ye may not know where ye come from Nell, but I'll tell ye true 'twas never service. When a mistress lets ye go without a reference, ye'll not find good work, not the kind that would make ye parents, bless their souls, proud."

"Oh, Katie." I reached out to soothe her, but something in Katie's glance stilled me.

"Don't ye be jumpin' to conclusions now," she said, sniffing. "I was poor, but I had me pride. I slept for a few months in the church-yard where me family's buried. Beggin' for food and the like, livin' best as a poor lass can. Then I got sick meself. Never sick a day in me life, not even when me parents and sisters died, but afore long, I was coughin' and sneezin' and had not the strength to stand.

"The father of the church next door found me lyin' there on me ma's stone like the poor wretched babe I was, and before I knew it, I was off to Bellevue. Holy man he was, the father, but he sent me over the river into this hell sure as them doctors at Bellevue done." "When was this?"

A shrug. "Six, maybe seven months ago. I don't know exactly because I was so sick I don't remember the days passin'. I do know they did the bloodlettin' in the infirmary and it made me weaker every day. 'Twas a miracle I came through. Lord knows it weren't from no treatment or kindness they give me at this place. I needed a good beef broth to fix me proper, but they serve the same fare to the ill as they do the haler ones. 'Tis a crime to be sure."

At breakfast, I'd tried a spoonful of oatmeal and spat it out. It was sour and grainy. I could endure the lack of seasoning, the lack of taste, but I couldn't eat what was spoiled. My companions had eaten no more than I. This morning, Tillie had run from the table retching. When she returned, she was ashen and shaking, frightened Nurse Grady would notice and turn her malevolent eye on her now that Louise had been sent to the Retreat.

"Does Nurse Grady often choose one of the women to pick on?"

Katie made the sign of the cross. "Lord, but that nurse is the vilest witch that ever walked the earth. There's not a day goes by she isn't up to something foul, to be sure. Poor Louise. Grady's as evil as they come, but Louise is young, and she's in me prayers." In an uncharacteristic show of compassion, Katie touched my arm. "I came out of me sickness, and Louise will too."

I turned away, unable to speak. If I was honest with myself, I was worried about Tillie too, and Anne. I didn't want to be. I hadn't come to form attachments; I'd come for a story. I dipped my brush into the grayish water and forced my mind to think of something else. What would Mama say if she could see me now, scrubbing on my hands and knees with a filthy brush, saddened by the declining health of a girl who might just die here? And Albert, what would he think of me in rags, toiling away in an asylum, all for a job he didn't think me suited for? And Fannie and Viola, had they guessed I was the girl the papers were writing about? All were questions I couldn't answer. Even so, images of their faces came to me often, familiar ghosts that brought sadness to my waking dreams.

Katie gave me a sidelong glance. "Ye've had some schoolin', I think. Ye don't sound like ye've been in service. Your speech is too refined."

I couldn't tell her the truth, that I very much remembered the formal education I'd had, what little of it there had been. After

Papa's estate had been settled, the court had entrusted a man named Samuel Jackson to manage my inheritance. Jackson was a distant relative, wealthy, and head of the Apollo Savings Bank. When I'd reached thirteen, I'd enrolled at the Indiana State Normal School in Indiana, Pennsylvania, so that I could one day become a teacher. But after just one term, I'd been forced to drop out and return to Apollo. My guardian had squandered the funds he'd assured me would get me through all three years of school.

"Goodness, Nell," Katie said, breaking my train of thought, "you're mad as a wet hen."

I'd been pressing down hard on the brush and making violent strokes across the floor. *Damn Samuel Jackson.* Katie was right—there was something therapeutic about putting your anger into scrubbing.

"Tell me," Katie said with a mischievous glint in her eyes, "do ye think ye have a beau at home?"

I went still. A face materialized from memory, a pair of keen gray eyes. Laughter. The scent of carnations. It was too much.

Katie's smile faded. "Heavens, ye look as though ye've seen a ghost."

I shook my head. "I . . I don't remember." I changed the subject. "Did you hear the screams last night?"

"Ye think I'm deaf? Raving mad, she is."

"Who?"

"Sounded like Old Bess to me. You've seen her. Poor blind thing. Been here for years. No family neither." Katie stopped scrubbing and glanced at the nurse just outside the door. She said more quietly, "She does that now and again, screams like hell's inferno is nippin' at her toes. They give her laudanum to keep her quiet at night, but when they don't, she's a banshee."

"Laudanum?"

"Oh yes, and more besides. And she ain't the only one."

"What do you mean?"

"They give us medicine that make us see things, some of us. Things that make us vomit and soil ourselves." Katie leaned closer. "Ye've seen the women who beg for water? I've heard 'em beg all night for a drop and get none. 'Tis the drugs that bring the thirst. They give so much morphine and chloral that the patients go crazy. Ye've heard about the Lodge, haven't ye? The Retreat's a holiday compared to the hell that goes on there."

I gaped at her. "What kind of things?"

"I hear the women are chained up, for one. There're beatings too. The women on the rope are put there because they're not fit to be anywhere else." I stared at her in disbelief. "Ye think I'm tellin' tales? Ask any o' the others, they'll tell ye. There's a contraption there, some kind o' chair—"

The sharp report of footsteps brought our attention to the end of the hallway.

"Hush, you hear?" a nurse said, approaching us. "You're to work, not gab. I hear you again, I'll send you straight to the lavatory to clean the reeking toilets."

Time stood still in the sitting room, its pace marked only by the movement of sunlight across the floor or the call to the dining hall. No standing or slouching or moving or stretching. No talking or reading or sewing. It was a torture in itself, the inactivity. A million moments that stretched to infinity. An interruption in the monotony was a relief. I welcomed the reprieves as much as the others, except when suffering or abuse was the cause. And there was always plenty of that.

So it was when, after Katie and I returned to the sitting room after scrubbing the floor, loud voices in the hall broke the silence. Two nurses entered, dragging an old woman with a slack head between them.

"Oh, where are you taking me!" the woman cried, thrashing her head from side to side. "I cannot bear it anymore!"

They pulled her to a bench, where she landed with a thud. Occupants seated there scurried and found seats elsewhere. She righted herself and began to pat the bench. Her skin was clammy, but her nervous restlessness was most alarming. When she lifted her head, her milky, sightless eyes traveled around the room.

Old Bess. Was she under the influence of laudanum now?

"Oh, what are you doing with me?" Old Bess cried. "I'm cold, so cold. Why can't I stay in my bed or have a shawl? Have you no mercy for a poor old woman?"

The nurses watched with interest. Bess stood up and patted air to the center of the room. In a trice, the nurses dragged her back, her heels scraping the floor as she went. Again and again Bess stood and flailed her arms ahead of her until she hit a table or a bench. The nurses only laughed.

"My feet ache!" Bess screamed. "Have pity on an old woman!" She removed her shoes. Her feet were swollen and horribly misshapen. The nurses, one sitting on Old Bess and the other holding Bess's feet, soon had her back in her shoes. The ruckus brought more nurses, including Nurse Grady.

Old Bess collapsed into a heap of sobs, lying down on the bench. Nurse McCarten prodded her to sit up, saying, "You can't sleep here. Now get up!"

"Oh, give me a pillow and pull some covers over me." The blind woman wrapped her arms around herself, huddled and shaking. "I'm so cold. I can't bear it."

Nurse Grady approached. "Why, if it isn't blind Old Bess."

The old woman tensed and shrank back. "I'll be good. I promise I'll be good."

Nurse Grady sat down beside her and ran her fingers over the old woman's face and inside the neck of her dress. When Old Bess shrieked, Nurse Grady only laughed. She was like a cat who had caught a mouse.

Finally, Nurse Grady stood. "Take her to the Lodge. That should straighten her out."

My mind was unraveling. There were no mirrors, but I knew the vapid look of listlessness, of despair, was written on my face as plainly as it was on the others'. Anyone who arrived at Blackwell's Asylum who endured the long days, the inadequate food, the harsh treatment, would eventually succumb. It was only a matter of time.

Now that I knew that going outside was a possibility each day, I was devastated to awaken to foul weather. I wasn't fooled, though. The doctors didn't restrict our time outdoors on cold, wet days to preserve our health; it was the nurses who didn't like to venture outdoors when it was too raw for their comfort, though they wore more layers and heavier coats than the inmates.

We talked of food, Anne, Tillie, Molly, and I. We voiced our cravings and tried to outdo each other. We concocted exquisite delicacies—roast mutton, cured ham with pineapple, bread pudding, apple pie with ice cream—to amuse ourselves. It spiked our hunger, but it passed the time.

Anne's persistent request was for nothing more exotic than a fresh red apple. We laughed. Surely she could think of something more delicious than an apple! Pork chops perhaps. Or stew. But Anne was steadfast.

Like a diminutive Ellis Island, Hall Six bustled with activity when new inmates arrived by ferry. Each day I awaited the hour when it arrived to see if any new unfortunates would join our ranks. Molly considered it her personal mission to offer sympathy and ask questions of the latest arrivals. As long as she was sly about it, the nurses didn't meddle. As I wanted to learn as much as I could from the newcomers, I sat next to Molly often.

On the fourth day, a young woman arrived. After she handed over a small suitcase and her coat, she took a seat. Her eyes darted around the room, and the restless energy of her limbs kept her moving on her bench almost constantly. She reminded me of a deer, ready to run from the room at the slightest sound. Most telling, however, was the large bruise on her cheek, and another on one of her wrists, which, when she saw that I had noticed, she attempted to hide by pulling her shirtwaist sleeve down.

Nurses McCarten and Grupe, seated at the nurses' table, were reading through the woman's paperwork, which a nurse had handed over when she'd arrived. The newcomer didn't appear to notice.

"I'm Molly." She reached over and offered her hand. The young woman shrank back. Molly dropped her arm. "I'm sorry. I don't mean anything by it. I was just trying to be a friend." A quick glance at the nurses' table, then "You'll need one in this place."

The woman paled and met my eyes. "She's right," I said. "You're among friends here."

For a brief instant, she seemed to relax.

Nurse McCarten looked up, her eyes narrowed to slits, as she considered the woman. A devious smile formed on her face. She rose and waddled over, stopping in front of her, hands on her ample hips. "What you run away from your husband for, eh, Urena?"

The woman, Urena, looked away, crossing her arms and hunching into herself. "I . . . he was . . ."

"Your papers say he went lookin' for you and you was with another man."

"My brother," Urena said. Her face blushed red. "It was a misunderstanding."

"Is that right? That ain't what your paperwork says. It says you're a hussy, out with all kinds of men, and your husband got wind of it."

"That's a lie. I never."

"No lie," Nurse McCarten said. She then said louder for all the women in the room, "This girl is a hussy. Her husband sent her here to make sure she wouldn't lay with nobody else." The room was silent. The women knew better than to contradict McCarten. "Urena, how many men have you had in your bed, hmm? How many were you entertainin' like a bitch in heat when your husband went to work?"

Urena looked shocked. "That's not true." She turned away, dismissing the nurse as a lone tear traveled down her face.

"You're a lying slut, girl. We got a place for whores like you."

"You're the liar!" Urena cried. "You mustn't say such things! My husband beat me and I ran away—" Her mouth clamped shut. She'd said more than she'd intended. I saw her hand go to her belly, her palm splayed across her midsection. I considered her clothes. Her shirtwaist and skirt had seen better days. More importantly, there was a small bump at her waist. I could see it plainly now. *No. Not here. Not at Blackwell's.*

"Lying whore. Whose babe you carrin' now, eh? Bet you got no idea," Nurse McCarten spat. "Nurse Grupe, does this girl look like a hussy to you?"

"Of course. I knew it as soon as I looked at her. Vee all did." A wicked smile from the nurses' table.

"I will not have you say such things!" Urena shouted. She leaped from her seat and flew at Nurse McCarten, who caught her and shoved her back onto the bench.

"I won't stay in this place! You know nothing about it!"

"You'll stop that now," Nurse McCarten said, her face reddening. The laughter was gone; she'd gotten the response she'd wanted, and her mood had turned.

But Urena's cries didn't abate. "You're heartless people! Just like my husband. He's the one that was whoring around, not me!"

"I dink he beat you good to teach you a lesson," Grupe said with a devil's smile. "You can't blame a man for taking a hand to his vife when she can't keep her legs closed."

McCarten nodded. "Bet you'd be tryin' to rut with one of the doctors soon enough, if it wasn't for the bastard in your belly."

Urena glared at her in horror. "That's a lie and you know it, you . . . you vile cow."

Nurse McCarten responded by snatching Urena by the wrists. "You idiot woman. You don't talk to me like that!"

Urena tried to wring herself from the nurse's grasp, but McCarten had a death hold on her prey. In the end, Urena spat instead, the glob landing on McCarten's cheek. The nurse froze, a muscle working in her jaw.

I started to stand, but Molly tugged me down.

In one fluid movement, McCarten shoved Urena to the floor.

The young woman landed flat on her back. The nurses bent, Grupe attempting to get hold of Urena's arms, McCarten her legs.

"Stop, Urena," McCarten said, trying to clamp her hands on the other woman's ankles. "You'll only make it worse for yourself, you filthy whore."

Heedless to McCarten's warning, Urena used her body to full effect, bucking to avoid being trapped by McCarten and striking out at Grupe by clawing and scratching at her face. In the next instant, however, Grupe had pinned Urena's arms to her sides.

Urena screamed. Her skirt had ridden up enough to allow her to raise her leg, and she kicked out, landing a blow square in McCarten's gut. For a moment, the large nurse nearly fell backward from her squat position, but she managed to catch herself with her hands.

"You'll pay for that, bitch." McCarten lunged forward again, and, in an effort to prevent Urena from landing more kicks, laid her knees across Urena's thighs.

Urena grunted in pain and went still. She lay prone, unprotected and vulnerable.

Your job is to observe, nothing more.

"You should never have kicked me in the stomach, Urena," McCarten said. "Do you know why?"

Around the room, not a one of us stirred.

"Because here, it's an eye for an eye."

No.

Urena's whole body tensed. McCarten's arm came up. She made a fist and then, with all her might, drove it into Urena's stomach.

No.

There was an appalling thud. Urena convulsed and cried out, and then the life went out of her. She lay still, her eyes closed, tears tracking her cheeks. Grupe released her hold, and McCarten slid from her legs. Urena's shirtwaist was torn at both sleeves. She rolled her face to the side, unwilling, or perhaps unable, to get up.

"There'll be no more screaming and ranting from you," McCarten said. She cleared her throat and spat on Urena, a globule of her own saliva hitting the other's cheek. "An eye for an eye."

With a nod to Grupe, the two pulled Urena to her feet. Her shirtwaist and skirts needed adjusting, and her hair had tumbled from its pins, but Urena was oblivious. She seemed far away, insensible to everything around her. Grupe led her to a bench, and the women there moved to make room. Urena took a seat and then suddenly pitched forward, squirming in agony. Her hand flew to her stomach and she looked down, her brows twitching together. She seemed to come to herself, and then, eyes falling on Grupe, who was an arm's length in front of her, tore herself from the bench, screaming. Grupe reacted quickly, her hands encircling Urena's neck as the latter bore down on her.

"What have you done?" Urena roared. "My baby, my—"

Her speech was cut off as Grupe squeezed, Urena's face reddening, her eyes widening. But she hadn't the strength left to fend off Grupe, and when the latter finally released her grip, Urena fell slack against her, gulping air. But it wasn't the end. As Grupe came behind her and placed her hands beneath her arms and McCarten lifted her legs, Urena screamed anew. She kicked and yelled, again to no avail, as they carried her from the room. Urena's cries grew fainter and fainter as they bore her down the hallway, until we could hear no more.

As sickening as the fight had been, as vile the screams and the sound of McCarten's fist drumming Urena's stomach, there was nothing more terrifying than that silence. Where would they take her now? What would become of her? What would become of her baby?

I locked eyes with Anne, who sat across from me. I knew her revulsion mirrored my own, but I could offer no comfort. All I could do was look away.

The nurses returned a few minutes later, panting, their faces red with exertion. Grupe's face bore the welts and scratches from the scuffle with Urena. As for McCarten, she scanned the room, glaring at each of us in turn, daring us, any of us, to meet her eye. "You see what happens when you go against us, don't you? You get what's coming."

Mrs. O'Keefe, the snowy-haired senseless woman, took this inopportune moment to cackle. She could not have been aware of what she was doing. The nurses knew it, but they couldn't back down, not when it looked like she was deliberately goading them. They were upon her in an instant. Mrs. O'Keefe cried out, shocked. They carried her out into the hall, where her cries, too, soon ceased. What would become of her, Old Bess, Urena, and so many others when there was no one to come to their aid?

I spent the rest of the afternoon still as stone. Inside me, hate and turmoil roiled. I cursed the doctors, the nurses, the asylum itself. I prayed for God to condemn them all. I prayed for the women of Blackwell's to find succor in each other and to remain courageous, to endure, even if only for one more day. How had I ever believed I could remain uninvolved, merely to bear witness as Cockerill had instructed me to do? Suddenly the care and safety of the women were vastly more important than my own selfish interests, even if acting on my concern meant I could be found out.

Alone in the thick darkness of my room that night, I made a resolution: I would stop my show of madness. I had fooled police officers, a judge, numerous doctors and nurses—all links in the chain that had bound me here. Now I had to convince the doctors I was sane. I'd continue to profess my memory loss, but I wouldn't feign insanity. I wanted to learn if release was possible.

I wanted to know if, once admitted to Blackwell's, there was hope of ever getting out.

16

*P*unishment seemed to awaken their
desire to administer more.

BLACKWELL'S ASYLUM, SEPTEMBER 1887

The foul weather was unrelenting, as if it had conspired with the
asylum to cloak us in misery. Wind pressed against the windows
and found its way through the sills, persistent to embrace the
weakest among us. In Tillie, it had found victory; she shook without
cessation. She was terrified to bring attention to herself, but each
convulsive shudder was worse than the last. Her body itched with
the need to move. Each time a nurse came in or glanced her way,
she looked as if she would jump from her skin.

"She's worse," I whispered to Anne, seated next to me in the
sitting room. "We've got to do something."

"Something was done." Anne's own health hadn't improved;
she had lost more weight, and the crescents under her eyes had
darkened.

"How do you mean?"

"Superintendent Dent came to our room last night. Tillie was
sitting on the bed shivering like she does. Like we all do. He spoke
to her, and she started to cry, poor lamb. He got angry. He told
her to stop behaving as if she were any worse off than the rest of
us. Then he took his hands—" Anne's voice caught; a tear welled,

then spilled down her face. "He took his hands and squeezed like this." She placed the palms of her hands against her temples and pressed. "He kept squeezing and squeezing until Tillie cried out. He told her to shut up or she'd get worse."

I can assure you this is a very safe place, he had said. "What happened?"

"Tillie fell back on the bed, half faint. She's had a horrid headache ever since."

I saw them now, faint bruises at Tillie's temples, like dark, stormy clouds. How had I missed them?

I couldn't bear it any longer. The scene with Urena had filled me with a rage I couldn't seem to quell.

I approached McCarten and Grupe, who were huddled in coats at the nurses' table playing cards. "If you'd be good enough to tell me where the extra garments are stored—a blanket or shawl, anything—I'll get them myself. Some of the women are freezing."

Nurse McCarten didn't lift her eyes from the cards. They were filthy. The queen of hearts stared at me from behind an oily sheen. Confiscated from an inmate, no doubt—someone naive enough, as I'd been with my notebook, to believe an innocent diversion would be allowed here. "She's got on no less than the rest of you," McCarten said. "If you can get by, so can she. Sit down."

"Tillie was ill before she came," I said, trying to keep my voice even. "She worsens every day. If you think a shawl is too much trouble, think how much more work there will be when she worsens."

Just then, Tillie moaned and collapsed onto Molly's lap. Molly stroked her hair and tried to soothe her, but when Tillie saw that the nurses' attention was on her, she forced herself to sit up, eyes wide.

"Let her fall on the floor next time," Nurse McCarten called, resuming the game. "That'll teach her a lesson."

"And speaking of lessons," Nurse Grupe said, "sit down or it vill be Urena all over again for you."

My hands balled into fists. My heartbeat was a thud in my ears. *This is what it is to see red.* I wanted to hit Nurse Grupe so hard her head would strike the floor. One satisfying crack, like a watermelon hitting pavement. I took a step closer to the table.

"*Psst.*"

I turned. It was Mrs. Fox. She'd made room for me beside her and was waving me over. I could feel Nurse Grupe's eyes on me, waiting.

The air thickened. Time seemed to stand still. In the end, it was the silent imploring of Tillie's eyes to do nothing that bade me take a seat next to Mrs. Fox.

"I tell you my story, yes?" Mrs. Fox said after the nurses had resumed their card playing.

"You can speak!" I said, shocked. She nodded. Her eyes were deep brown chestnuts. "You're Italian. But your name—"

"—is Volpe, Signora Volpe. But nobody can say or remember, so I tell them Mrs. Fox. *Volpe* is 'fox,' yes?"

"I see."

"So, I tell you my story, and maybe at the end you no angry no more and you no want to kill somebody."

"Forgive me," I said, still stunned. "I thought you were mute."

A shrug. "I want everyone to think so."

"Why?"

"Because I got nothing to say."

"But you're speaking now."

"Because you hit a nurse, you no come back. We never see you again."

Like Old Bess. Like Urena and Mrs. O'Keefe.

"The others here, the women on the rope? They crazy. There is nothing nobody can do for them. But you, you no crazy. You listen, yes? They take you away, then we have less *signore* right in the head." She tapped at her temple with a pudgy pointer finger. "Ah, you no look so angry. You feel better already, yes?"

"I wish it were that simple."

Mrs. Fox followed my eyes to the nurses' table. "The German, *la avvoltoio*? How do you say? Vulture. Bah. She go to hell for what she say. The big one too. You listen to my story."

Mrs. Fox unfolded a tale of loss and grief. She had emigrated from Italy with her husband, Tomás, fifteen years earlier. He was a stone mason who built Catholic churches in the city, a craftsman with an eye for detail who could mold saints from stone. And then, one day, he was gone. Thirty years of marriage ended when he fell from scaffolding during the construction of St. Anthony of Padua. It was a bad fall; his neck broke. The man she loved, who was her life, was dead. Mrs. Fox took to her bed for weeks. There wasn't much in the way of savings—Tomás made little from his immigrant wages, and money soon ran out. Mrs. Fox wasn't educated; she knew no trade and spoke heavily accented English. And she was nearing fifty, not an age when women easily found work. She had no family to pay the rent or help with the bills; theirs was a marriage that had produced no children.

"There was no one in your community to take you in?"

"Oh, I have friends, I have many friends. But no husband. They tell me I can no stay with them. They think their husbands pay too much attention to me. They think I steal one of them for myself. But I no live without my Tomás. I stop eat and they tell me I steal somebody's husband maybe so I can live again."

"They must've been very jealous."

Mrs. Fox made a face. "They have little tiny hearts of stone, like my husband carve."

A devout Roman Catholic, Mrs. Fox turned to her church. She was sent to an almshouse for a few months, where they tried to mend her broken heart.

"I no eat or speak," Mrs. Fox said. "I lose my faith in God. I no want to live. After two months, they no know what to do, and so they send me to Bellevue. The doctors there? No good. They have same hearts of stone."

"I'm sorry."

"Bah." A dismissive wave. "The story of many, many who have lost someone *prezioso*. And you? You have no memory? I trade with you, Signorina. All I have is memory, and it give me much pain." There were tears in her chestnut eyes. "I wish I have a heart of stone. Then I no care. No more sad. No more tears."

I felt it then—the absurd pretense of my memory loss. The guilt, the weight, of my lies. As despicable as the asylum was, I had no grief, no loss like this woman's. What would Mrs. Fox say if I told her it was all a ruse?

⁂

"How fares Miss Nellie Moreno Brown this afternoon?" young Dr. Ingram asked.

"Not so well."

"Oh? Does your fear of fire continue?"

"Naturally," I said. "Nothing has changed."

My second examination by Dr. Ingram was progressing similarly to the first, with the exception that he had weighed and measured me, as if mental stability could be measured in the fluctuation of pounds and inches. I would not feign hysteria this time.

"Stick out your tongue," he said, placing a tongue depressor in my mouth.

"Does the tongue of a lunatic look any different from that of a sane person?" I asked when he had withdrawn the depressor.

"Not particularly, no."

"Then why ask to see mine?"

"To see how obliging you are for one, and to see if you have any sign of sore throat for another. Some of the patients have come down with colds."

"I could have told you I don't have a sore throat."

"Patients do not always have the ability to know what they feel and what they don't."

"You mean insane patients." He shrugged. "I'm not insane."

He stood looking at me for a moment and then returned to his desk and took a seat. "Indeed, your eyes are very clear. You don't appear to have the countenance of one afflicted so."

"I'm glad you think so."

A chuckle. "Tell me, Nellie, do you know what day it is?"

"Friday."

"Correct."

"I have been here five days."

"Also correct."

"Do you think me insane?"

Dr. Ingram did not immediately reply. Whether he was studying me to form his opinion or stalling to think of a proper reply that wouldn't fluster me, I couldn't say. "I think there are circumstances that brought you here that are unusual. Have any memories returned to you?"

He seemed to be genuinely concerned for me, and if I owned to it, I thought him rather handsome. "Not a one."

"Ah, so you still do not recall how you came to be at the Temporary Home."

"No."

"The world is a dangerous place for a woman with lapses in memory."

The world was a dangerous place for any woman, lapses in memory or not, and I rather thought the women here were in far more danger than whatever awaited them outside Blackwell's. "And if my memory doesn't return, is there no persuading you I'm sane?"

"I should like to see someone come forward for you, Nellie, someone to take care of you. The papers are most anxious to see you put into the arms of those who have lost you. I'm certain someone will come forward."

No one would come forward because no one was looking. Nellie Brown did not exist. The *World* would have me released in a matter of days. In the meantime, how could I convince him I wasn't mad? And there were so many others who weren't crazy—did he realize these women were simply victims of circumstance? I wanted to tell him what Superintendent Dent had done to Tillie, how the nurses had treated Old Bess, Urena, and Mrs. O'Keefe, but could I trust him? Did he know these things went on?

I remembered our first meeting, when he'd looked out the window and indicated that he'd made recommendations for improvements to no avail. And there was the way he referred to the women as patients, never as inmates or lunatics.

"What is it, Nellie?"

If I said too much, I might endanger the others and myself. But what was to be gained if I said nothing?

"We are all unbearably cold here," I said finally. "The garments we wear are adequate for summer perhaps, but the days are growing colder. And there's no heat."

"The boilers are not turned on until October," Dr. Ingram said. "A budgetary issue, I'm afraid."

"All the more reason an extra layer of clothing would be greatly appreciated, especially at night. So many of the women suffer. And there are other things you—" A floorboard creaked behind me, and I clamped my mouth shut.

"Yes? Go on."

I shook my head and looked down at my hands. Best to wait, for now.

"Very well. Nurse Grady, you may return Nellie to the sitting room. Please bring in the next patient."

I avoided Nurse Grady's eyes when I rose from my chair. I was almost out the door when I heard Dr. Ingram say, "Oh, and nurse, see that you find some extra clothing for the patients. They're cold and will rest better if they are warmer."

"Of course, Dr. Ingram," Nurse Grady said. "That shan't be a problem."

Sleep had become a fickle thing; it didn't come when I willed it, and when it did come, it didn't stay long. The nurses and their persistent rounds saw to that. Like hunger, it taunted me with an exhaustion that never waned. Each night, alone in my little room, I lay down and curled into myself, a futile attempt to ward off the ubiquitous cold. I closed my eyes and listened to the sounds of the ward settling: the groan of floorboards, doors shutting, a muffled cough. And I listened for the occasional shriek or scream, wondering what or who had provoked it. In the darkness, I thought of Mama, of Fannie, of QO. I wondered if Colonel Cockerill was keeping track of the days I'd been away, if the papers persisted in their stories of the poor lost girl on Blackwell's Island. And inevitably, I thought of George McCain, wondering if he thought of me and then chastising myself for being such a fool.

But that night, I thought of none of those things. That night, I waited.

True to her word, Nurse Grady, with the help of Nurse Grupe, had handed out clothing in the sitting room after supper, congenial as they dispensed extra underskirts and blankets and shawls, behaving as if they were the milk of human kindness. The inmates snatched them up without a word, looking at the nurses askance. Tillie had taken a shawl and clutched it to herself, fearful it would be snatched away in the next instant. Anne and Mrs. Shanz had accepted theirs and mouthed a silent thank you to me as they threw them around their shoulders, grateful I'd spoken up.

My thoughts scattered as footsteps stopped in front of my door. The key turned and the door creaked open. Lantern light spilled into the room.

I was already sitting up in bed.

"Can't sleep?" Nurse Grupe said. "Guess she figured out dey all get vat's coming to dem sooner or later."

Nurse Grady was monstrous in the lantern light. "Hush. Nellie will think us unkind. We've come with something to help you sleep, Nellie." In her hands was a glass of reddish brown liquid.

I felt my heart beating fast. "I won't take it."

"Oh, I think you will."

"I don't need anything to help me sleep."

"Nonsense," Nurse Grady said. "What will your family think when they realize you're here and see you haven't slept a wink in days?"

They lunged. I scrambled, but I wasn't fast enough to leave the bed. Nurse Grupe managed to get hold of my leg, though she was impeded by her grip on the lantern. Nurse Grady had a death hold on my wrists, but in the end, she, too, was hampered by the glass.

"Very well," Grady said, more to her companion than to me. She gave me a scathing glance, and they left.

Terror raced through me as their footsteps retreated.

I heard Mama's voice in my head: *Oh, Pinkey. What have you done?*

Albert: *No fool would commit herself to such a place. Have you lost your mind?*

McCain: *I beg you, do not put yourself at risk for the* World.

Three filled the doorway when they returned. This time the nurses were joined by Superintendent Dent. In the glow of the lantern light, his face was murderous with contempt.

"The nurses tell me you are refusing to take your sleeping draft."

"I don't need it."

"You are a lunatic with no memory in an insane asylum. You have no idea what you need. Hold her down."

I struggled, but in the end, the nurses held my ankles and wrists fast, and I could only stare up at Dent, who was holding a hypodermic needle up to the light. I was a fool. If I had only drunk the medicine, I could have vomited it up the moment the nurses left. Now I had no recourse.

I felt the prick of the needle, and then they were gone. I was alone in the cold darkness. Presently, I felt the bed begin to pitch. Darkness whirled around me, and I screamed.

I float on the wings of a recurring dream, my mind fevered and glancing off memories long repressed. I am fourteen, and it is New Year's Eve. The smell of wood smoke is heavy in the air. Fresh snow on the ground, and more coming down in great, lazy flakes. We are arm and arm, Kate and I, as we follow Mama and Albert downtown, laughing, sidestepping patches of ice on the sidewalk, lifting our skirts to keep our hems clear of mud. Kate slips, but I catch her just in time, and though this is a disaster narrowly averted, we laugh harder.

Behind us, Charles is teaching little Harry how to catch snowflakes on his tongue. "Stick it out as far as you can, like this," Charles says.

"I can't get one!" Harry shouts. For a second, he is a petulant nine-year-old, afraid that he will fail to capture one of the thousands of snowflakes drifting down like feathers around us.

"Silly, they won't come to you. You have to catch them."

Harry runs ahead of us giggling, mouth open and tongue extended, following wayward flakes in haphazard zigzags. His white stockings blaze in the darkness.

The scene dissolves, and I am in a crowded room on the second floor of the Odd Fellows' Hall. Doorways festooned with evergreen boughs and crimson bows. Mistletoe hanging from a gas lamp over the bar. A buffet table emptied of most of its bounty, save for a few crumbs of spice cake. The band is taking a break and dipping punch into white cups decorated with green and red holly branches. I know every face: Pastor Leonard and his wife, Agnes; the Harrisons, our neighbors; John Bair, the grocer recently widowed; Ada and Alvina Lovelace, old sisters who never married. Their faces come to me in floating waves, then disappear, and then Mama is suddenly at my elbow. She is dressed in the finest dress she owns, a deep blue satin gown that matches her eyes. It is eight years old, a throwback to the days of Papa and a finer wardrobe. The dress is fancy, and thus something that has stood the test of time, because it has been worn on spare occasions.

I know she is rallying herself, for she has joined our company to take off the mantle of unhappiness she's been wearing for too long. She has held herself apart from the festivities all evening, seating herself at a table away from the dance floor. When she turns to me, her attempt at a smile saddens me more than if she had frowned.

Hate wells up in me, fierce and consuming. I know what is coming, but I am powerless to stop it. Always, always, the scenes must play out, even if I know the end. Even if I dread it.

There is a burst of laughter from a group of men smoking near the windows that look down onto Main Street. Beyond the panes, snow is still falling. Beside us, the Lovelace sisters talk in animated tones about the weather. Will there be more snow? Will carriages be able to get down Warren Avenue? Albert and Charles are flirting with Carolyn Brammer and her sister near the Christmas tree. I don't know where Harry and Kate are. It shouldn't be important, but this is more memory than dream; I know in my gut it is very important.

The band strikes up again, a jaunty tune with a banjo and fiddle. Better suited for a summer picnic than the holidays. The dance floor fills once more. The music is infectious. I want to dance, but no one has asked me. A few girls from school are dancing together. Perhaps it isn't too inappropriate to dance with one's schoolmates instead of a boy. I turn to Mama, ready to reach for her hand and pull her onto the floor, but when I see her face, I know he is here.

I follow her gaze to the door. Jack Ford is at the threshold, leering about the room. He wears a heavy overcoat, and his cap is pulled low. He makes no move to remove them; he doesn't plan to stay long. No one has noticed him yet, except Mama and me. For a moment, nothing changes. The band plays on, the dancers twirl, the partygoers chatter on above the strains of the music.

Jack spots Mama at last, his eyes dark slits of rage. A small sound escapes Mama. Her face is lily white. One hand has come up to clutch her throat. She is shaking.

My stepfather advances into the room, his mouth curled in a sneer. His eyes are red from drink, but his gait is steady. He has eyes only for Mama. He bumps into a couple dancing and creates a ripple among the dancers. They stop moving, and for a second the band plays on. But when someone from the crowd—one of the Lovelace sisters? Carolyn Murphy?—gasps, the music ceases.

And it is then I see that he has taken a pistol from his overcoat and is pointing it at Mama.

"You filthy whore!" Jack thunders. "Didn't I tell you not to come here?"

The scene shifts to our kitchen, where we are all seated at supper.

"You aren't going to the party, none of you," Jack says, gnawing at a turkey leg. My siblings and I sit like wooden dolls at the table, unable to take our eyes from the spectacle that is Jack. He reeks of sweat and is drunk again, having come home only minutes before and sitting himself down to eat. Jack is rarely home evenings these days, so Mama hadn't expected him and hadn't laid a place.

"We haven't been for three years," Mama says quietly. She moves her food around on her plate with her fork. "The church has rented the Odd Fellows' Hall. It's a perfectly respectable gathering, and it will be good for the children."

Jack stops chewing and pulls a piece of gristle from his mouth. He is like an animal when he comes home drunk: ravenous and predatory. "I said you aren't going, and that's final."

"Nonsense," Mama says. "We shall be home by—"

With a quick flick of his wrist, Jack flings the turkey leg at Mama. It strikes her in the face. She flinches and throws it back. Jack's fists pound the table so hard the dishes rattle.

"You will listen to me, woman, or I'll slit your goddamn throat!"

Hate rises inside me, pawing to get out. Oh, how I loathe him.

"What's it to you?" Albert blurts. He is nineteen—no longer a boy but not quite a man. A muscle twitches in his jaw. He is poised to spring. He hates Jack as much as I do; it is the one thing that unites us, the loathing of a man whose only love is drink.

Harry grabs my hand under the table as Jack rises. "What did you say?"

Mama is up so quickly that her chair overturns. "Never mind, Jack." To Albert, she says, "Hold your tongue. This is between Jack and me."

"You're a bunch of ungrateful curs," Jack sneers. "Every fucking one of you."

"And you're a drunk." All eyes turn to me. It is not the first time

I have spoken out, but it's the first time it hasn't been to Jack's retreating back. The blood drains from Mama's face.

Jack comes around the table for me, but Mama and Albert move quickly, placing themselves between us. Harry scrambles from his chair and hides behind Kate. Albert balls up his fists, ready to hit Jack square in the jaw. Jack's face is red. A sheen of sweat glistens from his upper lip, and his eyes are wild.

"Children, leave the kitchen. Now," Mama says, low. No one moves.

"I've had my fill of all of you!" Jack screams. Spittle flies from his mouth, and with one fluid sweep of his arm, he whisks the dishes from the table. Glassware and china crash to the floor. Behind Kate, Harry is whimpering.

"You're an ungrateful bitch of a wife, Mary Jane," Jack sneers. "And as for the rest of you, I'd sooner cut off my own leg than spend another night in this filthy hovel with you. I'm leaving. I can't stand the sight of you anymore. Rot in hell."

The kitchen scene melts into the Odd Fellows' Hall once more. Jack is so close I can smell the whiskey on him. I step in front of him, blocking Mama from his view.

"Move," Jack says, waving the gun.

"No. You're not going to lay a hand on her again. Ever."

Jack's eyes darken. *"Bitch."*

The next thing I know, I'm on the floor, and my cheek is on fire.

Astonished cries from the room bring Jack's attention to the crowd. "Well? What are you all staring at? I've come to teach my wife a lesson, and it isn't anyone's damned business."

Pastor Leonard calls out, "Now, now, Jack. This can all be settled peacefully if you'll just put down the gun."

Albert and Charles are slowly sidling up behind Jack. I am relieved to see Kate by the Christmas tree, out of the path of the gun. Where is Harry?

"You'll keep out of our business if you know what's good for you," Jack says. "I told Mary Jane not to come, the willful slut. I warned her, I warned all of them." He hasn't taken his eyes off Mama. "I'll kill you, you little cunt, if it's the last thing I do."

Pastor keeps talking. "As I say, this can all be settled safely if you'll just put down the gun. No one has to get hurt."

Jack half turns and spies Albert and Charles at the same time I see that Harry has latched on to Mama's leg. She is furiously trying to tuck him behind her.

Cold determination comes into Jack's eyes as his head whips back around, and I know what I must do.

I lunge for Mama as the pistol goes off. Cries, angry shouts, scuffling. Mama, Harry, and I crash to the floor. As the men wrestle with Jack, the gun goes off again. More screams as people scramble for the door.

"We must go, Mama," I say, pulling her up. "Hurry, Harry! There's no time." Kate appears at my side, and together we usher Harry and Mama from the room. We are down the stairs quick as a whip. A cold blast of air hits us as we dash into the street.

We run. It is not until we are blocks down the street that I feel the first throb in my upper arm, a sticky wetness that clings to my sleeve. And then the world tilts and goes black.

17

*Love blooms, with a new-found beauty in
every clime.*

NELLIE BLY

PITTSBURGH, JULY 1885

It was a beautiful day for a ride in the country: farmland to the
left, plush and dotted with cows, and to the right, the verdant
lawn of Allegheny Cemetery. It was warm. Fortunately, I'd chosen
my lightweight polonaise—a skirt of sky blue that draped in the
latest fashion, revealing a white underskirt beneath, which I'd
paired with a matching jacket of blue and white stripe. I was just
reflecting that I'd chosen wisely when the cab lurched to a stop.

"Far as I go, ma'am," the driver announced.

"But we've only just reached Stanton Avenue," I replied. "You
must take me all the way up the hill."

"It's just farms beyond," the driver said, indicating the fields
with a sweep of his arm. "I won't go any farther. Can't risk my horse
losing a shoe in the middle of God's green earth."

"I should have liked to have known that before I hired you," I
snapped.

"You'll be wanting to find a cab again along the highway here
if you want to go back to the city, unless you want me to wait."

"But I don't know how long I shall be, especially now that I
must walk the last mile on foot and back." I shot an angry glare at

his back. He hadn't the decency to address me directly. "I don't suppose you'll exclude your waiting time in my fare back?"

"No, ma'am."

"Then good day to you." I climbed down from the cab and dropped ten cents into his palm. He tipped his cap, whistled to his horse, and rode away.

I cursed him, wishing now that I hadn't worn the polonaise. I suspected the road might turn to dirt before I reached the house at the top. I took a deep, calming breath. A foul mood would get me nowhere. In front of me, the road stretched up to meet the sky, a startling deep azure. The countryside unrolled into grassy fields the color of emeralds. It had been a long time since I'd left the smoke-filled streets of the city, where the steel mills belched dark clouds into the air that came to rest as a black powder on everything in its path. The fresh air and the sweet smell of milkweed were a welcome reprieve.

Twenty minutes later, I stopped to catch my breath in the shade of a linden. It was insufferably warm now. The road was like a hot iron. Why hadn't I thought to bring a parasol? My feet ached, and my hair was escaping its pins. Surely the house couldn't be much farther.

On my right, the marble shafts and sloping mounds of the cemetery lay in calm repose, as if ridiculing my travail up the hill. How lovely it would be to sit on the grass beneath the old oaks in the shade there, rather than climb the road in the heat of the day.

A cabriolet within the grounds was approaching the road. I had removed my hat and was putting my hair back into its pins when the driver emerged from the lane onto Stanton. I left him a wide girth to pass, and as he did, he dipped his head politely. I nodded in turn and resumed my walk. Almost immediately, I heard the horse's hooves halt behind me.

"Miss Cochrane?"

George McCain jumped down from the carriage, his appearance like a mirage in the heat. How odd to find him here. He was dressed in a white suit and boater. A fleeting image of flinging myself into the rain the last day of the flower show swam before my eyes.

"A strange coincidence," he said, echoing my thoughts. He had removed his boater, and the sun glinted off his dark hair. "What a pleasure to see you here, away from the teeming streets of the city. What brings you to the country?" If he remembered the circumstances of our last meeting, he didn't show it.

"I'm gathering information for a story," I said. "Schenley

mansion." I couldn't possibly look as crisp as he did in the heat, and then I cursed myself for caring.

McCain's eyes wandered behind me up the hill. "Oh yes, Schenley. At the top, isn't it?"

"You know it then?"

"I've heard of it, yes. A fine place, they say." His eyes assessed me. "May I ask why you are endeavoring to make the trip on foot?"

"My driver refused to take me up. He thought his horse might lose a shoe."

"The devil, leaving a woman alone on the road and in this heat. Allow me to take you up the hill. It's wretchedly hot." His kind gray eyes implored me.

I lifted my chin. "I can bear the heat, Mr. McCain."

"Perhaps, but chivalry demands I inquire nevertheless."

"Well, you have done so admirably and are excused." He looked wounded, and so I added, "It isn't much farther anyway."

"All the more reason to allow me to take you. It shan't take but a moment."

I would almost certainly be late if I didn't accept his invitation. For reasons I refused to consider, I blushed to the roots of my hair when McCain assisted me into the carriage, his hands strong but gentle on my waist as he guided me up. In another moment, he was making a wide turn in the road, and we were on our way up the hill.

I thought of the flower cards back home in my Bible. Red poppy. Ox eye. Flax. Cape jasmine. They were a silent mantra to me now, the blooms and their meanings, in my waking and sleeping hours.

I said, "To whom were you paying your respects at the cemetery?"

"No one. I have no relatives buried here. My purpose is less noble than that. I like to take a ride on days like this, when my schedule allows, and my brother-in-law's cabriolet is available. I find it peaceful in the way the city is not." I felt his gaze on me. "You must think me crazy."

"Not at all." I looked down at my hands neatly folded atop my notebook and reticule. "There is solace in nature when one is alone. I find it quite invigorating for the soul."

Our eyes met. "How alike we are, Miss Cochrane." Something in his face altered. For a moment, it was as if we were at the flower show again, at ease in the presence of each other. Quite suddenly, as if to change the undercurrent between us, he said in an altogether different tone, "Tell me: is Schenley a story of your choosing, or is it Madden who has sent you into the wilds of the Eighteenth Ward?"

I smiled at the recollection of Madden's confusion when I'd announced I wanted to write about the lonely mansion on the hill. "If you were to guess, Mr. McCain, what would you say?"

He was silent for a moment, then said, "I think the Schenley manse is your idea."

I watched two white butterflies flit across the road and into the trees. I was happy to be sharing this moment with him, as if it were perfectly normal having a conversation with a married man who'd been sending me esoteric messages on flower cards. "Why?"

He swiveled his head to look at me, a smile playing at the corners of his mouth. "I think it would intrigue you, a woman with a keen mind and abundant curiosity. Madden, in my opinion, has little enough of both."

I laughed.

He continued. "A mansion with a mistress, if memory serves, almost never in residence, who prefers England to her native Pennsylvania. It intrigues you, and so you think it would intrigue your readers. Am I correct?"

"You are." Why did I feel so exposed by the admission? He had merely guessed correctly. Yet it was more than that. He understood me. He knew how I thought. The realization was both thrilling and terrifying. "There should be a turn-off soon," I said. "The housekeeper was rather vague about the directions."

No sooner had I spoken than we slowed to a halt. A line of ducks was crossing the road in front of us. "Now there's something we don't see in the city," McCain said. "I suppose before our journey ends, we'll see chickens, geese, cattle, and pigs."

"You don't enjoy God's creatures, Mr. McCain?" I said, teasing. I stole another look at him. The hands clutching the reins were strong and muscled. Twice the size of mine.

"As a matter of fact, I do. Imagine the life of a duck. Quacking, lolling about on a pond, eating at leisure. Watching us humans going about our business at great speed while he floats on the lake, wondering what all the hullabaloo is about."

I smiled. He had the uncanny ability to make me laugh. And yet I wondered if he could sense my unease beneath the facade. And the flower cards. Why was he sending them? Would he speak of them now?

"See that one there?" McCain was pointing at a fat duck that had stopped to stare at us. "Right now, he's wondering why, on such a fine day as this, we care to go about in a cabriolet when one can traverse the countryside with one's family, each behind the other."

I laughed again, a bubble-like ripple that reminded me of summer days long ago, before Jack Ford. When Kate and I had waded in puddles and skipped stones in the creek until it grew dark.

"And the pig," McCain went on, "imagine him lying about in the mud, gorging upon anything the farmer cares to throw his way. It's his lot in life to be lazy, to lie in the sun and eat. There's a lot about the pig we can all aspire to."

"You surprise me, Mr. McCain. I thought you a civilized man."

"Civilized?" He looked over at me, his eyes dancing. "Not in the least. But I am a city man. I'm more accustomed to seeing pigs and cows and the like on my plate." He gestured to the ducks still making their way to the other side of the road. "At this rate, I'll be famished by the time we crest the hill. Do you suppose the farmer will mind if I take a few home for supper? Ah, there's a farmer just there. I'll ask."

The ducks were at last off the road. McCain slapped the reins, and we approached a man on a roadside footpath carrying a bucket.

"Sir!" McCain called.

I hid my smile behind my glove. "You *mustn't*. He'll think us daft!"

"Kind sir," McCain called down. "Can you tell us how far it is to the Schenley place?"

The man removed his hat and gestured up the road. "See that chimney through the treetops yonder? That's it."

"And have you seen it?" McCain asked. "Is it as grand as they say?"

"Don't know," the farmer replied. "I've never set foot in the place." He nodded, replaced his cap, and was soon out of sight.

"You were teasing, Mr. McCain," I said. "You had no intention of asking him for a duck."

"The day is young, Miss Cochrane. Should one wander this way, you may find one on the seat between us."

A few moments later, we took a narrow plank road and found ourselves on a shaded lane girded by oaks. Leaves shifted in the breeze, a hushed silence descending on us. We rounded a bend, and a sprawling brick home with a two-story pillared porch revealed itself through the trees, as enormous, as grand, as I'd imagined. As we drew nearer, however, I saw that it looked deserted: tall weeds lined the lane and sprouted through the planks, dead branches littered the ground, ivy had strayed from the trellises and was winning the battle to own the yard. Sadness draped the place, solemn and final as a shroud.

"Is this what you expected, Miss Cochrane?"

"No."

McCain pulled to a stop at the house, climbed down, and came around to my side. I couldn't bring myself to look at him when his hands found my waist and lifted me down, but he didn't remove his hands until I met his eyes. He was so tall that I had to use my hand to keep my hat from slipping from my head when I looked up at him.

"I shall wait here for you," he said. "It's no trouble."

"That won't be necessary."

"And if I read of a woman overcome by heatstroke on Stanton Avenue in tomorrow's *Dispatch*?" Laughter shone in his eyes. "Imagine what a wound that would be to my pride."

A cricket chirped. Somewhere in the distance came the faint drone of bees. Sunlight shimmered. I smiled up at him like Eve in the Garden. It was only a carriage ride. "Then far be it from me, Mr. McCain, to injure your vanity."

He broke into a wide grin just as the front door opened. A slender, gray-haired woman waited on the porch. "Mrs. Kohler?" I inquired. "I believe you're expecting me. May I present George McCain, also of the *Dispatch*."

"Very well. You can leave the carriage where it is. Come along." She disappeared into the house, leaving the door open.

"I believe the housekeeper has mistaken you for my touring companion," I said.

"If that's an invitation, Miss Cochrane, I accept."

An hour later, we were traveling back down the drive. Alone with McCain once more, my shoulder grazing his as the cabriolet bumped along, I was acutely aware of him, a sensation that grew the more I tried to dismiss it. McCain was silent, and I wondered what he must be thinking. Touring the mansion, each room grander than the last, I'd been uncomfortably aware of him. I'd asked questions and taken notes, yet beneath the facade, my nerves had hummed with something I couldn't quite describe.

When we pulled out of the drive back onto Stanton Avenue, McCain broke the silence. "A satisfactory interview, Miss Cochrane?"

"I think so," I said. "I had no idea Mrs. Kohler once served as an under maid to Queen Victoria. I've come to find, as a journalist, that surprises are almost always a good thing when it comes to a story."

He nodded. "In my opinion, a journalist too sure of a story

often has nothing to say. But a journalist who stumbles across something rare, something unknown, that's where the magic is."

"QO once told me," I said, "that it is a journalist's job to tell the reader something he doesn't know, and if she's truly successful, the story will teach the writer something she doesn't know about herself."

"And what, pray tell, have you learned of yourself from the lonely mansion on the hill and its reclusive housekeeper?"

I thought for a moment. "That I should go absolutely mad keeping house."

McCain burst into laughter.

"It's true," I said. "Can you imagine cleaning those rooms each week as if Mrs. Schenley will return any day, when she hasn't been there in over twenty years?"

"No," McCain said, sobering. "But I imagine Mrs. Kohler is paid well. She's been in her mistress's employ most of her life. And it cannot be a bad life, living on the grounds as she does. What's your angle, Miss Cochrane? Is your story about the mansion or Mrs. Kohler?"

I considered the question. "I don't know if the two can be separated, or should be. I suppose the real story is about relationships. One cannot understand Mrs. Kohler unless one understands her loyalty to the family."

McCain's smile vanished. After some moments, he said, "May I take the liberty of stealing just a bit more of your time, Miss Cochrane?" There was something beseeching, something haunting in his eyes that seemed to take the breath from me. Was it something I had said? Before I could even consider it, I found myself nodding, eager to spend what time with him I could.

Frederick Gillespie had accosted me this morning before I'd left the house asking me if I would sit with him in the parlor before dinner. *He is perfectly agreeable,* Mama had told me more than once. *You are lucky to be pursued by the likes of such a man.* I had scoffed at her words. Would I always be comparing eligible men to George McCain? Would they always be somehow wanting?

A few minutes later, we entered Allegheny Cemetery, and McCain slowed the horse. The air was sweet with the smell of clover. The paved road stretched out before us, a twisting gray ribbon threading among the tombstones. McCain halted the horse under the shade of a tree near the lane, jumped down, and came around. He had not asked permission to stop. I didn't know his intentions, but I didn't care. Somehow, it seemed right to be with him in this lovely place, on this lovely day. It was all I wanted.

He led me to a round, dome-shaped mausoleum standing alone atop a small mound. It was a beautiful, brown sandstone structure weathered with age, its pillared entrance columns and quatrefoil windows a testament to a bygone era. McCain gestured to a sheltered porch before the door. "Please. Have a seat."

I should have protested. I should have told him I needed to get home and write my story. But none of it mattered, nothing but the imploring look in his eyes. It seemed in that instant that fate, that providence, had brought us together. I lowered myself onto a stone bench and tucked my legs to the side.

"I shall be blunt, Miss Cochrane," McCain said. His back was to me, and he was looking out across the cemetery grounds. "I never reckoned I'd ever have the chance to speak with you alone again. I certainly didn't think I'd find you on Stanton Road today, but as I did, perhaps it is providence."

Providence.

"I've been thinking a great deal about you these past few months. I was, in fact, thinking of you when I saw you walking up Stanton."

"I shall take that as a compliment." It was a fleeting attempt to be lighthearted, but it seemed to fall flat.

"You may retract that statement when you hear what I have to say."

I waited. A bird twittered in a tree, calling to its mate.

"You left in a rush after meeting my wife. I imagine that learning of her must have been a shock to you."

Slowly, my comprehension dawning, I realized why he had brought me here. "Think nothing of it, Mr. McCain," I said tightly.

"You must understand I am at war with myself at the moment, Miss Cochrane. If I don't speak the truth, I shall burst. If I do, I may alienate you forever."

"Naturally, I prefer that you speak the truth," I said icily. One, two, a million heartbeats passed between us. The bird called to its mate again and was answered.

"Mary and I . . . we have known one another since we were children. Our families always believed we would marry, and I suppose because everyone expected it, that is why I asked her. We are not . . . we are not unhappy."

"You needn't explain."

He turned. His face, so handsome, was ravaged with pain.

I came to my feet. Had I misunderstood him? "Mr. McCain? What is it? Is your wife ill?"

A small, twisted grimace. "Not in the way you mean, no."

I was confused. "I don't understand you."

"Please tell me that you will not disappear."

"Disappear?"

"Leave the *Dispatch*. Leave the city."

"Why would I disappear?"

"To take a job elsewhere."

"Why would I do that?"

"Because I fear I shall overstep my boundaries, if I haven't already done so."

"The flower cards."

His face was a mask of grief. "Yes."

It was his guilt, his *guilt,* that compelled him to send the cards. He thought me so wounded by his marriage that he sent them to assuage my pain. I glared at him, so angry I could spit.

"Please don't look at me like that," he whispered.

"You are vain beyond all measure, Mr. McCain. I care not a whit for your cards, and if you think I suffer because you are married, you deceive yourself. What do you think? That I lie awake at night and cry myself to sleep? Is your vanity so deluded that you think I cannot live without a message from you, some crumb you can throw my way to give me hope that you have not forgotten me?"

His face altered, his lips drawing down into a frown. "No, that's not it at all."

"Then what is it?" I stepped to him, my anger a hot coil inside me. "Perhaps your darling Mary prompts you to send them. 'Poor Miss Cochrane, the lonely girl without a suitor. Do send her something, pitiful thing.'"

"Miss Cochrane, stop."

"I won't," I said. "You judge me incorrectly, Mr. McCain. I don't need you or your infernal cards. And you may stop sending them. I no longer care to see them."

"I love my wife, Miss Cochrane—"

I spun away from him. "Bravo, Mr. McCain. You have made that fact quite clear."

"But I am not in love with her. I believe . . . I believe I have fallen in love with you."

The world tilted. I turned, my body in slow motion, the sounds and colors around me suddenly muted and blurry. I saw only the man before me. He stood ramrod straight, his feet planted slightly apart.

"It's true. From the moment I pulled you from the street. I cannot rid myself of you. You are all I think of. I don't send the cards out of pity or guilt. I send them because I cannot help myself. Because those cards are all I can do."

"But you love your wife," I breathed.

"Yes," he said. "Because she is good and kind and would never hurt anyone. But she isn't you. She will never be you."

I had tried, since those three days of the flower show in April, to keep myself together, to clear my mind of this man, and now, now. . . It was too much. I was shaking. Hollowed out and shaking. My knees buckled, and I began to sink.

He was at my side in an instant, pulling me to him, his breath in my ear. He was warm and strong, and I was crying, drowning in sobs. With the tip of his finger, he lifted my chin.

"I feel as if I barely know you and that I've known you forever," he said. "You are all that I have ever wanted and I cannot have you."

I nodded, my tears still falling. "Does she know?"

"No. Mary isn't well. She has had a weak constitution since she was a child. Her lungs are fragile, and she's often bedridden. The knowledge of this, my feelings for you, would kill her."

I closed my eyes, an image of Mary McCain swimming into my vision. A tiny, sickly woman who had reminded me of a timid rosebud. Yes, it would kill her. I asked the question I dreaded, the one that had haunted me more than any other. "Have you children?"

"Yes."

It was a shot to my gut. "I see."

"I've said too much."

"You've spoken the truth." I gave him a weak smile; it was all I could muster.

"Do you hate me, Miss Cochrane? Do you despise me?"

"You know that I do not," I said. "But you are married. That is a barrier to anything more that I could say."

"Not if you don't return the sentiment. It's easy enough to say that you don't."

I stared at him, our eyes locked in understanding. Finally, I looked away. "Saying I return your feelings won't remove the obstacle of your marriage. Nothing can do that."

"I know." He rubbed my bottom lip with his thumb. "I've lived with that fact since the day we met." McCain took my hands in his. "I've told you this because I can't keep it inside any longer. But I won't act on it. I would never do that to Mary; I could never do that to you. But I ask that you allow me to keep sending you the cards. They're the only way I can communicate with you. I won't ask you to answer them or meet with me in clandestine places. Nothing like that. It would cheapen what little we have."

I nodded and gazed down at our clasped hands.

He placed his finger under my chin again and lifted my face. "Promise me one thing."

"Yes?"

"You won't disappear from my life." He tightened his grip on my hands and placed them against his chest. "We are a dyad, the two of us. I can bear living without you as long as I know where you are, what you are doing. You mustn't shut me out."

I smiled through my tears. "I don't think I could do that if I tried."

His eyes fell to my lips. "My dear Elizabeth." For a moment, I thought he was going to kiss me. The sound of my given name on his lips was itself a caress. Then, as if pulled by some invisible force, he stepped back. I could see how much it cost him.

"I must be getting you back," he said.

18

*I saw by the sudden blanching of his face
and his inability to speak that the sight
of me . . . had shocked him terribly.*

NELLIE BLY

BLACKWELL'S ISLAND. SEPTEMBER 1887

"Are you sure it was laudanum?" Anne's amber eyes were enormous as they stared back at me. I glanced in the direction of the nurses' table, where Nurse McCarten was occupied in playing solitaire.

"I'm not sure," I whispered back. My dreams had been so strange. I hadn't dreamed of Jack Ford in ages. The sharp images—his red face contorted in rage, Mama's cries, the report of his pistol—still lingered, filling me with exhaustion. But then, perhaps they were the effects of the drug. I was almost certain the glass Grady had brought to my room had contained laudanum, but I wasn't sure if that was what Dent had given me by needle.

Molly, seated on the other side of the bench, leaned in. "It could've been worse. They use drugs far worse than laudanum in the Retreat and the Lodge to subdue the women."

"So I've heard," I said, turning to Molly. "Do you know what kinds of drugs?"

She shrugged a thin shoulder. "Not by name. What does it matter? They're all designed to punish us and make us have fits."

I considered Molly, my eyes moving over her bare scalp. I wondered if it had been shaved inside the Retreat or the Lodge, if this was why she knew so much about what went on inside those buildings.

"I see you looking, Nellie," Molly said, running her hand over the stubble on her head. "No, I haven't been inside either one. I got this for mouthing off to one of the nurses when she told me I couldn't have another potato at dinner. Wasn't the first time they've shaved me, either, and I doubt it'll be the last."

"Tell me about the Lodge and the Retreat, Molly," Anne said.

I couldn't help wincing. I hadn't shared what Katie had told me about the buildings because I didn't want to frighten Anne. But she deserved to know. Staying innocent wouldn't protect her from the dangers here.

"The Retreat is where they keep the ones who might bring harm to themselves, but it's also the place they keep women isolated from everyone else. I've heard tales of women being locked away without seeing or hearing another living soul for months at a time."

"Not even a doctor?" Anne asked, horrified.

"Ha, there's not much talk of doctors there."

"And the Lodge?"

"For the real crazies, like the women on the rope. The violent ones who are like to bring harm to anyone who so much as looks at them." For once, Molly's defiance slipped, and fear seemed to overtake her. "There are other stories too. Women locked up without food, without fresh air or light. And beatings."

"It sounds more like a prison to me," I said. Punitive treatment without the hope for rehabilitation. How many women housed in those buildings belonged there? How many were simply languishing away because they'd been sent there for punishment like Old Bess?

"You can't complain anymore, Nellie," Anne said. She placed a hand on my arm, her eyes pleading. "Next time, they might very well send you to one of those ghastly places. It was good of you to tell Dr. Ingram we needed more blankets and shawls, but it's not worth it if they're going to punish you for it."

Kind, sweet Anne. She would never have lied to me about her identity as I was doing, never duped a friend to better her chances for a position. Even now, she would put me first before her own needs, which, as each day progressed, were growing increasingly evident. She moved to and from the dining hall more slowly now, each step an effort, and had asked during our last outdoor exercise if she could remain inside, claiming fatigue. The nurses had only laughed.

"It needed doing, Anne," I replied. "Besides, I'm here now, and none the worse for wear." Nevertheless, I shuddered inwardly at the memory of my drug-induced dream—the report of a pistol, the frightened screams. My hand came up to rub my left upper arm. I could feel the irregular tissue beneath the flimsy calico of my asylum gown. I'd been lucky the bullet had only grazed the skin all those years ago. Mama may have applied for divorce soon after that night, but the scars—for all of us—would always remain.

"Do you think they'll come again tonight for you?" Anne asked.

"I don't know, but if they do, I hope what they give me is in liquid form so I can spit it out after they leave."

"They're too smart for that," Molly said.

"I don't think Dr. Ingram had anything to do with drugging me. I have a feeling it was all the nurses. Nurse Grady overheard the conversation and conspired with Grupe, then they involved Dent because they needed someone else to hold me down."

Our discussion came to an abrupt halt when a harsh cry punctured the air.

"They've taken all of it, every last penny!"

Matilda was standing on a bench, gesticulating to someone out the window who wasn't there. She pulled at her hair, tore at her dress, and then took hold of the bars and shook them. Old, wizened, and toothless, she reminded me of the dried apple dolls Kate and I used to make when we were children.

"Poor thing goes off her rocker every few weeks or so," Molly said. "The nurses won't let us do a thing."

"Climb down, Moneybags," Nurse McCarten called, looking up from her card game. "You'll bust your head open, crazy loon."

Mrs. Cotter got up and began walking toward Matilda.

"Stop right there, Eugenia. She's a grown woman. She can climb off a bench good as anybody else."

"There's nothing left!" Matilda cried, eyes red with tears. "They took everything! Do you understand? I have nothing!"

Nurse Grady and Nurse Grupe entered the sitting room. "What's dis?" Nurse Grupe said. Nurse Grady was looking at Matilda with interest.

"Matilda's having one of her spells," Nurse McCarten told them. "Crazy bitch."

"They took it all, the filthy lawyers!" Matilda screamed, shaking the bars. "Filthy scavengers!"

The nurses exchanged glances. Nurse Grady walked over and crooked a boney finger at Matilda, coaxing her to bend down.

"Nurse McCarten shouldn't talk to you like that," she said, loud enough for all to hear. "Tell her she's the crazy bitch."

Matilda looked at Nurse McCarten but didn't make a move toward her. Instead, she turned to the window again and continued her assault on the bars. "I'm piss poor now, all because of those thieving lawyers. Every last penny gone! The house, the carriage, every last dress!"

"Go tell Nurse McCarten she's a vile hussy at once." There was no mistaking the order in Nurse Grady's voice. Matilda, who had likely suffered from not heeding Nurse Grady's instructions before, climbed down and walked slowly to the table.

"She's got something to tell you, don't you, Matilda?" Grady said.

Nurse McCarten smirked. "Well?"

Matilda looked at the floor.

"Get on with it," Nurse McCarten snapped, "else I'll box you to kingdom come."

"I . . . I . . . can't say," Matilda stammered. "It's too private."

For a woman as large as she was, Nurse McCarten was lightning fast. She turned in her chair, hoisted a meaty leg, and kicked Matilda square in the stomach. Matilda stumbled backward and went sprawling. The nurses laughed.

I was off the bench in a flash. "That's enough."

"Well, well, well," Nurse Grady said with a curl of her lip. "If it isn't the famous Nellie, the poor lost girl from the papers. Didn't you learn your lesson last night?" She folded her arms and looked imperiously down at me, black eyes twinkling.

"You call yourself a nurse, but you're nothing but a bully," I said.

I stooped down to Matilda and took her hand. "Can you get up? Let me help you to a bench."

"Bitch," Nurse Grady replied. "You'll pay for that."

I rose to my feet. The room was quiet enough to hear a pin drop. "I imagine I will, but before you punish me, consider what my family will have to say about it."

Nurse Grady's eyebrows drew together. "What?" It was the first time I'd seen her hesitate.

"There have been three parties who've come here already to see if I'm the girl from the papers. One of these days, someone will recognize me, and when they do, I'll tell them everything you've done. Everything. I don't imagine they'll like what they hear."

"Fool. You've been here almost a week. Do you really think someone will come for you?"

"Are you willing to take the risk they won't?"

For once, Grady had no retort. She was too consumed with

rage. I could think of no better way to foil the malicious nurse than to make her believe others were looking for me, people who would not only be angry over the treatment I'd received but willing to do something about it.

"You're on very thin ice," Nurse Grady said after some moments. "I shouldn't bank on a rescue if I were you." She leaned in to me and whispered, "And we're not finished with you yet." She bent down to Matilda and spat. A glob of saliva landed on Matilda's cheek. The old woman didn't dare wipe it away, not when Grady was looking at her like she was ready to throttle her if she so much as moved. She dealt a swift kick to the prone woman, who, in turn, groaned and lay still. With one last venomous look at me, Grady turned on her heel and sailed from the room.

⚘

Later that morning, I was sitting outside Dr. Kinier's office. Superintendent Dent was examining the doctor's patients. Apparently Kinier had the day off. A woman dressed in cook's attire bustled past me with a tray laden with fruit and cheese. For a moment, I wondered if it were a mirage. Were hunger and exhaustion playing tricks on my eyes? The cook entered Kinier's office, bid the superintendent hello, and left empty-handed.

As was customary, the door was left open; there was no such thing as privacy at the asylum. An older, plump woman named Mrs. Turney had just sat down to be examined, and as the nurses happened to be elsewhere at the moment, Mrs. Turney wasted no time.

"I've been beaten," she said, "beaten for no good reason."

Mrs. Turney's lip was split, and I'd noticed that her eye had been turning black since yesterday afternoon.

Dent bit into an apple and made no reply. "It was that vile woman, Nurse Grupe."

"Your word against hers," the superintendent said in a bored voice as he chewed. "I'm sure if I ask her, Nurse Grupe will deny it."

"'Course she will," Mrs. Turney said. "But what else can I do but tell you what happened?" Her voice had grown shrill. "You're the head of this place and it's you who should get to the bottom of it."

"I don't take kindly to being told what to do," Dent said, his words laced with ice. "For all I know, you're making it up."

"Oh, I'm making up my eye, am I?"

"Your eye indicates a physical altercation. It doesn't implicate Nurse Grupe. Come now, what lunatic did you quarrel with?"

"None of them," Mrs. Turney replied. "I was doing my private business in the lavatory yesterday. There wasn't no one about and before I knew it, when I was finished, Grupe come at me from behind the door. Waiting for me. I didn't do nothing."

"Just you and the nurse. No other witnesses."

"Just because there weren't no witnesses don't mean it didn't happen."

"And I'm to believe a nurse beat you, unprovoked?"

"They don't need no reason," Mrs. Turney declared. "And I swear on a stack of Bibles Nurse Grupe done it."

Dent chuckled. "An oath from an insane woman." There was a bang as the apple core landed in the trash can. "Get out."

⁓

At noon, we lined up in front of the windows outside the dining hall. Even dressed in extra shawls, we shivered, huddling into groups to fend off the cold. When the doors opened and we filed in, I took a seat across from Mrs. Turney, hoping to learn more of what had happened in the lavatory.

"Isolde asked me to thank you for our shawls, Nellie," Mrs. Roiger, Mrs. Shanz's German companion, said across the table. Mrs. Shanz smiled at me, nodding her agreement. "She wants you to know she thinks you have great courage."

"Mrs. Roiger, I wonder if you might tell me, assuming you know and Mrs. Shanz is agreeable, why it is that she is here. Other than her being unable to speak English, she seems quite sane to me."

"Indeed she is, and I do know the tale," Mrs. Roiger said soberly. "I shall ask her if it is okay to share it with you." After a short conversation between the two women, Mrs. Roiger turned back to the table. "She is fine sharing with you, with all of you. But I must warn you, it is a despicable tale. You see, Isolde's husband of twenty years, a man she met and married in Germany and soon after emigrated here with, found another woman a short while ago. Isolde was quite devastated, as you can imagine. She found out when a neighbor woman told her of the affair and sought the woman out to confront her. Naturally, she hoped to end the affair between them."

"Another German woman, I suppose," Mrs. Cotter said.

"Yes," Mrs. Roiger replied. "Younger and unmarried."

"How awful," Anne exclaimed.

Mrs. Roiger nodded. "Isolde did find the woman and gave her a piece of her mind."

"That's the way," Mrs. Turney, who had remained silent until now, said. "I hope she punched her in the face too."

There was a beat of silence, and then Mrs. Roiger continued. "She demanded the woman see sense. There were four children to think of." She sighed and patted her friend's hand. "Unfortunately, the younger woman went straight to Mr. Shanz and told her what his wife had done. Her husband got angry and felt she had meddled in his business. Can you imagine?"

"And then he threw her out?" I asked.

"Yes, in a matter of speaking. He escorted her to Bellevue himself, drumming up stories about her mental state so they would admit her. Dreadful."

I frowned. "But there was a young boy I saw come in with her."

Mrs. Roiger spoke to Mrs. Shanz, and when the latter had replied, she turned to me. "Her son. Her husband refused to accompany her across the threshold of the insane pavilion. He made their son do it because he spoke better English."

Mrs. Shanz wouldn't have been able to communicate her side of the story to the doctors. I wondered, though, even if she had, whether the doctors would have believed her. A man's word was often believed over a woman's, but that a man could have his wife committed on the basis of his sole testimony, not to mention his convenience, was unbelievable.

I reached across the table and took Mrs. Shanz's hand. "Please tell her how sorry I am, how sorry we all are." I could not imagine being placed here because my husband had found another woman and grown tired of me. How many other women were here with a similar story?

"Men have no shame," Mrs. Turney said, "no shame at all."

I took a sip of tea and eyed my plate: a withered chicken wing, a small mound of peas, bread topped with the gray substance that passed for butter. Mrs. Turney bit into her chicken and winced. The split in her lip began to bleed.

Nurse Grady prowled the aisles, moving among the women like a jackal among gazelles. Her black hair was drawn up in a more severe style than usual, which made her look even more malevolent. The keys dangling from her belt were a constant reminder of her presence in the dining hall.

"She's not the only one here put away by her philandering husband," Mrs. Turney said. She drew her sleeve across her mouth.

I thought of Urena, whose own husband had placed her here, ostensibly because she had been with other men, when Urena had said it was he who'd been with other women. Where was she now? I wondered. What chance had she to be released if her husband persisted with tales of her unfaithfulness?

"I'm sorry," I said. I could not help but think Mrs. Turney's lip and the small cut above her eye would become infected. When she made no reply, I went on. "I heard your story today, what you told Dent. I think it was very brave of you." I remembered something Katie had told me the other day. She'd spoken about a chair inside the Lodge, some sort of punishment device, but as Nurse McCarten had suddenly appeared, Katie hadn't been able to enlighten me. I needed to learn more about it. Perhaps Mrs. Turney knew.

The older woman grunted. "Brave or not, it had to be done." Her eyes cut to the door where Grupe sat on a chair overseeing the dining hall. "She's a menace to us all, that one. Weren't no reason for her to up and hit me. I was minding my own business."

I placed a pea in my mouth. It was tasteless, an unexpected windfall. I finished the rest of them, studying Mrs. Turney as I ate. She was still angry. Her face was mottled, and she kept darting thunderous glances in Grupe's direction.

"Is that the first time you've been assaulted by a nurse?"

Mrs. Turney swung her gaze to me and breathed out sharply. "You're new, ain't you? You don't know the way of things yet. Well, you're in for some surprises. To answer your question, no, it ain't the first time, and it won't be the last." She eyed me up and down and then said, "You look like a good girl. You'd do well to heed my warning: if you need to go to the toilet, don't go alone. I only went alone myself because I couldn't hold my water anymore. There's things that happen in the lavatory. Bad things."

Mrs. Roiger nodded. Whatever Mrs. Turney was alluding to, it wasn't something only she knew.

"What kinds of things?" My heart was beating rapidly. This was just the type of information I needed, and yet, there was a part of me that didn't want to know.

"For one thing, it's where the doctors get hold of young girls like you," Mrs. Turney replied. I felt the blood drain from my face. "It's empty most of the time, and there's plenty of room to do . . . what they come to do. To satisfy their lust, I'm saying."

"Which doctors?" Anne asked.

Mrs. Turney shrugged. "What difference does it make? You're

a sitting duck no matter who it is." She picked up a pea and placed it gingerly in her mouth, and then, finding she could manage it, took a few more.

Out of the corner of my eye, I glimpsed a hand on my tray, and then it disappeared. An extra piece of bread lay on my plate. I turned to see Matilda scurrying back to her place. She bobbed her head at me, her wizened face beaming. I picked up the bread and took a bite, raising it in salute. It was foul, but I swallowed nevertheless. Mrs. Shanz's and Mrs. Roiger's bread joined Matilda's on my tray.

"For Matilda," Mrs. Shanz said in heavily accented English.

"That's not the worst thing that happens in the lavatory," Mrs. Turney said. She was still looking in Grupe's direction. "You seen the broomstick end in the tub, the one they use for a plug? It comes in handy when a girl comes here in a family way."

It took me a minute to understand what she was saying. "You don't mean . . ." My voice trailed off. I couldn't finish the sentence. I thought of poor Urena. Where had they put her? Was she still with child? I felt sick. I pushed my tray away, bile rising in my throat.

"That's exactly what I mean," Mrs. Turney said. "I come upon it being done myself months ago. The girl weren't far along, but the nurses knew. Blood everywhere. Screaming like nothing I ever heard. Worse thing I seen in my life and that's saying a lot, being as I've been here four long years."

"Did you tell the doctors?" Anne asked.

"I told Dent. He said he'd question the nurses. I don't know if he did or not. The girl died a few days later."

I could not imagine the poor thing's pain and anguish. How could the nurses do such a heinous thing? The girl's death had almost certainly been the result of what they'd done. It was beyond comprehension.

Before I could comment, Mrs. Turney bolted from the table. In a flash, she was across the room, her cup in her hands. With an angry bellow, she flung tea in Nurse Grupe's face.

"You can burn in hell for beating me, you filth!"

Grupe sprang from her chair, sputtering. Tea dripped down her face. "How dare you, you conniving bitch!"

Shouting erupted as three nurses, Grady included, grabbed Mrs. Turney. A few inmates rose to their feet. Others began to bang their plates and cups on the tables.

A shout from one of the tables rose above the din. "You're one to call her a bitch!"

Grupe's eyes widened. The nurses holding Mrs. Turney exchanged glances as the clamor in the room built. It was the first time I'd seen the women stand up for one of their own. The nurses were justifiably wary; our number in the dining hall was seven times what it was in the sitting room. A fight would be difficult to stop.

Superintendent Dent stormed into the hall, his face livid. All commotion, all movement, ceased. One scathing look from him was all it took for the inmates to lose their courage. Those who had risen sat down.

"What the devil is the meaning of this?" Dent said. His pale blue eyes impaled Mrs. Turney, who was still breathing heavily from the struggle.

"She deserved it and you know it!" Mrs. Turney shouted, struggling to wrest free. "I told you and you did nothing!"

"She threw tea in my face," Nurse Grupe cried. "You can't let her get away with this!"

I could stand it no longer. I knew Mrs. Turney would be punished. It was only a matter of where they would send her—to solitary confinement at the Retreat or to the veritable hell that was the Lodge. I doubted my interference would make any difference, but I had to try.

Dent's eyes narrowed as I approached. "Sit down at once."

"I think Mrs. Turney has a sound reason to be upset, don't you?"

"*I said sit down.*"

I felt my heart constrict and that old feeling of hate return. I didn't think it possible to despise another person as much as I'd despised Jack Ford.

"The tea wasn't hot," I said. "It's only Grupe's pride that burns."

Dent's eyebrows rose in incredulity. "That's hardly the point. She assaulted a nurse." To Nurse Grady, he said, "Take Turney to the Retreat at once."

"I rather think it's the other way around, Superintendent."

"That is not for you to say," Dent said between clenched teeth. "You know nothing of the matter."

I took a step toward him. "Did you even consider looking into Mrs. Turney's story? Or perhaps it's too much trouble and you're here to punish the patients instead of the staff who abuse them."

"You see how unmanageable she's become?" Nurse Grady said, triumph in her eyes as she and Grupe held a struggling Mrs. Turney between them. "Next, Nellie will have the inmates up in arms."

The superintendent was taking a menacing step toward me when a nurse entered the dining hall. "Sir? There's a visitor for Nellie Brown."

Dent gave a curt nod, too consumed with the matter at hand to deal with me.

As the nurse escorted me down the hall, my mind raced. Someone had come to see me. Another family member looking for a lost daughter or wife or sister or lover. Since the Newlands, other aspirants had arrived on the shores of Blackwell's Island, dazed and hopeful, only to leave with anguish and regret. Two days before, a man had come looking for his fiancée, but his face had fallen as soon as he'd caught sight of me. The girl had taken the elevated train home one evening after work, got off, and disappeared into the night. Yesterday it was an Irish couple in search of their niece. They'd presumed she'd eloped, but upon locating her beau, they found that he, too, was in desperate search of her. It was soul crushing to witness a family's devastation when they saw I wasn't the loved one with whom they'd hoped to be reunited. Dent had been present each time, putting on a show of false sympathy for the visitors, only to return to his customary arrogance as soon as the guests departed.

Every unsuccessful reconciliation only strengthened his belief that I would never be claimed. I just hoped whatever punishment he had in store for me wouldn't be brought to bear before the *World* came to my rescue. I prayed Mrs. Turney was enough of a distraction to prevent him from following me. Then, with a wave of shame, I realized how horribly selfish I was being. If Dent wasn't going to make an appearance, it was because he was reprimanding Mrs. Turney. What form of punishment would he mete out to a woman who'd only wanted justice?

A cold breeze swept through the corridors as we approached the reception hall. The windows at the top of the tower were throwing no light down into the rotunda when I entered, for there was little sun that day. A man sitting in a chair stood as I approached.

My heart leaped at the sight of him. George McCain was as handsome as ever: impossibly tall, dressed entirely in black as if he were in mourning. He'd removed his hat and seemed unsure what to do with his hands. He clutched them, placed them behind his back, and finally dropped them at his sides. He had gone pale at the sight of me, but then how alarming I must look in my soiled asylum gown, my hair streaming from my loose braid.

"Well," the nurse, a girl I'd never seen before, said, "is she the one you're looking for?"

There was an interminably long pause. McCain was wondering, I supposed, what to say. He couldn't think I wanted to be rescued, could he? And yet here he was. Suddenly, the sun peeked from behind a cloud and streamed through the tower windows. For the briefest of moments, we stood in a golden haze, dust motes in the air between us. In the brilliance, I could see the shadows under his eyes, the drawn lines around his mouth, and then the sun slipped away again.

I said with slow deliberation, "I don't know this man."

"Well, do you know her?" the nurse said to McCain. "She's the one who don't remember a thing."

His gray eyes never wavered from mine. "Sadly, I do not. I'm looking for a woman I . . . have lost." His voice was strained. "The girl I'm looking for looks a lot like the illustration the papers printed, but this isn't she. It's sad no one has come forward yet. The papers are making quite a fuss over her."

My story was still alive. I didn't know whether to be relieved. What would Cockerill think?

"Good enough then." The nurse started to show him out.

McCain didn't move. He withdrew something from his coat pocket and held it out to me. "I brought this for my sweetheart, hoping I would find her here. I leave it with you, in the hope you find the one you've lost. Perhaps it will give you comfort until you are returned to those who love you."

I took the card. A deep purple bloom. Clematis. I turned it over. There was no message. McCain wasn't taking any chances.

"In the language of flowers, it means 'mental beauty,'" he said.

For a brief instant, I was standing at the mausoleum in Allegheny Cemetery. A beautiful day with the call of birds and the smell of clover around me, around us. *We are a dyad,* he had said. So long ago, but it seemed, in that moment, like yesterday.

The nurse barked a laugh. "There ain't much mental beauty around here. They're all nutty as fruitcake."

"Thank you, sir," I said. "You have given me reassurance that someone in the world will come for me soon."

He smiled ever so slightly, and I knew he understood.

The nurse was anxious to see him out, and, in any case, there was nothing more we could say with her looking on. In another moment, he was gone, his footsteps dying away in the distance and leaving me alone with my thoughts.

I was still looking at the card when the nurse returned and snatched it from me. "Ain't that nice." She leered at me. There was a gap in her smile where a tooth should have been. "Pity he didn't know you, eh? He was a looker. Well, you can't keep it. No gifts allowed." She slipped it in her apron pocket and led me from the room.

19

*That such an institution could be
mismanaged, and that cruelties could exist
'neath its roof, I did not deem possible.*

NELLIE BLY

BLACKWELL'S ASYLUM, SEPTEMBER 1887

Superintendent Dent lifted the knife and sliced through the cheese.
It was blue veined, the odor pungent and earthy. Pieces came away
in crumbles. One of these he placed in his mouth with the help of
his knife. "You had a visitor today."

I made no reply.

He put another piece into his mouth. "Whom was he looking
for?"

"His sweetheart."

"And you didn't recognize him."

"No, nor he me."

"I find it odd." He sliced through the cheese again, taking his
time. "He didn't sign the visitor's log. No name, no profession, no
address. A man of mystery."

I shrugged. "Perhaps he wasn't told—"

"Gertie instructed him to sign in while she was fetching you."

"I don't see what difference it makes. I wasn't the one he was
looking for."

Dent's knife glinted as he stabbed a piece of cheese and held it aloft. "Aged to perfection. Imported from England. Costly, but worth the extravagance. It takes three hours for a nurse to fetch it for me in the city. I pay five cents for the errand, twenty cents for the cheese."

My mouth was watering. After six days of weak tea and bread, I was hollowed out with hunger. "You should pay the nurse more and the grocer less."

The superintendent smiled. "Witty for an inmate."

"I shouldn't be an inmate. I'm not insane."

He chuckled. "And the criminals at Blackwell's Penitentiary don't think they've committed a crime." Those translucent blue eyes bored into mine. "Your little show in the dining hall was quite courageous. Courageous but unwise."

"You think because I acted out I'm crazy, but you're wrong. It's because I see the injustices here that I speak up. It's what a reasonable, sane person would do."

"*Injustices.* Such a grave word."

"So are *negligence* and *abuse.*"

The smile slid from his lips. He opened a drawer and withdrew a notebook, which he placed on the desk between us. It was the notebook inside my reticule that had been taken from me when I'd first arrived.

"Interesting drawings. Although, when I studied it closer, it appeared you might have been cataloging information. Why?"

"I don't remember names and places very well."

"You seem to remember all that goes on here well enough."

"It's a shortcoming," I said, with what I hoped looked like a dismissive shrug. "Sometimes my memory is poor."

"Interesting." Dent leaned back in his chair and steepled his fingers. "You see, people with a faulty memory don't remember they have a faulty memory."

"Well, some part of me does."

"And some part of me believes you're hiding something." He leaned forward. "You were agitated and nervous when we last spoke. Since then you seem to be far more . . . confident. And two times now you've come between the staff and the inmates. It's most irregular."

"Aren't lunatics supposed to be unpredictable?"

"Ah, but you've just told me you're not a lunatic. Or had you forgotten?"

I felt my heart skip a beat. I swallowed, my mouth suddenly dry. Dent reached into the drawer again and tossed McCain's flower card onto the desk. "What does it mean, Nellie?"

"'Mental beauty,' I think he said."

"No, I mean *what does it mean*, that he would give you this, a stranger who's never seen you before?"

He was perilously close to the truth. Even knowing that I would be released in four days did nothing to ease the erratic beating of my heart or the feeling of foreboding that was coming over me. But I would not let him see it. I refused to be cowed by this vicious, hateful man. I wouldn't give him the satisfaction.

"If I had to guess, I'd say he felt sorry for me. I am, after all, a patient in a mental asylum. Look at me. I'm dressed in a filthy gown. My hair hasn't been combed in a week. It's the way we all look, Superintendent—disheveled and ill cared for. Or haven't you noticed? No, I think not. You're too busy sending nurses into the city for Stilton. How silly of me."

A knowing gleam came into Dent's eyes, but not before I'd seen naked fury in their depths. "I can see we'll have to sedate you again this evening, Nellie. Excitement can be so detrimental to one's health, especially one as deluded as you. You do realize, with each passing day, the probability of someone coming forward for you lessens. Sooner or later, the papers will tire of you and move on, and when they do, you'll be forgotten. Yesterday's news. We shall have no other recourse but to keep you here. Such a pity. The poor, lost waif the papers have written of so fervently may never find her way home."

He called to a nurse. He'd made his intentions clear, and he was done with me. As I walked back down the corridor, one thought after another leaped through my mind. Dent strongly suspected I was sane but couldn't be sure. Either way, he was in a precarious position. On one hand, he needed to treat me reasonably. If someone claimed me, I might tell my story to the press upon my release. I had a hunch that the papers would like nothing better than to conclude the story with the mystery of my identity solved. My tale of the horrid world I'd witnessed behind asylum bars, the neglect and abuse, would not reflect favorably upon the superintendent and his staff. On the other hand, if no one came forward for me, he was free to do with me what he pleased—and it would not include releasing me.

He was simply biding his time, waiting to see which way the wind would blow.

I still had four days left. If the papers stopped printing anything about me, I would no longer have any protection. He would be bolder. There would be nothing to keep Superintendent Dent and his wrath at bay.

The wind coming off the East River nipped at my nose. Paired in
sets of two, we were marching in line like an army of ants. Leaves
skittered across the gravel yard. The day was cold and the wind
brisk, but it was always a fine day when we were allowed to leave
the stifling tedium of the sitting room.

"I hear there is news to celebrate," Mrs. Cotter said, low. The
nurses were about, ever watchful, and we needed to be careful
they didn't catch us talking.

"Oh?"

"When I was scrubbing the floor in the dining hall earlier, I
heard the nurses say Louise has been sent to the infirmary. She
is no longer in the Retreat."

"And that's good news?"

"I believe so," Mrs. Cotter replied. "The Retreat is a filthy
place. My guess is they've sent her there to clean her up before
she joins us again."

I was relieved. I hadn't expected to see her before I was released.

After some moments, Mrs. Cotter said, "You have turned,
Nellie. You were robust when you came to Blackwell's a week ago.
Pink cheeked, healthy. You're different now. Everyone eventually
succumbs. I'm sorry to see it."

My limbs did not seem to want to cooperate that morning.
My arms and legs felt weak and my head ached. Superintendent
Dent and Nurse Grady had come to my room the night before and
given me another shot. Something stronger. My nightmares had
been horrible. I'd awakened that morning in a daze, trembling as
I splashed water on my face. Knowing what I did now about what
happened in the lavatory, the place made my skin crawl. Every
crack, every stain, had new meaning. Anne had looked at me
aghast, knowing in an instant what had happened. "Oh, Nellie,"
she'd said, laying a hand on my arm until one of the nurses shouted
for us to form a line for the sitting room.

I regarded the dainty woman walking beside me. Mrs. Cotter
was perhaps a little older than Mama, her hair swept back and
graying at the temples. I remembered how she'd offered me her
bread the first day and how I'd declined because it looked so unappetizing. Now I ate it most meals because it was the only thing I
could stomach. Was there any benefit to telling her I was being
drugged? Would it serve any purpose other than frightening her?
The horror of it seemed something best kept to myself.

"You remind me of a woman I met just before I came here," I said.

"Oh?"

I told her of my stay at the Temporary Home before I'd been carted off to Bellevue, of a sympathetic woman named Mrs. Caine who had cared for me when the other women had shunned me for my crazy rantings. "I don't think I'll ever see her again. I wish I'd told her how grateful I was for her kindness."

"There are angels who pass in and out of our lives before we have a chance to tell them what they mean to us." Mrs. Cotter's eyes brimmed with tears.

"You've lost someone close to you," I said. Ahead, Nurses Grady and Grupe walked alongside our line, one on either side, the wind whipping at their skirts.

"My husband and I lost our daughter to consumption not long ago," Mrs. Cotter said. "Margaret was just eighteen when the good Lord took her." She stopped speaking. I thought she would say nothing more, but after some moments, she resumed. "She was our only child. My husband couldn't provide for me at home. You see, I . . ." Her words trailed off and were swallowed in the wind.

"You don't have to go on," I said. "I understand."

A week ago, I would've tried to wring every word from her. Gather details I could use for my write-up for the *World*. Now, it seemed cruel to encourage her to speak of something that brought her so much pain. My magpie's nest was chock full of details I wanted to forget. I didn't need any more.

"No, no," Mrs. Cotter said, placing a hand on my arm. "I must speak of it; I mustn't keep it in." She wiped at her eyes. "After Margaret died, I suffered from bouts of melancholy to such a degree, I didn't wish to go on living. My husband couldn't give me the care I needed. I was terribly ill and weak, you see. My husband is a laborer; he works all day at a brush factory. There was no one to look after me, no money to pay a nurse. He brought me to Bellevue and the doctors promised to restore my health."

"And sent you here instead."

We were making a loop back toward the building. A group of women from another hall was approaching the gravel. Coats flapped in the wind. Someone's hat was whisked away in the breeze and went careening through the grass. A sharp whistle split the air when the woman attempted to leave the line to fetch it.

"Bellevue is overcrowded," Mrs. Cotter continued. "They had no bed for me. I was brought here, and when my husband came to visit, the superintendent promised him he would restore my health.

Blackwell's isn't a place for recuperation, of course, but we didn't know that then. You may find it odd, but although I'm hungry and the abuse I've witnessed here is something I shall never forget, my will to live has been restored. I miss my daughter terribly, but I must go on. I belong with my husband. I'm ready to move on from this place. My husband is coming to fetch me in a few days when he has some leave."

My eyebrows rose in surprise. "Dent allowed that? He's letting you go?"

"Oh yes, my husband wouldn't hear otherwise."

It made sense. Superintendent Dent couldn't afford contradicting, much less angering, the relatives of his patients. He wouldn't risk the scrutiny that might lead to an investigation that would reveal the horrors that went on at Blackwell's. Concerned family members from the outside world looking in would be treated with respect, their relatives reasonably well looked after at the asylum. Which meant the large majority of the women here had no one. That, or their families had simply abandoned them. I gave Mrs. Cotter's arm a tight squeeze. "I believe yours is the only story I've heard with a happy ending."

Nurse McCarten was trudging toward us, eyes narrowed as she checked to see no one was talking. When she was satisfied, she returned to the front of the line.

"I fear most of the women here will never return home," I said.

Out of the corner of my eye, I saw Mrs. Cotter take a faltering step. She was looking straight ahead, a strange expression on her face.

"Mrs. Cotter?"

She didn't reply; she wasn't listening. And then, suddenly, she was running. Grady and Grupe spotted her, but not in time to grab her as she ran. She was headed for a man standing along the path that led to the west wing. A grounds keeper, by the way he was dressed.

Grupe blew her whistle. "Back in line, Eugenia! Stop right der!"

Mrs. Cotter drew up to the man, began to embrace him, and then took an awkward step back. The man looked flummoxed, staring down at her in surprise. The nurses were on her in an instant. Grady struck Mrs. Cotter in the face, and the older woman fell to the ground.

I ran to Mrs. Cotter, heedless of the whistles and the shouting around me. Her cheek was bleeding. I crouched down to her, stricken with fear. "Are you all right? Can you stand?"

All at once, I felt an excruciating pain in my side and fell to the ground. I nearly landed on Mrs. Cotter.

"Get up," Nurse Grady said. She looked venomous, poised to kick me again if I refused to obey.

I stood, helping Mrs. Cotter to her feet as I did so. A slow rage began to build inside me.

"My husband," Mrs. Cotter said, still panting. "I thought he was my husband. He's coming for me soon and I thought . . ." The man she'd mistaken for Mr. Cotter was disappearing down the path. A large tear traveled down her cheek, her face white with shock.

"She wasn't being defiant," I said to Grady. "She was acting on instinct. It was a mistake."

"Yes, for both of you." She pushed me in the direction of the south wing, while Nurse Grupe did the same to Mrs. Cotter.

"We'll get back in line," I said, trying to keep my voice calm. "As I said, Mrs. Cotter made a simple mistake."

Grady gave a bitter laugh. "We don't tolerate mistakes, nor excuses. Now keep moving or I'll kick you again, and harder."

The other nurses had stopped the women from marching to let us pass, halting them with the peal of their whistles. They stood, all eyes on us, as we left the yard. I glimpsed Anne and Tillie, clinging to one another as they shivered in the wind, and then suddenly, a cry broke the silence: "Bless you, Nellie! You give 'em what for!"

Nurse McCarten blew her whistle and then cried out, "That's enough! The next one who speaks joins them."

An eerie hush filled the yard. Not an inmate stirred. As we left the yard, I heard more whistles. The inmates were being commanded to resume their walk.

"He wasn't my husband," Mrs. Cotter murmured, shaking her head. She seemed to be confused, her brow furrowed, her eyes far away. "Not my Archie at all. It looked like him, but no, he wasn't my Archie."

"You can see Mrs. Cotter is confused," I said as we neared the south wing. "Let me take her back to the sitting room. She didn't mean to disobey. There was no harm done."

Grady kicked me behind the knees and I pitched forward, landing in a sprawl on the path. "Keep moving, bitch."

As we passed the south wing, a low, two-story rectangular building came into view, small compared to the main building and covered in unpainted clapboard. As we neared it, Mrs. Cotter seemed to come out of her fugue. She took a step back, horrified. "Oh, no, no, no," she cried, "I know what that place is. I've done nothing to deserve the Lodge. I'm leaving soon!"

"You should have dought of dat before you got out of line," Nurse Grupe said. "You break da rules and you get vat's coming to you."

So this was where patients were sent to be punished. The veritable hell spoken of in whispers. *Three days. Just three more days.* Whatever horrors lay beyond those doors wouldn't last longer than that. Cockerill would send someone to get me out. And then suddenly, I was ashamed. How selfish of me, thinking of my escape when I should be concerned for Mrs. Cotter.

Grupe unlocked the door with a key from her ring, and hands pushed us inside. A dim corridor stretched ahead, off of which were a series of closed doors with padlocks. Down the corridor we walked, my legs feeling weaker and weaker as we neared the double doors at the end. My head was aching in earnest by the time Grupe unlocked the door.

Unwashed bodies, urine, feces—the stench was a blow. I raised my hand to cover my mouth, fearful I might gag. The room was dim, the only light streaming through slats over the sparse windows. As my eyes adjusted, details took shape. The room was large, its floor covered with a thin scattering of hay. The clink of a chain brought my attention to the right. Through the gloom, my gaze met the sight of a woman slumped against a wall. Her hair was loose and hung in knots, her legs bent, her knobby knees exposed. She moaned piteously and reached out a trembling hand. A moan from the other side of the room—another woman. And another. I counted six chained to the walls amid their own filth.

"This is inhumane," I said, my voice slicing the air. "You've got to release these women at—"

Grady's hands were around my throat in an instant. I tried to gulp air, but her nails bit into my flesh, my fingers digging at hers to no avail.

"I may not be able to lay a hand on you now," she said viciously, "but your time is coming. For now, you can watch. Watch and learn." She spat into my face, a globule landing below my eye. "That's for Matilda."

She pushed, backing me up against a wall. When she released me at last, I gasped for breath, feeling faint. In the next moment, a heavy metal cuff enclosed my wrist, entrapping me with a resounding clang. I looked down and pulled. The chain was perhaps three feet long and heavy. I was trapped like an animal. Mrs. Cotter stood motionless staring at me, horrified by Grady's violence. Her lips were moving, but no sound was coming out.

A whimper brought my attention to the left. A woman stirred in the shadows, her silhouette familiar. Old Bess? In the next instant, Grupe was walking toward Mrs. Cotter, a broom handle in her hands.

"Don't," I cried. "Don't hurt her!"

Grupe thrust the end of the broom into Mrs. Cotter's abdomen and the older woman doubled over, crying out in pain. The next blow was to her ribs. The third, a horizontal slice across her neck, sent her crashing to the floor, where she landed with a sickening thud. Grady then bound her feet, tying the rope with such dexterity it was clear it was an act of long habit. Mrs. Cotter's hands were next. All the while, the poor woman mumbled on about her husband, that he was coming for her. In the next instant, the nurses were hauling her to her feet and placing a pillowcase over her head.

"What are you doing?" I shouted. "For heaven's sake, have pity on her! She's a poor defenseless woman!"

My screams made no difference. The nurses had their plan and they would see it through to the end. When the pillowcase was in place, they secured it with rope around Mrs. Cotter's neck. They lifted her to the barrel, stood her up next to it, and forced her to bend over it.

"Vee are going to give you a bath, Eugenia," Grupe said maliciously. "You know how much vee like to have da inmates clean."

"On the count of three," Grady said. "One, two, three."

The nurses pushed Mrs. Cotter's head down until it was completely submerged. Water sloshed over the rim of the barrel as she struggled, although with her hands and feet bound and Grupe and Grady holding her, there was little she could do to fight back. In another moment, they were tugging her up by the rope around her neck. Mrs. Cotter's sharp intake of air was audible, a wheezing sound that filled the room and brought laughter from the nurses. She struggled to breath, the pillowcase tight against her face.

How stupid I was to think this hideous display was over. They were only getting started. Down Mrs. Cotter went again and again and again.

20

ow nonsensical it is to blame or criticize people for what they are powerless to change.

NELLIE BLY

PITTSBURGH, SEPTEMBER TO OCTOBER 1885

The hands on the clock had not yet reached nine in the morning when I arrived at the *Dispatch*. The newspaper office never seemed to sleep, but the early hours were the most hectic, when all two hundred employees converged at once. It was the one time of day the reporters were all in, waiting to get assignments and see what the day would bring. I climbed the stairs to the third floor, sidestepping two reporters chatting so spiritedly they nearly ran me down as they descended. At the top, I headed for the mail slots. As usual, they were bursting with all manner of correspondence. My cubby, however, held a single envelope, which bore only my initials. I slipped it into my bag. I had glimpsed McCain in the office a handful of times since Schenley. He was in the company of others each instance. He had treated me with the gentlemanly solicitousness polite society required, without a hint of the man who had so ardently expressed himself to me two months before. It pained me to see him treat me as if we barely knew one another, but it was better than not seeing him at all.

I was about to leave when I glimpsed something else in my

slot. It was a single piece of note paper upon which were the words *See me*. Madden's signature was scrawled below.

I took the stairs to the fourth floor and knocked on Madden's door. The editor was seated at his desk and looked up.

"Morning, Miss Cochrane," he said. Unlike QO, he continued to refer to me by my real name, seemingly unconcerned with my identity being discovered in the office. He didn't dare do the same for Bessie Bramble; she wouldn't hear of it. So far, I had said nothing. I wasn't so vain as to think myself in the same league as the celebrated journalist. For another, Madden looked to be in a foul mood. Though he was generally discourteous as a rule, I'd never seen him look hostile. The eyes that stared at me from beneath the brim of his bowler were watchful and full of annoyance.

I arranged my face into an expression of demure innocence, hoping it would have a good effect on Madden. "Is this a good time?"

"Now is as good as any." He took a puff from his cigar and waved me in. The cigar had been smoked down to a stub, which meant, even at this early hour, tomorrow's edition was already pressing in on him. Thankfully, my latest contribution had appeared in yesterday's paper; I didn't owe him anything for a few days. Late copy had a way of sending Madden and his typesetters into bouts of apoplexy.

Sensing a compliment might soften his disposition, I said, "I'd like to thank you again for giving me a column."

A few weeks before, Madden had, at last, decided to award me a column with a byline. I had, thanks to hard work, carved out a niche for myself that had convinced him I had the skill and tenacity required to compete with his other reporters. I also suspected it had something to do with the large amounts of fan mail I received.

Madden grunted. "That's just what I wanted to talk to you about."

I felt my pulse quicken. Had he received more threats from advertisers? I'd never breathed a word of what McCain had told me in the spring, that a business had put pressure on Madden to let me go. I had thought that all behind me when he'd given me a column.

"I was of the impression," Madden said, "you were going to continue in the same vein as the William Sirwell piece."

Several weeks before, I'd journeyed to Armstrong County to interview the area's most revered Civil War hero. I'd been awed by the charming, if ailing, colonel who had led his cavalry to so many victories on the battlefield. I'd been crestfallen to learn of his death less than two weeks after my story ran.

"It was a thorough profile, Miss Cochrane. One that did a great man justice so close to his end, and it showed promise for your future. That piece, and a few select others, is why I decided to give you the chance at a column. As a test, to see if you had the grit, as it were." Another puff on his cigar. The room felt close. "To my surprise, the copy you turned in for your first column was . . . let's just say, less than stellar."

I'd written a series of short vignettes on city life: I'd poked fun at the way Pittsburghers gawked, described a drunken man's behavior, and expounded on dogfighting. "I was going for something light," I said. "I thought—"

Madden's fist came down on his desk, and I jumped. "Fluff. I don't pay my columnists to write fluff." He smashed the remains of his cigar into the ashtray, grimacing around the smoke.

He was right. I'd gone to Armstrong County with more in mind than interviewing Colonel Sirwell. I'd gone home to Apollo to start proceedings to prepare a suit against Samuel Jackson, the so-called guardian who had mismanaged my inheritance years before to the extent that I'd been forced to drop out of school for good. By the time I'd finished with the attorney I'd hired to go after Jackson and returned to Pittsburgh, my deadline was looming, and I'd cobbled disparate ideas together to make the column's deadline. A mistake.

"The only reason I allowed such drivel to go to print was because I didn't have a column and a half of content to put in its place. You've risen quickly here, Miss Cochrane. It's virtually unheard of for a girl of your inexperience to have a byline, much less a column in a newspaper—all in the span of seven months."

"I understand, and I'm grateful—"

"Then show it. If you want a column, write of themes that are worthy of one. There are two things in this world I despise. One is oysters. Do you know what the other is?"

"No."

"People who make me look a fool."

I walked down Wood Street in a daze. The day was crisp and clear, but the warm autumn sun failed to cheer me. I scarcely noticed the carriages and cabs-for-hire rushing past. I was ashamed of myself. Over and over, I played back the conversation in Madden's office. His cutting words, his sharp anger. I couldn't believe, after working so hard, that it had come to this. There was no one to blame but myself. Madden hadn't given me a column because I'd finally arrived at the top. He'd done it as a test to see if I had what it took to keep going, and I'd failed him. I'd failed myself. At Seventh Street, I turned west toward the river, toward home, and felt my shame turn to anger. Madden had given me every opportunity to succeed. He was rude and unpredictable at best, and I hated being tossed back and forth between the themes I felt were important and the trifling ones I abhorred, but he'd given me a chance. How could I have been so stupid?

The burn of angry tears pricked my eyes, but it wasn't until I heard the loud whinny of a horse that I came to myself. I wiped the tears away with the heel of my hand and looked around. I'd been so steeped in my thoughts that I'd paid no attention to where I was going. Where was I? The corner of Penn Avenue and Seventh Street. A grand, newer-looking building rose majestically from the street, its facade an elaborate stonework whose upper floors sported handsome red brick. The placard by the door identified it as the Young Men's Christian Association. Well, it was as good a place as any.

Under the shelter of the portico, I opened my bag and withdrew the envelope. The date on the back read "Sept. 6." Yesterday, the day of my column's debut. I tore it open. Printed on the card was a purple, crown-shaped flower. Coronella. I consulted the little book in my reticule for its meaning. *Success crowns your wishes.*

I began to cry in earnest. So far, my entry into the world as a newspaper columnist felt like no success at all.

❦

"For goodness sake, Elizabeth, you must give up on Jackson," Kate said peevishly. She swept a wayward lock of hair behind her ear. "He's a liar and a thief, but it's not worth the trouble."

The summer-like weather had spilled over into late September, and we were taking a stroll in Allegheny Commons. Thankfully, the easterly breeze was keeping the coal smoke that hung eternally over Pittsburgh from making its way over the river to Allegheny City. Pedestrians strolled at their leisure, enjoying the afternoon sun. Little Beatrice made a cooing sound from her pram, and I leaned down. She was bundled adorably in a pink coat with matching bonnet, a gift from me. I'd decided that when she got older, I'd allow her to call me Aunt Pinkey.

I said, "Mr. McClister thinks I have a very good case."

"They all say that," Kate replied. "Lawyers get paid whether they win your case or not."

"He thinks he can prove that Jackson forged my signature for withdrawals, Kate."

My sister stopped abruptly and turned to me. She was sporting a new hat I'd bought with my *Dispatch* earnings, money I kept separate from what I gave Mama each week to help with the boarding-house expenses. It had taken me more than two months to save enough, but it had been worth it. The brown-velvet-and-ostrich-plume concoction made her look older and more sophisticated. God knew her husband wouldn't have thought of it. As a train car conductor, he was rarely at home. I found it selfish of him to spend so much time away and leave her with raising a baby without a father, for surely he could find other employment that would allow him to spend more time with his family.

"Why can't you let it go, Elizabeth?" Kate said. "The rest of us have. You're not the only one of us he stole from, you know."

"I can't let him get away with it."

"You mean you *won't*. There's a difference."

Kate had no idea my trip to retain Mr. McClister had resulted in my substandard column, and I wasn't about to tell her. Neither she nor Mama knew Madden was unhappy with it, and I intended to keep it that way.

"It's just like with Papa," Kate said, resuming her walk. "You've never forgiven him for dying. You've got to let things go."

I breathed out a long sigh. *So much for a lighthearted conversation.* Ahead in the distance lay the Western Penitentiary, a sprawling edifice that looked, with its high, crenellated towers, more castle than prison. It was time to change the subject. "I've always thought it odd, a penitentiary in a municipal park."

"I think it beastly," Kate said, wrinkling her nose. "I feel for the poor souls who gaze out watching us stroll, while there they sit, locked away in prison."

"Well, it's no matter," I said, sidestepping a man with a dog on a leash. "There's talk it will be torn down soon."

"Oh?" Kate's pretty brows rose. "How did you—oh, of course. You're always reading some newspaper or other these days."

"I happen to like newspapers," I said matter-of-factly. "And besides, it's my job to keep up on what goes on in the city."

To the east, across the Allegheny River, the profusion of smoke-stacks that was Pittsburgh lay under a dim gray cloud.

Kate was quiet for some moments and then said, "You know, if you spent less time with your head in a newspaper, you'd find there's a lot to see right in front of your nose."

I stopped abruptly and put my hands on my hips. I knew where this was going. "I refuse to discuss Frederick Gillespie."

Kate laughed and picked up Beatrice, bouncing her on her hip. "Now just look how cross your Aunt Elizabeth is. Goodness, her face is going to get stuck that way if she keeps frowning at us like that."

"I mean it," I said. "I don't want to talk about him. I'm not interested and that's final."

Kate laid Beatrice down in the pram again and tucked the blanket around her little chin. "He's a very nice man. You'd see it if you gave him a chance."

"A page right out of Mama's book."

Kate sighed. "Well, perhaps I shouldn't blame you. You've never been in love. You can't possibly know how wonderful it is."

I stiffened and looked away, but Kate was on me in an instant, laying a hand on my arm. "Elizabeth?" She brought both hands to her cheeks and looked at me in astonishment. "You *are* in love. I might have known. Who is it? Tell me."

I made no reply. I couldn't look at her. The thing to do was deny it, but I found myself unable to speak, and even if I could have, what was there to say? *It turns out I'm very much in love, but he's married, you see. Oh yes, there is someone, but it's never going to be.*

"Someone from the paper? It must be. It's the only place you go."

I looked down at my gloves, blinking back tears. I needed very much to stop this conversation. In the end, I decided it was best to be honest—at least as honest as I was willing to be.

"Yes, someone from the paper. I will tell you in time, when I am ready. But not now."

"Very well," Kate said, taking a step back. Her eyes were full of sympathy. "I won't breathe word to Mama."

We walked on for some moments in companionable silence. Presently, we arrived at the fountain on the southwest corner of the commons. It had been closed for the winter, its basin dry and ugly without the sparkle of water to give it life. I sat down on the perimeter. "Kate, I need an idea for a story."

My sister's eyebrows rose. "You're asking me?"

"Yes, you. Why not?"

Kate shrugged. "I thought you found me dull. And you know I don't have a mind for such things."

"Nonsense." In truth, I was in a fix. I was still writing vignettes that were, I knew, falling pathetically short of the meaty content Madden was looking for. The court case against Jackson and my feelings for McCain had sapped my energy. That, and Madden's scathing words had rid me of whatever confidence I might have believed that I had. What was the word he'd used? *Grit*. The two columns that had run since my original one had featured my byline in larger type and prominent subheads summarizing the content—devices to draw readers in—yet Madden had cut considerable portions of my copy. The last entry, dropped two days ago, was a quarter the length of what it should have been. He was setting me up for success by attention-grabbing features, but I wasn't delivering the copy that deserved it. I was treading on dangerous ground. "The well is dry, Kate." If I hadn't felt so blue, I'd have laughed at the irony of my perch on the fountain.

"It can't be. You've been there less than a year, and, well, you're *you*."

"What's that supposed to mean?"

"You're a force of nature. When you've got a mind to do something, there's no stopping you."

She'd meant it as a compliment, but her words only made me feel like an imposter. "I know you think me strong, but trust me, I don't feel strong right now."

Kate sat down beside me, her shoulder touching mine. For a minute, we were back in Apollo on the creek bank, dipping our feet into the water. "I'll help you if I can, you know that."

"Good." I turned to her. "You've read my pieces. What would you like to read more about? What would interest you?"

She thought for a moment, her eyes distant as she gazed ahead. Then she turned to me and said, "I should like to know where a girl like me can go for diversion. I don't mean the theater or a restaurant. I can't afford those things. I mean a place where a married woman can feel comfortable without her husband, someplace fun. A place with other women."

It was a sound suggestion, and the seed of an idea began to take shape. I had no idea then, of course, that it would cause the path of my career to go from bad to worse.

⁂

As I sat drying my hair by the stove two weeks later, I couldn't help but think that my luck had turned. I'd taken Kate's idea and run with it. My crying fit in front of the Young Men's Christian Association had turned out to be a blessing in disguise. I'd arrived at the building the day after our walk in the park and inquired about a tour. My request prompted an arched brow from the manager being that I was a woman, but when I told the manager I was a member of the press, he'd been all too pleased to give me a tour of the facility, and what a facility it was.

The piece I scurried home to write that evening applauded the new YMCA and its considerable amenities—a two-story gymnasium; reception and reading rooms; an auditorium for 250 members; a parlor with a piano; a game room; classrooms; a bowling alley; and bathrooms with hot and cold showers, sponge baths, and dressing boxes. The manager had proudly informed me the building cost a pretty sum—one hundred thousand dollars—paid for in contributions ranging from one to thirty thousand dollars by enthusiastic Pittsburgh citizens.

But where, I asked my readers, was such an organization for females? Did they not deserve the same? Was there no place women, young and old alike, could go to enjoy life's pleasures—to exercise, read, or learn as they wished? To my delight, readers responded immediately, agreeing wholeheartedly that the women of the city merited a structure just as grand. Perhaps best of all, Madden was pleased. Though to my consternation, he'd been his typical ill-humored self when he'd stuffed a note in my box that read only *It's about time.*

I was vigorously rubbing a towel over my head when Mama walked into the kitchen. "Mr. Gillespie asked me to give this to you." She handed over a copy of the *Dispatch.* "This morning's edition."

"He needn't have done that," I said irritably.

"I told him the same," Mama replied with a sniff. She hadn't mentioned Mr. Gillespie in weeks. I only hoped it was because she realized at last that her matchmaking efforts were a lost cause, and not because Kate had spilled the beans about the mysterious man at the paper. I didn't think so; Mama would have been too overcome with curiosity to contain herself. No, if she was quiet on the matter, it was because she thought me too stubborn for my own good.

"Thank you, Mama."

I laid the paper on the kitchen table and began to read. When my eye fell some moments later on Bessie Bramble's column, I was surprised to see that she, too, had written about the YMCA. But my chest filled with dread as I read further. It was no coincidence she'd written of the organization. It was a rebuttal of my own piece:

> That they have no elegant building like the YMCA is from
> the lack of means, not of will and deed. Women in general
> have no money to speak of. It is doled out to them for family
> use, but they have little or none to bestow as they please on

other purposes. Still, the Women's Christian Association of Pittsburg is a large institution and its members have a home of their own, though a modest one, on Penn Avenue.

I looked up from the paper. Penn Avenue. The same street the men's facility was located on. I read on:

> And they have besides established homes in both Pittsburg and Allegheny to aid destitute women and to hold out help to friendless girls and orphan children. That they are so quiet and silent about their good works, that Sister Bly did not know such an association was in existence, shows how well they have been taught the silence and submission theory, so long held and enforced by the church.

Hot anger began to build in my chest, and I let out an angry bellow. Mama and Kate came running.

"What is it, Pinkey?" Mama cried.

"Bessie Bramble," I said, rising to my feet and indicating the paper. "She's . . . she's refuted my column."

Kate frowned. "You mean the piece about the Young Men's—"

"Yes, that one!" I ran my hands through my hair and began to pace. *Sister Bly. How insufferable.* I was nothing of the sort to her.

"Calm down, I'm sure there's a reasonable explanation." Mama picked up the paper and read, Kate peeking over her shoulder. "Oh dear," Mama muttered. "Were you unaware the women had their own organization?"

"Of course," I snapped.

"Oh dear," Mama said again.

"Why would your editor, what's his name, Malden—" Kate began.

"Madden."

"Why would he print this? Why would he allow Ms. Bramble to humiliate you like this?"

"Because she's Bessie Bramble."

Kate's brows knit together in anger. "That's hardly fair."

Mama looked perplexed. "Well, I'd like to know, if the women have a corresponding organization here, why Madden printed your piece in the first place. He might've told you."

"Because, like me, he didn't know."

"Which begs the question, once more, why print Ms. Bramble's piece?" Mama said. "It doesn't make you look good, but it doesn't make Madden, nor, by extension, the *Dispatch,* look good either."

I gave a bitter laugh. "Not necessarily. Madden likes to stir things up." Perhaps feuding columnists was exactly what the managing editor was after.

"Well, then, that must give you some relief."

I stared at Mama. "You're missing the point. *Bessie* is missing the point." I ran a hand through my hair again as I continued to pace. "All the interviews I've done with girls in the city—the factory workers, the ones who can't find work—none of them mentioned the YWCA. They don't know it exists. Not a single woman who wrote to me after reading my article mentioned it either."

"You must tell Madden," Kate said. "He'll understand."

"It's Bessie who needs to understand," I said. All of a sudden, I knew what I had to do.

"Oh, Pinkey." Mama looked aghast. "I hope that doesn't mean—"

I stopped pacing and beamed at her. "It does. I'm going to write my own rebuttal."

⁂

"Miss Bly! Oh, Miss Bly!"

I paused at the entrance to the *Dispatch*. A ginger-haired boy was running toward me, clutching a stack of newspapers to his chest.

"Hello, Timmy," I said with a smile. "How are you today? Selling any papers?"

"'Course! I'm the best seller on Fifth Avenue."

"And modest too." I ruffled his curls, a gesture I'd seen McCain do that first morning I'd met the tall, handsome stranger who'd swept me off my feet. I smiled inwardly at the double entendre and felt the pain that always followed such memories. It was impossible to go a single day without thinking of him.

"Mr. Wilson told me to tell you you're to meet him in the St. Paul's churchyard down the street."

"Oh?" I frowned. QO and I had never met outside the office. "Did he say why?"

"No, only that if I seen you, I was to save you the trip of going up and finding a note in your mail slot saying to meet him there."

"I see." I rummaged in my reticule and pulled out three pennies, two for the paper, one for my friend. "I'll trade you. How's that?"

We made the exchange and said good-bye. I wondered why QO had asked me to meet him at the church. Though it was reasonably warm, the sky was overcast, and the lack of wind meant the smoke from the refineries hung in the air like a dismal gray curtain.

Some minutes later, the wrought iron gate creaked on its hinges as I entered the churchyard. I wended my way through the tombstones and spotted QO on a bench under a tree. An older man with white whiskers was seated next to him.

"Thank you, Mr. Wilson," the man was saying as I neared. He took a few dollars from QO's hand and swiftly put them in his pocket, looking sheepish.

At the sight of me, they both stood. "Ah, Nellie. You got my note. How nice to see you," QO said.

The whiskered man did not meet my eyes or introduce himself. He simply nodded his head in acknowledgment and hurried away.

"Why does he look so familiar?" I said, staring after him. "I know I've seen him somewhere before."

"He was the receptionist at the *Dispatch* until a few months ago."

"Oh, that's right," I said. "The drinker. No one ever knew if he was going to show up or not. I didn't know the two of you were friends."

QO gestured to the bench, and we took our seats. "Not friends, exactly. Just acquaintances. Madden had to fire him. He was too unreliable. Now he's out of work and having a hard time of it."

"And still drinking."

"Yes."

"And you're giving him money?"

"He needs to eat, Nellie."

"You're too kind, QO."

"Is such a thing possible, to be too kind?" He turned to me, his features softening for a moment, and then looked away. "His wife is ill and can't find work herself. It's the least I can do."

"I once knew a man who drank and hit his wife." I rubbed absently at the scar on my upper arm. "He tried to shoot her with a gun but, thankfully, missed. It was awful."

"Not all drunks are mean and spiteful. Noah Gregson is a kind, gentle man."

I had never considered a drunk might be so. I had only ever known the viciousness of Jack Ford. How judgmental I was, how naive. Perhaps, like Kate said, I needed to let go, to stop clinging to memories of the wrongs that had been done me, and embrace the future.

QO removed a small brown paper bag from his coat pocket, placed his elbows on his knees, and tossed some corn down on the grass. Almost at once pigeons appeared and began to peck at the earth. Another came, then another, swooping down from the gothic arches of the church.

"Do you come here often?" I asked.

"From time to time. It's quiet here among the pigeons."

I'd never seen QO look so serious. He was the affable, gray-haired gentleman in shirtsleeves with a pencil tucked behind his ear who searched in vain for some item or other among the clutter around his desk, the cheerful man who churned out weekly content and chuckled at my jokes with equal measure. In a somber church-yard, wearing a hat and coat and a solemn expression I'd never seen before, he was a different man. He was QO and not QO, and it unsettled me.

"I thought we could talk out of the office today," he said.

"And here I thought you never left your desk."

My lighthearted attempt to make him smile fell flat. "I won't beat about the bush, Nellie. Maddie is pulling your column."

I felt the blood drain from my face. "What? And he was too cowardly to tell me himself?"

"Not at all. I asked him if I could do it."

"To spare me? I'm a grown woman, QO."

QO turned to me, his expression pained. "You've become like a daughter to me, Nellie. I wanted to tell you because I knew—because you and I both know—Madden wouldn't have been kind about it."

I couldn't disagree. "It's because of the YMCA piece, isn't it?"

QO flung more corn to the ground. For a few moments, there was only the sound of the pigeons cooing and pecking at the grass.

"He felt your pieces before it ran weren't up to snuff, and your YMCA reply to Bessie, well, it didn't go as expected."

In my written response to Bessie Bramble, I'd respectfully pointed out that, if Pittsburgh had services for women, why wasn't it common knowledge? I'd gone on to assert that if there were quiet, humble women going about their works, what good was it if women in need didn't know they existed? Madden had printed my write-up in its entirety, and I had felt, naively it now turned out, it was the end of the matter. McCain, however, must have sensed the risk. The day after my piece ran, he'd sent a card: oleander. *Beware.*

"It's Bessie, isn't it? She can't have anyone besting her, espe-cially someone new and inexperienced like me."

"You must understand, Bessie has been doing this a long time. She's well respected, not to mention well known. She brings in quite a lot of readers for the *Dispatch*. Madden doesn't want her going to the competition."

I stared at him. "She threatened to leave?"

"I rather think it was enough just letting Madden know she was unhappy with your response."

"And so it was about keeping her on, about the circulation."

QO gave a bitter laugh. "My dear girl, it's always about the circulation."

I felt the sting of tears. "Madden liked my YMCA stories, QO. I *know* he did."

"Yes, but he likes Bessie on staff too."

Bessie Bramble. Oh, how the name made me burn. *Never, ever apologize for your opinions in print,* she'd told me. *You must always appear the authority.* She'd been so worried I'd betray her by unmasking her identity. In the end, she'd betrayed me.

"Come now," QO said, "don't look so distraught. Madden's not letting you go."

QO fumbled for a handkerchief in his pocket, the sudden movement unsettling the pigeons. I took the proffered linen and wiped my eyes, feeling foolish for crying in front of him. When I had composed myself, I sniffed and said, "He's putting me back on fashion, isn't he?"

"I'm afraid so."

I burst into tears again, overcome with the unfairness of it all.

"Now, now, my dear girl," QO said, pulling me to him. "You have a good cry on my shoulder. Let it all out. I've got all the time in the world. When you're done, we'll go back to the *Dispatch* together, and you'll show Madden just what a girl with mettle looks like."

21

s the days passed Miss Tillie Maynard's condition grew worse.

NELLIE BLY

BLACKWELL'S ASYLUM, SEPTEMBER 1887

"What will happen to Mrs. Cotter, I wonder," Katie said. "She'll be in no condition to leave now, poor woman."

That I found myself sitting at breakfast the morning after witnessing Mrs. Cotter's torture was a shock to no one more than me. After seeing the brutal mistreatment of another inmate, it was unimaginable that I had escaped the clutches of the nurses. After the dark horrors of the Lodge, the dining hall was a welcome sight. Even the food seemed less repulsive.

It was only after Mrs. Cotter had fallen to her knees that the nurses had stopped dunking her. Grady and Grupe had whisked the pillowcase off her head, dragged her to the wall, and chained her there. Mrs. Cotter was by then only half-conscious, shaking and mumbling nonsense. For hours I listened as she murmured again and again for her husband. I called out to her several times to let her know that I was there. She never responded and fell at last into a torturous slumber. I called out to the woman I believed was Old Bess too. Whether the woman was herself sleeping, drugged unconscious, or afraid to answer, I didn't know. I'd eventually given up. By then night had fallen, for there was no more light coming in through the slats at the windows. I'd slept not a wink. How could I, with so many women miserable around me, the only sign that they were alive the clinking of the chains when they moved?

I'd had no choice but to leave them when Grady—begrudgingly, and using a stream of expletives—unchained me and marched me back to the main building in the dark. Snatching my neck from behind and giving me a shove as we crossed the threshold into the west wing, she'd said, "Like I said, your time is coming, bitch." She'd shoved me into my cell—for that was what it had become for me—and locked it, the light of her lantern growing fainter through the gap under the door until I saw it no more.

"I've heard rumors of the chained women," Molly whispered, bringing me from my thoughts. "Now I know they're true. I can't imagine any of them surviving, living like that."

"That's no living." We all turned to Mrs. Fox. The little Italian woman so rarely spoke that her words took us by surprise. "Chained like that, with no hope, it's a way to die, no live."

"How is it Mrs. Cotter is still in the Lodge and you're here, with not a bruise on you?" Tillie asked.

There was no mistaking the accusation in her tone. My ribs were, in fact, bruised, and my neck burned where Grady had choked me.

"Nurse Grady is biding her time," Molly said, fixing me with a knowing look.

Anne put down her bread and looked from me to Molly. "What do you mean?"

Nurse McCarten approached. We stopped talking, picking at our food until she had passed.

"It means," Molly said, leaning in after she'd moved away, "the she-devil is waiting to see if anyone claims Nellie. If nobody does, she'll beat the daylights out of her."

I shuddered. *Two more days.*

"If Grady lays a finger on her now," Molly continued, "she'll have hell to pay if a loved one shows up and finds out what goes on inside this hellish place. No one's likely to come for us and so the nurses can do what they want, but Nellie's different."

Oh, if they only knew. Would they even talk to me if I were to confess that I'd been lying to them, that my rescue had been planned from the beginning?

"But someone was coming for Mrs. Cotter," Anne said. "Didn't the nurses take a risk, harming her as they did?"

It was bothering me too. Mr. Cotter would be upset, to say the least, to see his wife in such a condition. Perhaps they would refuse to let him see her. Make up some terrible story about Mrs. Cotter's mental condition taking a turn . . .

"I don't understand what's so special about Nellie," Tillie said with a sniff. She turned to me. "What about Old Bess and Mrs. O'Keefe? They're still at the Lodge, aren't they?"

"I'm not sure," I answered, "but I think one of the women in the room with the barrel might have been Old Bess," I said.

"And you didn't save her?" Tillie questioned incredulously, bright spots of color blooming on her cheeks.

"Tillie," Anne said, aghast, "what a thing to say. You know very well Nellie could have done no such thing."

Before Tillie could react, Anne sat up straight, her attention drawn to something behind us. We turned in unison. Louise was making her way to our table. The young girl had lost even more weight, her shoulders, hips, wrists, and legs all boney angles. In the days that had elapsed since we'd seen her, she'd become a mere ghost of herself. In any other place, the sight of her would've brought doctors running, but this was Blackwell's. That she was considered robust enough to be released from the infirmary most likely meant nothing more than that she was able to walk without aid.

"I'm glad you're back," Anne said after Louise sat down. "I'd wondered if we would ever see you again. I hope the nurses weren't too awful."

Louise's only response was to stare down at the table. I doubted anything would be forthcoming. Whatever evil Louise had endured inside the Retreat wasn't likely anything she would want to share.

Just then, a woman sitting at the table next to ours leaned over and handed a piece of bread to me. "From Matilda, over yonder."

Three tables away, the wild-haired, toothless Matilda nodded to me, making hand motions to eat the gift she'd so generously given. I nodded acknowledgment, feeling wholly undeserving.

"A thank-you for helping her," Anne said.

"Or perhaps for Mrs. Cotter," Katie said. "All o' us were talkin' about ye bravery after we came in from the yard."

A nurse made the rounds again, pausing for so long near our table that I wondered if she would ever leave. When she had gone at least, Anne filled in a confused Louise. "Nellie came to Mrs. Cotter's rescue in the yard yesterday, or tried to, when she stepped out of line."

"It was nothing," I mumbled.

"That's not the way we see it," Katie said. "Ye got yourself sent to the Lodge on account o' stickin' up for Mrs. Cotter. That takes guts. There were whispers in the dormitory last night, Nell, after we'd all gone to bed. The women here think you're a hero."

"That's nonsense." *A hero would not have left Mrs. Cotter or Old Bess in the Lodge. A hero wouldn't be lying to you now.*

Two prunes appeared on the plate in front of me, passed hand to hand along the tables. "They disagree," Anne said, indicating the women in the room. "Food is precious here, like gold, and they're giving you theirs."

I had noticed this morning as we waited in the corridor outside the dining hall that many of the inmates had nodded to me. One woman had offered me a place on her bench this morning. It had all made me feel very uncomfortable.

"Mrs. Cotter's not in the Lodge." Louise had spoken so low, we almost didn't catch it.

I put down my tea. "What did you say?"

Without lifting her eyes, Louise spoke again. "She was brought to the infirmary early this morning."

"It's her own fault for being there," Tillie piped up. "You can't blame Nurse Grady for acting yesterday. Mrs. Cotter broke the rules." For a moment we all sat frozen, wondering what had gotten into Tillie. She was huddled into herself, but for once she wasn't shaking. Her eyes, glassy and enormous, roamed but never seemed to rest anywhere, and her hands kept smoothing the unruly tufts of hair that stuck out on her head. "It's just like with Mrs. Turney," she continued. "It was rude of her to throw her tea at Nurse Grupe. Where were her manners? If you ask me, she got what was due her."

"Well, aren't ye a prickly thing," Katie shot back. "One minute you're jumpin' on Nell for not savin' Old Bess, and the next you're sayin' Mrs. Turney got what she deserved."

Nurse McCarten was looking in our direction.

"The superintendent was in the infirmary this morning after Mrs. Cotter came in," Louise said, still speaking to the table. "He was angry. He said . . . he said something about getting Mrs. Cotter's health restored or the nurses were going to pay, and he was very cross with them for taking Nellie to the Lodge too."

Anne looked confused. "He's angry with the nurses?"

So they weren't going to turn Mr. Cotter away at the door and invent a story about his wife's decline; Dent planned to get her well. But he was worried. He couldn't bank on Mrs. Cotter's recovery, and he had Grady and Grupe to blame for the potential risk that posed.

Nurse McCarten lumbered up to the table. "I've seen you all blathering and I've had enough. Nellie, Tillie, you can stay after and scrub. You can work your asses for once instead of your damn mouths." She stomped off.

Around us, the inmates were leaving the tables. As I watched them go, I wondered about Grady and Grupe. It had been unwise to attack Mrs. Cotter when they had, and now Dent was furious. I couldn't help but think the nurses were becoming even more unhinged.

"You look a little better today, Tillie."

"Do I?"

As the last inmate left the dining hall, McCarten had handed us buckets, brushes, and a harsh stream of insults about what would happen if we did a poor job. She'd then plunked down on a stool to keep watch from the door, so I'd beckoned Tillie to start with me in the far corner, away from McCarten's prying eyes and ears.

"Your complexion is much improved," I told her. "Your eyes are brighter than I've seen them."

Those cornflower blue eyes, huge in her tiny face, regarded me. "They say you had a visitor yesterday."

"Yes."

"A reporter?"

"A young man in search of his sweetheart."

"What did he look like?"

A pang of longing bloomed in my chest. "He was very tall. Thirty perhaps." *Handsome and married and someone who will never be mine.* I dipped my brush in the water and winced. Even the slightest motion made my side throb where Grady had kicked me.

"Did he give his name?"

"There wasn't any need, Tillie. He didn't know me, nor I him." I began to scrub, making slow circles to minimize the pain radiating from my rib cage.

"I find it odd there are so many who come to see you."

The stench of lye burned my nostrils. "It's the papers. People are curious to see if I'm their long-lost relative they've been searching for." My arm was beginning to ache. The slightest activity wore me out these days. I had no stamina.

"Did your visitor ask for me?"

I stopped scrubbing. Tillie hadn't touched her brush. I was struck again how young she looked, how very much her chopped hair made her look like a boy. "Tillie, you must work or Nurse McCarten will complain." I plunged Tillie's brush into her bucket, pulled it out, and handed it to her. "To answer your question, no, he didn't ask for you. Why should he?"

Tillie set the brush down and wiped her hands on her dress. "My friends should have come to look for me by now. I'm certain of it. I think you pretend to be me so that you can see them."

I stared at her. "I don't know what you mean."

"Don't you?" Tillie sat back and put her hands on her hips. Voice raised, she said, "You pretend to care about us: Anne, Mrs. Shanz, me. You don't really care at all, do you? I think you pretend to be me so you can go home when my friends come to release me."

McCarten was frowning in our direction. "Lower your voice, Tillie," I whispered.

"Why should I?"

"You must know that I'm your friend. I would never do such a thing."

"I don't think you were really trying to help Matilda or Mrs. Cotter. I think you just want attention."

I noticed again her fine coloring, the sparkle in her eyes. How foolish I had been. Tillie wasn't improving; she was suffering from some nervous weakness, or—"Tillie, are the nurses giving you anything at night? By mouth or by needle?"

"That's none of your business."

"You must refuse it. You must spit it out when they leave you. Promise." Thankfully, no one had come to my room the night before with a hypodermic needle or otherwise. Perhaps the nurses thought watching the horrors unfold at the Lodge was punishment enough.

"She hates you, you know."

"Who?"

Footsteps approached. I bent my head and started scrubbing again.

"Nurse Grady," Tillie replied. "And so do I. She asks all kinds of questions about you, you know. The medicine they give me will make me well, she says. I—"

"Tillie—" I began, and then Nurse McCarten's boots appeared next to my brush. I looked up.

"Do you want to go back to the Lodge? I can arrange it." She shot a look at Tillie. "You too. There's plenty of room there for the two of you."

Tillie only glared at me, unmoved by the warning, unfocused on anything, it appeared, but my presumed betrayal. I couldn't bear it if anything happened to her. I had to protect her. She wasn't well. My presence here was a lie, and I owed it to her. I owed it to all of them. "I'll work over there." I pointed across the room.

"Get on with it, then," Nurse McCarten grumbled, lumbering away.

I carried my bucket to the other side of the room. It was the only thing I could think of to prevent Tillie from unraveling further.

22

I was too impatient to work along at the usual duties assigned women on newspapers.

NELLIE BLY

PITTSBURGH, JANUARY 1886

"What's this?" Madden picked up the sheets I'd slid across the desk to him and rifled through them. I didn't owe him a story, so he was immediately suspicious. For once, there was no lit cigar in the immediate vicinity of his mouth, and I could breathe. He raised his eyebrows at the headline then flicked his eyes back to me.

In the months following the death of my column, I had covered everything Madden had assigned me: the description of the art of tree graphs from the city's garden nurseries, the account of a local minister's collection of fifty thousand butterflies, and—worst of all—the latest in ladies' hair care. I'd accepted all his assignments without the slightest quibble. QO had been astonished, regarding me warily each time Madden handed me another tedious theme. More than once he'd asked me if I was feeling well.

The columnist popped his head through the door. "I understand I'm wanted here."

Madden frowned. "No, I—"

"Actually, that was my doing," I said. "I put a note on Mr. Wilson's desk and asked him to step in." QO's eyes looked a question, but

I only indicated the empty chair beside me. "I've just handed Mr. Madden a story I wrote up on the self-sacrificing Christian ladies of Pittsburgh. I thought a piece on the silent women who go nobly about helping others, such as the ones Sister Bramble mentioned in her reply to me, would be a good way to put right any antipathy I have caused between us."

Stuff and nonsense. Bessie's arrogant retaliation in print and Madden's subsequent pulling of my column as a conciliatory gesture to the sainted female journalist still rankled. My expression, however, was all doe-eyed humility. Madden nodded sagely, looking for all the world as if I'd finally had my comeuppance. QO, who knew how angry I remained over the incident, wasn't fooled, but I knew he would say nothing. I had deliberately planned this meeting as a surprise, and until he figured out what I was up to, he would be on my side. I only hoped after he learned what I was about that he would continue to support me.

"You don't have to run it, of course." I looked down at my hands. "But perhaps you could let Ms. Bramble have a look. I should like her to know how very sorry I am." It was a wonder I didn't choke on my own words.

"So you've written this by way of an apology, eh?" Madden said. He blew a stream of air from his mouth. "I'm sure Bessie will be quite pleased to see you've learned something from your little public shouting match."

That he had allowed my "little public shouting match" to run was apparently not the point, not when Bessie's ego was on the line. Assigning me tame, dull stories was his peace offering to Bessie. What better way to make certain she wouldn't go to another paper? That I had become the scapegoat to appease her bothered Madden not in the slightest. Since the YMCA debacle, I'd only seen her once in the office. I had quickly walked in the other direction. Best to keep a wide girth. Thank heaven Madden hadn't gone so far as to insist I make a personal apology to her. There was only so much playacting I could do.

I cleared my throat. "As you know, I've been occupied with the stories you've asked me to report on a good many weeks. I have also been working with the entertainment committee on hosting the Mexican delegation in town."

"And what a good job you've done of it, Nellie," QO said. Behind his spectacles, his eyes were full of questions. He really had no idea where I was taking this, but how could he? I had only hatched my plan this morning.

Madden grunted, thumbed open a drawer, and withdrew a

cigar. With a pair of scissors, he trimmed off one end. He had assigned me to the committee, though I suspected it had little to do with goodwill and more to do with his feeling that if he kept me occupied elsewhere, I'd be less inclined to get tangled up with Bessie again.

"It's the delegation that I'd like to talk about," I said. "You see, a few of the delegates have been kind enough to invite me to their country, and I can't think of a better way to serve the *Dispatch* than as a correspondent."

"Wait right there," Madden said, holding up his palms, the cigar balanced between two meaty fingers. "Nobody's going anywhere."

QO shook his head and looked pensive. "My dear girl, Mexico is no place for—"

"Wait, Erasmus," Madden cut in. "You'll have your say." He turned his attention to me. "Just because some delegates are here and being entertained by some lofty citizens and a few of my reporters doesn't mean you should go traipsing off with big ideas about—"

"I wouldn't be traipsing," I said. "I would be covering Mexico on behalf of the *Dispatch,* with your blessing, of course."

"And what makes you think you, a little slip of a thing, could handle that?"

"I'm twenty-one now, Mr. Madden. With a large following of women of various ages who would like to see me cover more than butterfly collections."

"Ah," Madden said. He struck a match and held the cigar above the flame, rotating it until a ring glowed around its tip. "Now we come to it."

QO shifted in his chair. "If I may, George?"

Madden didn't answer right away. Instead, he blew on the embers at the end of the cigar until ash formed. Only then did he take a puff, blowing out the smoke like a fire-breathing, bowler hat–wearing dragon with a pot belly. I resisted the urge to blow it back at him.

"Go ahead, Erasmus."

"Nellie, Mexico isn't like the United States. It is a wild, exotic place. A young woman alone there would be quite unsafe. It just isn't done."

I'd known he would raise this objection. I'd said not a word to Mama about Mexico, much less her accompanying me there, but I couldn't think of that now. I needed to get Madden's permission, and if I had to tell a little white lie to get it, so be it. It was for the sake of my career, after all. Who could argue with that? "That's why my mother has agreed to join me." Two pairs of eyebrows shot up in unison. "Yes, she . . . thinks it a wonderful idea."

QO looked flummoxed. "Your mother has agreed?"

"Oh, yes," I said, nodding. "She and I both think there is no end to the stories I could investigate. Pittsburgh readers would be most entertained."

"Even so, it's too dangerous," QO said.

Curiosity glittered in Madden's eyes. "Why Mexico, Miss Cochrane? Why now?"

"The delegates have been telling me wonderful things about their country, and it seems to me more people would benefit by learning more about it. We share a common border, after all. As to why," I shrugged, "no one else is doing it."

"Because I haven't told anyone to," Madden said, his mouth turning down into a frown. He puffed some more, the cigar's end glowing. He was sinking quickly into one of his morose moods. If I let that happen, all would be lost.

"Well, you don't have to tell me, Mr. Madden. I'm willing to go. Many of the reporters here have other obligations. I can understand if they might give pause to such an idea. They have their families to consider. I have no such impediment."

"You still haven't told me why you're the one to do this," Madden said, laying his cigar into the ashtray at last and crossing his arms in his chair.

"Because I'm the one who wants to go," I said. "And I'll be the first at *any* of the city papers to do it. That must count for something."

"You are very young, Nellie," QO said. He looked at Madden for support, but the managing editor's eyes were glazed over, a sure sign his gears were turning.

"I'm not asking for a column, Mr. Madden," I said. "Just give me six months, that's all. If you don't like what I write, you don't have to print it."

"I never print what I don't like, Miss Cochrane," Madden said, picking up his cigar and taking a long draw. "You can be sure of that."

"What if I were to ask my readers what they think?" I pressed. "If there isn't much interest, I'll drop the whole thing. I won't bring it up again."

After a short silence, QO leaned forward. "George, you're not seriously considering this, are you?"

Madden sat back in his chair, his cigar dangling precariously from his lips. "I don't see that it hurts to find out what interest she can drum up, Erasmus. This may not be such a bad idea after all. She's right. No one else is doing it. It might very well be a feather in our cap." He turned to me, his eyes narrowing. "See what readers say. Perhaps, if the response is positive enough, I may be persuaded. *May*, mind. That's not a yes."

I stood abruptly. Better to leave the office before Madden could change his mind.

"Before you go," Madden said, "don't think I don't know for a minute why you wrote this." He picked up the pages of my story. "I'm not that stupid."

≈≈≈

Not only did my readers fully support my six-month adventure in Mexico but they sent along story ideas I should investigate while there. Could I write about the bullfights? What was the food like? Was it true the women and children rarely wore shoes? I collected the letters and put them in neat piles on Madden's desk. They didn't remain there long: he promptly moved them over to QO's office, where they came to rest in leaning piles on the floor, but it didn't matter. It was plain the city—at least the women who read my pieces—were behind me. Even the Pennsylvania Railway offered to cover the cost of our tickets through to St. Louis.

"I don't like this one bit," QO said. He stood and came around his desk, grasping my elbows and looking intently at me. "You naughty little kid. You knew very well I'd never agree to go to Madden on your behalf about Mexico."

"Can you forgive me?" I gave him a pained smile. "I've got to get out from under this Bessie Bramble thing. I can write stories that *matter* in Mexico, QO. If I stay here and keep writing what Madden's been giving me, I'll wither away and die."

He pursed his lips. "I doubt it would be that bad." Despite his attempt to smile, he didn't look pleased. He hugged me to him for a brief instant and then pulled away, holding me at arm's length. "Remember what I said, what you promised me now."

"I'll be very careful."

"And?"

"I'm to meet up with Mr. Gestefeld and his wife as soon as we reach Mexico City. He's expecting me." Gestefeld ran a paper in Mexico City, and as he was an old friend of QO's, QO had tasked him with looking after me.

"Thank heavens he's there to keep you out of trouble." The amusement in his tone didn't match his eyes.

"I'll be fine. Now what did you promise me?"

"I will forward all your mail to you on a weekly basis. You have my word."

I paused at the door and looked back. "I'll miss you, QO."

He nodded once, his eyes a little misty, and then waved me away, taking a seat at his desk once more.

A few minutes later, I paused in front of the mail slots. Looking up and down the hallway to make sure no one was around, I pulled a small envelope from my reticule. The message inside was brief:

> Allegheny Commons 5 o'clock this evening. Southwest fountain.
>
> —E

The memory of George McCain swam before me. In his white summer suit at Schenley, birdsong around us on a hot summer's day. *We are dyad,* he had said. *I can bear living without you as long as I know where you are, what you are doing. You mustn't shut me out.* And I wasn't. I would meet him one last time before I left for Mexico. I owed him that. There had been no time to speak to him of Mexico in the two weeks that had passed since the meeting in Madden's office. At best, I'd glimpsed him in the hallways, but he had never been alone. I placed the envelope in his slot and was just going when I remembered something else he had said that day. *I won't ask you to meet me in clandestine places. It would cheapen what little we have.*

I couldn't do it. I couldn't ask him to meet me. It wasn't right. And anyway, I would be back in six months' time. He would understand. I knew he would. I wasn't leaving the city and going somewhere else, as he had feared. I was just going away for a while.

It would do. It would have to do.

MEXICO CITY, MEXICO, FEBRUARY TO MARCH 1886

"Thirty minutes to dress for breakfast!"

I heard the warning repeated next door as the porter made his way down the moving car. I attempted to sit up and then remembered I was packed like a tinned sardine inside my narrow berth. I swung my feet over the side of the bed, came to a sitting position as best I could, straightened my legs, and elicited a monstrous yawn. Mama was seated in her dress and coat on a chair before the window, an expanse of flat, dry land flying by outside. Blue smudges of fatigue lay beneath her eyes. "I didn't sleep at all well," she sniffed. "You, on the other hand, slept like a babe."

I jumped down and grabbed my skirts and petticoats from the empty seat facing Mama. I yawned again and began to dress. We had traveled three days on a series of trains from Pittsburgh to Texas and had arrived in El Paso two days before in the dead of night fatigued, out of sorts, and looking for lodging. In the darkness, and led only by a man carrying a lantern, we managed to find a house for rent because the hotels had closed with the lateness of the hour.

Outside in the clear Mexican air as far as the eye could see, the land was a bare, flat wasteland. Only the cacti, which rose up at random in great clusters with exquisite yellow and red blooms, broke the monotony.

Since crossing the border, we had stopped at several stations, alighting each time to take in the sights. Hucksters sold their wares and beggars awaited us at every stop. The former offered up flowers, avocados, goat's milk, and strange fruit in paper-like husks called *tomatillos*. Women and children offered only their empty palms and were silent. In the poorer towns, the Indians were barefoot. Along the gutters by the railroad, women washed clothes and bathed their children. Many of the homes were tiny structures with simple straw roofs. Everywhere the air carried the scent of cook fires and dry earth. I'd viewed it all with hungry eyes, eager to return to the car each time so I could jot details in my notebook to write of later.

I sat down in the chair and began to button my boots, pausing when I saw Mama dabbing her eyes with a handkerchief. I reached over and patted her arm. "It's only a few months, Mama. It will go fast, you'll see."

"And then?" Mama said, sniffing once more. She turned from the window. "If Mr. Madden doesn't take you back?"

I leaned back against the seat and sighed. "Why shouldn't he? I left on good terms. I'm a foreign correspondent now."

"I think if you had just apologized to Bessie Bramble, none of this would have happened," Mama said, turning to the window again.

"I did nothing to apologize for." Why must she be so stubborn? "We simply had a difference of opinion."

"Yes," Mama said simpering, "and because of that, here we are, bound for some godforsaken country we know little to nothing about." She gestured to the bald earth out the window. As if on cue, a lone buzzard circled in the near distance to mock the tragedy Mama believed our lives had become. "We don't even speak the language! Really, Pinkey, that Mr. Madden demanded you come here was quite rude, even if you did upset Ms. Bramble. Imagine sending a young woman to a foreign place, and for six months! What else could I do but come with you? Goodness, we shall be among the savages!"

"We must think of it as an adventure, Mama." I said. "My readers certainly are."

"Your readers did not have to spend four days cramped in one Pullman after another. I shall never get the kinks out of my legs."

"I think it a small price to pay. Once we arrive, we shall be very comfortable, you'll see. Besides, do you really think you're going to miss running a boardinghouse? I saw the toll it took on you."

Mama sniffed again and picked an imaginary piece of lint from her sleeve. "I admit, it was hard work. However, it remains to be seen if the 'adventure' you surely believe is before us will be as entertaining as you say. I rather think we shall be like fish out of water where we are going. Surely Mr. Madden could have assigned you stories in Pittsburgh that would have kept you well away from Ms. Bramble."

"They weren't stories that interested me, Mama. You know that."

"Beggars can't be choosers, Pinkey."

Oh, how I wanted to tell her I *had* chosen, because Mexico had been my idea. But that would have only made things worse. "It's better this way, Mama. As long as Bessie is angry and Madden wants to placate her, I'll be writing about skirt lengths and Hall's Vegetable Sicilian Hair Renewer until the cows come home. It's best to move on and hope things are better when we return. There's nothing for me in Pittsburgh."

Despite my words, a vision of George McCain swam before my eyes—dressed in a white summer suit, lifting me from the carriage, the sun glinting off his hair. How long ago that summer day seemed! I believed in the beginning that he would be fine with my six-month sojourn. As my departure day neared, however, I'd wondered if he would feel betrayed that I'd said not a word to him. He must have known of it. Once Madden had given me his blessing, it had been common knowledge. Why then hadn't McCain approached me? Probably for the same reason I hadn't approached him: there hadn't been a private opportunity. Now it was too late. In leaving, I had betrayed the one promise I'd made him: not to disappear from his life.

Tucked away in my satchel was my Bible. Inside were McCain's flower cards. Eight in all now. McCain's way of reaching out, of communicating. And now that I'd betrayed him and left without saying good-bye, I was sure I'd seen the last of him and his cards.

"—and what will that poor young man think with us off to Mexico and closing our boardinghouse?"

I blinked, catching only the tail end of Mama's words. For a moment, I thought she was referring to McCain. "Pardon?"

"Mr. Gillespie," Mama said. "He may very well find a sensible young woman while you're away."

"If I'm insensible, Mama, Mr. Gillespie is better off without me." The last meeting I'd had with Frederick Gillespie had been an embarrassing episode in which he'd professed his devotion and told me he would wait for me to return from Mexico. Unwilling to feed Mama's anger, I'd said not a word of it to her. I planned to write him as soon as we were in Mexico City and tell him he was wasting his time. Then, when he ceased correspondence, Mama would think he'd changed his mind.

"Don't look so smug, Pinkey," Mama said. "I know very well he told you he would wait for you."

"I don't *want* him to wait for me, Mama. I am not at all interested in him, or in getting married for that matter."

Mama scowled. "You will be one day and, as I don't see a line of suitors behind Mr. Gillespie, you would be wise to consider him."

"Because surely if no man wants me, I'm not worthy of anything, certainly not a career of my choosing."

This last seemed to lower the temperature in our compartment by several degrees, and neither of us said anything more.

☙

From atop his gelding, Joaquin Miller ran his hand down his long auburn beard and grinned. "Every day is Sunday in Mexico, yet no day is Sunday and Sunday is less a Sunday than any other day of the week."

Mama pulled on the reins of her prancing horse. The mare was growing agitated with the throng of tallyho coaches, dogcarts, English gigs, and carriages streaming by on the Paseo de la

Reforma. Perched on a sorrel mare and dressed in a fawn-colored riding habit and sombrero—both borrowed this morning from our landlady—I felt almost as Mexican as the ladies promenading down the *paseo*. The grand boulevard, built by Emperor Ferdinand Maximillian, was wide enough to drive four or even six teams abreast. On Sundays, it was packed with pleasure seekers who desired nothing more than to flaunt their conveyances, horses, and fine dress down the avenue on the most religious day of the week.

The past two months had passed quickly. Madden had printed my Christian ladies story a few weeks after I'd left for Mexico. Whether or not it had had any effect on how Bessie Bramble felt about me, or the kind of reception I'd get at the paper once I returned, I didn't know.

"Pittsburgh has no rival," I said.

Miller leaned his elbow on the pommel of the saddle as his horse shifted beneath him. Ever since Mama and I had been introduced at a dinner party at the end of January, Joaquin Miller had become our almost constant companion. If he was rough around the edges and rather blunt, it was a price well worth paying for being in the company of an entertaining, rather famous forty-eight-year-old poet from the American West. "My dear Nell, when will you cease comparing all things here to America?"

"Pittsburgh is the only comparison I have at my tender age," I said, shooting him a sidelong glance. "I'm not the seasoned frontier poet you are, but give me a few more decades and you'll see."

Miller broke out in a hearty laugh.

We swung our horses toward the gate of Chapultepec Park and passed below the arch. High on a hill above us, peaking above the trees, sat Chapultepec Castle, once home of the deceased Maximillian. Wagons loaded with supplies were snaking up the hill, and higher above, men gazed down from the castle walls.

"What's going on?" I asked.

"President Díaz is making renovations," Miller said. "The castle hasn't been occupied by a president since Maximillian's fall some twenty years ago, but Díaz is making it his now. I hear he's hired a New York firm to do the work and the Mexican people are footing the bill. Something in the neighborhood of one hundred and sixty-five thousand dollars."

"The more I hear about President Díaz, the less I like him," I said, wrinkling my nose. For a leader to fund his residence, built off the backs of Mexico's poor through excessive taxes, was unconscionable. "You must tell me more about him."

"Well, as a member of the press, you'll need to be careful about what you print about him and his regime."

"Oh, dear," Mama muttered.

How much better she looked. Whether or not Mama wanted to admit it, Mexico agreed with her. Now that she wasn't slaving away at boardinghouse work, she had put on some much-needed weight, and there was less strain around her eyes.

"But I'm not writing to a Mexican audience, Mr. Miller," I said. "My readers are in the States. Why would Díaz care a whit about what I'm writing?"

"Another day, little Nell," Miller said, chuckling. "It's Sunday, not a day to discuss politics." He swung his gaze to Mama. "Don't you agree, Mrs. Cochrane?"

"I do indeed, Mr. Miller."

He nudged his gelding, and we followed him through the grounds to the other side of the castle. Twenty minutes later, we entered what appeared to be another shaded park.

"El Panteón Civil de Dolores," Miller said. "The City of the Dead."

There were graves decorated with flowers, others with altars. Some had tiny summerhouses built over them. Most of the tombstones were coffin shaped, though in some areas, only white wooden crosses marked the graves. "For the poor," Miller explained. Oak, spruce, and apple trees dripping with Spanish moss dotted the landscape, interspersed with fountains and statues.

I had tried hard over the preceding months to put my mind from McCain, but here, in a place that reminded me so much of Allegheny Cemetery, I was suddenly overcome. I tethered my mare to a nearby tree and sat down on a bench. On the occasions I'd endeavored to write him, no words had come.

"What is it, Pinkey? Are you ill?"

I jumped. "Mama, you startled me."

"If you're ill, we must turn back."

"I'm sorry, I—" I broke off, my eyes filling with tears.

"What is it?"

"Nothing. I just find cemeteries . . ." My voice trailed off. I didn't want her to see me crying, for I could never explain my tears.

"You look like you've seen a ghost. Tell me what's upsetting you, my dear." The blue eyes beneath the brim of her hat—she refused to wear a sombrero because she thought them hideous on a woman—were watchful.

I sat up straight and took a deep breath. "It's nothing. I'm fine now."

Once, when I was putting McCain's cards back in my Bible in our shared bedroom back in Pittsburgh, Mama had come in. I was certain she'd seen them, but she'd said nothing. I hoped she never would. I didn't want to lie to her, but I would do so to keep George McCain a secret.

I put down my pencil. It was past eleven o'clock at night—late by most standards, yet still early for the Mexican upper class, who never seemed to fall into bed until the early hours of the morning. Mama would be at the theater until midnight at least. I'd begged off Miller's invitation to go, insisting they attend without me. I was glad she'd accepted; I needed quiet time to catch up on my correspondence. But that wasn't my primary reason for staying home.

For the past hour, I'd been committing to paper the day's excursion at the floating gardens of La Viga, an enchanting place of boats, flowers, food, and music. I scanned my last paragraph:

> In blocks of fifteen by thirty feet nestle the gardens surrounded by water and rising two feet above its surface. The ground is fertile and rich and will grow anything. Some have fruit trees, others vegetables, and some look like one bed of flowers suspended in the water. Around the little canals through which we drifted were hundreds of elegant water lilies. Eagerly we gathered them with a desire which seemed never to be satisfied, and even when our boat was full we still clutched ones which were the prettiest yet.

I'd written it in haste, getting the words down as quickly as they came to me. I couldn't help but think Madden would find my penmanship too difficult to read. I pictured him frowning over it, his red pencil poised, as cigar smoke swirled around him like fog. Well, I would just have to rewrite it when I was finished. Confound the man. Eighteen hundred miles away and he still irritated me. I couldn't complain, however. Every story I'd sent north to the *Dispatch* had been printed almost in its entirety. He had also put them under a large heading: NELLIE IN MEXICO. It was the column I'd never believed I'd get again (and one that would likely disappear once my adventure was over). My readers were responding wonderfully. Their letters began arriving with regularity soon after Mama and I had settled in our small apartment in Mexico City. QO was forwarding them just as he had promised. A good many of them had been opened and read, something I'd expected Madden would do. He was testing the barometer of my stories. I was immensely relieved to find so much of the mail favorable. I rubbed my eyes. With an exasperated sigh, I unlocked the desk drawer and picked up the letter that had arrived that day from Frederick Gillespie. In my enthusiasm to begin writing about Mexico and its people, and with the regularity that Madden demanded stories, I hadn't had time to write the good-bye letter I'd planned to send him from Mexico. Mama had demanded I not "break things off completely" with him when we'd left, though I wasn't sure what "things" she was referring to. The envelope felt lighter than his previous correspondence. Perhaps, now that nearly three months had passed since I'd left, he was at a loss for words. I tore open the envelope. The letter was short and to the point:

Dear Miss Cochrane,

It is with some embarrassment that I write to tell you that fate has intervened. As I had made it known to you that I would wait until your return to resume our growing friendship in hopes that it would blossom into something more, I feel it paramount that I inform you immediately that I intend to ask for a most charming young lady's hand in marriage.

I remain most respectfully yours,
Frederick W. Gillespie

Oh, Mr. Gillespie, you were never most respectfully mine. Thank heaven the poor fool had found someone who returned his affections. Would he break the news to Mama himself or leave this sticky business to me? Well, Mama couldn't blame me now for botching the match, no matter how ridiculous the possibility had been in the first place. Relieved, I removed my Bible from the desk drawer and opened it to the page that held the flower cards. Since Schenley, McCain had sent several more, three of which he'd slipped into my mail at the *Dispatch,* which QO had forwarded to Mexico each week. I'd never dared think he would continue to send them, not when I'd broken my promise and left the country without so much as a note to him. Yet he had. The flowers stared up at me. As always, arranged in order, left to right. A poker hand of bright blooms.

Clotbur: *Pertinacity.* McCain's reaction to Madden's swift withdrawal of my weekly column after the incident with Bessie. Red columbine: *Anxious and trembling.* McCain's reaction for not having seen a single word in print from me in December other than my query to readers about my trip to Mexico? I didn't think it could mean anything else. I had been scarce in the office too, spending time getting ready for the trip and helping Mama prepare to sell the boardinghouse.

The three cards I'd received in Mexico troubled me most:

White catchfly	*Betrayal*
Red carnation	*My poor heart*
French marigold	*Jealousy*

White catchfly had arrived two weeks after my first write-up from south of the border, entitled "Adieu to the United States." I had moped for weeks, following in Mama and Joaquin Miller's wake in a state of listlessness, as I wrote of the disappointing food, incessant cigarette smoking, modes of travel, and the butchery of bull-fights. I was certain it was the last I would ever hear from him. To my surprise, another appeared a month later following my story on theatergoing, an exposé in which I'd stated that, upon entering our box, I'd been presented with a bouquet of flowers by an avid admirer from the pit below. How my heart had soared at the sight of an envelope postmarked from Pittsburgh in McCain's elegant hand. His heart was weeping! My "Love and Courtship in Mexico" produced the third card. I had never intended to make him jealous. I could only assume no handwritten note accompanied the cards because he was aware Madden was opening my mail.

I gathered the cards to my chest. I needed to reassure him that he need not be troubled; my heart had not changed. I snatched the flower book from the desk drawer, flipping through the entries. I picked up my pencil and continued my description of La Viga:

Such roses! I can yet inhale their perfume, and how they recalled kind friends at home: daisies, honeysuckle, bachelor buttons, in variety unknown in the States. Surely no other spot on earth brings forth such a variety of shade, color, and size. They are even finer than the peonies of the States . . .

Roses	*Love*
Daisies	*Innocence*

Honeysuckle	*Devoted affection*
Bachelor buttons	*Celibacy*
Peonies	*Shame and bashfulness*

It was my first attempt at an esoteric message through the *Dispatch*. My first love letter to George McCain.

23

A fter several months' confinement the thoughts of the busy world grow faint, and all the poor prisoners can do is to sit and ponder over their hopeless fate.

NELLIE BLY

BLACKWELL'S ASYLUM, OCTOBER 1887

Outside Hall Seven's second-story window, the day was clear. The river was a roiling blue-gray mass that carried ferries and tugboats from north to south along the eastern rim of Manhattan. The skyline beyond was a serrated edge of structures: hotels, a firehouse, the four-story rectangle of a ladies' shoe factory, judging by the large heeled boot painted on the bricks. A ferry passed, ASTO-RIA painted in bold red letters on its side. Bound for Queens, then, and crowded with passengers. Who were they? Did they cherish the freedom they had to do as they pleased? Did they shudder as they passed the island with its penitentiary, its charity hospital, its asylum for the insane? The world outside the window seemed so distant. Ungraspable. A whirring cog of events and experiences of which I was no longer a part. Hours, days, marched ahead, while behind asylum walls, time stood still.

McCain was out there somewhere. What was he doing? Did he think of me as often as I him? He had looked so anguished, so wrecked. How I longed to have the card he'd given me and that the nurse had snatched. I fought back the sting of tears, willing myself to concentrate on something, anything, else.

Just outside the window, a couple was making their way across the lawn in the direction of the ferry dock. The man had his arm around the waist of a woman who was walking with great care. I brightened. I was almost certain it was Mrs. Cotter. Bless her. She was gone from this place now, never to return again. But how had Dent managed to pull off her release after she'd been brutally beaten and nearly drowned? She must still bear the signs of the attack. He'd most likely accused an inmate. Far easier to blame her assault on one of them, for who would suspect a pair of nurses could be responsible for such a monstrous thing?

I turned from the window. Nurse Conway, gray haired and squinting through glasses, sat at the nurses' table in the center of the room, flanked by thirty women or so sitting idle. The sitting area was slightly better appointed. Instead of the ubiquitous benches of Hall Six, there were chairs, a newer piano, and artwork on the walls that depicted the Brooklyn Bridge and Central Park. There was light chatter too, something the nurses tolerated as long as it was low. I didn't know what Anne and I had done to warrant being moved here, but I suspected, in my case, it had something to do with the superintendent wanting to a put distance between Grady, Grupe, and me. Perhaps, like Mrs. Cotter, he wanted me out of harm's way, if for no other reason than to protect his own interests. Or perhaps I was just being fanciful. It was hard to say.

Were the papers still following my story? McCain had hinted as much during his visit, but that had been days ago. How could they be when there was no progress? Dent certainly wouldn't be feeding the reporters information, if in fact they had tried contacting him at all. In the beginning, I'd been afraid of the papers' interest in me, fearful they might discover who I was. Now, it was vital the papers continued to follow my story. It was the only thing that would keep Dent from laying a hand on me.

At the far end of the room, a young girl sat next to Anne sewing. The two women had been absorbed in conversation most of the afternoon, talking quietly as the girl stitched. That she was allowed a needle was a testament to how much more lenient Hall Seven was. Already the nurses seemed kinder.

"Nellie, this is Bridget McGuiness," Anne said as I approached.

The girl's hands trembled as she clutched her fabric and needle. There was something in the jerky movements of her hands and the rest of her body that reminded me of Tillie. But she appeared more composed, without Tillie's recent flightiness and wild-eyed demeanor.

"I've been telling her of your stay at the Temporary Home before you came, and your lack of memory," Anne said. "I hope you don't mind."

"Of course not." There was no privacy here. United in their misery, the patients listened to each other's stories and held little back of their own. Except for me, of course. I had my secrets.

"You're the one from yesterday, the brave one in the yard," Bridget said. "I'm surprised you're here. It's uncommon for someone to be back from the Lodge so soon, if she comes back at all." There was something haunted about her bluish green eyes. I wondered how long she had been at Blackwell's. "I was very fortunate."

"And the other woman?"

"Sent to the infirmary yesterday after a night at the Lodge," I said, "but I just now saw her making her way to the ferry with her husband."

"Oh, I'm so happy for her," Anne said.

"Thank goodness for that," Bridget said. "She's no longer in hell."

"You sound as if you know from personal experience," I said.

Bridget looked down at her hands. "I was brave like you too, once. Now, I have these." She held up her hands. They trembled without pause. Her whole body, including her head, shook slightly. "I suppose you'll want to know my tale as well."

"Only if you wish to tell it," Anne said.

"Why not?" Bridget said with a wan smile. "I prefer you hear it from me instead of someone else." She patted the seat next to her, indicating for me to take a seat. When I had, she began. "When I was twelve, my parents died of influenza. My sisters, being older, had already gone into service, but I was too young and we hadn't any family who could take me in. My sisters tried to get me hired on as kitchen help or as an errand girl where they had positions, anything to keep me under a roof and put some food in my belly, but nobody would hire me. I was always small for my age and looked more like nine or ten than twelve." A faraway look came into Bridget's eyes. "I wish I'd told the housekeepers I'd work for nothing. Just food and a bed. Maybe they'd have taken me in and things would've been different." She seemed to come to herself, saying after a moment, "I ended up at the poorhouse and eventually got sent to Bellevue. That was six years ago." She was clutching her hands, as if to keep them from moving of their own accord.

"I wonder why you weren't sent to the workhouse on the island," I said.

Bridget lifted a thin shoulder in a shrug. "I was too young, I suppose."

"Well, if I may say so without being rude," Anne said, "you look very well for one who's been here so long."

A bitter laugh escaped her throat. "You think so? Would you believe I've been in the Lodge?"

"For what offense?" I asked.

"Throwing a piece of bread at one of the nurses," Bridget replied. "She insulted me about my dress. Said I looked like a whore in it. Can you believe such nonsense? The beatings I got there were dreadful. My first, a nurse jumped on me and broke two of my ribs. After that, they put me on the rope gang. There's nothing worse than being tethered to the truly insane. But that wasn't all. I was pulled around by my hair, strangled, and held underwater until I thought I would drown."

Just like Mrs. Cotter. "And the doctors?" I asked. "They did nothing?"

Bridget shook her head. "The nurses made the inmates keep a lookout by the door for the doctors."

Anne's eyes widened. "No."

"Oh, yes." Bridget picked up her sewing. It was an inmate's dress, tattered and missing buttons. Suitable for the rag bag anywhere but Blackwell's. "The nurses made us do it. They'd hold us under the water and threaten us if we ever breathed a word. We all promised. We knew the doctors wouldn't do anything anyway. There was a German girl. I don't remember her name. She was sent to the Lodge because she was sick, of all things. She fought the nurses for putting her there because it was so filthy. One night they took her and, after thrashing her good, held her down in a cold bath. They threw her on her bed just like that: wet and with no gown or blankets. The next morning, she was dead. The doctors said she died of convulsions, and after that, nothing more was said of her."

Rage welled up inside me, raw and smarting. There was no end to the stories. No end to the tales of cruelty and suffering.

"You remind me a bit of myself when I first came," Bridget said to me. "I see the fire in your eyes. It can be your enemy, the anger, the hate. Even here, in Hall Seven, where we're treated better than most, things can change. My tremors? The beatings and the starvation, not even the dunkings, had anything to do with them. I try so hard to keep my hands still, but I can't."

Bridget's voice quivered with emotion, and for a moment I thought she was going to break into tears. What could have caused her shaking? What could be worse than what she had already described?

As if she'd heard my thoughts, she said, "I'll tell you what did this to me." She glanced at Nurse Conway. The nurse was half-dozing at the table, and so she went on. "In the Lodge, they've got a contraption. The rotary or spinning chair, they call it."

The rotary chair. The one Katie had mentioned.

"I don't know what death smells like," Bridget went on, "but it can't be far from the stench of the room where they keep it. Human waste and vomit. The room is empty except for that chair and the stairs that lead up to it. The 'stairway to heaven,' the nurses call it. They haul you up those steps to the platform and strap you in the chair with belts. Then they start it moving."

Anne's eyes were saucers. "Moving?"

Bridget nodded. "One of the nurses stands on the platform and twists you round and round until the ropes are taut, and then lets you go. You spin and spin in the other direction until your head is floating and you can't do anything but vomit, again and again. And when you stop spinning, she twists you again."

"How many times did they do this to you?" I asked.

"I don't know. More times than I could count. The shaking in my hands started soon after."

"And how long would they do this? Spin you like that?" Anne asked.

"If it was a doctor's order, maybe ten or fifteen minutes—which is to say, an eternity. It's the vomiting they're after. They say it's cleansing, that it will rid you of your madness. But sometimes, if you anger a nurse, she and her witch's coven will put you in the chair without a doctor's permission, and you'll be spinning around much longer. And once you've recovered, they make you clean up the mess you've made, which only makes you sick again."

"Dent allows this?" My voice was barely above a whisper.

"Dent orders it done and watches," Bridget said. "'Therapy,' he calls it. Therapy with a nurse cackling while you're up there and throwing up something awful. The drugs they give you just before make you vomit all the more and let loose your bowels. You spin up there retching and shitting yourself and there's nothing but laughter in your ears. Those steps aren't the stairway to heaven, they're the gateway to hell."

❦

Nurse Conway led Anne and I, along with the other women of our hall, to the dormitory as the sun was setting. At the entrance to the room, the inmates began removing their clothing. As this was the first night in our new hall, Anne and I looked a question at the nurse.

"Do like the others," Conway said, her spectacles glinting in the lantern light. "Get yourselves undressed."

Anne and I exchanged glances. Even in the poor light, I could see my friend had gone pale. "You mean we must undress here in the hall?" she said.

"No, I meant everyone else but you two. I've got a separate boudoir just for you that's heated."

"Nurse, surely you don't expect us to sleep without anything on," I said.

Conway stepped closer, raising her lamp. "I saw you in the yard yesterday helping that poor woman. If you know what's good for you, you'll mind yourself. There's no good that can come of making trouble here. No good at all." She looked at me as if she wanted to say more but shook her head and stepped back instead.

Without a shred of clothing, the cold was all the more invasive. Dr. Ingram had told me the heat was turned on in October, but so far, that hadn't been the case. Yet another detail that added to the depravity that was Blackwell's.

When all the inmates stood naked, Nurse Conway unlocked the door. Women rushed for the beds farthest from the windows, echoes of the first night Anne and I had been shown into a dormitory and my adventure had begun. I was relieved, at last, to be sleeping in the company of others. I had never looked forward to the nights when I was alone with my thoughts in the darkness. I lay down in a bed near Bridget and pulled the blanket over me. I had never slept in the nude. Even in Mexico with the oppressive heat, I'd never slept without a chemise. How senseless, the nudity. But then, that was the intent: to rid us of any semblance of propriety or common decency.

The women were restless. One of them, an older woman, muttered to herself, ramblings that made no sense. Another sat up in bed, wrapped her arms around her knees, and rocked herself back and forth, so that her bed made a horrible grating sound against the floor.

"Bridget?" I called softly into the darkness.

"Yes?"

"Why do they make us sleep in the nude?"

"There was a woman in Hall Seven who got out once. One of

the nurses forgot to lock the door. She ran all over the asylum in the dark screaming her head off, dodging the nurses for hours. After that, they made us remove our gowns. They think we won't run if we're naked because of the cold. That and the humiliation of being found without a stich on."

I thought of that poor woman dashing cold and frightened through the halls, the darkness closing in on her as she ran. I thought of Mama, of McCain, and of QO. Were Fannie and Viola worried for me? Did my friends wonder how I fared? Most of all, I wondered if they would have dared take the risk I was taking.

When at last I fell into a troubled sleep, I dreamed of being strapped into a chair as vicious laughter swirled around me in the darkness.

24

*he Mexican papers never publish one
word against the government or officials,
and the people who are at their mercy
dare not breathe one word against them.*

NELLIE BLY

MEXICO CITY AND PITTSBURGH, MAY 1886

"You are a follower of this new Christian Science?" I asked the woman seated at the head of the table next to me.

Ursula Gestefeld smiled, an effect that heightened the warm brown of her eyes. "Indeed I am, Miss Cochrane."

"Now, Ursula," her husband, Theodore, said from the opposite end of the table, "you mustn't bore our guests with your newfound fascination."

I smiled. This was more jest than admonishment. It was clear Mr. Gestefeld was enormously fond of his wife.

"Nonsense," Joaquin Miller said, his eyes dancing in amusement. He was in good spirits this evening, eating and drinking with relish. "If there's a bore at this table, Gestefeld, it's you." The guests burst into laughter. Above us a chandelier flickered, its glow reflected in the fine china, serving dishes, and glassware. "Let the kind lady speak."

"Thank you, Mr. Miller, you're most kind." Mrs. Gestefeld looked around the table at her guests. "Have you heard of Mary

Baker Eddy? I read her book *Science and Health* not long ago. I found it fascinating. I met her when she came to Chicago last year to teach when Theo was working at the *Chicago Tribune*. I listened to her lectures and soon became one of her most avid students. I find the combination of scripture and science riveting. One of these days, I shall write of my own findings on the subject."

With an almost imperceptive nod of her head, Mrs. Gestefeld motioned for the servants to clear the plates for the next course. I caught the eye of Hector Alvarez and smiled. He did not return it. I wondered vaguely if he was ill—the tall, courteous widower always had a ready smile. What a lovely coincidence it had been that the polite gentleman Mama and I had met on the train in January when we'd first arrived in Mexico City was a close friend of the Gestefelds. We had passed many pleasant evenings in his company. Seated next to him was his mother, Consuelo, a somber if kind woman whose black lace mantilla was a sharp contrast to her white hair.

"Tell me, Mrs. Cochrane," Augustus Baker, the English consul at Vera Cruz, said, "did you and your daughter enjoy Orizaba?"

"It's the most picturesque place I've been since our arrival here," Mama said. "The churches were so lovely. There was an earthquake while we were there, you know."

A murmur passed around the table.

"Your first earthquake?" Señora Alvarez asked.

"Oh, yes," Mama said. "And do you know, Elizabeth and I both thought it a wonder that the locals paid it no more attention than we would a spring shower at home."

Mr. Gestefeld dabbed at his mouth with a napkin. "And will that particular detail find its way back to Pittsburgh, Miss Cochrane?"

"I don't see why it shouldn't. It seems innocent enough for President Díaz and his police."

Mrs. Gestefeld made a face. "Bah, Díaz."

"We hear so many stories," Mama said. "Is it true that poor man—Cabrera, isn't that his name?"

"Daniel," Señor Alvarez volunteered, his tone solemn, "Daniel Cabrera."

Mama's hand rested on her chest. "Is it true he still languishes in prison?"

"*Sí*," Señor Alvarez answered. "I do not think he will see the light of day again." For a brief moment, his eyes flicked to me and then down.

"Well, he asked for trouble, did he not?" Señora Alvarez replied. "If the editor of the *Ahuizote* was thrown in jail for his satirical cartoons of Díaz and his administration, how could Señor Cabrera think he should be treated otherwise for doing the same?"

"Some news of Cabrera has reached Vera Cruz," Mr. Baker said, nodding. "Sadly, we haven't heard all the details. Was there a specific incident that caused the police to throw Cabrera in Belem?"

"He printed a caricature relating to the *Ahuizote*'s demise," Mr. Gestefeld said. "He entitled it 'The Cemetery of the Press.' In the background were the graves of the different papers who denounce Díaz's regime. In the foreground was a large cross engraved with the words 'The Independent Press, R.I.P.' The police were ordered to find and destroy every copy. Cabrera was thrown in Belem the following day."

"You must be careful of what you write, Miss Cochrane," Mr. Baker said. "Or is politics something you do not broach in your correspondence for the States?"

"Not primarily, no," I said, "but I've already written of President Díaz and the way the people feel about him."

For a moment, no one said a word. Mr. Gestefeld set down his wineglass slowly. "I thought we agreed, Miss Cochrane, you would refrain from Mexican politics while you were here. It's unwise to get the attention of government officials."

Mr. Gestefeld was well aware of what little liberty existed in the press. He was the editor of Mexico's *Two Republics* and had spoken with me at length about his own tenuous role as a newspaperman in Mexico. It was a difficult position for him, a man from a country where freedom of speech was a way of life.

"We did agree," I said. "But I felt, after hearing story after story, that I owed it to the people at home to tell them Mexico isn't the republic many think it is. How could I not report on my discoveries, when my role is to write faithfully of what I see and hear?"

Mrs. Gestefeld fingered the black beads at her throat. "What did you write, my dear?"

"I wrote about the absurdity of the government-subsidized papers. How the citizens have nothing but contempt for them and refuse to read them. The editors are too lazy and live too comfortably on government money to print the truth. These sheets then circulate among the only people who read them—foreigners, who don't realize how false they are."

"*Dios mio,*" Señora Alvarez muttered, making the sign of the cross.

Her son looked down at the table, fingering the stem of his wineglass. Mama looked white. I could feel Mr. Gestefeld's disapproval at the end of the table. "Is that all?" he asked.

I lifted my chin. "No. I mentioned the two editors, the ones who worked for the subsidized papers and weren't getting paid because the government funds have run out to pay them."

"And?" Mr. Gestefeld was scowling.

I smoothed the napkin in my lap. I couldn't look at Mama. I had kept these things from her, knowing she would've done her best to prevent me from putting them in print. "I wrote of how the editors, since they were no longer getting paid, began to write much more truthful accounts of what the government was doing."

"These editors, if I recall correctly, were thrown in Belem, weren't they?" Joaquin Miller asked, looking from me to his host.

"Yes," Mr. Gestefeld said. "Did you write about that too, Miss Cochrane?"

"I did."

"What in heaven's name were you thinking, Pinkey?" Mama hissed. Her eyes were shooting daggers at me, an effect exaggerated by the flickering lamplight on the Gestefeld's porch. I had never seen her look so angry. "How could you write against the *government*?"

"They were small mentions, both times, Mama. A paragraph or two buried among other details of my experiences, not lurid exposés. Besides, my accounts are being well received in Pittsburgh. QO told me so himself." He had also warned me to be careful, even in the smallest instances, from writing anything that might get back to Mexico, at least while I was living south of the border. McCain, too, had sent a warning, a card depicting rosebay: *Danger.* Madden, on the other hand, had been silent on the matter—which was as good an indication as any that he was satisfied with my content.

"Well, we have gone right from the frying pan into the fire," Mama said, pacing in frustration. "I have put up with living in a virtual desert for the past five months as your chaperone, believing this 'adventure,' as you put it, would advance your career. Now I see the error of it."

Through the filmy white curtains at the window, we could hear the other guests talking in the sitting room over port. Miller broke out in boisterous laughter. "Well," Mama said presently, "I'm glad we said our good-byes. You could have cut the tension with a knife at dinner. Come, our carriage is waiting. We'll speak more about this when we're home."

Just then the door opened and the shadowy form of Señor Alvarez appeared. He walked into the lantern light, bowed his head in greeting, and said, "I thought I heard the two of you speaking out here." He turned to me. "Might I have a word before you go?"

Mama took the hint and bid good-bye, saying that she would wait for me in the cab. The lantern threw wavering shadows across Señor Alvarez's features. It was difficult to read his expression. He produced a folded newspaper from beneath his arm and held it out to me. "I meant to show you this earlier, but by the time I'd arrived this evening I could not get a separate audience with you."

"What is it?"

"An article, in Spanish, denouncing one Nellie Bly of Pittsburgh, Pennsylvania, who is in this country as a correspondent for the United States and spreading false and malicious propaganda to that country."

I felt the blood drain from my face. "What?"

"It appears your stories about Díaz and the press are being circulated here."

"How—" I stopped. I could guess. My pieces had likely been picked up by other papers in the States until they made their way, in all likelihood, to a Texas paper, where they fell into the hands of an editor sympathetic to Díaz and his cause. Or perhaps a Mexican editor had found it there himself. "When did it print?"

"Yesterday. There is a phrase in it you would do well to heed, Miss Cochrane. *Un botón es suficiente.* 'One button is enough.' It means one story of yours is enough for them to know what all the others are like. It is all the evidence they need."

"They weren't really stories. Just, just comments—"

"It makes no matter."

"But it's true, all of it," I whispered. "Every word."

"It has never been about the truth, Miss Cochrane." I could not see him clearly, but I could hear the quiet urgency in his voice. "Our government, you well know, does not take kindly to these things. We have a law here, Articulo Treinte-Tres, Article Thirty-Three. It defines the fate of malicious foreigners who speak or write too freely here. In practice, the government has, once or twice, been kind enough to march the offending foreigner, with a regiment of soldiers, across the border, that is, if they do not throw him in jail. I say 'him' because the instances I know of were men, but I would not put it past Díaz and his *officiales* to stop at a woman."

"You are saying they will do that? Send me across the border or throw me in jail?"

"It is in their power to do so."

I stood gazing down at the newspaper, unable to read the print in the faint light but feeling the power of it nevertheless.

"I have not breathed a word to Mr. Gestefeld," Señor Alvarez said. "I thought you should know first. You should tell him soon, however, before he learns of it elsewhere. I would not want him to be, what is the English word? Blindsided. As an American editor who is known to be acquainted with you, I would not like to see him questioned by authorities—or worse. I am sorry to say it, Miss Cochrane, but you must, for you and your mother's safety, leave this country at once."

"But it's only May. I still have another month."

"Better to leave a month early, señorita, than find yourself inside Belem."

⁂

Images flew by the window: the brick facade and columned arches of the station, a group of men standing in a half-circle smoking cigars, a woman with a large bustle pulling a small white dog on a leash. Before I knew it, the train was lurching to a stop. I was home at last.

Ever since QO had arranged for someone from the *Dispatch* to meet us at the Liberty Avenue Station, my mind had been awhirl. Would McCain maneuver to be the one to greet us? Would he dare? Would he even know QO had planned for someone to meet us?

"Come, Pinkey," Mama said from the aisle. "Don't forget your things."

I'd been looking forward to this moment, picturing myself alighting from the train in the new spring hat I'd purchased in St. Louis on the return trip. I fingered the brim, making sure it was set just right, pleased with the way the yellow and green ribbons matched my coat.

We alighted into the warm air, the smell of pavement, steam, refuse, and burning coal converging at once—Pittsburgh welcoming us home. We stood for a moment on the platform. Dozens of people moved about, no one paying us any attention.

I wondered if McCain had changed, if he would see a change in me. Would he notice my golden skin, touched by the Mexican sun? Would my hat call attention to my careful toilette and betray that I wished to look my best?

"Mama!" a male voice boomed. "Elizabeth!"

Albert stepped forth into our vision. Beside him was Kate, little Beatrice balanced on her hip. Mama ran to Kate, embracing daughter and granddaughter in one broad hug. "Oh my dears! How I have waited for this moment. How Beatrice has grown!"

"You look well, Albert," I said over Mama's exclamations.

"So do you," Albert said. He looked me over, taking special note of my face. "You've been in the sun."

"It was difficult to stay out of it."

"You shall be unpopular among the females here who dare not emerge from beneath their parasols and large-brimmed hats."

Just one minute in his presence and Albert was already finding fault. "Popularity is overrated," I said. "Where's your wife?"

"Jane is at home with a headache, I'm afraid. She sends her regards."

Mama bounced Beatrice on her hip while Kate and I embraced. We drew back, clasping each other's hands, and looked at one another.

"You're brown!" Kate said, laughing. "Did you have a safe journey?"

"You're thinner," I said, "and yes, though it was interminably long. Mama was fit to burst the last hour. She missed all of you very much, especially Beatrice."

Beatrice, not yet three, squealed and reached for her mother.

"You see?" Mama said, handing over the child to Kate. "I've been away far too long. She doesn't know her own grandmother anymore."

"A fact which shall soon be remedied, Mama," Kate said.

"Albert, see to our luggage, won't you?" Mama said. "I'd like to get out of this crowd and wait inside."

Albert moved off while I followed Kate and Mama toward the station. Standing in the crowd was a teenage boy holding a sign with my name on it.

"Someone from the paper," I said, waving Mama and Kate on. "I shan't be a moment." I turned to the lad. "I am Elizabeth Cochrane."

"Robbie, from the *Dispatch*, ma'am." He tugged the brim of his cap. "Mr. Wilson sends his welcome."

"How nice of him to arrange for you to meet the train." Not McCain, then, but a boy. QO had sent a boy.

"These are for you." He withdrew a bouquet of flowers from behind his back. Daisies, lilies, carnations. How well I recognized them now.

"Was there a card with these?"

"A card, ma'am?"

"Yes, a card."

"No, Mr. Wilson didn't give me a card. Just the flowers."

I frowned. "The flowers are from Mr. Wilson?"

"Why, yes, ma'am."

My heart sank. "Please tell him thank you and I shall see him tomorrow at the office."

I was moving away when I heard my name. My eyebrows rose at the sight of the ginger-haired boy I hadn't seen for months. "Timmy! How you've grown!"

Timmy blushed and grinned at the same time. "Did you have a good time in Mexico, Miss Bly?"

"I did."

He screwed up his face. "Are there really savages there who'll scalp you if you look at them the wrong way?"

I tilted my head. "I think you have your geography mixed up."

He nodded, his question forgotten, and withdrew an envelope from his pocket. "Mr. McCain give me instructions to meet you here. He told me to give you this."

"Thank you, Timmy." I held out two pennies for him.

"Oh, there ain't no need. He paid me already, before he left."

I took the envelope. It was unmarked. Turning it over, I saw there was no date either. "What do you mean, before he—" But Timmy had already vanished into the crowd. I returned my attention to the envelope and tore it open with shaking hands. Inside was an illustration of a yellow trumpet-shaped flower. Carolina jasmine. After checking that Mama and Kate were nowhere in sight, I withdrew my flower book from my reticule and quickly found the meaning. *Separation.* What did it mean? I was replacing the card in the envelope when I noticed something written on the reverse.

Scrawled in George McCain's now-familiar hand were two words. "New York."

25

I had looked forward so eagerly to leaving the horrible place.

NELLIE BLY

BLACKWELL'S ISLAND, OCTOBER 1887

The next morning we were awakened, as ever, by the turn of keys and the throwing of the bolt.

"Get up," a nurse by the name of Hart said as she flung open the door.

I sat up and felt the room sway as the walls closed in. I swung my legs over the bed, my feet hitting the cold stone floor as spots swam before my eyes.

"What is it?" Anne whispered, coming to me with her blanket wrapped around her shoulders. The others crept into the hall, found their asylum uniforms, and began to dress in the semidark. "Are you unwell?"

"Light-headed, that's all."

"I'll get your things," Anne said, squeezing my arm. "Don't move."

I dressed in slow motion. I'd lost more weight. The ties of my underskirt no longer kept my skirt at my waist. I had to hitch it up constantly to keep it from slipping off. The overdress was now so large that I was lost inside it. Hunger pangs no longer racked me. It was as if my body had given up signaling its need for sustenance. I was weak all the time now; not even the tea and bread restored me. Perhaps most horribly of all, I was too exhausted to care anymore. Yesterday, when Bridget had seen me pulling up my skirts, seen the way I struggled to stand, to climb over the benches in the dining hall, she told me all the women succumbed this way, even the younger, healthy ones. "Soon you won't have your monthly trouble," she'd said. "It happens to us all."

At breakfast I ate as much of my bread as I could manage, eating around the rancid butter. The sight and smell of it turned my stomach. I'd learned to drink down the tea, as water was never given at meals and was refused us when we asked for it.

A short time later, when my dizziness had mostly passed and Anne and I were in the sitting room, a nurse came in.

"Nellie Brown, you're wanted in the superintendent's office."

Moments later, I entered Dent's lair. There was a man seated there I had never seen before.

"This is Mr. Hendricks," Dent said from behind his desk. His light blue eyes were cold with contempt. "He is an attorney from the city and has come to ask you a few questions."

Mr. Hendricks had a neatly trimmed mustache and dark hair shot with gray. But it was his polished shoes and the smell of leather and expensive cologne emanating from him that made him seem exotic and so entirely foreign from Blackwell's. He took in my disheveled hair, my unsightly dress, my filthy boots. I resisted the urge to fix my skirt. It would make little difference; I had taken on the cloak of the asylum in ways no mere adjustment could alter.

Hendricks, for his part, seemed displeased by what he saw but did not remark on it. Instead, he said to me, "I represent a client whose dear friend vanished some ten days ago. It is his belief you may be the one the papers are writing about. Can you state your name for me?"

"Nellie Brown."

"And do you remember how it is you came to be here, Miss Brown?" Hendricks listened intently as I told him of my stay at Bellevue, which had come about by way of Judge Duffy at the Essex Market Police Station. "And how is it you came to the station?"

"I was staying at a home for women, somewhere on Second Avenue I think. I don't remember how I got there, but the assistant matron was eager to be rid of me."

Hendricks nodded. "And do you recall anything before that? Such as whom you might have been with?"

My pulse quickened. This was surely Cockerill's doing, wasn't it? Or was this man really representing a client looking for a woman of my description? How was I to answer? "I just remember the Temporary Home," I said at last.

"*Y hablas español, verdad?*" Hendricks asked.

"*Sí, claro.*"

Mr. Hendricks turned to Dent. "This young woman's name, age, and physical characteristics match the description my client gave me. She also speaks Spanish, which my client assured me she would."

My mind raced. The Temporary Home was a detail from the papers, as was my ability to speak Spanish. Hendricks was using what had been printed to establish my identity, or so it seemed, which could mean he'd been sent from the *World* to fetch me. Evidently my 'dear friend' was not coming forward to identify me himself, perhaps because he didn't exist. But would these details be enough to convince Dent?

Hendricks withdrew a slip of paper from his briefcase and handed it to Dent. After the superintendent inspected it, Hendricks held it out to me. It was not a sheet of paper but my photograph. Seated and wearing a black dress with a matching hat edged with ostrich feathers, my own eyes stared back at me. I wondered how Cockerill had gotten hold of it.

"Do you recognize yourself, Miss Brown?" Hendricks said kindly.

Cockerill had thought of everything. "I do."

"I believe I have everything I need to have Miss Brown released, Superintendent."

"Not quite," Dent snapped. "We cannot let our charges go to just anyone who comes to claim them. Your client is not her husband?"

"No."

"Then you must have her consent."

I wanted to laugh out loud. Any woman left here for more than an hour would leave with anyone, absolutely anyone, who came to get her.

Hendricks turned to me, seemingly perturbed that his motives were in question and impatient to be done with Dent. "My dear Miss Brown, do you consent to be released into my custody so that I may escort you to the home of your friend who is ready and anxiously awaiting your return?"

"Yes." *More than you know.*

"I'm afraid there's a bit more to it than that," Dent said. He reached into the file cabinet behind his desk, rummaged among the files, and withdrew a sheet of paper. "This affidavit must be filled out in its entirely for our records, including the signature of your client. We do things to the letter here, Mr. Hendricks. We do not cut corners."

Hendricks took the paper, looked over the rim of his glasses at the superintendent, and said sardonically, "Have you many attorneys who come on behalf of their clients looking for long-lost loved ones, Superintendent?"

Dent gazed levelly at the attorney, his eyes blazing distain. "The infrequency does not diminish the necessity."

"I see," Hendricks drawled. "And is it a necessity that your patients be kept in filthy garments?" The superintendent merely stared back at his opponent, rage emanating from his every pore. When it was clear he had no intention of responding, Hendricks went on. "Well, then, as I represent my client in matters both personal and professional, I assure you my signature can act in his stead."

"I'm afraid that would be in violation of asylum rules, Mr. Hendricks." Another chilly smile. "You may, of course, take the matter up with the commissioner, but I rather think that will take longer than simply obtaining the signature of your client."

Hendricks glanced at the sheet, exhaled an exasperated sigh, and put the paper and my photograph in his briefcase. "Miss Brown, I will be in communication as soon as I have my client's signature. I beg your forgiveness that I'm not at liberty to take you with me now."

I stood there like a cow, too stunned, too disappointed, to move. I had the sudden urge to attach myself to Hendricks's leg and never let go.

"I should like to know, Mr. Hendricks, who this mysterious friend is. This is all most irregular."

"My client, for now, wishes to remain anonymous," Hendricks said with a shrug.

"These circumstances are most unusual," Dent repeated with a scowl. "How am I to know I'm not releasing my patient into the hands of a criminal?"

His patient. As if he, or any of the other doctors on staff with the exception of Dr. Ingram, had ever behaved like doctors treating their charges with care or a thread of human decency.

"I am a representative of the law, Superintendent. I assure you—"

"And I am Nellie's doctor and superintendent of this asylum. I demand to know why your client wishes to be veiled in secrecy and waited over a week to come forward to claim her."

Dent suspected something. Otherwise, why would he care? He'd never let me leave, not if he could help it.

Hendricks sighed and set down his briefcase. "I am not compelled by law to tell you anything of the matter, but I shall give Miss Brown peace of mind, as she has, from the looks of her, been through a great deal." He turned to me and said in a kinder tone, "The boardinghouse you stayed at on Second Avenue is in the vicinity of an accident in which my client and you were involved. A carriage accident. When my client's carriage collided with a wagon that failed to stop before entering the intersection, there was a crash sufficient to throw the both of you from the vehicle. My client was rushed to the hospital, as was the driver of the wagon. He believes you wandered off for help, and when people arrived and realized what had occurred, no one realized there had been anyone else involved besides the drivers. He was only just released from hospital yesterday and sought my assistance at once. Do you recall any of this, Miss Brown?"

The two men waited as my mind raced. What was I to say? I cleared my throat. "I-I have had the most awful headaches. Do you think I hit my head when I was thrown from the vehicle?"

Hendricks gave me a swift wink. His back was to Dent, and it was over in flash, so quick I might have missed it, but I knew I'd said the right thing. He stood up and made to go. "I have your word, do I not, that this young lady will be kept safe and sound in your care until I return tomorrow? My client should hate to find otherwise."

"Naturally," Dent said. "Safe and sound." Despite his words, a shudder ran through me. Dent was not a man to take threats, however veiled they might be. Yet even he had to know he had lost in the long run. Hendricks would be back, and I would leave with him. Dent couldn't, wouldn't, dare do anything to me now. I was untouchable.

I passed the rest of the day in a state of delirium. I fantasized of things I had long gone without: lamb stew, lavender-scented baths, soft cotton sheets, cozy shawls, fitted gloves. I should have been thinking of the story I would write. I should have been worrying about the companions I would leave behind. I felt horribly selfish, but I couldn't help it.

Anne inquired about my meeting with Superintendent Dent. I saw no reason to keep her from the truth—as much of it as I could tell.

"How wonderful!" Anne exclaimed. "I knew you'd be released. Of all of us here, you deserve to be here the least."

"No one deserves to be here, Anne."

"Perhaps 'deserve' is the wrong word," Anne replied. "What I meant to say is that you never belonged here. How wonderful it is you have a friend who has come to your rescue. How strange it must be not to remember who he is! Do you think," she looked at me, all hope and kindness and incredulity, "that he's a suitor? Oh, Nellie, wouldn't that be grand?"

An image of George McCain swam before me, his head bending over my hand at Central Park not so very long ago. I swallowed. "He's not a suitor, no. I mean, I don't think so."

Anne looked at me askance. There was not a trace of jealousy on her face. How much like Fannie and Viola she was. How fortunate I was to know women so entirely without cunning. Poor Anne. If she only knew the truth about who I was, knew how I had lied and was lying to her still, she wouldn't feel me so deserving.

News of my impending release spread.

"Nurse Hart!" a woman called Mattie exclaimed in the sitting room. "Please allow me to play something for Nellie on the piano. A celebration is in order."

"Nonsense. I'll not have you banging on and the rest of you crooning like sick cats."

"But yesterday—" Mattie began.

"Yesterday was different, and that's final."

After so many days and nights of constant hunger, worry, and dread, I felt as if a great weight had been lifted. The knowledge of my impending release brought a feeling of intense goodwill for the inmates I had come to know. I ate more at dinner—not because the food tasted any different but because I wanted, in what little time I had left, to boost the spirits of those who remained.

"Keep up your strength," I told them at dinner. "You mustn't stop eating. Even a little food is better than none."

Across the room, my Hall Six companions acknowledged their congratulations by raising their cups. All but Tillie. She remained aloof, unwilling to meet my glance. With the exception of Anne and Bridget, the ladies at my own table said very little. Anne squeezed my hand and smiled, but the others were less cheery about my departure. How could I blame them? What would they say if they knew I was here under false pretenses, that my release had been guaranteed from the beginning?

Any uneasiness I may have felt after Hendricks left had melted away when Dent sent me back to Hall Seven without a word. In fact, he'd failed to make an appearance in the sitting room or at dinner. Nurses Grupe and Grady prowled the dining hall with their usual malevolence, but neither paid me the slightest attention. Now that someone had come for me, I was no longer of interest. At bedtime I was strangely relaxed. *I am going home. I am leaving at last.* Even sleeping in the nude didn't disquiet me. For the first time in ten days, I fell into a sound sleep.

26

The insane asylum on Blackwell's Island is a human rat trap. It is easy to get in, but once there it is impossible to get out.

NELLIE BLY

BLACKWELL'S ISLAND, OCTOBER 1887

I was jarred awake by the sound of hinges creaking. Whoever was checking the room carried no lantern. An inmate turned over in bed. Another let out a loud snore. Anne was fast asleep in the cot next to me. After a moment, the door closed. I sighed and closed my eyes, only to open them again when a floorboard creaked. *Someone was still in the room.* Before I could come to a sitting position, a hand covered my mouth. More hands clamped onto my arms and legs, pinning me to the bed.

No. It can't be. They wouldn't. I struggled and tried to scream despite the hand over my mouth. Surely the others were awake now. *Someone will help.*

I sensed at least three of them. I lay on my back, squirming, trying to recognize them in the darkness. Fingers pinched my nose closed. So this was it. No drugs but suffocation. It wouldn't leave a mark on me. The hand moved away from my mouth, and I spied a cup coming toward me. I responded by clamping my mouth shut and jerking my head to the side, only to have it forced back by a hand gripping my jaw. I writhed, desperate for air.

"Swallow it."

I knew that voice.

With my nose pinched closed, the only way to breathe was to open my mouth, and I did, only to feel liquid against my gums. I coughed.

"Drink. *Now.*"

Nurse Grupe? Conway? I struggled again for air. I heard, or perhaps only imagined, the other women waking, sitting up and wondering what to do, knowing it wasn't wise to help me.

I opened my mouth again, sucked in air, and again felt liquid enter my mouth. Thin and bitter. I turned my head to the side, half choking, half spitting. I closed my mouth again, shutting off the oxygen I so desperately needed.

The next time I waited longer to open my mouth, until I felt faint from the lack of oxygen. Deep inside me, a small, rational voice said, *If you drink it, you can vomit it up. They'll only use a needle if you resist.*

I went limp and opened my mouth. My lungs filled with blessed, life-saving air. Before I could inhale again, liquid splashed into my mouth. I swallowed—three, four, five gulps—until the cup was empty.

It was finished. In the scuffle, the blanket had slipped and revealed to them my nakedness. I snatched it up and covered myself. Why weren't the nurses leaving? They'd finished what they'd come to do. I still hadn't identified them; I saw them only as a collective hatred, a group of spiteful ill will. Suddenly, through some unspoken command, they threw a dress over my head, forcing my arms into the sleeves. When I'd been clothed, they pushed me onto my side, wrenched my hands behind me, and bound them with rope.

Why now? Hendricks was coming back for me tomorrow. But then, with a slow dawning, I realized they still had one more night, and that was as good a reason as any. I opened my mouth to speak, but my stomach lurched as pain shot through my abdomen. They then hauled me from the bed. Most of the women were sitting up, watching the nurses do their work. Anne was slumped against the wall. Had it been she who'd tried to help me? With a mighty push, I was propelled to the door and into the corridor. I leaned my shoulder against the wall to remain upright, for the room was pitching. Laughter behind me. I turned, felt another knot tighten in my stomach, and leaned forward. Sick, I was going to be sick.

I looked up. It was then that I recognized them. Grady and Grupe were sneering down at me.

"Not feeling yourself, my dear?" Nurse Grady said. In the darkness she was a witch in white, her dress and cap aglow in the gloom. "This is as far as I go." I turned to the voice behind me. Nurse Conway. "I ain't taking her any farther." With one last look at me, she disappeared down the hall.

"Where—" I couldn't finish. My stomach clenched again so tightly that I felt as if an invisible vise were crushing my midsection.

They pushed me down the corridor and along another. I stumbled once, twice. Each time they hauled me up by the rope at my wrists. My stomach was a roiling cauldron. Grupe unlocked a door at the end of the corridor. A cold wind blasted me, and my bare feet raked against the sharp gravel of the yard, but this was the least of my worries. My bowels were about to let go. I stopped and bent over in pain.

"I . . . I . . ."

My bowels released. A flood of warm liquid swam down my legs. Almost at once my stomach erupted, and I vomited onto the gravel. "Now, now," Nurse Grady taunted, "let's not spoil all the fun in one go." I sank to the ground, but the nurses pulled me up and dragged me across the yard. The scrape of my feet against the gravel was nothing compared to the churn in my stomach.

Ahead, the low building waited like a thief: dark, silent, and still. I knew this place. Of course. How could I have been so naive?

We were perhaps thirty feet from the entrance when a scream cut the air. The nurses stopped. I used all my energy to lift my head. The building was dark. As far as I could tell, the grounds were deserted.

"Dat's as good as any velcome you vill get from da Lodge," Nurse Grupe said when her cackle had subsided. "Aren't you special."

Another scream rent the air, just as bloodcurdling as the first. This time, however, there were shouts from within the building.

The nurses exchanged glances. "Check it out," Nurse Grady snapped. Grupe hesitated, looking from me to Grady. "Look at her. You think I can't handle her on my own?"

Grupe ran to the building, unlocked the door, and disappeared inside.

Now was my chance. I wouldn't get another. I had to run. Instead, I retched again, bread and bile coming forth in a thin stream. I felt again the hot stickiness between my legs.

"Look at you," Nurse Grady spat. She released her grip and

shoved me to the ground. "Stinking heap of shit." She crouched down and grasped my hair at the top of my head, pulling it up so that I was forced to meet her eyes. "You may be leaving this place, but not without seeing the chair. We'll see how special you are then."

The chair. The rotary chair. Of course. The vilest of the vile.

Another scream split the air, then another. Shouts rang out. A flickering orange glow at a window. Muffled shouting.

"Fire!"

"Bring water!"

"Get the doors!"

Now was the time to run, but I had no strength. I couldn't move. Nurse Grady yanked me up by my arm and dragged me toward the building. The stench of something burning hit my nostrils just as Grady flung open the door. A cloud of smoke billowed from the building, but the sounds were what terrified me: screams and pounding. The inmates were trying to break free of their prison. Somewhere down the corridor, a fire burned. I thought of the women in the room at the end of the corridor, the ones chained to the wall. They would be too weak to get to their feet, much less free themselves of their binds.

I mustered my strength and pulled away from Grady, who responded by pushing me down the smoke-filled corridor. I landed in a tangled heap. The angry beast that was the fire roared somewhere ahead of us. I could feel its heat, smell the acrid stench of burning wood. Grady fumbled with her keys as I lay sprawled.

She's going to leave me here to burn. Me and all the others.

"Get up," Grady said, turning.

"Please . . . ," I croaked. My throat was parched from the smoke, and my eyes stung. It was difficult to see in the corridor now; the hall was filling with more smoke. Grady pulled me to my feet. Clumsy and disoriented, I tried to take a step in the direction of the exit.

"Oh, no, you don't," the nurse snapped. "It's the chair for you. Not even a fire is going to keep me from giving you what you deserve, you bitch!"

Grady unlocked the door and pushed it open. Inside the room, thinly masked by a veil of smoke, was a wooden stair. Above it, hanging from ropes attached to a crossbeam, was a chair suspended in the air. Empty. Waiting.

I felt my throat tighten. It had all come to this. My heart was beating like a wild thing, and I took a step back. *Run. You'll die here if you don't.*

I didn't see Nurse Grady move behind me. All at once she

kicked me head first into the room. I landed with such force that my temple struck the ground. My vision swam: smoke, the floor, the white blur that was Grady. I gagged again and tried to crawl toward the door.

Shrieks spilled into the room. Somewhere down the hall, glass shattered. Through it all was the insistent pounding of the women imprisoned in their rooms.

"We'll burn alive!"

"Save me!"

None of it stopped Nurse Grady. She dove for me, yanked me to my feet, and pulled me to the stairs. "We call it the 'stairway to heaven'!" she cried. Her black hair had come loose from its bun, and this, combined with the altogether different fire that burned in her eyes, made her look more deranged than any inmate I'd ever seen at Blackwell's. "Climb!"

I was too dizzy and nauseated to move. Enraged, Grady lugged me up a few steps, then a few more, her rage lending her extra strength. I felt like a rag doll as she maneuvered me higher and higher. We were halfway up when Grupe burst into the room, face black with soot. Behind her, inmates flew past, running for the doors.

Thank God. They're getting out.

"Are you mad?" Grupe cried. "Get out! Dere's no time!"

In the lull, I found my opening. I pulled free from Nurse Grady and, in the process, half stumbled, half fell down the steps. To my relief, Grupe didn't respond; she simply turned on her heel and ran. With a sudden surge of adrenaline, I followed her.

"Come back, you bitch!" Grady bellowed.

I was in the hallway then, the inmates' screams deafening in my ears. *I have to save them.* More women—nurses and inmates both—ran past. The floor shook as something—a timber? the ceiling?—crashed to the ground. Two more inmates flew by, headed for the exit doors. I squinted through the smoke, trying to get my bearings, when out of the haze, a glowing figure appeared, arms outstretched, body aflame. Even through the smoke, I recognized the face.

"Save me! Oh, God, have mercy. Save me!"

It was too much. I dropped to my knees, choking, gasping for breath, feeling the hot burn of the fire just doors away. I watched the burning woman fall and roll until she was no longer a woman but a blackened body.

꿈꿈꿈

Bright morning sun illuminated the yard. Across the gravel, a few plumes of smoke rose from the roof of the Lodge, the air pungent with an acrid stench that burned my eyes and nose. The building still stood. Only half a dozen broken windows with char marks above them and a portion of the roof showed signs of damage. Grounds keepers were piling smoldering debris.

Not even a fire, however, had changed the exercise routine. Our hall was walking in formation, two by two. Perhaps it was a way for the staff to minimize what had happened, to gloss over the horror that only a few knew had occurred within those hellish walls.

"It's a miracle everyone got out safely," Anne breathed.

I couldn't look at her. This morning the nurses had declared that everyone had fled the Lodge in safety. I knew better but had said nothing. It seemed the wisest course; I was leaving. I wanted nothing to stand in the way of my release. Who knew, after all, what Dent would do if I proclaimed I'd seen at least one woman burn to death? Anne knew only a small portion of what had happened—that I'd been drugged, as she had witnessed herself, and that I'd been led outside. I'd explained that the fire had thwarted the nurses from any further mischief. I couldn't bring myself to tell her that I had been dragged inside the Lodge to the rotary chair. If I had, she would wonder for the rest of her days here if such a thing could happen to her. How could I leave her with that knowledge, that horror, knowing that I was getting out and she was not?

It was Nurse Conway who'd helped me from the burning building, draping my arm around her neck as she half carried, half dragged me to the doors. She had saved my life. The nurse had cleaned me with a wet cloth and combed my hair by the light of a single lantern until every sign of what I'd endured was gone, all the while cursing the nurses for what they'd done. She'd even dressed me in a gown so I didn't have to endure what was left of the night naked and shivering. I'd passed the remainder of the time back in the dormitory, with only my frayed nerves for company, until dawn had arrived, crisp and clear and bleak.

I watched, transfixed, as the men continued working. The heap of burned wood, blackened mattresses, and charred bed frames was growing, each trip inside yielding more and more for the pile. I hoped the rotary chair had burned. I hoped it was now a pile of smoking ash.

Just then, movement from the south wing caught my attention.

A few grounds keepers, shovels in hand, approached the Lodge, but they didn't stop at the building. Instead, they walked past and disappeared into the trees beyond.

The doors of the west wing banged open, and McCarten and Grady led Hall Six onto the gravel. There was no sign on the nurses' faces of the mischief from the night before. If they noticed me, they paid me no attention. Tillie was at the front of the line and walking with her head high, as if those behind her paraded for her alone. Behind her a few rows, Mrs. Fox and Mrs. Shanz walked together. I longed to go to them to say good-bye, but there was no opportunity without leaving the line, and Mrs. Cotter's mistake was still fresh in my mind. When Hall Six made a turn and came closer, I waved and tried to get their attention. Katie and Molly waved discreetly back. Tillie ignored me.

The women on the rope, temporarily transferred inside the main building, were led out soon after. From their number, it looked as if they had survived the fire. The nurses had managed to set them free. I caught sight of the strange woman with the bedraggled appearance and broken teeth who had leered at me the first day, which now seemed so long ago. This time, I did not look away. The sight of her, of all of them, was no longer as alarming as it had once been. I had become immune to the shock of madness. The realization saddened me more than their tethers and belts, their cries and filth, ever could. The horrifying had become mundane.

A sudden shout pierced the air. There was a faltering of forward movement in the group; one of the women had lost her footing. Those behind her continued forward, marching on, each stumbling into the woman in front of her in line. The forward nurses were trying to keep the group moving, unaware there was an impediment.

Anne touched my arm. "Look. There. I think she's calling your name."

At the end of the gravel yard, a nurse was waving. Beside her stood Mr. Hendricks.

With an encouraging nod from one of the Hall Seven nurses, I stepped from the line and approached them.

"I've just given the superintendent the paperwork he needed," Hendricks said with a tight smile when I reached him. "He was none too happy about it." He shook his head. "It doesn't matter now. Get your things. The ferry's waiting. You're going home, young lady."

I emerged from the west wing and joined Hendricks. As we made our way across the grass, I peered up at the second-floor windows. No women looked out as they had days before. I looked behind me at the patients still marching in the yard. They were all the same. An endless parade of women dressed identically in drab, ill-fitting coats. I waved. There were Anne and Bridget. And Louise, Tillie, Mrs. Fox, and Mrs. Shanz. And Molly and Katie. I wanted nothing more than to leave this place, but now that my time had come, I was overcome with sadness. I may have gained my freedom, but I'd done nothing to grant them theirs.

My mind was awhirl as I walked with Mr. Hendricks down the rutted road that led to the ferry. I had to do something, something that would guarantee that the poor woman who had perished wouldn't be forgotten. I owed it to her.

"Mr. Hendricks, I'd like to make a stop before you take me home."

"Oh?" His eyes searched mine.

"Yes. I'll tell you everything once we're across the river. It's terribly important."

27

*It seemed intensely selfish to leave them
to their sufferings.*

NELLIE BLY

NEW YORK CITY, OCTOBER 1887

I awoke to a murky room. Images swam into focus: the footboard, the dresser, clothing folded in a neat square upon a chair. The curtains were closed, but I could see light around the edges. I lifted my head, and suddenly Mama was coming to me.

"What day is it?" My voice sounded rough. It didn't belong to me.

"That's not important." Mama brushed hair from my forehead.

"Have long have I been sleeping?"

"Two days."

Two days. I was aware, in some nether part of my brain, that two days was too long to be abed. I should rise immediately and begin, and begin . . . what?

"You must rest," Mama said. "Then you can bathe and eat. I'll not allow you to do a lick of work for Cockerill or his infernal paper until then."

Of course, Cockerill. *I need to start writing.*

I didn't argue, though; I didn't want to move. I didn't want to write. I didn't want anything at all.

My eyelids were growing heavy. So heavy. I closed my eyes and fell into a deep, black hole. I dreamed of fire and smoke and screams. I dreamed of a woman burning, begging for mercy that no one offered.

When I woke again, I was alone. With some effort, I sat up. I was horribly weak. I held out my hands, palms down, and examined them. My nails were ragged and dirty, my fingers blistered from scrubbing floors. Bruises and broken skin marked my wrists where they had been bound. I swung legs that didn't quite feel like my own off the bed and came to a sitting position. Shakily, I crept to the window and pulled back the curtain. Narrow boardinghouses and a large elm losing its leaves across the street. The little wrought iron gate before Mrs. Tuttle's front stoop. Home. And yet, it didn't feel like it. I felt like an interloper in someone else's life, wondering how it was I got here. Or perhaps it was that I was no longer the girl I'd been when I'd last looked out that window.

A thin waif in a chemise stared back at me from the dressing mirror in the corner. Pale skin, sunken cheeks, enormous eyes. My hair had dulled to a lackluster brown and hung flat and heavy around my shoulders. And I was dirty. My face and neck were filthy; I looked as if I had been rescued from the streets. A bruise darkened my temple. With a finger, I felt under my chin for the cut I'd received when Grupe had sent me sailing over the lavatory tiles. It would scar; I was certain of it. I would always bear the mark, a horrid brand from Blackwell's. I closed my eyes. I opened them at the sound of Mama coming into the room.

"I thought I heard you stirring. How are you feeling?"

Like I have emerged from a nightmare. "Better."

Mama led me back to the bed. Propped up on pillows, I poured out my story in a flat, listless monotone. I couldn't muster the energy for more than that. I left nothing out. Mama bore it all with quiet resolve, her eyes closed much of the time, reliving my nightmare as it unfolded.

When I was finished, she said, "I won't pretend I was happy with your assignment, but I'm relieved you're back. The horrors you have witnessed . . . but you're safe now." She held my hands and squeezed, then lifted the corners of her mouth in a smile. "How dull my days have been without you." The lines around her mouth and etched into her forehead indicated a much harsher trial than she was willing to admit.

I bathed, with Mama's help, in water as hot as I could stand. She scrubbed until my skin was red and raw. She helped with my hair: wetting, soaping, scrubbing until my scalp throbbed. Though she was gentle and the water clean, I couldn't help but shudder, memories flooding forth: icy water, the greasy soap, the nurses' laughter, my naked humiliation as Grupe did her worst. Later, when I stood before the mirror, I felt like a girl playing dress-up; my clothes hung like a sack. The mutton sleeves and lacework at the collar of my dress seemed wonderfully elaborate after the plain, ugly uniform of the asylum.

A tray of food waited for me in our little front room: a pork chop, potatoes, peas. After dreaming so long of food, I found the smell oddly unpleasant. After some moments, I took a small bite of pork chop. In the end, tea was all I could manage. It was good and strong and sweet after the asylum's weak substitute.

"Mrs. Tuttle will be none too pleased you've wasted food," Mama said gently. "Do you want to write?"

I didn't answer. Instead, I stared out the window. A horse car passed outside. Dishes clanked belowstairs. The normal sounds of the boardinghouse, yet they seemed somehow alien and remote.

When I turned at last from the window, Mama was studying me. I noted again the deep lines on her forehead. Always in the face of adversity—when Papa passed away, when our funds were low and we didn't have much food growing up in Apollo, and later, when Jack Ford came into our lives and made it all worse—my motivation and sheer force of will had propelled me into action. She had never seen me like this. My listlessness was something new, and it frightened her. "I hope that your time here alone didn't pass too unpleasantly," I said.

"I wasn't alone. I had letters from Kate. Mrs. Tuttle came up every day to see how I was getting on. Fannie, the dear girl, visited every day too. She can't wait to see your story in print."

But I couldn't write my story. I left those poor women there. *I'd let a woman burn.*

A knock on the door. I gathered my shawl around me as Mama opened it. A young boy stood on the threshold in knee breeches and a cap.

"Is that her, then?" he asked, his eyes sliding to me and then back to Mama. My mother nodded and took the envelope he was holding.

"He refuses," Mama said, "to leave the colonel's letters at the front door with Mrs. Tuttle. Isn't that right, young man?"

The boy nodded, looking at me. "I have strict instructions, miss, to give 'em only to you and nobody else."

"You can imagine the time I've had of it while you've been asleep." Mama pressed a penny into his palm and he was gone, footsteps reverberating down the hall as she closed the door. "Two others he delivered are on the table."

In my mind's eye, I saw Colonel Cockerill sitting at his massive desk, his penetrating eyes willing me to write. *Well, Miss Cochrane. Let's have it.*

"Don't look so glum, Pinkey." When I didn't stir, Mama's eyebrows drew together. "Perhaps you should lie down a bit."

I walked to the table where the two envelopes lay, each with my name written in a hurried hand. The first note was short and to the point:

Miss Cochrane:

> First of two installments due immediately for Sunday edition. Do not delay.

—J. Cockerill

I hadn't anticipated two installments. Cockerill would likely print the second the following Sunday—another week. Dent could cover up a lot of things in between the first and second printing. But what else could I do? If I insisted to Cockerill he print it all in one run, he'd want to know why, and I couldn't tell him. Secrecy was key to my plan.

The second note bore no salutation and looked as if Cockerill had penned it in a hurry:

> Why have I not heard from you? Need story posthaste for Sunday—

—J. Cockerill

I couldn't open the last. Without a word to Mama, I withdrew to the bedroom and closed the door. The shadows deepened in the growing darkness. I thought of Anne's kind face, her whispered dreams in the sitting room of one day getting out. I thought of Tillie and the sickness that had left her increasingly emaciated, restless with fear and suspicion. I thought of quiet Mrs. Fox and Mrs. Shanz, who, for no fault of their own, had been committed to a mental institution, in all probability, for life. What chance did any of them have? I'd lied to them. I'd led them to believe I was someone I was not. But more than that, no matter what I wrote, no matter what the outcome, I couldn't save them. I couldn't save any of them. I doubted that even my errand with Hendricks after we'd docked at the Bellevue pier could do that.

The bedroom was dark and still, the half of the bed where Mama slept empty. In the asylum, it had never been quiet. Even in the dead of night, in the small predawn hours, there was always stomping and slamming, cursing and crying. I'd hated it at first; it had frightened me. Now the silence was unsettling. It was as if the house was waiting to see what I would do, or what I would fail to do.

Faint conversation drifted to me from the sitting room. The clock on the dresser read half past eight. Who could be visiting Mama at such a late hour? I reached for my shawl and pulled the door open a few inches.

"—dangerous. I don't understand."

"Don't fuss, Albert," Mama said. "She's home now."

"Yes, but at what cost? She'll write her lamentable story and forever be the girl who had herself committed to an asylum."

"It's what she wanted."

"Yes, but is it best for her? I must say, I don't see women in journalism, Mama. This man Cockerill is dabbling at this idea of women reporters. In the end, it will be a passing fad, mark my words. Then where will she be? How will she afford to—"

I opened the door fully and pulled it closed behind me with a bang, making my presence known. "Albert, I thought I heard you complaining."

My brother turned in Mama's rocker and assessed me. "You look dreadful."

"And you are blunt."

"Pinkey, Albert has come all the way from Pittsburgh to see us," Mama said. "He's going to stay a few days. Please be courteous."

"Mama and I were just discussing your . . . stunt. I hope, for your sake, you haven't ruined your health."

"How kind of you to consider it."

"If you have, you shall never find a proper match, and—"

"I will not discuss such things with you," I snapped. "It's none of your damn business."

Albert's eyebrows rose. "Did you learn that language in the asylum?" He shook his head. "Never mind. Mama says you haven't started your story yet."

"All the more reason for you to leave so that I can begin."

Mama, seated on the davenport and watching us in despair, interrupted, "Pinkey, Albert came all this way to see us," she repeated. "Please don't be cross."

I looked from her to my brother. "Well, he has seen." I walked to the door that led to the hallway and pulled it open. "And now he must go."

⚬⚬⚬

I awoke to the sound of the door opening. Mama held a lamp, and for a moment, I was reminded of Nurse Grady in the flickering darkness with a glass.

"Fannie is here," Mama whispered. "Would you like to say hello?"

I sat up, forcing Nurse Grady from my mind. "Give me a moment."

When I entered the front room, the smile slipped momentarily from Fannie's face as she took in my appearance. She recovered quickly, coming to me in a rush.

"Oh, Elizabeth! I'm so relieved to see you home at last."

We sat on the davenport. A beat of silence; neither of us seemed to know quite what to say. A small stack of newspapers lay beside Fannie.

Mama said, "I'll go tell Mrs. Tuttle to prepare some beef tea for you, Elizabeth."

When she'd left, I turned to Fannie. "Thank you for looking in on her."

"It was no problem at all. We had a lot to talk about." At my quizzical look, she elaborated. "I now know a great deal about your childhood in Apollo. I found the tales of you and your brothers quite humorous. You had a much richer childhood than me."

So Mama had said nothing of our troubled years with Jack Ford. Like his last name she had acquired, she had let it go, never to be revisited, perhaps except in disturbing dreams. It was just as well. "If by richer you mean arguing a lot with Albert and getting in a lot of trouble for trying to keep up with him and my other brother Charles, then yes."

Fannie frowned. "Losing your father, and that awful man who stole the money for your schooling. But you never gave up, did you? You only got stronger."

She was attempting to bolster my spirits. It was admirable of her, but Fannie couldn't know how her words wounded me. I wasn't brave now. I hadn't done enough. I was a coward.

"I guessed you were the woman with the lost memory at

Bellevue right away. It sounded like something you would do, and it certainly sounded like something that scoundrel Cockerill would want to see carried out, no harm done to him, of course. Still, how frightened you must have been when you were sent to Bellevue, and on to Blackwell's!" When I made no reply, she said gently, "It may be too soon for you to write, Elizabeth, but I think you should have a look at these."

Fannie picked up the papers. "The *Sun* reported this morning that you were released a few days ago, and there's this." She leafed through another paper, its broad pages spilling off her lap. "The *Times* ran this today. It's longer than what the *Sun* reported, with an interesting detail." She folded the page and held it out to me.

"Tell me," I said, looking away. I couldn't read it.

"It says the 'mysterious lost girl' has been released after more than a week of confinement, though the facts of why you lost your memory or where you came from are still unknown. It doesn't stop there, though. It says your treatment for insanity achieved 'gratifying results' and with a doctor's care, your full sanity will soon be restored."

"Is, is that all it says?"

"Yes."

So the story had focused on me and not on events at the asylum. I couldn't think a reporter from the *Times* had been allowed on the island, yet the story had the unmistakable feel of being master-minded by Dent.

I turned to Fannie. "Has the *World* printed anything?"

"Not a word. That's the interesting part. You'd think, just from that, the other papers would've caught on. The *World,* the largest, most prestigious paper in the city, hasn't said a word about you, yet the others have been following your story since you appeared in Judge Duffy's courtroom. One would think the other papers would be suspicious. It's unlike Pulitzer to let a story go that the *World*'s competitors are talking about. The other papers have no idea they're going to get the biggest surprise—that you went inside Blackwell's on behalf of the *World!* They've only helped hype the story you'll deliver in full. Cockerill must be thrilled. When is your story due? Has he said?"

"He wants something for the Sunday edition."

"Sunday! Good heavens, that's the day after tomorrow! You must get to work immediately." Fannie leaped from the couch and crossed to the little table in front of the window where she retrieved a large stack of newspapers and brought them to me. "You haven't seen these yet, have you?"

"No."

"I've been saving them for you." Fannie placed the stack on the davenport between us and gave it a pat. "Every piece that's been written about your stunt. I thought you'd want to read through them before you write your own account."

And what, exactly, was my own account? The story of a woman who'd witnessed the horrors of Blackwell's, without doing a single thing about them.

The soft click of the door announced Mama's return. On a tray she carried a bowl of beef tea. There was something else there too. An unmarked envelope.

"I've just shown Elizabeth the editions that have reported her release," Fannie said with enthusiasm.

I rose from the couch. "Hail to the 'lost girl' who left the island, her treatment producing 'gratifying results.'" I couldn't keep the rancor from my voice. I tore a sheet of paper from a tablet on the desk and scratched out a note to Cockerill. "Fannie, would you be so kind as to deliver this to Cockerill first thing in the morning? He'll have what he needs for Sunday."

⁂

I lit the desk lamp in the sitting room. The two unread letters were where I'd left them beside the tray: Cockerill's and the unmarked one Mama had brought in earlier. I opened Cockerill's first. There was neither salutation nor signature.

> It is apparent from your lack of communication that
> you are not fit for the man's job of journalism.

I muttered an oath as hot tears stung my eyes, though his words hardly surprised me. Had I abandoned my dreams? I used to be unstoppable. A force slowed only by those who impeded my progress—men who didn't understand me, men who didn't understand that women had the same goals and motivations they did. I was not unstoppable now. My guilt for leaving Anne, for leaving the others, filled me with a bitter blackness, and I could not rid myself of the memories of the women in the Lodge pleading for help. I picked up the other envelope. George McCain's. It had to be from him. It had been hand delivered too, not by a delivery boy, but left on the doorstep. No postage, no address, just my name. How had he learned where I lived? How many times had I been thus, poised to open another of his missives with my heart hammering in my chest?

What would you think of me now, Mr. McCain? I'm not a champion of the downtrodden. I am a champion of my own cowardice.

I fingered the envelope open. Inside was an illustration of an exotic yellow flower with thin, needle-shaped petals. Black poplar. I consulted the book. *Courage.*

The word was a silent plea. No, I had not abandoned my dreams. More than ever I was sure of what I must do. I must tell the story of the women of Blackwell's—women who, by a large majority, were not insane at all. Blackwell's was not so much an asylum as a prison for women who fell outside of society's norms, women who did not, for one reason or another, meet the expectations class structure forced upon them. Who but I, a woman who for most of her life had railed against established customs, could tell the story best?

Mama had retired for the night, leaving me to the pile of newspapers Fannie had collected for me. Within the hour, I was well versed on what the city's papers had made of the woman who'd landed in Judge Duffy's courtroom with no memory. It had all the makings of a thrilling story: a young woman, amnesia, the necessity of medical intervention, suggested madness. It was both irritating and thrilling to read about the doctors' "accurate diagnoses" of my mad condition. With the exception of Dr. O'Rourke and the kind Dr. Ingram, how inept they had all been in finding me a lunatic, yet how perfectly their incompetence had served me in my endeavor to get to Blackwell's.

Thanks to the reporters who'd visited me at Bellevue, my sketch had been published in most of the papers. All pondered where I could have come from, who I might be, how I might have lost my memory. That the *World* remained silent through it all did look curious given that all the major papers had dedicated so many column inches to the story. McCain had easily put two and two together and decided to visit me under the guise of a man who had lost his sweetheart.

After two days of sleep and avoidance, I was amazed how my pencil flew across the page. Once I began, I couldn't stop. I was surprised at the strength of my memory. Recollections tumbled forth quicker than my pencil could scrawl. I didn't exaggerate; the tale spoke for itself, the details covering the pages without artifice. I hoped the strength of my narrative, combined with my errand after leaving Blackwell's Island, would produce the result the women of Blackwell's desperately needed. If not, everything

I had done would be in vain. I couldn't, *I wouldn't,* accept that. I had risked too much to see things fall apart.

Morning light was coming through the window as I finished. My right hand smarted and my fingertips were smudged with lead. My back ached from hunching over the desk.

The bedroom door opened. The surprise on Mama's face turned to relief. "How long have you been working?"

"A few hours, I suppose. I lost track of time." I gathered the pages. "Cockerill expected me yesterday. I must go at once." I put the first installment in my bag but left the second on the desk. Cockerill would want it all, of course, but I wasn't about to make it that easy for him. He would just have to wait.

"Would you like some company?" Mama's hair was in a long braid. She looked younger, more vulnerable. "I'd be happy to go with you."

"Thank you, Mama, but it's not necessary. And there's no use spending the extra fare. I'll be back before you know it." In truth, my refusal of her company had less to do with saving money and more to do with my need to make the trip to Newspaper Row alone.

"You are late, Miss Cochrane," Colonel Cockerill intoned from behind his desk. "I told the typesetters to leave ample space when I got your note this morning, but your story better be sound. As it is, I'll have to run this downstairs immediately for it to print in tomorrow's edition."

I did not reply. How tired of him I was.

"Hendricks shared with me the meeting with the doctor when he came to fetch you. What was his name?"

"Superintendent Dent."

"Beast of a man. Hendricks said you looked ghastly."

I waited. When Cockerill said nothing more, I let out a long breath. So Hendricks had made good on his promise to me that my errand would stay between him and me. The attorney had said as much as we'd traveled by carriage to our downtown destination, but I knew now for certain that he hadn't betrayed me to Cockerill. I handed him my story. He snatched it up, began to read, and said, without looking up, "You have formed this into two installments?"

"Yes. This is the first. It details everything up to the point of stepping onto Blackwell's Island."

"And the second?"

"At home."

Cockerill narrowed his eyes. "I expected both."

"The second half won't print for another week," I said. "I want to get it just right."

He regarded me with a cold stare and then returned his attention to the story, his eyes moving over the page. "Excellent. This should whet readers' appetites for the island ordeal."

"Precisely."

He set the pages on his desk and interlaced his fingers together on top of them. "The timing is perfect. The tale of the young girl with the lost memory has not yet grown cold, yet the competition hasn't had any real news since your release." He chuckled. "When this hits the streets tomorrow, we'll shock them all. I'll have my editors make any necessary changes immediately."

He reached into his desk and handed me bills. "Another twenty-five for your efforts thus far. Do not disappoint me with the second installment, Miss Cochrane."

I made no move to take the money. "Colonel, I hope what I've given you is the beginning of an understanding between us."

"Don't fear, Miss Cochrane. Now, I must get this downstairs." He pushed back his chair and stood.

"Then you're offering me employment?"

He paused at the door. "Miss Cochrane, while I have every hope in your success, it still remains to be seen what effect your first installment will have on our readership. And, of course, we must see what the second installment renders."

Confound him. But then, I had my own card up my sleeve. If my plan succeeded, he would be—after he got over the fact that my second installment would have crucial details missing—appeased. If not, I seriously doubted I would ever work for the *World*.

28

If you want to do it you can do it. The question is, do you want to do it?

NELLIE BLY

NEW YORK CITY, OCTOBER 1887

Late morning on Friday, five days after the first installment of my story had run, I found myself fleeing Central Park under ominous clouds. With my hand on my hat, I dashed down Ninety-Sixth Street, the wind buffeting my skirts and blowing leaves and debris into the street. By the time I arrived at Mrs. Tuttle's boardinghouse, it was sprinkling.

I burst through the front door and was heading for the staircase when a movement in the front parlor caught my attention. Mama sat perched on a chair by the fireplace. Seated on the davenport was George McCain. I'd never expected him ever to look again as sad and bleak as he had at Blackwell's, yet he did. He eyed me anxiously, his face white, as he rose to his feet. I'd imagined our first meeting outside the asylum would be one where he congratulated me on the success of my story, but this was not the face of a man who was delighted that I'd so cleverly fooled doctors, nor was it the face of a man who was happy that I was the talk of Newspaper Row.

"Mr. McCain?" I said feebly, fear rising in my throat.

"Let me take your things, my dear," Mama said in a cheery tone that belied the tension in the room. I allowed her to remove my coat while I stared at McCain. "I shall just have Mrs. Tuttle put on some tea," she said, and then she was gone.

We knew each other too well to go through the usual greeting. This was not a social call. "What is it?" I whispered, stepping into the parlor.

He beckoned me to the davenport. Outside the sprinkle had become a steady downpour. The light at the window cast an imprint of rain on McCain's face, the water dripping from the glass like tears on his cheek.

"How did you find me?" I asked, taking a seat beside him.

"Your friend Fannie. I chanced upon her in Newspaper Row. I knew she worked for the *World* and thought perhaps the two of you had met. I explained who I was and she gave me your address. I think she thought you'd like me to come see you when you returned."

Of course. It explained how McCain had known where to hand deliver the card he'd sent. Fannie would have encouraged a fellow correspondent working for the same out-of-town paper to visit. She didn't know the complicated history between us.

I searched his face. "Is it your wife? Has something . . . ?" I trailed off, unable to finish.

"My . . . Mary? No, she's well. In fact, she sends her love."

Love. The word burrowed its way inside me, twisting like a serpent. Pretty Mary McCain, who had for her own the only man I'd ever wanted.

McCain cleared his throat. "I take it you haven't seen the paper?" He lifted a folded newspaper from the armrest beside him and laid it between us. He took my hand. "The *Sun*. Today's edition."

"Tell me."

"They've reported on your stay in the asylum. In its entirety."

My heart skipped a beat. "They can't have. My second installment doesn't run for two days." Suddenly, hatefully, I wished McCain had come to tell me his wife was ailing. That her death was eminent. It would have been easier to bear.

"They managed to speak with the asylum staff and get hold of your medical examinations," McCain said, stroking the top of my hand with his thumb. "They tell of rumors after you left that circulated about you being a pretender."

So Dent had allowed at least one reporter on the island. Now that the first part of my asylum piece had dropped, in which I'd maneuvered my way to Bellevue, been pronounced insane, and been carted off to Blackwell's, he wanted to appear as reasonable

and obliging as possible. *As if there was nothing to hide at the asylum.*
Footsteps approached. We withdrew our hands.

Mrs. Tuttle waddled into the room with a tray and set it down
on a table. Mama followed in her wake.

"I'll pour for the two of you and be on my way," the housekeeper
said, setting to her task. "Sugar? Milk?" We declined, both eager
to be rid of her. "Would you like me to light a fire, Miss Cochrane?
Won't be no trouble, no trouble at all. Dreadful weather."

"No, thank you, Mrs. Tuttle. That won't be necessary."

When the housekeeper had finished pouring, she stood with
her hand on her hips. "You sure you don't want a fire? Day like
this, a good fire will take the chill away." She smiled at McCain.
"I'm not one to go without tending to my boarders, or their visitors."

"You have already outdone yourself in that regard," McCain
said gallantly, gesturing to the tea service.

Mrs. Tuttle beamed and stepped back. Thank heavens. I was
ready to burst with impatience.

"Elizabeth," Mama said, "I have a bit of a headache. If you don't
mind, I shall go have a lie-down upstairs."

A maneuver to grant us privacy and a signal to Mrs. Tuttle
that Mama was forgoing her role as chaperone. Mrs. Tuttle didn't
allow her unwed female boarders to entertain gentlemen unless
they were family or accompanied by an older adult. In this case,
Mama evidently felt the rule could be waived. McCain must have
told her why he was here. That, or his serious countenance had
signaled the need for privacy.

"Of course, Mama," I said. "I hope you feel better."

When they were gone, McCain unfolded the paper. The story
was spread across the front page of the *Sun*:

PLAYING MAD WOMAN.
———

Nellie Bly Too Sharp for the
Island Doctors.
———

NINE DAYS' LIFE IN CALICO.
———

The Sun Finishes Up its Story of
the "Pretty Crazy Girl."

Across six columns of type on two pages, an unnamed reporter
had recounted my story—my examinations, my complaints of the
food, my attempts to have blankets and extra layers of clothing

provided for the inmates. He'd got the number of days I'd spent there wrong, though. Glaringly missing from the piece were my trips to the Lodge. There was only a passing mention that a fire had taken place there, and no mention of the rotary chair or any of the other despicable things that went on inside. The *Sun* hadn't uncovered the whole truth. The access Superintendent Dent had granted had gone only as far as he'd allowed, which was to say that none of the real horrors of Blackwell's had been exposed.

I still had revelations of my own that would top the *Sun*'s account. My remaining installment—what had actually taken place once I was inside the asylum—might secure a job at the *World,* but it wasn't as important as catching out Dent. I had a feeling, given the lack of the reporter's interest in the Lodge, that Dent had glossed over the fire while he was visiting. This surprised me not in the least. From what Louise had overhead while she was in the infirmary, Dent had strongly reprimanded Grady and Grupe for allowing me inside the Lodge with Mrs. Cotter. For this reason, I believed the two had acted alone when they'd drugged me and pulled me from my bed, which meant Dent would have been outraged to learn that they'd done it again.

"Miss Cochrane?"

I blinked, returning to the present. McCain was watching me curiously. "They haven't reported the whole story, not by a long shot," I said. At his look of surprise, I took his hand. "There were things I experienced I need to tell you. It will all come out soon enough anyway, and I'd prefer you hear it from me." I launched into the tale of what I knew of the Lodge: what had happened during my first visit with Mrs. Cotter, and what I had undergone on the last night of my stay. I told him I'd been drugged by the nurses, dragged to the building, the fire, the chair, watching an inmate burn to death—all of it. "I don't think Superintendent Dent knew what the nurses were planning to do that night. Mr. Hendricks was coming back for me the next day. He wouldn't have wanted to risk exposure like that."

"It doesn't matter," McCain said angrily. "He runs the asylum. He's just as responsible."

"Which is why he'll do anything to cover for them. He'll deny it happened, I'm certain of it. He'll say it's all for the sake of a sensational story."

"Dear God." McCain shook his head. "You're lucky they didn't leave you to burn." He got up from the davenport and ran a hand over his hair. "You're lucky you got off the island at all. What hell you've been through."

"All the more reason to expose Blackwell's for what it is." Something in his eyes shifted. "What? What is it?"

"Speaking of exposure, you need to read the rest of the *Sun's* story, to the end," McCain said, indicating the paper. "There's more."

I frowned and continued reading, cursing under my breath as I finished. As if it wasn't enough that the *Sun* had stolen my story, they had unmasked me. The newspaper had printed my real name, citing my former work at the *Pittsburg Dispatch* and even Papa's career as a judge in tiny Apollo. I was no longer Nellie Brown the daring reporter but Elizabeth Cochrane of the Upper West Side.

I rose to my feet in a rush. Suddenly, the parlor seemed too small, the walls too close.

"I believe you are the first reporter, certainly the first female one, to get your name in a rival paper," McCain said. "Astounding."

I whirled, skirts swishing, hands clenched. "Is that what you call it, 'astounding'? Pulitzer must be livid. He abhors Charles Dana and his paper. As for Cockerill—"

"Listen to what they say about you," McCain said, snatching up the paper. "'She is intelligent, capable, and self-reliant, and, except for the matter of changing her name to Nellie Bly, has gone about the business of maintaining herself in journalism in a practical, business-like way.'"

"That intolerable charlatan of a publisher," I seethed. "Dana went on record with me saying he didn't believe women had the skill to report like men. Now, to boost his circulation numbers, he's doing an about-face. And *of course* I had to change my name! I'm not allowed to use my own!"

McCain lowered the paper. "My point, Miss Cochrane, is that the *Sun* applauds you and your efforts. You mustn't overlook that."

"Of course they applaud me." I began to pace. "I delivered a story, a newsworthy one at that, right into their hands, and they have, have—"

"'Scooped,' I believe, is the proper term these days."

"—*scooped* my story, right out from under my nose, not to mention the *World's*." I brought a hand to my hair, realizing that I still wore my hat. I withdrew the pins and flung it to the floor.

"The *Sun* may have disclosed some of your tale, but not all of it," McCain offered. "Not the most salient parts."

"Yes," I said, biting my thumbnail. "But Dent can't see those in print. If he does, all is lost."

McCain's eyebrows drew together. "Why ever not?" And then his face changed. "Ah, you mean to trap him."

"Yes, but I'm not doing it on my own. I have . . . help." I then told him of my errand with Hendricks after I'd left the asylum and what I had agreed to do there. "For now, you mustn't say a word of what I've told you to anyone. Not even Madden or QO. I have been sworn to secrecy, as you can imagine. The story—the whole of it—must break here first, from the *World.*"

"And what does Cockerill have to say about this?"

"He doesn't know. I still owe him my second installment. But if I tell him everything that happened that night, and what I suspect, he'll—"

"Demand it all go in the story."

"Yes."

"I don't like this, Elizabeth. Cockerill could refuse to hire you if your plan should backfire."

"I know," I said, letting out a long breath, "but that's a risk I'm willing to take."

After a thoughtful pause, McCain said, "As you wish, as long as you promise me you're not putting yourself in any danger."

"None." At least not with Dent. Cockerill, I wasn't so sure. "I need to get to the *World.* I've got to speak with Cockerill and get the second installment in his hands. I can't imagine what he'll think now that another paper went to press with my story first."

"It's hardly your fault they did." McCain moved to me and placed his hands on my shoulders. "You mustn't lose hope."

I searched his face, the man who gave me so much pleasure and pain in equal measure, and felt a pang of animosity flare within me. "That's why your wife sends her love, isn't it? Because she pities me. Both of you do. You think that because of the *Sun*'s exposé, Cockerill won't hire me."

"You would resent me for pitying you, would you not?" He gripped me, looking as if he wanted to fold me into himself. Outside, the rain pounded. "I don't pity you," he said, his voice low. "You're too much a fighter, too much a winner, to be pitied. You're a survivor, and you'll survive this."

"You can't know that."

"I don't know what Cockerill's response will be, no," McCain said. "But I do know that if you don't end up at the *World* for the asylum piece, you'll end up at another paper. The *Sun,* perhaps. That's what I've been trying to tell you. There isn't one word in their story that besmirches you or what you did. Quite the contrary. They hail your prowess as a reporter. If that damned idiot Cockerill doesn't see it, Dana does."

Tears stung my eyes, and I looked away. I didn't know if I believed him.

McCain cupped my chin and turned me to face him. "Go fetch the rest of your piece. I'm taking you to see Cockerill. You must ask him directly what he's going to do. If he gives you the slightest hesitation, go see Dana." Slowly, as if loath to do it, McCain released me. He reached for his hat and gloves and in another moment was moving for the door.

"Where are you going?"

"To hail a cab. I don't want you showing up in Cockerill's office dripping wet."

I bounded up the stairs and seized the second installment off my desk. I ran my eyes over the pages. I'd continued my habit of writing in pencil from my days at the *Dispatch*. It would be so easy to add in the parts of my ordeal the *Sun* had missed, the parts Cockerill would be most keen to print. My story—the whole unvarnished truth—would scoop the *Sun* and make their own exposé laughable. But I couldn't do it. I owed it to the women of Blackwell's to let things play out as I'd planned. I only hoped that, when all was said and done, Cockerill would understand.

By the time I returned downstairs, McCain was back. I threw on my coat and hat, and he ushered me under his umbrella and into the cab. I sank back into the seat. McCain climbed in after and shut the door. Outside, the rain was a violent thing, rattling the windows, lashing against the cab, thundering on the roof. I was relieved we hadn't taken the el, though I was nervous being so close to McCain. Inside the cab, we were alone in a way we had never been. Even Allegheny Cemetery had been less isolated. The interior of the cab felt exciting and forbidden.

To ease my nerves, I looked out the window, but I could feel his eyes on me, and when I couldn't bear it any longer, I swung my gaze to his. There was no need for words. George McCain understood me, and I him. I could have protested his presence, told him I was capable of making the trip to Newspaper Row on my own, but I didn't. I needed him. And I knew he wanted to see this through, that whatever result lay at the end of the ride, he would be with me. He wouldn't have it any other way.

For six miles we uttered not a word, alternating between looking out the window and turning our gazes inward to each other. McCain took my hand and didn't let go until the cab stopped in front of the *World*.

He alighted, opened his umbrella, and helped me to step down. Inside the lobby, he said, "I'll be waiting here when you return."

To my relief, the guard didn't impede my approach to the elevators. In a few minutes I was outside Cockerill's office, inquiring of his secretary if the managing editor was in. He was. The secretary opened the door to his office.

"I've seen today's *Sun*," I said without preamble after the door shut behind me.

"Ah, Miss Cochrane." Cockerill set down his pen and gestured for me to have a seat. "What do you think of the story they snatched from us?" As usual, his features betrayed nothing. He might have been a poker player in another life.

"I came here to see what you think."

Cockerill leaned back in his chair. "I think an anonymous reporter has been very clever, and Charles Dana is having a superb cigar right now on our behalf. He'll stop at nothing to trump us." He glanced over at the *Sun*'s exposé, which lay on top of the pile of newspapers on his desk. "Damn good bit of reporting, the uncovering of your real name. I wonder how they managed that."

"I have no idea."

"Your first installment did very, very well for us, and Dana thought, no doubt, he'd capitalize on it too. Do you know what hubris is, Miss Cochrane? Are you familiar with the term? 'Pride goeth before destruction, a haughty spirit before a fall.'"

"Pride or not, Colonel, the *Sun* recognizes my talent."

"And that's where they made the biggest mistake." Cockerill smiled. "Tell me, Miss Cochrane, who will tell the better story? The *Sun* and its anonymous reporter for telling it first, or you, by telling it from your own perspective?"

"I will," I replied, my face growing hot. "I *have*. I'm the one who endured the ordeal firsthand, I—"

"Precisely," Cockerill said, drumming a fist on his desk. "For once, the *Sun* has done us a good turn, though I can't believe they think so. While they rest on their laurels and think they've stolen the story, every *Sun* reader who sees today's front page will be turning to the *World* to get the story from you. Firsthand, as you say. Dana and his reporter have done such a fine job of dressing you up as a first-class reporter that readers will come scrambling for the second installment come Sunday. *Yours.* I have already told the pressroom to print twice the editions for Sunday, Miss Cochrane. You're to be commended."

My head felt full of cotton, and I was dizzy. *Twice the editions.* Some moments passed before I realized Cockerill was speaking.

"Miss Cochrane?" I stared at him. His hand was outstretched. "Your story?"

"Not so fast," I said, cocking a brow. "I should like an offer for a job." Cockerill made no reply. He only sat looking at me, a small smile playing at the corners of his mouth. "You paid me twenty-five dollars with the understanding I would go nowhere with my list, instructions, which I followed to the letter," I said icily. "A second twenty-five for the first installment, which has done quite well, as you've so admirably admitted. If we can't come to terms, I think Charles Dana will be more than happy to see this." I brandished the story.

Cockerill let out a long sigh and sat back, his smile even bigger now. "I commend you. I admit I didn't think you would be able to carry out the assignment I gave you. I was wrong. I underestimated you. Your skills are admirable and you've certainly proved you have pluck." He regarded me over steepled fingers. "I planned to tell you we are hiring you on *after* you gave me your story, but I see I need to make the matter of your employment clear before you hand it over. Therefore, you may now consider yourself employed by the *New York World*. I shall have a contract drawn up straightaway." He held out a hand. "And now, may I?"

"Well," I said, my face suddenly warm, "in that case." I handed over my story.

I'd written of the horrible food, the lack of heat, the brutality of the nurses. I'd gone into detail about the cold baths and the first two times I'd been drugged. I had described my first visit to the Lodge and the horrid details of the second, but I hadn't disclosed everything. Had Cockerill known of the omission, I was quite sure he wouldn't be smiling.

I'd been forced to turn the other cheek with Bessie Bramble. It had been the same in Mexico with President Díaz, where the stakes had been even higher. I did not, once again, want to find myself at the mercy of someone who conspired for the upper hand at the expense of what was right. But, unlike with those prior experiences, I realized that some things were more important than the story.

"I shall give this a read and then take it downstairs straightaway," he said. I nodded and made toward the door. "Oh, and Miss Cochrane?" I turned, my hand on the doorknob. "Were I you, I would consider approaching a publisher for your asylum series. It may well prove to be a nice supplemental income to your salary from the *World*."

McCain was leaning against a marble pillar near the doors. He straightened immediately when he spied me. Seeing him so anxious brought tears to my eyes, and I fought to maintain my composure. Fearing the worst, he ushered me away from prying eyes and straight into the rain, where a cab waited at the curb. As soon as we were inside, I fell into tears. He reached inside his coat for a handkerchief and handed it to me. It smelled of him: leather, soap, and an elusive scent I couldn't name that was all his own. He hugged an arm around my shoulders, and I lay my head against his chest, letting my tears flow. After I had somewhat composed myself, I sniffed and wiped my eyes.

And then I launched into my meeting with Cockerill, though much of it may have been incomprehensible, as I was still blubbering miserably. "He said he was doubling the print run Sunday because of the *Sun*'s story," I said. "He said I should look into having my asylum series published into a book."

McCain's face was thunderous with anger. "Did the scoundrel offer you a job?"

"Yes," I said, smiling through my tears. "Yes, he did." I told him the rest, including how I'd withheld the second half of my story and threatened to go to Dana if he refused to hire me then and there.

McCain's body relaxed. He smiled, his gray eyes filling with warmth and not a little bit of mischief. We were sitting very close, our knees touching, as we jostled back up Eighth Avenue. "Then may I ask why it is you're crying?"

"Because I'm relieved." I returned his smile, my eyes refilling with tears even as I said the words. "It's funny. I thought when I came here, I should be rid of Madden soon enough. Now I fear I've simply found the New York equivalent of him. Cockerill is exasperating beyond measure and twice as disagreeable."

He nodded. "Madden is mercurial and shortsighted, but Cockerill . . . Cockerill is an altogether different man. You mustn't underestimate him, do you hear?"

"That's the second time you've warned me," I said, the back of my neck prickling as I recalled our conversation in Central Park. "What is it you know?"

McCain took my hand in his. "Five years ago, when Cockerill was working at the *St. Louis Post-Dispatch* for Pulitzer, he shot and killed a man."

I inhaled sharply. "No."

"I'm afraid so," he replied. "A man called Slayback, an attorney. Slayback was a rather shady fellow and eventually aroused Cockerill's enmity for his crooked politics. Apparently, Cockerill was printing insults Slayback couldn't abide, and he charged into the newsroom one day and, in front of a few witnesses, drew a revolver.

Cockerill, evidently expecting such an altercation, drew his own gun. There was a scuffle, and Cockerill fired. The bullet pierced Slayback's lungs, and he died shortly thereafter."

I had never liked Cockerill. I found him discourteous and arrogant at best, but that he had killed a man was beyond my imagining. "Did he serve jail time?"

McCain shook his head. "Pulitzer pulled some strings and saw to it that he was released on bail. A grand jury chose not to indict him, convinced Slayback had provoked the shooting by entering the newsroom with a weapon. However, rumors have been circulating around Newspaper Row of late."

"What kind of rumors?"

"The normal kind, completely unsubstantiated ones." I waited. McCain looked down at my hand. "One of the witnesses to the scuffle now asserts Slayback never had a gun. According to him, Cockerill saw to it one was planted on him before the police arrived to strengthen his self-defense story."

"Do you think it's true?"

"Whether it is or isn't, Cockerill shot someone to death. While I don't think he'd ever pull a stunt like that again, he's dangerous. As happy as I am that you're working for the *World,* it makes me uneasy you'll be working closely with him, especially knowing that you're keeping information from him he'd very much want to see in print."

Cockerill had slain a man over newspaper business. What if my secrets, once they became known, stirred his wrath? "You tried to tell me in the park that day."

"Yes," he said, "but I was afraid if I said too much, I would alienate you completely." His eyes were so beseeching that my heart ached.

"I'll be careful. I shall just have to stay one step ahead of him." And then, because I wanted to change the subject and I was emboldened, I suppose, by the intimacy of the carriage, I said, "I've missed you. When I returned from Mexico, the *Dispatch* was a very dull place without you darkening its door."

He grinned wolfishly. "Darkening? This from a woman I saved from being trampled by a horse on Fifth Avenue." I laughed. "Tell me, what would you have done if Cockerill had thrown you out on your ear today?"

I lifted my chin. "Hit him soundly, I suppose."

His hand came to rest on the side of my face, his smile gone. "If you were any other woman, I wouldn't believe you. But you, you, Elizabeth . . ."

The sound of my given name on his lips sent a thrill through me.

Oh, the pleasure of the moment, to be understood in the way that only he could. I'd been tethered to him since he'd pulled me from certain death the day I'd met him, linked to him by the language of flowers, which in two years had only strengthened my love for him. This was what it was to be a prisoner to love. To be fully rapt in the very thing that fulfilled you, yet had the power to be your undoing.

He bent his head and kissed me. I expected him to pull away immediately, but he did not. The kiss deepened, and my lips parted. The rain drummed on the roof and thunder sounded in the distance, but it was of no matter now. My hands found his hair. I was aware of the strength of his body, the erratic beating of my heart. It was as if, with his touch, my body had come to life. My senses had always been stimulated by his nearness, but now, with his lips on mine, every inch of me hummed. His hands came around me, pressing me into him at the same time that they traveled down my spine. I gave myself over fully to his embrace. It only increased his ardor; McCain let out a groan as one hand stroked my exposed neck, his fingers trailing to my breast.

The cab lurched, and we were suddenly thrown forward, then back.

"Fifty-One West Ninety-Sixth!" the driver barked, rapping on the roof.

My eyes flew open. We had stopped.

I came to my senses. My skirts were in disarray, my hat askew, my reticule on the seat opposite. A warm flush of embarrassment flooded my cheeks. McCain grabbed the umbrella and jumped out, while I fussed with my hat and gathered myself as best I could. When I leaned out to step down, McCain offered his arm. To my astonishment, he didn't look at me.

"Thank you," I said. I searched his face, but still he avoided my eyes. He was holding himself rigidly, almost detached. That buoyant feeling that had thrilled me moments ago was gone, leaving in its wake an excruciating sense of dread.

"Miss Cochrane," he said, nodding. For all the lack of feeling in his words, we might have been strangers.

We walked under the umbrella to the porch, where he left me with a curt nod. I turned at the door and glimpsed McCain's silhouette through the cab's window as it drove off. It was the profile of a man struggling to keep his emotions in check.

I wiped a tear from my cheek with his handkerchief. I hadn't thought to return it. Now, it seemed a precious thing, something to lock away with his flower cards. Why had he behaved so? What thoughts were tumbling around in his head?

I couldn't think about the answers now. If I did, they might very well destroy me.

29

*Could I pass a week in the insane ward
at Blackwell's Island? I said I could
and I would. And I did.*

NELLIE BLY

NEW YORK CITY, OCTOBER 1887

"Listen to this," Viola said, reading from the paper in front of her and ignoring the waiter delivering tea to our table. "'We all know that in times not so very remote men and women were sent to insane asylums on the certificates of doctors who were in collusion with relatives interested in having them put out of the way.'"

Newspapers cluttered the table: the *New York Sun,* the *New York Tribune,* the *Mail and Express,* the *Boston Globe,* the *St. Louis Post-Dispatch.* Were it not for the petite salt and pepper shakers, the delicate lace tablecloth, and the fine upholstered chairs, it might have been the surface of an editor's desk and not a table at the Cosmopolitan.

"'Not so very remote'?" I replied. An image of poor Mrs. Shanz arose in my mind. "I know for a fact it's still going on."

"Dreadful," Fannie remarked with a shiver. "To think how many people have languished without a single champion to protect them."

My second installment had run three days earlier, and since then, papers all over the country had lauded my achievement. Cockerill was right: the *Sun*'s story had only fueled interest in my own account. The *World,* two days running, had carried excerpts from dozens of papers congratulating me for my spunk.

I leaned forward, trying to see which paper Viola had read from. "What paper is that?"

"The *Hamilton Times.*" Beneath a brown hat trimmed with black and brown ribbon, Viola looked up, beaming. "Your story has reached Canada, Elizabeth."

"And that correspondent from Pittsburgh, George McCain," Fannie said. "It was so lovely of him to mention you in the *Dispatch.* All the fan mail you've been getting, he said!"

"Oh, speaking of the *Dispatch,*" Viola said mischievously, "do let's read that part again Bessie Bramble wrote. I do believe," she quirked a brow at me, "that woman is eating humble pie." She sifted through the papers. "Here it is. 'Behold! Nellie Bly steps in and performs a feat of journalism that very few men of the profession have more than equaled. She has shown that cool courage, craft, and investigating ability are not monopolized by the brethren of the profession.'"

After our spat in Pittsburgh, I could hardly believe Bessie had written so graciously of me. Perhaps it was her version of offering the proverbial olive branch. Of course, I hadn't received a word from Madden. I wondered if my success in New York brought him relief or a sense of loss for letting me slip through his fingers.

Most of the papers were astounded by how easy it had been for a girl with no special training to fool so many doctors. Superintendent Dent and a few of the other doctors had denied charges of abuse and continued to defend themselves, though in my opinion, they were clutching at clouds. Sixteen hundred women on Blackwell's Island could attest differently.

Fannie poured tea and handed cups around the table. "I propose a toast." The three of us lifted our cups. "To the fearless Nellie Bly, who, through her courage and ingenuity, has hoodwinked every paper in the city, except the one for which we work."

I winced inwardly as we sipped. I had hoodwinked the *World* too, but not, I trusted, for much longer. The trap was set. I only hoped that the account I'd written had given Dent confidence to believe his secrets would remain hidden.

Viola picked up the day's *World.* "I still can't get over Pulitzer's comment. The man is hard-pressed to compliment any of his staff, much less a woman. It's remarkable to say the least, Elizabeth."

On his return to New York by rail via Pittsburgh's Union Station, the revered Joseph Pulitzer had been questioned by a *Dispatch* reporter on his assessment of my feat. The publisher was quoted as saying he was pleased with the performance of his "bright" and "plucky" new staff member and had rewarded me with a "handsome check." Now, at last, I could afford to pay our rent at the boardinghouse and for many other things Mama and I had gone so long without.

"She is well-educated and thoroughly understands the profession which she has chosen," Viola read. "She has a great future before her."

"I must be very careful of all this attention," I said. "It may go to my head."

"Nonsense, Elizabeth," Viola said. "You're finally getting your due. Bask in it—you deserve it. And now, if you two don't mind, I'll just go powder my nose." She rose. "Don't read anything else until I come back. I don't want to miss anything."

As soon as Viola had gone, Fannie turned to me. "All right, out with it. What's the matter with you?"

"What do you mean?"

"You've been quiet ever since your installments ran. You look troubled. I can't imagine why. Everything has gone swimmingly for you, as far as I can tell." She narrowed her eyes. "You aren't yourself. Has Cockerill given you another unpleasant story?"

That I could answer honestly. "Not at all. He's going to let me choose my next theme. I have a few scandalous ideas rolling around in my head."

My attempt at lightheartedness didn't fool my friend. "Then what is it?"

I bit my lip. So far, everything was going to plan, but each day, I took the train to Newspaper Row and bought every daily, scouring the papers for any news of what was happening on Blackwell's Island. I'd found nothing. So far, Dent had only fielded questions from reporters about my visit. He continued to state that the asylum wasn't abusive—it was only lack of funding that prevented the inmates from getting better food and heat during the winter. There had been no further mention of the fire. I took a deep breath and let it out, fixing a smile on my face. "I'm just a little nervous my next attempt won't be as exciting as the asylum piece, that's all. Cockerill is expecting big things from me now. I don't want to let him down."

Fannie said, squeezing my hand, "Goodness, you don't have a thing to worry about."

"I'm glad we came in when we did," Viola announced as she slid back into her chair. "Otherwise, there wouldn't have been a table for lunch."

The Cosmopolitan was a popular haunt for the press, and it was crowded. Fannie leaned forward and said in a conspiratorial whisper, "Let's just hope Pulitzer doesn't use Elizabeth's success to pit us against one another in the name of 'friendly competition' like he does the rest of his staff. I hear you can cut the tension in the newsroom with a knife these days."

"We won't let him turn us into rivals," Viola said much more loudly. "We're all in this together, with the same purpose, waging the same war against narrow-minded, old-school buffoons."

Her voice attracted the attention of a man and woman seated nearby, who raked us with their eyes and then resumed their conversation.

I changed the subject. "How goes the battle with Cockerill?"

"I took a cue from you and Fannie," Viola said. "I gave him a list of story ideas—brave and daring ones. He's incubating. We shall see what he says."

"Tell me you didn't suggest a story on another mental asylum," Fannie said. "I don't think I could take another friend disappearing for ten days."

"If I'm committed," Viola said dryly, "it will be because I strangled Cockerill."

We were all laughing when an attractive woman in a bottle green coat and hat entered the café. Elizabeth Bisland surveyed the luncheon crowd, waved to a few reporters, and was making her way to a table in the corner when she caught sight of me. The book reviewer for the *Sun* changed course so quickly that she nearly collided with a waiter engaged in clearing a table.

"And we were having so much fun," Fannie muttered at her approach.

Bisland was on us in an instant, like a fox spotting prey. "Good afternoon, ladies. May I sit down?" She didn't wait for an answer. She seated herself, adjusting her voluptuous skirts around her. "I must congratulate you on your shocking story, Miss Cochrane." She batted her lashes. "Viola, your hat is charming. Brown is such a good color on you, my dear." She surveyed the table strewn with newsprint. "My, my. Such a lot of papers. It looks like you've been scouring all the dailies." She fixed her deep brown eyes on me. "You must be looking for a new story idea."

"We were just looking at the papers that have been commenting on Elizabeth's story," Fannie said. "There are so very many."

"Indeed. And to think, when last I saw Miss Cochrane, she was a correspondent from Philadelphia."

"Pittsburgh," I said, "and I don't believe we've ever met."

Perhaps it was my tone that stopped her sugary repartee, or maybe she'd caught on that we were watching her with hostility. Though the smile remained, Ms. Bisland's eyes became hard, dark stones. "Tell me, Miss Cochrane, what will you write of next?" This was not, I was certain, the rhetorical question she'd disguised it to be. I shrugged. "I don't know yet."

"Ah, resting on your laurels. Milk it for all it's worth."

Viola looked aghast. "What ever do you mean?"

Bisland's eyebrows shot up. "Surely you've been approached for speaking engagements and appearances, Miss Cochrane? I'm sure everyone wants to catch a glimpse of the girl who fooled everyone."

"The story isn't about me," I said, frowning. "There are still many women on Blackwell's Island who need justice."

"Ever the champion for the underprivileged," she drawled. "How good of you." She lowered her voice. "If I may give you some advice, the public is best served by reporters who print news. Wielding the sword of social conscience won't get you very far. You'd best move on to something else. Let others fight the messy battles."

"That must be why you write book reviews," Fannie said. "I can't imagine a lot of 'messy battles' in that."

Before Bisland could transform her venomous look at Fannie into words, I said, "I'm afraid you and I disagree."

"Perhaps we do. Well, when you decide what it is you're going to tackle, I'm sure it will be interesting. I for one shall be glad to see your asylum piece put to rest. Such a fuss over it, all for the poor lunatics who dwell there. Now, if you'll forgive me, I shall just go say hello to some friends. It was so nice to catch up."

Fannie watched Bisland retreat and then returned her attention to the table. "Don't you pay her any attention. I just know something good will come to Blackwell's because of what you've done, Elizabeth."

I hoped so too. It all depended on what would happen in the coming days.

30

The trip to the island was vastly different to my first.

NELLIE BLY

BLACKWELL'S ASYLUM, OCTOBER 1887

A brisk wind from the west blew across the East River, attempting to unseat my hat as six uniformed policemen and I waited at the shoreline of Blackwell's Island. The ferry swayed in the water like a drunken goose, threatening to take flight from its mooring. One by one, twenty-three gentlemen jurors stepped gingerly from the boat, aided by Vernon Davis, the assistant district attorney. Standing at the end of the pier in a black windswept robe was Judge Gildersleeve. Beside him was the court recorder, his little black machine peeking out from a bag that hung from his shoulder.

McCain was the last to step from the boat. In a well-fitting overcoat and top hat, he looked every inch a juror. The only evidence he was a reporter was the small notebook he carried. I'd watched him board at the Bellevue pier from a window inside the ferry, but we hadn't had a chance to speak. The boat had been too crowded for me to make my way to him, and in any case, it offered no opportunity for a private conversation. I hadn't seen him since the cab ride home from the *World,* but the memory of his kiss, and of his tormented profile as the driver pulled away, was a wound that had festered in the three days that had elapsed. As he stepped off the pier, I searched for a sign that things between us hadn't changed. A flicker of pain registered in his eyes when he saw me, but he recovered well, giving me a tight smile. Whatever feelings lay below the surface, he wouldn't display them now; we were hardly alone. Yet, I feared it was more than that. Something had altered in him when the cab had stopped, and I was afraid I'd never see the passionate man who'd embraced me ever again.

Which is as it should be. He's a married man, and I am a fool.

Davis approached McCain, and the two shook hands. The assistant DA launched into a discussion that brought first surprise, then understanding to McCain's face. A little way away, the court aide, a short, inconspicuous man with ginger hair and a tweed coat, met my gaze and nodded in silent understanding, as if to say, *And so it begins.*

The previous morning, I'd received a subpoena—based in large part on the facts I'd revealed in the second installment of my story—to appear before a grand jury to answer questions about my ten days' stay at Blackwell's Asylum. Much of the morning's proceedings had been my testimony before the jury. Davis had put all sorts of questions to me, clearly laying out for the jury what life behind asylum walls had been like. I had told them everything—from the vile food and dirty uniforms to the despicable abuse by the nurses and my own account of being drugged. The jury had listened carefully, and, after hearing of my experience inside the Lodge on the final night of my stay, reacted with disgust and outrage. To my surprise, they had petitioned me to accompany them to the island following. I could not have asked for a better outcome. From my errand in the city, I'd known that my story would lead to an investigation, but a front-row seat to the jury's evaluation of the asylum and its staff was a windfall that I hadn't imagined. It remained to be seen how Dent would answer the questions put to him, but I fervently hoped the result would be the unmasking of his unsavory methods and his more recent schemes.

Davis gave McCain a final clap on the back, then the two joined Judge Gildersleeve, who instructed the group to follow him up the tree-lined, rutted lane that led to the asylum. The officers brought up the rear. I waited until everyone had passed before following. McCain fell into step beside me.

"You got my message," I said. I'd scratched a quick note at the courthouse and given it to Fannie, asking her to find McCain at Park Row.

"In the nick of time," McCain replied. "Another minute and I'd have missed the ferry." He cocked an inquisitive brow. "I take it all is going as planned? There's been nothing but a scant mention in the papers of the fire."

I breathed a long sigh. "Yes, I've been on edge for days." I lifted my skirts and stepped around a puddle. "Our appearance here should be a complete surprise."

"And you're along for the ride."

I nodded and told him how the jury had asked for me to accompany them.

"And me? I can't think it was the jury's idea to have another reporter present. Davis just threatened me within an inch of my life if I print a word before the proceedings are fully concluded."

"I requested—quite strongly, I might add—that you come. Mayor Hewitt was good enough to allow it. It's irregular, but the city is pleased I didn't break the whole story and ruin their chances of discerning the truth before Dent could act. They owed me a favor, as it were." I paused, searching for the right words. "I-I wanted you to break the story, if all goes as planned today. Well, after the *World* does, of course. I thought I owed it to you."

McCain's gray eyes widened in surprise. "You owe me nothing."

"You didn't reveal me when you were here. The game would have been up if it weren't for your silence."

"Miss Cochrane," McCain said, his mouth downturned, "I do not, in general, make a habit of betraying those for whom I care."

He winced at his words, and I realized their irony, for with their utterance, he had unintentionally evoked his wife. Love me he did, but he would be disloyal to her no more. Tears welled in my eyes, and I blinked them back. I had to endure this wretched tour, the stares of the jury, the scathing looks of the staff that surely awaited me. But I couldn't bear the change in him. Walking side by side with his body so close to my own, and feeling his restraint, was more difficult than anything I'd endured inside the asylum.

The tower was now visible through the trees. I remembered how cold and wet I'd been the first time I'd seen it, riding in that horrid open wagon with two nurses looking on and my companions shivering in the cold rain. Unbidden, the woman on fire in the Lodge, her tortured screams, filled me, blotting out all else. My step faltered. I took a deep breath and closed my eyes. When I opened them again, McCain was watching me.

"The memories must still be very fresh," he said, low.

I rallied myself and gave him a thin smile. "Perhaps, but I wager it will be far easier to be Elizabeth Cochrane now than it was to be Nellie Brown then."

The jurors, who'd been talking among themselves as we walked, quieted as we reached the clearing. The wind rippled across the grass that led to the gravel, but the grounds were vacant. No nurses blowing whistles, no women walking in formation. Rising up in the distance was the circular tower with its mullioned windows and mansard roof. Flanking it to the west and south were the long wings of the asylum. A strange quiet hung in the air, as if the building were waiting for us.

We crossed the lawn. As we neared the building, I couldn't help but look once more at the upper stories. However, as it had been the day of my departure, no skeletal faces looked down from the windows. At the main entrance, we mounted steep steps. One of the policemen barely had his knuckles to the door when it was swept open. Nurses Grady and Grupe stood before us in pristine uniforms and starched aprons without blemish.

A hot coil of anger rose in me. "They know," I said, low. "Someone informed them we were coming." McCain turned to me in surprise but said nothing, as Judge Gildersleeve began to speak.

In a booming voice, without introducing himself or the purpose of our visit, the judge demanded to see Superintendent Dent. Without so much as a question or look of surprise, the nurses stood aside and allowed our party to enter. We were led through a series of hallways to the receiving room rotunda with its winding, three-story staircase. Nurse Grady instructed us to wait there and disappeared in the direction of Dent's office. He appeared almost immediately, followed by Dr. Ingram and another man I'd never seen before.

Judge Gildersleeve stepped forward and introduced Davis and himself, gestured to the jury, and informed the superintendent what Dent and his staff apparently already knew: we were here as part of an official investigation into the happenings within the asylum, that the grand jury would be touring the facility, and that he and his staff were in no way to impede the investigation. Dent received all this with bland acceptance that only confirmed to me that none of this was a surprise.

"Judge Gildersleeve, Mr. Davis," the superintendent said, extending his hand, "I'm so glad you've come. We are at your service. Allow me to introduce Dr. Ingram, assistant superintendent, and Dr. MacDonald, superintendent of Ward's Island. This is Head Nurse Grady and Nurse Grupe." Dent then turned to me and gave me a look of such amusement I had to take a deep breath to calm my rage. "Welcome back, Miss—Cochrane, isn't it?"

I lifted my chin, his delight over the *Sun* reporter's discovery of my real surname evident. "Tell me, Superintendent, where is the ferry that escorted me here a few weeks ago?" The filthy ferry at the Bellevue pier my companions and I had ridden to the island was gone, replaced by a far newer and cleaner one. I'd assumed the newer one had been for the benefit of the *Sun* reporter he'd allowed on the island. Now I knew better.

"In for repairs, I'm afraid," Dent replied. He then addressed the jury, altogether dismissing me. "Gentlemen, shall we get to it? How may we be of assistance?"

"And the nurses?" I asked loudly. "I suppose they just happened to be standing at the door just now waiting for visitors?"

"Miss Cochrane," Judge Gildersleeve said, "you must refrain from speaking directly to the staff. Mr. Davis will do the questioning."

But Superintendent Dent, his eyebrows raised, said, "Are you complaining your knock was answered too directly, Miss Cochrane? Should we have kept your party waiting longer?" He scanned the men to see if his joke would catch.

I was about to reply but checked myself when Davis gave me a warning look.

"We'll begin with a tour," the assistant DA said. "We'd like to see the dining hall and the sitting rooms."

Dent gave a short bow, all courtesy. "Allow me to lead the way."

The jury followed Dent, the nurses, and Judge Gildersleeve down the corridor. Davis fell into step with McCain and me at the rear and said, "Someone must have alerted them while we were at the courthouse."

"Most likely," I said, "though I suspect they've been suspicious something like this would occur since my story ran."

If we are too late, all my plans will have been for nothing.

Davis was nodding. "What do you make of Dr. McDonald? Did a doctor from Ward's Island ever visit when you were here?"

"Not that I know of. Perhaps he wants to learn what to expect should the jury decide to tour the facility there."

When we arrived at the sitting room for Hall Six, it was empty. The piano was still there, but the floor and benches looked freshly scrubbed, the nurses' table laid with a clean white tablecloth. I turned to Nurse Grupe. "Where is everyone?"

"Supper."

Her hair, tucked primly under her cap, was as neat as her uniform. I wondered if all the nurses wore new things now in anticipation of our visit. Would the inmates, too, be dressed in new uniforms, their hair neatly tidied? "Supper? So early?"

Nurse Grupe didn't respond. The group was moving on. The smell of food assailed my nostrils as soon as we turned the corner. The windows near the dining hall were closed, and I realized for the first time how warm it was. The coal-burning furnaces were finally being put to use.

More than three hundred heads swiveled as we entered the dining hall, low conversations breaking off abruptly. My story must have made the rounds, for none of the women seemed in the least surprised to see a group of men with a former inmate-cum-reporter in their midst. The food, though far from appetizing, was not the meager fare I remembered. A piece of boiled beef, a small potato, green beans, and dates rested on each plate. Even the tea looked different, dark brown instead of the odd pink color. Sugar bowls and salt and pepper shakers were present at each table. I couldn't help but think that Dent had adjusted the supper hour so the grand jury wouldn't be privy to so many women sitting idle in the sitting rooms. I mentioned as much to Davis in a low tone, my eyes scanning the tables for a familiar face. I spied Molly and Louise. And then Mrs. Shanz and Mrs. Fox, who both gave a discreet nod of recognition when they saw me. Katie was staring at the jury with such concentration that she didn't appear to see me. And then at last, I saw Anne. How pitiful she looked, as pale and thin as ever, and yet she smiled, giving me a quick wave, which I returned. A stab of guilt pierced me. I had left her here. Her and all the others.

And then I spotted Tillie sitting off by herself at another table. Her wild crop of hair had grown out a little, but her face looked just as wan and pinched, her eyes as big as ever in her tiny pixie face. Her eyes held anger and, I thought, a challenge. And then she looked away.

"Nurse McCarten, have you ever used force with a patient?" David asked.

With the help of the officers and the court aide, the Hall Seven sitting room had been transformed into a makeshift courtroom. To the right, the jurors sat in two rows of chairs under the windows. Nurse McCarten sat on the opposite side of the room. A short distance away were Judge Gildersleeve and the court recorder. The court aide had vanished. Superintendent Dent, Drs. Ingram and MacDonald, and the nurses had been asked to wait outside.

"No."

"Not ever? Even when a patient was being difficult?"

"No." McCarten shook her head, her jowls wobbling. Her arms were crossed over her enormous belly, forearms resting on her stomach.

"You've been employed here for, how long is it, six years, you said? That seems like a long time not to have ever used force." Davis paused and let his comment sink in. "Perhaps I can jog your memory." He consulted his notes. "Miss Cochrane has testified you and Nurse Grupe were involved in a physical altercation with a new inmate named Urena. She began shouting after you provoked her. Urena spit on you."

Silence.

"Come now, Nurse. You were angry, were you not? You punched her in the belly—a pregnant woman no less." The jury stirred. Davis waited for a moment, then resumed. "You then dragged her from the room. Didn't Nurse Grupe also put her hands around Urena's neck and choke her?"

"I don't remember."

"I will remind you that you are under oath," Davis warned. "There were many witnesses to the skirmish—not just Miss Cochrane but all of the women seated in the sitting room, some forty women. I'm sure I can find someone to corroborate Miss Cochrane's account."

"We had no choice," Nurse McCarten spat, suddenly leaning forward in her chair and glaring at the district attorney. "Urena was crazy!"

"So you admit to provoking her and using force to subdue her?"

Nurse McCarten eyed the jury for the first time. "She was causing a disturbance. We had to remove her from the room."

"Prior to which you silenced her by punching her belly—after making obscene remarks about who the father of her child was."

"Some of the women here are unruly. They don't listen to orders. At times we must settle them down. It's our duty to keep the peace."

"To 'keep the peace,'" Davis repeated, musing. "Did you ever 'keep the peace' by dragging an inmate to the Lodge and torturing her there, say, by submerging her underwater?"

"No."

"It stands to reason Miss Cochrane—never content it seems, and always making suggestions for improving the patients' comfort here—would make enemies with the nurses. Wouldn't you agree?"

"No," Nurse McCarten said with an emphatic shake of her head. "Me, the nurses, Dr. Kinier, and Superintendent Dent all agreed she didn't make no enemies of us. She was just the complaining sort and we done our best—"

"When you all agreed?" Davis took a step closer. "So you discussed Miss Cochrane in preparation for this visit?"

Silence.

"Nurse McCarten?"

The nurse mumbled something under her breath.

"The witness will speak up," Judge Gildersleeve said.

"We had a meeting, yes. Just in case we was questioned."

"In this meeting, did Superintendent Dent tell you what to say?"

"'Course not. He just wanted to make sure we was all of the same mind."

"Meaning?"

"Meaning we all thought Miss—*her,* was the complaining sort, never satisfied, always asking questions and wanting more for the others. But we didn't take it out on her. We just did our job, just as we always do."

"You sound, Nurse McCarten, as though you are trying to convince yourself of these things."

The nurse squinted at Davis, not sure whether he was calling her words into question.

"Mr. Davis," Judge Gildersleeve said mildly, "please refrain from making statements and keep your discussion to questions."

"I withdraw the comment. Please send in Nurse Grupe."

Sitting in her immaculate uniform, her hair tidy, Nurse Grupe might have been the picture of a professional, kindly nurse. Except, of course, she was neither. With the exclusion of Nurse Grady, she was the cruelest individual I had ever known. She shot the assistant DA a look of loathing and ignored the jury altogether as she was sworn in.

"Did you ever come into Miss Cochrane's room to administer laudanum?"

"Vunce," Nurse Grupe said. "Miss Brown or Moreno or Bly, vatever her name is—"

"Cochrane," Davis said, "Miss Cochrane."

"—didn't sleep well. We dought it vould do her good to have a peaceful night's rest."

"'We,' Nurse Grupe?"

"Nurse Grady and me."

Davis's eyebrows shot up. "Just the two of you? You didn't need a doctor's assistance to give a patient medicine?"

Nurse Grupe's cheeks reddened. She glanced furtively around the room. "Vell, of course we needed a doctor's permission." Her

German accent seemed more pronounced now that a judge and jury were scrutinizing her. Dr. Kinier, the flirtatious fool, couldn't save her now. "Superintendent Dent sent us, Nurse Grady and me, to give it to her."

"And?"

Grupe bit her lip. The court recorder's hands stilled on his little black machine.

"Nurse?"

"She took it straight down."

Murmurs from the jury.

"Miss Cochrane did not refuse to take the laudanum?"

"No."

"She's lying," I whispered.

"Let her speak," McCain said, leaning on the wall next to me. "Davis knows what he's doing."

"Miss Cochrane has testified otherwise," Davis said. "She claims you and Nurse Grady attempted to pin her to the bed to make her drink it. That you fetched Superintendent Dent for help and he gave her a shot through the arm instead."

"Dere vere two of us, sir. Vee didn't need to pin her down, but if vee'd tried, vee vould have succeeded vidout a doctor's help."

"You have used force before?"

"I didn't say dat," Nurse Grupe replied, her voice rising. "I just said vee vouldn't have needed help from da superintendent."

"Did you ever hold Miss Cochrane underwater in the bathtub?"

"No."

"Have you ever done so with other patients?"

"No."

"Did you ever push Miss Cochrane with such force in the lavatory that she slid on the wet tile and banged her chin?"

"No."

Davis paused and consulted his notes. "Are you familiar with Eugenia Cotter, who was discharged recently?"

"Yes."

"Did she spend some time in the Lodge before she left?"

"I don't know."

"Did you, with the help of Nurse Grady, take Mrs. Cotter there and beat her with a broom handle, then hold her underwater, while Miss Cochrane looked on?"

"No."

"Was there a fire in the Lodge on the night of October 3, the night before Miss Cochrane was released?"

"Yes."

"Where were you when it broke out?"

"Sleeping in da nurses' dormitory."

"Did anyone summon you to help get any of the women out?"

"No," Nurse Grupe said, crossing her arms. "It vas a small fire. Da nurses in da Lodge put it out in no time."

"Miss Cochrane has testified before the jury that on the night of the fire, you and Nurse Grady drugged and then dragged her to the Lodge with the intent to strap her into the rotary chair."

Grupe lifted her chin, but there was fear in her eyes. "I don't know anyding about dat."

"Is that what Superintendent Dent told you to say when you all met to discuss how you were to answer questions?"

Nurse Grupe narrowed her eyes. "Dere was no such meeting."

"Nurse McCarten has said otherwise, which means, of course, one of you is lying."

"Mr. Davis," Judge Gildersleeve said, glowering. "Questions only, please."

"I apologize to the jury," Davis said. "That will be all, Nurse Grupe."

Nurse Grady walked into the sitting room with the air of a woman who knew her mind. Her black hair was swept severely back in a tight bun that accentuated the hard angles of her cheekbones and the hooked beak of her nose. Hers was not a pretty face. Her power lay in her self-assured arrogance. Her witch's eyes swept the jury and the judge, and when they at last came to rest on me, they lingered, a challenge in their depths. *See if you can trap me, you little bitch,* they seemed to say. I refused to look away. I'd had my time on the stand at the courthouse; now it was her turn. Her manipulation and lies had ruled for years at the asylum. I doubted they would last long before the jury.

"Nurse Grady, how many meetings did you have with Dr. Kinier and Superintendent Dent in which you discussed Elizabeth Cochrane in the event you might be questioned about what she reported in the *New York World*?"

A sudden, fleeting widening of the eyes was the only indication that Davis had taken her by surprise. "One."

"And in that meeting, were you or the other nurses instructed what to say?"

"Certainly not."

"What did you discuss?"

"We discussed what we could recall of her time here."

"As it related to her narrative in the papers?"

"As it *differed* from it. Miss Cochrane has quite an imagination." Nurse Grady's eyes slid to me and back to the attorney.

Davis launched into the night I'd been given laudanum. Nurse Grady confirmed Nurse Grupe's story of visiting my room with one important difference. "She refused to take it," she said. "As we do not use force with the inmates, we went in search of Superintendent Dent."

The jurors began to murmur among themselves once more. Judge Gildersleeve banged his gavel.

"As you were saying, Nurse Grady?" Davis prompted.

"We often call upon the doctors to help us administer medicine. Oftentimes, a doctor can persuade an inmate when we cannot."

"Persuade," Davis said.

"Yes."

"And the superintendent gave her a shot in the arm when you returned with him to her room?"

"Yes."

"Was she compliant in allowing him to do so?"

"Miss Cochrane wasn't the compliant sort. In the end, we had to hold her down. But I will remind you, it was all for the sake of giving her a good night's rest."

Mutterings from the jury. Judge Gildersleeve banged his gavel again and called the men to order.

"Nurse Grady, Miss Cochrane has testified at length about an episode with patients with reduced mental faculties who were teased, rather ruthlessly, by you and some of the other nurses."

"I'm not surprised." Nurse Grady's eyes sought mine again. "As I said, she has quite an imagination."

"There was an instance of a blind woman," Davis said, "a woman called Old Bess, whom, according to Miss Cochrane, you teased and humiliated. Can you explain to the jury what occurred?"

"I cannot explain what did not occur. I do not provoke the patients."

"You do not recall Bess complaining of the cold after suffering through a long night screaming, a night she spent asking for blankets?"

"Old Bess complains of many things," Nurse Grady said. "She is delusional and often thinks we're trying to molest her. She's been here for many years, and though she is generally harmless, she is quite mad."

"Was Old Bess moved to another ward while Miss Cochrane was here?"

Nurse Grady narrowed her eyes. "Yes."

"And to which area was she moved?"

"The Lodge."

Davis consulted his notes. "There were a few other patients sent elsewhere while Miss Cochrane was here. A woman named Urena and a Mrs. O'Keefe. Where are they now?"

There was only the slightest hesitation. "In the Lodge."

"Ah, it would appear Miss Cochrane's recollection of these transfers is proof that she didn't imagine everything."

Judge Gildersleeve cleared his throat. "Mr. Davis."

"Strike the comment," Davis said with a dismissive wave. "Nurse Grady, when did you become aware that Miss Cochrane was being discharged?"

"I believe Superintendent Dent informed me the day she left."

"I find that hard to believe because, you see, Miss Cochrane has testified that the night before she was to be discharged, you took revenge on her. It was her last night, and you wanted to get even before it was too late, isn't that right?"

"I've read her account in the paper," Nurse Grady replied. "Neither I nor Nurse Grupe drugged her and forced her inside the Lodge."

Davis stepped closer. "Miss Cochrane has testified that you, Nurse Grupe, and Nurse Conway entered her room and gave her something that made her sick. Miss Cochrane was immediately overcome with severe vomiting and diarrhea. You dressed her and, with the help of Nurse Grupe, dragged her to the Lodge, a facility used to house the most violent inmates. Isn't that true?"

Nurse Grady turned to the jury. "No, it's all nonsense. Every word."

"I understand there is a special apparatus in that building, a spinning or rotary chair, that is suspended from the ceiling and made to whirl patients around until they become quite ill, is that right?"

"The Lodge is not my area of responsibility. I wouldn't know."

The jury began to murmur. Judge Gildersleeve gave them a stern look, and they settled down before he could bang his gavel.

"So you didn't take Eugenia Cotter to the Lodge with Nurse Grupe and torture her by dunking her in a barrel of water while Miss Cochrane watched?"

"Certainly not. She made that all up too."

Liar.

"And yet I suppose you *are* aware of the fire that took place on October 3, just hours before Miss Cochrane was released?"

"It was a small fire started by a lantern, that is all."

"Any injuries or deaths?"

"None."

Liar.

"Miss Cochrane has testified that as you, Nurse Grupe, and she neared the building, the fire was already under way. You ordered Nurse Grupe to investigate. When she didn't return straightaway, you dragged Miss Cochrane into the building. You led her toward the room with the rotary chair, didn't you?"

"I have said I did not."

"Even with a fire raging, and women crying out to be unlocked from their rooms, you dragged Miss Cochrane up the stairs to strap her into the chair, isn't that right, Nurse Grady?"

"She's making it all up. You have no proof of any of it."

The door opened. The court aide entered the room and approached Davis. The two had a short, whispered discussion. My heart was beating rapidly now. Everything hinged on this. Everything. But neither man was betraying anything. The aide took a seat in the back. Davis returned his attention to his witness once more. "Very well. Send in Superintendent Dent."

A moment later, Dent entered the room as Grady was just leaving. In the briefest of instants, anger swept Dent's face as he passed her, and then it was gone. She had crossed him once by marching me to the Lodge to see Eugenia Cotter abused; he must be even more furious that she'd forced me to the Lodge again. Now, he would have to lie before the jury to corroborate her story. I could only imagine that the reason he hadn't fired her and Grupe was because he would've had to explain, should anyone outside the asylum inquire, the reason why. So far, my intuition was correct. I only hoped I was right about everything.

After Dent was seated and sworn in, Davis approached him. "Superintendent, I'm hoping you can set us straight on what happened the first night Miss Cochrane was drugged. We have two testimonies from Nurses Grady and Grupe that contradict each other. Did you or did you not enter Miss Cochrane's room and administer a drug by hypodermic needle against her wishes?"

"I did," Dent said matter-of-factly.

McCain came off the wall and balled his hands into fists.

"Such maneuvers are necessary," Dent continued, "when an inmate refuses to obey instructions."

"Did you also approve a second dose of medication a few nights later, something stronger, which Miss Cochrane has testified gave her terrible nightmares?"

"No."

Stirrings from the jury. McCain muttered an oath, and Judge Gildersleeve looked questioningly in our direction. "Order," he interjected. "I will have order."

"You must remember that we believed, during Miss Cochrane's time here, that she was mad," the superintendent said. "Now, of course, we know that was not the case, but at the time our actions were justified. I gave her an opiate to relax her. Using a needle was necessary when she refused to take it by mouth. Lunatics are prone to be incorrigible. In such cases, it's standard medical practice."

"Standard medical practice, you say," Davis said. "Such as freezing cold baths?"

"Cold baths are therapeutic," Dent replied, speaking to the jury. His tone was even, without malice, as if he were an instructor before his pupils. "Though they may seem cruel to those unfamiliar with therapies for the insane, those in my profession believe them to restore the humors to the body and equilibrium to the mind."

"Tell me, Superintendent, does holding patients underwater until they nearly drown restore humors to the body and equilibrium to the mind?"

"I was quite shocked to learn this was happening when I read Miss Cochrane's account in the newspaper. Had I known, I would have seen that an end came to it immediately."

Liar.

"Let's move on. Medicine that makes the patient violently ill with vomit and diarrhea. Is this also considered therapeutic?"

Dent frowned. "Purgatives are used to cleanse the body, Mr. Davis. Mercurous chloride, commonly known as Calomel, has been shown to have a positive effect on the insane."

"And what kind of patient would need a purgative?"

"One who is violent or incorrigible."

"And which was it in Miss Cochrane's case?"

"Neither."

"And so why was it, then, that Miss Cochrane was given a purgative her last night here?"

"Just because she told the tale for the *New York World* does not mean it occurred, Mr. Davis."

"So you deny that she was drugged and led to the Lodge by Nurses Grady and Grupe on the night of October 3?"

"I do."

"Does the rotary chair exist?"

"It does—although it is used sparingly." Dent turned to the

jury. "For the most severe insanity cases, it is used to rebalance the mind."

"Causing extreme discomfort to the patient," Davis said, "including vertigo and vomiting?"

"Unfortunately, in such cases, the end is worth the means."

McCain swore under his breath. The jury began to stir. Judge Gildersleeve banged his gavel.

"Miss Cochrane has testified that nurses often set up an inmate to warn them of a doctor's approach so that they won't be caught out when harassing patients. If the patients refuse, they are severely punished. Are you aware of this practice?"

"Not before Miss Cochrane's story ran, no."

"Why—" Davis began.

"Just a moment," Superintendent Dent interrupted. "Had I known your purpose, Miss Cochrane, I would have aided you. It is unfortunate, but the doctors often have no means of learning the way things are."

All eyes turned to me. "Mrs. Turney informed you directly she was beaten in the lavatory by Nurse Grupe. You did nothing."

"Miss Cochrane," Judge Gildersleeve interjected, "you cannot address—"

"It was her word against Nurse Grupe's," Dent cut in. "When Mrs. Turney responded with violence, she was punished. We do not condone violence against nurses here."

"No, only the other way around," I shot back.

Davis moved to obstruct the sight line between us. The jurors mumbled among themselves, and once more Gildersleeve's gavel went to work.

When the noise had died down, Davis continued. "Superintendent, did a fire occur here the night before Miss Cochrane was released?"

"Unfortunately, yes."

"Nurse Grady has testified there were no injuries as a result of the fire. Is that correct?"

"Yes."

"And there were no deaths?"

"No, not even Miss Cochrane invented that for her newspaper piece," Dent said sardonically.

"Superintendent, is Nurse Conway, a recently hired nurse who works in Hall Seven, the hall to which Miss Cochrane was assigned before she was released, still employed here?"

Dent did not immediately answer. When he did, his voice was low. "No, she is not."

"She gave notice?"

"Yes."

"The day Miss Cochrane was released?"

"I can't say. I shall have to check my records."

"For what reason did she leave?"

"She didn't say."

"Perhaps it was because she was one of the nurses who helped Nurses Grady and Grupe enter Miss Cochrane's room on her last night. She had a key. Then, seeing what they planned to do, she refused to help them any further. Did Nurse Conway say as much when she gave her reason for leaving, Superintendent?"

"As I told you, she gave me no reason at all."

"Do you think it might be because she was frightened of what Nurses Grady and Grupe were planning for Miss Cochrane and thought better of working here? Perhaps because she was frightened if she said anything to you she might be in danger?"

Dent did not reply, but a flush had crept onto his face.

"Superintendent, in your opinion, do you believe Miss Cochrane has awareness beyond the normal senses? That she could, say, know something was occurring somewhere else without seeing it?"

Dent snorted. "Certainly not."

"Then how is it Miss Cochrane is aware of the death of at least one inmate on the night of the fire?"

A floorboard creaked. McCain's pencil froze on his notepad. Dent's eyes flicked to the policemen scattered about. The room was deadly quiet.

And then I was once again in that smoke-filled corridor. I could barely breathe, nor see through the haze, and yet, there she was: arms outstretched, body covered in flames, moving toward me. *Save me! Oh, God, have mercy. Save me!* I would have known those unseeing eyes anywhere.

Bess. Old Bess.

The smell of burning flesh singed my nostrils, my throat. Bess collapsed and rolled, but it was too late. Her body was engulfed in fire, her skin bubbling, blackening beneath the flames.

"Elizabeth? *Elizabeth*," McCain whispered, grabbing my arm. His voice catapulted me back into the present.

"She never wrote that," Dent said. "None of that was in her write-up." He looked at me, realizing too late he'd been caught out.

"I'm going to ask you to step down and have a seat right over there," Davis instructed, pointing. "Your honor, I call Jacob James to the stand."

The court aide was sworn in. In less than a minute, the jury learned that the assistant DA had tasked James, who was really a policeman, with searching for Old Bess during the nurses' testimonies.

"Couldn't find her," James said. "I looked in the Lodge, the Retreat, and the infirmary. No Bess. I asked the nurses if they'd seen her. They wouldn't say a word, not a word, but when I asked a few of the women at the Lodge, the inmates, they told me straight out."

"What did they tell you, Mr. James?"

"That Old Bess died in the fire that night."

The jury didn't stir. They had already heard as much in my own account at the courthouse.

"And then what did you do?"

"I searched the grounds. Didn't take me long to find what I was looking for. Freshly turned soil. Not in the graveyard to the east of the south wing where they bury the dead but back in some little-used area behind one of the outbuildings surrounded by brush. Not so much as a cross or a marker either. By the looks of it, it was more than Old Bess who died that night. There could be another four, five bodies buried there."

The jury erupted. Gildersleeve was on his feet, banging his gavel for order.

I felt the room sway and closed my eyes. Four or five more. It was worse than I'd imagined. *I didn't save you. I didn't save any of you.*

McCain took my hand. He looked aghast, his mouth open, his eyes wide. "You might have been one of them."

The jury quieted down once more when Davis turned to Dent. "Miss Cochrane never wrote about Bess's death, Superintendent, but she witnessed it. She has testified that when the nurses declared the next morning that there had been no fatalities, she suspected that Bess's death would be covered up. She also believed the fire would be dismissed as a trivial matter, if not covered up altogether. And there were the grounds keepers she saw with shovels the morning after the fire, which led her to believe they might be burying Old Bess, and perhaps others, somewhere on asylum grounds. Miss Cochrane knew, from what the other inmates had told her, that Old Bess had been an inmate here for years and had no family. It was unlikely anyone would visit her and learn of her death, which meant her passing wouldn't be missed, let alone investigated, by anyone from the outside. Perhaps the same can be said for the other casualties.

"Miss Cochrane wrote her story for the *World,* but she decided to hold back that she'd seen Old Bess die. That information she took to the police immediately upon her release. She knew if she revealed in print everything she had witnessed, you would likely destroy the evidence of the bodies—by burying them off the island or depositing them in the East River perhaps—before the police could arrive. In light of this, the New York City Police Department, in cooperation with the mayor's office, saw to it that this grand jury investigation got under way.

"As luck would have it, Nurse Conway went to the police just before Miss Cochrane did—that next morning, after she'd given Dent her notice. She described her observations in her short time here. She told the police Miss Cochrane was, in fact, drugged and let out of her room that night for the purpose of placing her in the rotary chair."

The jury began to chatter again. Dent was red with fury.

"Gentlemen," Davis continued, addressing Judge Gildersleeve and the jury now, "I move to open a formal trial to investigate further the conditions inside Blackwell's Asylum and, more specifically, the events that occurred the night of October 3, when Miss Cochrane saw Old Bess burn to death. It is my belief that an investigation will further reveal what happened the night of the fire, as well as the names of the other women who were unfortunate casualties that night. Furthermore, a formal investigation will also expose Superintendent Dent's long-running mismanagement of this facility, which has resulted in extreme cruelty to the sixteen hundred souls who reside here."

Just then, the sitting room door banged open, and Katie rushed in. Her eyes scanned the room until she spotted whom she was looking for.

"Judge Gildersleeve, sir," Katie cried, rushing to him. "I'm so glad I found ye. I never thought I'd see the likes o' ye again!"

31

*S*he was not sworn, but her story must
have convinced all hearers of the truth
of my statements.

NELLIE BLY

BLACKWELL'S ASYLUM, OCTOBER 1887

"Katie told me she worked for a family whose head of household was a man of the law," I said. "I never dreamed it was Judge Gildersleeve."

Anne and I were seated on one of the davenports in the rotunda at the foot of the winding staircase. The others, including McCain, had gone to view the Lodge and the Retreat. I'd declined to go; they were the last places I wanted to see. The horrors I'd witnessed inside the Lodge would be with me the rest of my life, and I had no desire to add to them. Instead, I'd waited for the jury to finish questioning Anne and asked that we have some time together while the jury was occupied elsewhere.

"Will the judge take her back?" Anne asked.

She was a bag of bones. It looked as if the slightest wind could blow her over. Still, she was more concerned for the welfare of others than she was for herself.

"Yes." I said. "He told me his family has been looking for her for months. They're still recovering from his daughter's death, but his wife has been in a panic about letting Katie go."

"When will she be released?"

"Today. Judge Gildersleeve wants to make sure she doesn't get a night like I did."

Anne shivered. "You didn't say a word that morning after the fire, about what they'd done to you. Why didn't you tell me?"

A stab of guilt hit me, and I felt ashamed. "I was getting out, Anne. It didn't seem fair to scare you and then leave you here, knowing there would be little you could do if they came for you. I'm sorry. I should have been more honest."

"Don't trouble yourself. I've survived." Anne gave me a weak smile that quickly vanished. "Nell—I mean, Elizabeth—I've heard the inmates whispering. Is it true about Old Bess?"

I nodded. "And there were probably others, I'm afraid." She'd heard the details of what I'd written for the *World* through the nurses' gossip, but I told her everything my story hadn't mentioned, including how I'd gone to the police to see that justice was done. "They knew from what Nurse Conway told them just hours before I showed up that things were bad here. She realized what kind of place this was and wanted nothing to do with it. Because of her, they were already planning to put an investigation together, and so once they heard my story, we agreed that I would leave any details of the fire out of my exposé. They wanted to see if Dent would inform the city commissioner of the fire and file a death certificate for Bess."

"Which, of course, he never did."

"No. They told me to assume the worst and that they would start proceedings and assemble a jury as quickly as possible. Mr. Davis told me the police chief went straight to the mayor after my visit. They'd heard of rumors for years about Blackwell's, and now they had the opportunity to gather evidence of wrongdoing. The grand jury was convened quickly after that. Their hope was that what I left out of my story would create a false sense of security for Dent."

"Oh, Elizabeth. You took such a risk for us." Her amber eyes filled with tears.

"It was worth it. The judge and Mr. Davis were kind to you, weren't they?" I'd seen Anne before she'd entered the makeshift courtroom, with her auburn hair hanging limp and the look of terror on her face.

"Oh, yes," Anne replied. "I was scared at first. Speaking out is always dangerous here, but I realized, because you were with them, that they were on the good side and only wanted the truth."

"Dent won't be a threat here anymore," I said, taking Anne's bony hand in mine. "They'll be bringing him into custody before the day is out, along with Nurse Grady and Nurse Grupe. There will be a lot more scrutiny into what goes on here in the future."

Anne closed her eyes. A tear traveled down her cheek. "I'm so glad, Elizabeth."

"Tell me you are well—at least that they aren't beating you or giving you drugs."

Anne shook her head. "No, nothing like that. I'm as well as one can be here. The nurses in Hall Seven are better."

"Anne, is there no one who will come for you? Is there anyone in the city I can go to, anyone who will vouch for you? You mentioned an uncle when I first met you."

"A cousin." Anne looked away, her eyes distant. "For all I know, he's still without work. Even if he's found employment, I doubt he could afford to keep me, and—" She stopped and swallowed. "I don't know where he is. He may not even be in New York anymore."

"Perhaps I can find him."

"You mustn't do this."

I drew back. "What do you mean?"

"It's not your duty to get me out. I don't expect it, nor should you."

"*Anne.*"

"Please don't pity me. When I'm stronger and able to convince them I'm well, I shall be released. And then I'll find employment. There's always a need for a maid-of-all-work."

My eyes brimmed with tears. Did she really believe she could convince the doctors she was of sound mind—they who never seemed to consider it might be so—or was she putting up a good front for my sake?

"When your story ran, it was all the nurses could talk about," Anne said. "They told us it was all lies, that you'd done nothing but scheme your way here, but they were nervous. Superintendent Dent and Nurse Grady wanted to know if you'd told me anything, but of course you hadn't said a word. And then a reporter came from another paper."

"The *Sun.*"

"He was asking all sorts of questions, but they forbade us to speak to him."

"I wanted to tell you, Anne," I said. "It was hard keeping up the masquerade with you, Molly, and the others. I'd grown so fond of you all." But that wasn't enough. I needed to tell her the whole truth, ugly as it was. I took a deep breath. "I planned the whole ruse to get hired on at the *World.* I didn't have any other designs beyond that. It was about me. To get the story so that I could pay the rent. I was broke." She stared at me, trying to understand. "Somewhere along the way, I realized I couldn't stand idly by and watch the abuse. Suddenly the care and safety of you all was more important than my own selfish interests." I wiped tears away with the back of my hand. "I had it all wrong. The women here weren't the means to an end, they were the point—the way that I could make change. Do you hate me, for lying to you?"

"Oh, Elizabeth. How can you ask that?" Anne's own eyes were welling up. "I think you're the bravest person I've ever known. I haven't half the courage you do."

"Don't put me on too high a pedestal." I smiled through my tears and then remembered something. "Oh, I brought you this." I pulled a small bundle wrapped in paper from my reticule. "There isn't much I can give you the nurses won't take, but this, I hope, is something that will give you cheer and remind you of our wild fantasies in the sitting room."

Anne unwrapped the bundle to reveal a large red apple. "I remember." She laughed. "How perfect it is. Thank you." She hugged me and then began wrapping it up again.

"You must eat it now, Anne," I urged her. "They'll take it if you don't."

As if on cue, we heard footsteps. Anne quickly slipped the apple into her pocket. "I will, as soon as I'm able. I shall relish every bite."

A nurse approached us. Behind her walked a tiny skeleton of a girl with short fair hair sticking out in tufts. Tillie, aware of my scrutiny, brought her hand up to her head and regarded me with open hostility. Her wrist was boney and bore a thin bruise.

Anne and I exchanged glances.

"I shall leave the two of you to chat," Anne said. She stood and hugged me. "Don't be surprised if I show up at your newspaper one day. You haven't seen the last of me, I promise you."

"Five minutes," the nurse said. "That's all you've got."

"Don't bother, Nurse," Tillie said, raking me with her corn-flower blue eyes. "I don't know this girl."

"Nonsense, Tillie, it's me."

Tillie took a step forward and looked me over: my navy coat and boots, the new winter hat perched on my head. "Those are mine. Did my friends give them to you? You've convinced them that you're me, haven't you? They'll never look for me now."

"Tillie," I said, reaching for her hand, "please—"

She jerked away. "Take me back, Nurse. There's nothing more I wish to say to this pretender."

The three of them departed. The last sight I had was Tillie's head held high as she glided like a queen from the room and Anne looking back with tears in her eyes.

≈≈≈

The sun was an orange lozenge sinking behind a dusky Manhattan. The wind was up, and I shivered, my skirts flapping around my legs. The jury waited at the shoreline for the ferry a short distance away.

McCain, standing beside me, said, "I commend you. I understand how ghastly coming back must have been. You've given me a hell of a story to break. Madden will be pleased."

I arched a brow. "I didn't do it for Madden, and besides, you'll hardly have an exclusive. More than one reporter was here today, you know."

He grinned broadly, his white teeth flashing in the growing dusk. The old McCain. And then, just as quickly, his smile faded. "Cockerill will be none too pleased you kept him in the dark. I fear you won't have a job waiting for you once you tell him the news."

"If it got Dent into custody, it was worth it."

"Even if Cockerill fires you?"

"Do you think he will?"

"No. He doesn't want you going to the competition. There's also the fact that you've got Mayor Hewitt in your pocket. You worked with him and the city, and now, you'll have another story—just as shocking—to put on Cockerill's desk tomorrow. He won't be happy, but he'll get over it."

I smiled. I liked the thought of surprising Cockerill very much.

"Would you say now, on the other side of things, that it was worth it?" McCain asked.

"To get employed by the *World*? Yes." I tucked a stray lock of hair behind my ear. "You know, I never thanked you for taking me to see Cockerill the day the *Sun*'s story broke."

McCain looked out at the water, his eyes distant. "There's no need."

"You would have done it for anyone?"

"I did it for you," he said softly, "and you are not just anyone." And then he turned to me. I was aware of his body, the great tall mass of him. My pulse quickened; it was as if we were in the carriage again. Our own private space, hidden from the world.

And then suddenly, he tore his gaze away, his lips turning down into a frown.

On the pier, a policeman held a rope, ready to tether the ferry to shore. Torches flickered onboard, casting pools of light on the water's surface. It would be dark soon.

"Miss Cochrane, I once made a promise to you. I told you I would never act on my feelings for you, that I would never ask to meet you in clandestine places. I broke that promise the other day in the carriage. I want you to know—"

"Please don't apologize. I can't bear it." Tears stung my eyes. I wished for the light to fade completely so he wouldn't see. How had I really expected this, us, to end after all?

"It would be dishonorable of me if I didn't."

Damn him and his honor. I'd had my fill of it.

The jury was boarding.

"Miss Cochrane?" Davis called. "McCain?"

We had to go. It seemed there was so much left to say, and yet I couldn't speak. There wasn't time. There were no words. I saw the pain in his eyes for a brief second, and then it vanished. The wall was up; he was distant again. A man of honor.

McCain placed his hand on the small of my back and beckoned me toward the pier. "Come," he said.

Epilogue

Love! That wonderful something—that source of bliss, the cause of maddened anguish!

NEW YORK CITY, DECEMBER 1887

"What a beautiful evening," Mama said, looking out the window. "It will snow again before the night is over."

Our cab-for-hire was making its way down Broadway, the horses' hooves muffled in the snow. It was dark, half past seven. The vehicle's lanterns cast a golden hue onto the world outside. New York City was a glittering, frozen fairy tale—a spotless white terrain devoid of the grime, coal stains, and filth normally so ubiquitous in the streets. When we'd passed the Museum of Natural History with its castle-like turrets and domes and stone facades, I'd felt like an interloper in a foreign land. Farther south, we'd turned left at Roosevelt Hospital, another massive structure of stone and roof lines beautified by the snow, and caught Broadway, where we'd joined a stream of broughams and landaus heading into the theater district.

"If it does snow, traffic will be a beast after the opera," I replied. In truth, I didn't mind. On this, my first night at the opera, a gift bestowed on us by Joseph Pulitzer, nothing could douse my spirits. Not three months ago, I had been an inmate inside a lunatic asylum going hungry; tonight I was riding in a carriage bound for a night at the Metropolitan.

Cockerill had seethed for two days when I told him the whole story: that, upon my release, I'd gone to the police to tell them of the fire, that at least one death had resulted from it, and that I suspected Dent and the rest of the staff would try to cover it up. Fortunately, the exclusive I wrote a few days after my return visit to Blackwell's brought him around. In fact, I believed my efforts had won me some respect in his eyes—something he would be hard-pressed ever to admit.

Since my Blackwell's Island exposé, Cockerill had given me free rein to report on stories of my choosing. Gone were banal women's topics I'd covered during my time at the *Dispatch*. So far, I'd reported on the underground trade of newborn babies, a story in which I pretended to be unwed and pregnant. More recently, I had written of the young women who toiled in the paper box factories for a pittance. Both were well received by Cockerill. As he had advised, I'd had a small press print my asylum story into a bound book titled *Ten Days in a Mad-house*. It had sold through quickly and added a nice little income to my salary at the *World*. Thanks to it and my weekly stories, my readership was growing. Even Albert had congratulated me on my success during his last visit.

My luck had spread too. Cockerill had allowed Fannie to report on the women who rolled tobacco into cigarettes for sixteen hours a day. Viola impersonated a beggar for a day and wrote of her adventure through the eyes of the city's poor.

"There is the St. Cloud Hotel," Mama said. "We will be there soon. How nice of Mr. Pulitzer to think of us."

I smiled inwardly. In Mama's mind, Cockerill and the publisher had risen to the level of saints. They'd recognized her daughter's skill at last. She'd quite forgotten the enmity she'd felt toward them when my prospect of a career as a newswoman looked bleak. As for my own thoughts on the matter, I was enormously relieved. Cockerill and Pulitzer had elevated my financial and social standing beyond what even I could have imagined.

I looked down at my gown, a deep maroon taffeta trimmed in black that threatened to overtake the interior of the carriage. What space my dress wasn't occupying was taken up by Mama's voluminous skirts. Both gowns were new and purchased for the event, cut and tailored so precisely that we dared not eat for fear of bursting our stays.

"I am not the only reporter on his staff he rewarded with tickets tonight, Mama," I said mildly.

"But he didn't reward *all* of them, Pinkey," Mama replied, "and that is quite a feather in your cap."

The carriage pulled to a stop, and the driver jumped down to open the door. We alighted into the whited air and rushed beneath one of the grand central arches. In another moment, we were inside.

A large crowd milled about the reception hall, which was filled with the reverberating echo of a thousand conversations. Men in well-tailored suits with tails, impeccably groomed and pomaded, stood alert. Millionaires, many of them. Made of money. But it was the ladies, the pretty flowers who adorned the men's arms, who held my attention. Women in low-cut, bustled gowns worth more than a year of my salary paraded about, their perfume wafting through the air. White gloves spotless, tresses arranged in intricate coils, they were the epitome of the upper class, and they knew it. I watched them talk animatedly with their partners, while all the while their eyes darted about, evaluating every dress, every jewel, every coiffure of the women in the room.

I took in the ivory marble floor, the glittering gaslights, the gold, ornamented ceiling. It was a palace unparalleled to anything I had ever seen. Wide, serpentine staircases led to the upper floors. Built just four years before by the city's *nouveaux riches,* the Metropolitan had thumbed its nose at the older, heretofore unrivaled Academy of Music, whose patrons represented the old guard of New York. The Academy's snooty, wealthy subscribers would not allow the city's *arrivestes*—the Vanderbilts, the Morgans, the Rockefellers—to infiltrate their opera house. I had read that even thirty thousand dollars of William Vanderbilt's money couldn't buy him a box. Angry and belligerent, the newly moneyed industrialists and bankers of New York financed their own opera house. Now the Metropolitan was not only a larger, grander version of operatic entertainment; it was the place to be and be seen. It was exactly the rags-to-riches story I admired. That a new set could redefine the old ways and reshape them to fit its own was a testament to the land of opportunity that was New York. Joseph Pulitzer, a penniless Hungarian Jew who emigrated and found fame and fortune here, was himself a prime example.

We checked our wraps and followed the crowd into the auditorium, a vast, high-ceilinged room of gold and ivory. Two tiered balconies rose above a row of the *baignoires* carved elaborately in gold. Wide, red-carpeted aisles led down to an enormous stage, above which hung a proscenium arch that reached to the ceiling. Gaslights flickered at every level but were unequaled by the crystal chandelier that held court over three thousand six hundred seats.

"I have never seen anything so magnificent," Mama whispered.

"The diamond horseshoe," I said, looking up at the U-shaped layers around us. The phrase was not for the grand chandelier nor the lights at each level but for the jewels that sparkled from the throats, wrists, and earlobes of the ladies seated in the boxes. It had been widely reported in the papers that the combined wealth of those attending on any given night was estimated at five hundred million dollars.

We took our seats in the parterre, content to watch ladies lean over balconies to chat with neighbors and peer through lorgnettes at the gallery below. At last the lights dimmed. The great gold curtain parted, and *The Trumpeter of Säkkingen* unfolded. It was in German, yet from the first note, I was spellbound. Even in a foreign language, the story—a love triangle between the trumpeter Werner, his love Maria, and the spineless, aristocratic Damian—emerged. For two acts, I scarcely moved. When the curtain descended for the intermission, I couldn't believe so much time had passed.

The lights came up, and the boxes began to fill with more people—patrons making the rounds.

"Would you like some refreshment, Mama?"

"I'm quite content here watching the ladies."

Gentlemen stood, shook hands, gestured to the women seated in front, who in turn lifted a hand or a cheek to be kissed by a guest. It was a *de rigeur* display I found both fascinating and ostentatious, but I was thirsty. "I shall just go and get something cold to drink, if you don't mind." I fanned myself with my hand. "It's getting rather warm in here."

I followed the throng to the reception hall. It was crowded, but as the box tiers had their own salons and dressing rooms, less so than before. I found my way to a large room off the hall where refreshments were available and decided on champagne. Why not? I reasoned. I'd never had it before, and it was a special night, one I hoped would be repeated should Pulitzer's hospitality continue.

I was just leaving the line, intent on making my way back to the reception hall, when I stumbled into a broad chest. "Pardon me," I said, trying to save my champagne as I looked up.

"Miss Cochrane."

He was resplendent in black tails, his hair slicked back in the fashion. He swept a formal bow, and my heart missed a beat.

"Mr. McCain. I didn't expect to see you here." My face was aflame. I took a sip from my flute, hoping to disguise my trembling hand. Bubbly goodness traveled down my throat, but I couldn't relish it, not now.

"I heard Pulitzer gifted his best and brightest with tickets to tonight's performance," McCain said. He smiled warmly, his gray eyes merry, and yet I felt somehow that he, too, was as nervous as I.

Was this why he'd come, hoping to run into me? I hadn't seen him since our tour of Blackwell's Island more than two months ago. An eternity. I didn't know what to say. The room was hot, too hot. I took another sip and felt my nose prickle as the sweet burn descended.

"Your first glass of champagne, I wager."

I brought a gloved hand to my mouth. "It is that obvious?"

"A guess." He smiled.

I couldn't help but smile back. Oh, how I had missed him. How quickly, I thought, I could slip back into an easy repartee with him, how easy it would be to forget that the flower cards, the lovely, damnable flower cards, had stopped.

McCain lowered his gaze, his eyes sweeping over me appreciatively before they met mine again. "You are lovely this evening."

I blushed. "Tickets to the opera dictate a new dress. We could hardly attend in everyday attire."

"We?" McCain's brows drew together. I wondered fleetingly if he thought I might have come with someone else, another man perhaps, and then scolded myself for such vanity.

"Mama," I said. "She's watching the ladies glitter in their boxes as we speak."

"A show in itself."

"Yes."

An uncomfortable pause stretched between us. We were two acquaintances who'd bumped into each other at the opera and exchanged pleasantries. We had performed the social expectations custom demanded, no one else in the room the wiser that something had happened between us not so very long ago. It was expected now, of course, that we part, and yet I didn't want to say good-bye. Even more, I didn't want McCain to. I feared that if he did, I might never see him again.

"I've been reading of your exploits," McCain said at last. "I'm glad Cockerill is letting you explore themes of your own choosing."

"As am I." Another sip. He was playing for more time then. Relief washed over me. "Thank you for your article in the *Dispatch*. You were very generous."

McCain had applauded my efforts in my asylum stunt, lauded my invitations to speaking engagements, extolled my mountains of fan mail the *World* had so boastfully reported. Mama had read his piece out loud to Fannie and me, both unaware how uncomfortable I was as Mama gave voice to a man's admiration that went far beyond his praise in print. In the write-up, he'd mentioned not a word of his visit to Blackwell's Island. It would have been hard for him to explain why a man covering politics had gone to see a madwoman in an asylum.

"I was happy to write it," McCain said. "The Board of Estimate and Apportionment did the right thing. A million dollars isn't pocket change."

"To you and me," I said, taking another sip. I was beginning to feel light-headed. "To the people here, it's nothing."

"Don't make light of what you did, Elizabeth." McCain's tone was grave, and yet I reveled in his use of my given name. "The money will go far—clothing, food, medical care, more qualified staff. Perhaps a larger facility. The inmates have you to thank for improving their plight."

"One million dollars for all the New York asylums—I fear it won't be enough. How can it be, when so much still needs to be done to improve the treatment itself? There is so much to be learned still, to understand—"

"The beast that is madness?"

That he could so easily finish my sentences, understand me, made me feel again that acute, sweet pain I'd only ever experienced with him.

He took a step closer. For an instant, I thought he would reach out and touch me, grasp my arm the way he had done that glorious afternoon at Allegheny Cemetery when he'd laid his heart open to me. And then it was too much. I looked away before he saw how much I wanted him to, how raw my feelings were, feelings that even now keep me up at night for things left unsaid between us.

"You did a noble thing," he said, low. "I hear Judge Gildersleeve himself donated a large amount to Blackwell's on account of your story. His family is delighted to have their maid back—what was her name?"

"Katie, and she's only one. So many of them will never see freedom again. It's one thing to find fault with the medical community, quite another to change the culture that locks immigrants, the sick, and free-thinking women away because they don't conform to society's standards."

"You can't save them all, Elizabeth. You've raised the curtain. It's up to the doctors and lawmakers in the city to do more. It will take time, but it will happen. It's a beginning."

Tell that to the women I left behind. Tell that to Old Bess.
Laughter broke out around us. Glasses clinked in a toast. All
the room was alive and festive, and yet we held ourselves apart.
I sensed his discomfort, his need to say something that would
lighten the heaviness between us. "It must give you some peace
of mind," he said, "to know that Dent has been charged with being
an accessory after the fact and gross negligence. He'll never hurt
those women again."

"With the exception of Dr. Ingram, all of them were poor
excuses for doctors." I shuddered. "You know, sometimes I imagine
Dent shackled and being thrown into an asylum himself. Wouldn't
that be poetic—"

"Justice," he finished for me.

It had the effect of a sudden, hidden intimacy, something
McCain and I had shared from the beginning. For a moment, it was
like old times. I could believe things hadn't changed, that perhaps
only a busy schedule had kept him from sending the flower cards.

"There you are!"

I turned, the moment fizzling as quickly as the bubbles in my
champagne flute. I hadn't seen Mary McCain in more than two
years, but I recognized her instantly.

"You've found Miss Cochrane! How dazzling you look."

George McCain's diminutive wife was dressed in blue and
gold brocade, a color scheme that heightened her fair complexion.
She looked well, more robust, than when we'd met at the flower
show in Pittsburgh, when she was overcome with coughing. In
fact, beneath the gaslights, her skin was glowing.

"You look dazzling yourself," I said with more kindness than
I felt. I resisted the urge to throw back the rest of my champagne.
I wanted to disappear into the floor.

Mary looked between us, a strange glint in her eyes. I wondered
if she knew. Surely he hadn't said anything. Surely he had put this,
us, behind him, as I had done. *No, as I had failed to do.*

"Congratulations on your success, Miss Cochrane," Mary said.
"I am now even more an admirer." Something in her eyes belied
the words. "We are celebrating tonight, George and I."

McCain stiffened. "Mary, please—"

"Oh, don't be boorish, George," she said, looking up at her
husband as she wound her arm through his. "She's a friend, after
all." Her gaze swung to me. "George is embarrassed to speak of
such things, but I think you'll be happy to hear our news."

I didn't want to know the McCains' news. It was not something,
I sensed, I'd be happy to hear at all. McCain looked as if he wanted

to carry his wife from the room.

"News?" My hand was trembling again. I took another sip, clumsy in my efforts this time.

"Mary—" McCain said. Half plea, half warning.

"Oh, very well, I shall whisper it in Miss Cochrane's ear. Would that suit, George?"

McCain looked very much like it would not suit, but Mary bid me lean down anyway. I obliged, my eyes fluttering up to McCain.

"I am five months along," she whispered. "Can you believe it? I am expecting! Another child!"

McCain's face was pale, his lips white. Time seemed to stand still. It was bad enough to learn such news, ghastly I should learn it while looking directly into his eyes. The champagne stirred in my stomach, and I wondered if I might be sick. By sheer force of will, I straightened. "Congratulations, Mrs. McCain." I flashed a smile. "How happy you must be, Mr. McCain, to be a father again."

I glanced at Mary's gown. It had been fashioned expertly, with gathered layers around the midsection to hide her slight girth. Yes, I could see it now. Something no one would notice unless she knew to look.

Another five minutes of banal, meaningless, maddening conversation. Mrs. McCain was the only one talking. I could barely grasp what she was saying. I studied the oil painting on the far wall without taking in the scene. I glanced around the room and saw everyone and no one. All the while, I smiled and nodded, smiled and laughed, at Mary's witty chatter. I refused to look at McCain; I couldn't bear it. I excused myself as quickly as courtesy allowed. Head high, posture erect, I advanced toward the door and downed the rest of the champagne in a final gulp, depositing the flute on a waiter's tray.

The final act of *The Trumpeter of Säkkingen* unraveled on stage. A blur of colors, moving figures, musical notes. Later I would not be able to recall any of it. I didn't know it then, but for years to come, I would be unable to stomach the smell, the taste, of champagne.

Later that evening, Mama and I waited in line for a cab-for-hire. Three times Mama inquired if I was all right. Was I unwell? Did I not enjoy the opera? I assured her that I had, all the while wanting only the dark interior of the cab so I could think.

Expecting. Another child. Five months along.

Mary had been with child the day in the carriage when McCain had checked himself after our fateful kiss. He must have known then. This gift of a child, this precious thing, was what had given him pause. Or perhaps it was his moral character, his promise he made to me, to himself, so long ago.

A doorman beckoned us down a snow-encrusted sidewalk to a waiting cab. Halfway there, I heard my name. I turned to see McCain standing alone in the snow.

"Elizabeth?" Mama called.

"Go ahead," I said without turning. "I'll only be a moment."

Snow swirled as he approached. His top hat was speckled with flakes. I wanted to brush them away. I wanted to walk into his arms and pretend this was the beginning and not the end.

He reached inside his coat pocket and withdrew a card. A glorious card. *I heard Pulitzer gifted his best and brightest with tickets to tonight's performance.* He'd brought it in anticipation, then, expecting to see me. To deliver it by hand.

He held it out to me, his black gloves a sharp contrast against the paper. The snow was falling faster now, glancing off the envelope.

I took it and opened it with fumbling hands. Inside was an illustration of a flower of vivid blue. I had no need for the flower book. The flower's meaning was clear in its name: *forget-me-not.* When I looked up, I saw that McCain's face was grave, his eyes hooded. Suddenly his hand was on the side of my face, his thumb caressing my cheek.

I had suffered so much at the hands of men: my father's untimely death, my financial guardian's betrayal, my stepfather's abuse, Madden's and Cockerill's doubt. I had grown angry and mistrustful, wanting more than ever to succeed, to rise above, to prove to others I was more than the past I had endured. And I had succeeded. Despite them all, I had triumphed. Each had, in his own way, helped make me who I was, and I was deserving. I was resilient. I was strong.

I had survived them, and I would survive George McCain.

"You take it," I said, slipping the card back into its envelope and holding it out. "I don't need it."

His eyes held mine for a long moment, and then he nodded and took the envelope. In the next instant, he was gone.

I turned and walked toward the carriage, into the blinding snow.

Author's Note

When Elizabeth Cochrane arrived in New York City in 1887, Joseph Pulitzer had owned the *New York World* just four years. In that time, he'd transformed it from a dying newspaper with a 15,000 daily circulation to a towering monument to American journalism that boasted a daily circulation of over 250,000. As European satellite offices opened and circulation continued to rise, Pulitzer, never one to do anything by halves, was eager to show the city and his competition that his paper was unrivaled. He did this, in part, through the *World* building itself. When he embarked on a plan to construct an all-new building, he demanded it be at least fourteen stories—a number he knew would place it higher than any other building in the world at the time (it ended up at fifteen stories). He also stipulated it be "at least as good as the *Times*," which was itself being refurbished on Newspaper Row. When the building was complete, it contained two miles of wrought iron columns, sixteen miles of steel beams, and enough iron and steel to lay nearly thirty miles of railway. Below ground, printing presses were installed that were fast enough to supply every New Yorker with a copy of his paper in just a few hours. Also below, Thomas Edison's new electric dynamo supplied power to the building.

If the exterior was a technological marvel, the interior was a nod to refined aestheticism. The three-story lobby was laid in stone imported from Scotland and featured fast-moving elevators and bronze statuary. The cherry on top was an 850,000-pound gilded dome that housed Pulitzer's office and those of his editorial writers. The final bill would come to $2 million (about $55 million in today's money). Pulitzer paid for it all without borrowing a penny. I like to think he thought it well worth the cost just to read the words of a *Times* reporter who commented on a rival publisher's office

---

Facing page: Nellie Bly, circa 1890.

juxtaposed with Pulitzer's new digs, "The room of Mr. Charles A. Dana in the *Sun* building overlooks the foundations of the Pulitzer building."

I readily lapped all this up in my research but was disappointed that construction wasn't completed until 1890, three years after Elizabeth came looking for a job. However, I felt her description of the building's facade, with its golden dome that rose higher than Lady Liberty's torch, was important symbolically. Moving up the building's construction didn't alter the story and in fact helped illustrate why it was the *World* for which she most wanted to work. That, and how impressed she would have been when she approached it the fateful morning she gave Colonel John Cockerill her list of story ideas.

There is no record I could find that Pulitzer ever met his intrepid female reporter. It's possible, of course. Pulitzer was well known to be a nuisance of a micromanager, and it would not have been above him, wealthy elitist though he was, to scrutinize a new reporter, even one who wasn't yet on his payroll. However, I think it unlikely. A tête-à-tête with Pulitzer would have been a boon Elizabeth would have been all too glad to dish to her readers, yet no such record exists.

Second, Pulitzer's health began to seriously decline around the time Elizabeth began her asylum story. Fatigue from insomnia and overwork had plagued him for years, but when his eyesight began to diminish in 1887, he spent increasingly less time at the office. There would simply have been less opportunity for a meeting to have taken place. (Sadly, the luxurious digs of Pulitzer's new building would be lost on the near-blind publisher. He only made three visits to it after its completion and withdrew completely from his duties that same year. Total blindness soon followed.)

Whose idea was it to investigate the Blackwell's Asylum? No one knows for sure. Cockerill was credited in a private *World* memo from 1888 as the originator. Two years later, a *World* biography on Elizabeth gave Pulitzer the credit. Elizabeth would say later that the idea was one among a list she herself concocted. I decided on a three-way compromise: Elizabeth's idea, Cockerill's twist of impersonating a lunatic instead of a nurse, Pulitzer's ultimate blessing. It was a solution that paid homage to all three and gave each some acknowledgment.

The tale of Cockerill shooting and killing a rival in his office at the *St. Louis Post-Dispatch* is factual. He did manage to escape prosecution, thanks in no small part to a robust defense Pulitzer wrote and published in the *Post-Dispatch*. But then, Pulitzer was familiar with fending off the scandal of a shooting. He'd also shot a man, a political rival named Edward Augustine, in 1870. Luckily, the wound wasn't fatal. Pulitzer was fined $11.50 for "breach of peace" and settled out of court a year later for $400.

The fire that took place the last night of Elizabeth's stay at Blackwell's is my own invention. However, the conversation that took place between Elizabeth and Dr. Ingram, in which she expressed her concern for her fellow inmates in the event of a fire, is not. Given her unease about the survivability of a blaze when no measures were in place to release the inmates in the overcrowded asylum (it was built to house about 850 inmates but had 1,600 at the time), a fire seemed like a natural course of events. I decided to put Elizabeth through the paces. There's no better way to test a character's mettle than to throw her in over her head.

One of the most fun aspects of writing for me is when I get to fill in the gaps where the historical record is silent. Along this vein, there were a few odd little ambiguities when it came to George McCain. He was indeed an editor and later a New York correspondent for the *Pittsburg Dispatch*. Elizabeth and he would have been acquainted while she was working at the paper in Pittsburgh—her own writing attests to the fact. I first stumbled upon McCain in Elizabeth's account at the asylum. She says, upon coming into the sitting room where she'd been told a visitor was waiting, "There sat a gentleman who had known me intimately for years. I saw by the sudden blanching of his face and his inability to speak that the sight of me was wholly unexpected and had shocked him terribly."

There was a lot of good stuff there, but most interesting about the passage was what it didn't contain: the man's name. I got goosebumps. Who was this gentleman whom she'd known "intimately" and yet hadn't named? It almost certainly had to be McCain. She hadn't been in New York long enough to get to know anyone intimately, but she'd known McCain since 1885. Who else from Pittsburgh but McCain would be in New York City?

I then turned to McCain's account that he wrote for the *Pittsburg Dispatch* after Elizabeth's story broke. He bragged about her feat, extolled her fame, mentioned her fan mail, and hyped her forthcoming book. All this, but he never once mentioned he'd gone to the asylum to see her. Why?

In the sealed archives at Carnegie Library in Pittsburgh, I read Elizabeth's handwritten letters to Erasmus Wilson, which she wrote after her asylum stint. In one letter, she writes that she and McCain had "buried the hatchet" and that she had thanked him "for not betraying my secret." What had happened between these two that eventually ended with her telling Erasmus they had parted good friends? I was now on the hunt to find out more about George McCain. This eventually led me to Ancestry.com, where I learned three things that helped solidify him in my mind: first, they were close to the same age (McCain was eight years older); second, he was quite handsome; and third, he was married.

Well, there went the idea of some sort of former courtship. But (more goosebumps) what if something had happened between them anyway? His marriage would explain their circumspection. His unavailability would explain why Elizabeth never named him as her shocked and blanching visitor (even in later years), and why McCain never mentioned visiting Elizabeth at the asylum. It could also explain why there had been some tension between them in New York.

If I followed the path of a brief romantic entanglement between them, how would the two have communicated during a time when there were strict social rules about relationships between the sexes? I pored over the stories Elizabeth covered for the *Dispatch* when she began there. Arbor Day, the annual flower show, florists, the floating gardens of La Viga in Mexico. The idea of the couple's communication through the popular Victorian language of flowers began to take shape. George McCain's flower cards are, therefore, my invention. I hope they provide a window into what his correspondence with Elizabeth might have been like.

The grand jury investigation in which Elizabeth testified, and the subsequent island tour, did happen. The jurors asked Elizabeth to accompany them, and she did. She knew right away that the asylum had gotten wind of their impending visit; too many things bore the signs of improvement—a newer ferry, better food, warmer clothing, heated rooms, and improved treatment from the nurses, to name a few. A juror confided to Elizabeth that "in conversation with a man from the asylum, he heard that they were notified of our coming an hour before we reached the island."

Under oath, the nurses did indeed offer contradictory testimony and admitted to a preparatory meeting with Superintendent Dent in anticipation of their visit. As for Dent, he blamed the conditions of the asylum on lack of funding and said that he had no real way of knowing "the way things are." Anne Neville was reported as saying, "Strange to say, ever since Miss Brown has been taken away everything is different."

The million dollars awarded to the city's asylums did not have a substantial impact on Blackwell's. While many believed the money would solve the problem and turned to other things, Elizabeth knew better. "I left them in their living grave," she would later say. The asylum's allotment only increased the inmates' per diem from twenty-three to thirty-one cents. There wasn't enough funding for any significant building to take place. A new structure for the attendants was erected, though this was as much for necessity (they'd always been housed with the inmates) as it was to attract a higher caliber of staff. The Lodge was destroyed. The Retreat was refashioned so that all rooms ran along the perimeter, each with a window. A fire escape was planned, a feature that would have much relieved Elizabeth. A bathhouse and pavilion followed later. Interestingly, twenty-five canaries were bought for the wards the following year. One can hope that the companionship of the birds had a soothing effect on those who remained.

Acknowledgments

Many people helped this book become a reality; without them, *A Feigned Madness* might never have happened. Holly Monteith of Cynren Press, for your vision and guidance, I thank you. Jenny Quinlan of Historical Editorial, for your careful edits that made the manuscript shine, I am so grateful.

Heartfelt thanks go to the folks who allowed me to view Nellie's letters in the Manuscript Collection of the Carnegie Library's Pennsylvania Department. The letters were most helpful in solidifying Nellie in my mind. I also thank the Apollo Area Historical Society of Pennsylvania for spending an afternoon with me going through the contents of the "Nellie box."

To my beta readers I give grateful thanks for their patience and diligence in the early stages, including my sister Connie, for her honesty and wisdom. For the record, you will always be the smart one. To the coffee shops within a twenty-mile radius of where I live, thank you for the caffeinated energy and for keeping me company in the solitary effort that is writing.

I thank all my friends and family, near and far, for their support—including Melissa and the rest of the Mahjesties, who encouraged me through every setback. Thanks for the laughter. I wish I could have shared this with my parents, who I know are looking down and smiling.

To my sons—Thomas, Nicholas, and Christopher—who never stopped asking when I'd be done, well, here it is. And most especially, I thank Ron, who offered love and encouragement in equal amounts. I love you all.

Select Bibliography

Berdy, Judith, and the Roosevelt Island Historical Society. *Roosevelt Island*. Charleston, S.C.: Arcadia, 2003.

Bly, Nellie. *The Nellie Bly Collection*. Edited by Tri Fritz. Bloomington, Ind.: Xlibris, 2011.

————. *Ten Days in a Mad-house*. New York: Norman L. Monroe, 1887.

Burrows, Edwin G., and Mike Wallace. *Gotham: A History of New York City to 1898*. New York: Oxford University Press, 1999.

Fredeen, Charles. *Nellie Bly: Daredevil Reporter*. Minneapolis, Minn.: Lerner, 2000.

Greenaway, Kate. *Language of Flowers*. 1884. Reprint, New York: Gramercy, 1978.

Homberger, Eric. *The Historical Atlas of New York City*. New York: Henry Holt, 2005.

Horn, Stacy. *Damnation Island: Poor, Sick, Mad, and Criminal in 19th-Century New York*. New York: Algonquin Books, 2018.

Juergens, George. *Joseph Pulitzer and the New York World*. Princeton, N.J.: Princeton University Press, 1966.

Kroeger, Brooke. *Nellie Bly: Daredevil, Reporter, Feminist*. New York: Times Books/Random House, 1994.

Morris, James McGrath. *Pulitzer: A Life in Politics, Print, and Power*. New York: HarperCollins, 2010.

Reed, Henry Hope, and Sophia Duckworth. *Central Park: A History and a Guide*. New York: Clarkson N. Potter, 1967.

Sachsman, David B., and David W. Bulla. *Sensationalism: Murder, Mayhem, Mudslinging, Scandals, and Disasters in 19th-Century Reporting*. New Brunswick, N.J.: Transaction, 2013.

Reading Group Guide

1. In the beginning of the novel, Elizabeth is desperate to find work. Why is this the case? Had you been in her position, would you have done what she did to get a job at the *New York World*?

2. Elizabeth arrives at the Essex Market police station and must answer questions before a judge. Were you surprised that her route to the asylum included this stop? Why do you think it was necessary that she go there first?

3. At Bellevue Hospital, Elizabeth is given two examinations, the results of which will determine her fate. What was the nature of these exams? Do you think they were capable of revealing whether she was mentally ill?

4. Elizabeth encounters a range of women at Blackwell's: immigrants, orphans, the elderly, the poor, the women on the rope. Would a mental institution of today have similar patients? Why or why not?

5. Elizabeth's relationship with George McCain plays out in flashbacks as well as the current story. What was McCain's way of showing his feelings for Elizabeth? How would you have felt toward him if you were her? Have you ever "fallen" for someone who was unsuitable or off-limits?

6. Superintendent Dent wants very much to punish Elizabeth. What kept him in check? Why did Nurses Grady, Grupe, and McCarten behave differently?

7. Why do you think Nurse Grady was so intent on taking Elizabeth inside the Lodge on her last night at Blackwell's? Why did Nurse Conway come to her rescue?

8. When Elizabeth returns home, she struggles with writing down her account of what happened at Blackwell's. Why? What made her finally write her story?

9. When McCain tells Elizabeth that the *Sun* has "scooped" her story, she goes to see the *World*'s managing editor, John Cockerill. What was Cockerill's response? Did it surprise you?

10. What important detail did Elizabeth not reveal to Cockerill and leave out of her asylum exposé? Why? How did this omission get resolved during the grand jury investigation on the island at the novel's conclusion?

For Further Reflection

1. A main theme of *A Feigned Madness* is women's equality. Elizabeth struggles with wanting to enter a man's profession—journalism. In the 1880s, few women were working at newspapers. Have women today made any inroads into being treated fairly when it comes to their professions of choice? In what ways are women still fighting for equality today?

2. Mental illness was little understood in Elizabeth's day. What progress has been made in the causes and cures of mental illness today? Do misconceptions and confusion still exist?

A complete downloadable Readers' Guide
is available from the publisher at
http://www.cynren.com/s/feigned-madness-guide.pdf

CPSIA information can be obtained
at www.ICGtesting.com
Printed in the USA
LVHW050545291220
675237LV00013B/2563

9 781947 976207